Martyrs' Tomb

Mack R. Hicks

Splenium House, L.L.C.
Pinellas Park, Florida

Front cover illustration: "Kneeling Slave at Melbourne" (Van Nost, 1700). Painting by Mack R. Hicks from a photograph by James Pipkin in *The Country House Garden—A Grand Tour,* 1987. (Used by permission.) Cover typography and interior design by Pete Masterson, Æonix Publishing Group, www.aeonix.com.

This is a work of fiction. With the exception of historic facts, places, and persons, all names, places, characters, and incidents are entirely imaginary, and any resemblance to actual events or to personso living or dead, is coincidental. The opinions expressed are those of the characters and should not be confused with those of the author.

Publisher's Cataloging-in-Publication
(Provided by Quality Books, Inc.)

Hicks, Mack R.
Martyrs' Tomb / Mack R. Hicks. -- 1st ed.
p. cm.
LCCN 2001118211
ISBN 0-9712587-5-9

1. School choice--Fiction. 2. Educational vouchers--Fiction. 3. Public schools--Fiction. 4. St. Petersburg (Fla.)--Fiction. I. Title.

PS3558.I256M37 2001 813'.6
QBI01-7008913

Published by
Splenium House, L.L.C.
6710 Eighty-Sixth Avenue North
Pinellas Park, FL 33782-4502
Fax: 727-544-8186
web site: www.martyrs-tomb.com

First Edition, September, 2001

Printed in the United States of America

To Susan: Thanks for giving me time and space. Also to Jeb Bush and his brother for their courage in championing poor kids. Special thanks to Milton Friedman who told us to open the tomb to the fresh air of competition, Annette Polly Williams who pried the tomb open, Jeanne Allen, Center for Educational Reform, William J. Bennett, Chester E. Finn, Tommy Thompson, Bret Schundler, Lamar Alexander, Clint Bolick, Institute for Justice, J. Patrick Rooney, John T. Walton, Fritz Steiger, C.E.O. America, Quentin L. Quade, the Reverend Floyd Flake, Dr. Howard Fuller, George F. Will, Cal Thomas, Matthew Miller, Stan Marshall, the James Madison Institute, John McKay, Patrick Heffernan, Ph.D., Floridians for School Choice, John Kirtley, Joe Magri, Kent Corral, Larry Keough, Skardon Bliss, Phil Gailey, and, of course, "The Gipper." Much gratitude to American teachers and students. They comprise our country's greatest hidden asset but are martyrs in a system that just won't listen.

Acknowledgments and thanks to Philip Hicks, Andy Hicks, Doug Hicks, and Joe Waters for feedback. Mark Anderson, Laurie Rosen, Paul Thayer, and Pete Masterson, who provided professional advice and support. Thanks to Detective Sheldon Sayles, James Pipkin for permission to use my painting of his photo of "Kneeling Slave at Melbourne," Jim Nannen, and the USF Writer's Conference.

He shall cover thee with His feathers, and under His wings shalt thou trust; His truth shall be thy shield and buckler.

Thou shall not be afraid for the terror by night; nor for the arrow that flieth by day.

Thou shalt tread on the lion and adder; the young lion and the dragon shalt thou trample under foot.

He shall call upon me, and I will answer him; I will be with him in trouble; I will deliver him and honor him.

With long life will I satisfy him, and shew him my salvation.

—*From the 91st Psalm*

Prologue

Damn brute—sorry, sorry Lord. But men—not fair—such damn apes. Jenny ducked another slap and twisted her red-blotched arms from the boy's fist. But he pulled her in and wrapped his arms around her. Gagged and smothered, she couldn't move. He pinned her in a human cast. So helpless. Why did tears humiliate her even more?

She stuck her feet out in front of her like rigid stilts and dug her heels in near the rough rock wall. But he easily lifted her, twisted her around, and carried her to the edge of the steps. He dangled her over the cavernous graveyard.

She flopped upside down. Tombstones and markers pushed up out of the black earth to form a circle in the darkness. He pulled her down the steps to the bottom and along the uneven floor of the ancient graveyard. They came to a dark catacomb marked "Padre Cancer de Barbastro." A damp, musty odor clogged the air, making it difficult to breathe.

The young men's crisp military uniforms and blue-gray shirts blended into the half-light of the vast burial chamber, but the girls' full-length white, linen robes seemed at home among the gray tombstones and washed-out burial mounds.

Jenny looked at the others. She knew they could feel it, too. Someone was out there all right. Watching.

"You girls are wimps," Billy Ray said. "Some holy roller's out of action a few hundred years and you're worried about ghosts, for Chrissake. Jesus, they're made up. That's all, just made up."

Jenny edged in closer to the other two girls. Moving her head slowly from side to side, she peered into the darkness. The burial cavern spread out in all directions, maybe a hundred yards wide; the ceiling disappeared in shadows about forty feet over their heads. Broken tombs and decaying Indian mounds were scattered about the packed clay floor, forming a loose circle.

"Here, drink." Billy Ray pushed the frosted glass quart of Beefeaters in her face. She took hurried swigs of the peppery-hot liquid. It scorched her tongue and watered her eyes.

"Maybe we ought to—"

"No! Hell no, we're going through with it like I said. You and me, on top of one of them Indian mounds. Jenny Grant and Billy Ray Thomas--that'll give 'em something to think about."

"I know we—"

"Yeah, and we're gonna do it, just like the Hammer said. I'm a Lion now, and don't you never forget it." He fingered the silver necklace, exposing a medallion with intersecting triangles. "Hammer's idea, but it don't bother me none. I can do it, not afraid of ghosts." He raised his voice to a shout. "Especially dead priests." Billy Ray bent forward and kicked his way up the steep burial mound, boney fragments and loose clay bits crunching under his stiff boots.

She peered over Billy Ray's heaving shoulders into the blackness above. Thick strands of twisted vegetation hung in uneven lengths like giant rope ladders. Hundreds of small, brown bulbs dotted the dense tendrils. Flowers? Jenny shuddered. Could anything normal grow in this place?

Fluttering wings bolted past her face. Bats! She jerked downward, covering her head with her hands. A sour, dusty odor burned her nostrils.

Jenny tightened the grip on her hair, but hard, sandpaper hands pried her fingers apart. Billy Ray twisted her hair close to the scalp, and the searing pain dug into her skull. He pushed her toward the dark, shrouded tombstones.

That was when she heard the first yelp. When she knew. Someone was watching. Like a sobbing infant's cry, the vulnerable tones grew more shrill and insistent with each bark.

They all froze.

"Probably just some mutt who got hisself lost down here," Billy Ray said. But the eerie cries didn't sound canine or animal. Or even human.

The vast chamber sat in silence except for the haunting whine. Even the flutter of bats' wings seemed to retreat from the mournful symphony. Sounds of hurt and fear reverberated from the windows near the lofty ceiling down to the crushed relic bones supporting ancient Indian mounds.

"It's just a joke," Billy Ray said. He peered into the darkness. "It's the Hammer—his idea of a joke, all right." Billy Ray raised his voice. "Okay, Eric, I know what you're doing. I'm not afraid. You can stop anytime now, Eric. It won't work."

He ran the tips of his fingers along edges of intersecting belts that crossed his chest and looked at each of the adolescent boys. Unbuttoning his top button with trembling fingers, he took a deep breath and stepped into the darkness.

Jenny didn't wait. She ran ahead of the others and sprinted over the rough clay surface toward the steep stairway. When she reached the bottom she scrambled up the worn steps, careful to hug the moss-covered wall.

Two-thirds of the way up, Jenny slowed her pace and looked back. She saw nothing, but heard a small, plaintive voice between waves of deep, lamenting cries.

"It's me, Eric. Me, Billy Ray.

"It's just me, Eric.

"Come on, Eric.

"Eric? Is that you?"

She turned to continue her climb, then stopped. The eerie yelps had ceased. Silence fell over the vast cemetery.

But it lasted only seconds.

Muffled footsteps sounded in the darkness. Silence again. A stifled scream. A scream that reached inside her stomach with a cold, squeezing hand. Echoes of the paralyzed voice died out, but the icy, twisting fingers would not let go.

Jenny fled up the steps, then stopped near the top to swallow gulps of salty, humid air, her eyes searching the blackness. She tried not to listen, but the soft yelping sounds had returned like a drumming headache that would not go away.

But this time the sounds were different... lighter, happier, victorious. Satisfied.

Jenny raced to the top. She didn't look back again.

Chapter 1

Peter's fingers caressed the phone he'd just held, his mind on automatic.

"Who is it?" Kathleen rolled over and switched on the reading lamp.

"The service."

She struggled with the alarm clock. "It's not even six. Why can't they—"

"I'll take it downstairs, hon. Go back to sleep." He fingered the security code buttons and stepped into the hallway. No sounds from the kids' rooms. He struggled to remember Monday's appointment card. Or was this Monday? Wake up, Peter. Wake up. He rubbed his eyes.

His toes dug into the cool, carpeted stairs. A sliver of strawberry red sun brightened the kitchen. "Okay, I'm back."

"It's a Sterk Trump, Doctor. Says he's a friend."

Peter knew the energetic detective was an early riser, but he wouldn't call unless it was urgent. "Put him on." The phone hummed. A cell phone?

"Peter—had to call. They got David Mendola. Can you believe it?"

"David Mendola?"

"You know, the gang leader—Bloods, L.A. Bloods. I was in on the bust. Goddamndest thing. FDLE, locals, even some reps from the governor's office."

"I read about the accident." Peter's brain shrugged off sleep and moved into gear. A big pileup near the Gandy Bridge, or was it the Howard Franklin? No... wait, it was the Tampa Airport exit. Someone had torn down the one-way sign. "But what can I—"

"Hey, you think I'd call just to chat? Better get your boots on, pal, 'cause you're in it up to your friggin' earlobes. The select committee—ho, ho, I sure as hell use that term loosely—already picked you out. Wanted me to call. Now. Half the psychiatrists are loony-tunes, and half the psychologists are hired guns. Guess what? You're the only friggin' virgin in wrinkle city."

Peter reached for the message pad. "You got a name I can call? They've got the wrong guy on this one. The big school grant's coming up, and Kathleen did the series on gangs for the *Times*."

"Hell, I know all that, and no, there's nobody to call. Better get your rear end down to the office and jump on this thing. Let me know if I can help."

~

Peter pulled into the office parking lot at seven-fifteen and parked next to Linda's Honda Accord. A former police dispatcher, his industrious secretary usually arrived early to get a head start on insurance forms and billing statements. The small lot had room for only six cars, but on-street parking was good for two hours. Otherwise, patients would have to walk two or three blocks through a run-down, marginally safe neighborhood. Peter opened the back door near the small staff kitchen to the aroma of ground hazelnut coffee. He filled one of the chipped mugs and walked down the hallway, past the activity room, to the waiting area.

Linda looked up from her computer, eyebrows raised. He nodded and smiled, but moved past her desk to the fax room. Inside the open door a green "ready light" illuminated the empty facsimile tray. He took a deep breath and exhaled. Good. Maybe Sterk was overreacting. Then he glanced at the carpet below. A couple of dozen papers formed an unruly heap below the tray. One word jumped out and stood him up straight. His throat tightened.

COMMANDED.

Peter picked up the papers and shuffled them into a loose pile. He read:

> SUBPOENA DUCES TECUM. YOU ARE WITH THIS COMMANDED upon the motion to Compel Independent Psychological Evaluation. David Mendola, a minor, shall be psychologically evaluated by Peter Sheppard, Ph.D.,

> who shall conduct such psychological evaluation and file with this court a written report containing findings and recommendations in order to assist this court with resolution of criminal charges pending before this court.
>
> J. Harry Rolfson III
> Circuit Court Judge

He folded the papers and stepped through the side door into his office. His spacious office felt like home, almost better than home. At least here it was quiet. Usually. He eased into the large recliner and stretched his legs over the corner of the walnut desk.

Dark wooden beams and gold-wheat carpet projected warmth and reliability to both Peter and his troubled clients. Narrow rays of sunlight danced through stained glass windows, igniting the pale yellow carpet to a red autumnal glow. The aroma of burnished leather mingled with the smells of lemon cleaning wax and freshly vacuumed carpet.

He set down the faxes, took a sip of coffee, and looked around the room. Built in the 1920s, the lovely old home had seen better days. It needed restoration. And so did Peter's clinic. It all depended on one thing. The school reform grant.

The intercom buzzed.

"It's a Judge Rolfson. Wouldn't say what it's about," Linda said.

"Okay, I'll take it." He pushed the blinking button.

"Judge Rolfson? This is Peter Sheppard."

"I'm calling about the Mendola boy. Got a real mess on our hands here, Doctor. You get my fax?"

He glanced at the inch-thick report. "I haven't done much with drug problems lately. I'm afraid he needs—"

"His mom wants you. Saw you on TV or something. Look, we've been trying to nail this kid for a while now. You see the *Times* this morning?"

"Yes, sir. Accused of vandalizing street signs, three kids killed when their car went up an exit ramp to—"

"No accused about it. He did it. Hard to believe. This kid brings L.A. gangs to St. Pete and gets tripped up on a prank. Talk shows will eat this up."

Peter nodded.

"But the real problem is, who gets him? Public school folks want him in the Good Soil. It's one of their sponsored programs, and they've got a big grant coming up. This would be a damn nice feather in their cap.

Justice wants him, too, and so does HRS. Hell, everyone wants a piece of this kid."

"I know about the grant, Judge. My center is applying for it, too. We're supporting scholarships that will let parents transfer their kids to other public or private schools if their kids are trapped in failing schools. So I obviously have a clear conflict of interest—"

"Oh, I wondered who was behind that voucher nonsense. You're just wasting your time, Doctor. Don't you know the teacher's unions will crush you like a cockroach and never look back? The school system is the largest employer in the county. No, make that the largest employer in every county in America. And the Selby Isle parents don't want poor kids in their well endowed public schools. We all know that. Anyway, you need to see this kid. No time for niceties. Hell, legislature's reviewing our juvenile justice money right now, today, as we speak. No time to dilly-dally."

Peter fingered the subpoena. "I'll do my best, Judge. Maybe I can work him in next—"

"On his way over now. Really appreciate you fitting him in. Good luck."

Click.

Peter stared at the receiver and shook his head. What in heck was going on? He ran his fingers along his tongue and shuffled through the pile of faxes. David Mendola. Violent rage reactions and night terrors from early childhood. Impulsive, overactive, diagnosed ADHD at age five. Ritalin prescribed, but his father refused to give it. Peter shook his head. Why did some parents refuse to look at the side effects of not taking prescribed medications like Ritalin? Math and writing problems. He attended one of the worst public schools in the system and was then shipped off to Liberty High, an alternative school for dropouts and troublemakers.

He dog-eared the test summary sheets. David was a bright young man, no doubt. But when his father had pulled out in '90, he fell apart. The school claimed that David headed the Lions, a cousin of the L.A. Bloods. Drugs, drive-by shootings, and possibly murder. But no solid proof until his prints showed up on the stolen traffic signs.

Linda buzzed. Her voice was muffled. "Mrs. Atkinson is here with Kimberly, but they just brought in that Mendola boy. They've even got him in leg irons. Ah, now they're taking them off."

Peter cracked the office door. The adolescent boy looked tiny between the burly Good Soil orderlies. When David leaned back into the blue couch, rays of sunlight cascaded through the large stained glass window and washed his Desert Storm fatigues in reds and greens.

David pulled out a king-size Camel and smirked at little Kimberly, who sat on her mother's knee and stared at David with round doll eyes. Mrs. Atkinson lifted an open book to her daughter's face to block the girl's view.

Peter took a deep breath, swung the door open, and stepped into the waiting room. "Okay, David, looks like it's your turn. I'm Dr. Sheppard. Guess we'll have a little talk now."

The baby-faced youngster gave Mrs. Atkinson a bored smile and struck a long wooden match on the zipper of his fly. A purple and black tattoo glimmered for an instant on the back of his left hand. A five-pointed crown

Peter turned and took slow steps into his office. He had learned long before to communicate through gestures rather than words. The tactic usually worked. He was careful not to look back, and he heard David shuffle to his feet and follow him the ten or so steps to his office.

"Anywhere over there is okay." Peter pointed in the direction of an oversized leather chair with heavy, rounded arms. David dropped into the chair with a thud. Crossing his legs, he glared at Peter.

Peter looked down at David's file. No eye contact just yet. He would set the rules of this game, not a sixteen-year-old.

"It looks like things haven't been going too well. They been given' you a rough time over at Liberty High?" David was still in the special school for potential dropouts.

David stared at Peter while cigarette smoke curled into his caramel-colored hair. He sure didn't look that tough. A handsome face, almost pretty, and beautiful hair. A good reason for the macho act? And he was short—five-six at best. Peter scooted lower in his chair.

"Well, I don't suppose it was your idea to come here."

A slight flicker of David's left eyelid.

"If you didn't volunteer, then I suppose your mother volunteered you."

This time not even a slight lifting of the flat, bored expression.

"Okay, David, look. I imagine what you'd really like is for me and everyone else to get off your back. You didn't want to come in, and if you talk it means you give in, and your mother wins. You lose. The shrink and your mother win and you lose. Screw them, right?"

A flutter of eyelids. David's eyes moved to the left. Was it just the smoke or was there a glimmer of wetness?

"I'm with you. I wouldn't talk either. You've got enough people pushing you around without giving in, for God's sake. I hope you don't. I wouldn't respect you either if you gave in and quit. But—ah, we've still got a problem here. I mean, you do. I'm not going to con you." Most teens were easy to fool. Thank goodness.

David studied the ceiling.

"I'm not going to tell you we're sharing this problem, 'cause we're not. The problem is that you know there's no problem if people would just get off your back, but your mother thinks you've got a problem, so you've got one even though you don't or didn't or shouldn't. Heck—now you've got me confused."

Almost a smile as David sat back and let a thin column of bluish white smoke spiral to the ceiling.

"I can't talk."

"Good. Don't talk. I don't want you to talk if it means giving in. Tell you what. Why don't you leave here today and think about whether to come back and talk, but only because you decide and not 'cause you're forced to. Judge wants me to decide what's in your best interest and that's exactly what I plan to do. I'll give it my best shot no matter what you do, although I suppose everyone would feel better if we talked at some point down the road."

Peter stood and stepped toward the door.

"What's that?"

Peter stopped and turned, careful not to change his expression. "That's a model of an F-101 Voodoo, from when I was in the Air Force over in England."

"You fly?"

"Yeah, some."

"Combat?"

"Nah. When I was in there wasn't too much goin' on."

David nodded. "I'll fly someday."

"I've got models of other planes I flew. Wanna take a look?" Peter took deliberate steps toward the side exit. Out of the corner of his eye he saw David hesitate, hands gripping the sides of the chair. Then he heard the muffled sounds of footsteps behind him.

Peter's playroom was loaded, and the informal and cluttered room was built to absorb punishment. Surrounded by dart guns, barbells, and an old-fashioned pinball machine, a professional pool table occupied the center of the room. A plywood board that leaned against the far wall converted the pool table to a ping-pong table.

"Here's an A6 Intruder. Want to work—"

David looked up, his expression hard and vacant. "That's kid stuff." For a full thirty seconds David just stared at the floor, shoulders hunched. Peter said nothing.

David ambled over to the three-story dollhouse and reached in with both hands. He moved the furniture from room to room.

Poor kid, poor damn kid. The A6 model was kid stuff, but now he was in the dollhouse.

David pulled the large toy bed from the master bedroom. He placed it in the kitchen and quickly piled the family figures onto the bed. Peter used the anatomically correct dolls to interview and counsel sexually abused children. David laid the mother figure and the father figure on their back and piled the siblings and toy dog on top.

"Looks like they're all in there together," Peter said.

David stared at the bed with a sad, open-mouthed grin. His eyes reddened, but no tears fell. He jerked the father-figure doll from the bed and tore off its trousers. Spreading its legs, he placed it on its back on top of the chimney. Turning, he reached to a nearby shelf and retrieved a high-powered, rubber-tipped dart gun shaped like a German Luger.

David cocked the gun, placed it an inch from the doll's realistically designed genitals, and pulled the trigger. The impact drove the doll off the house and onto the carpet below. David put the gun down carefully, reached onto the toy bed, and picked up the infant doll.

My God, he's going to kill them all!

Again he methodically stripped the doll and spread its legs. Looking around, he found the toy castle, a favorite of five and six- year-olds. Bending, he opened the moat and shoved the naked infant into the castle dungeon.

Crash! David slammed his foot into the side of the castle. He kicked it again and again, smashing it against the wall. Peter reached out, but David pulled away. He darted across the room to the model airplane desk.

"So this is it, huh?" David picked up the model, whirled, and hurled it against the wall. It exploded, bits and pieces ricocheting across the room.

"Okay, David, I know you're upset, but we've got to talk. This doesn't do any good. If you can talk, it may help."

"Talk? Shit." David pushed him away and kicked open the activity room door. He stopped in the hallway. "You can keep this crap. It, doesn't do any good." His childlike scream was more sob than protest.

Peter reached the waiting room in time to see the orderlies escort

David out the front door. Little Kimberly and her mother moved closer together and peered at Peter.

"What happened?" Linda asked.

Peter held one finger to his lips and motioned her to his office. They stepped inside, and Linda closed the door.

"I don't know, but this kid's hurting big-time." He unlocked his bottom desk drawer and removed a large red canister marked "Drug Alert." He sprayed it on the seat and arms of David's chair. After a few seconds he wiped the chair with a folded cloth. The residue changed to reddish brown and blue.

"I thought so." He took long strides to the activity room. Linda hurried to keep up. He kicked through the clutter and went to one knee. Then he sprayed back and forth, covering the dollhouse and castle area. "Reddish brown and blue. That means one or more milligrams of crack cocaine or PCP. And probably marijuana."

"But isn't he locked up? Leg irons and all, I thought..." Linda shook her head.

"He's in the Good Soil for a few days until we decide what's best for him. No way he should have access to drugs, but this is one clever kid. You know, he was a lot softer than I expected, but those mood swings are something. Coming along fine, then bang. Good-bye."

"You going to see him again?"

"First thing Friday. That should give him a day to cool down. Call the judge's office if there's a problem, even the smell of a problem. This boy really wants help. Call it a long shot, but I'm going all the way with this kid."

Chapter 2

An hour later, Peter peered down at an empty file folder.

Linda had scrawled the letters "NP" on the name tab, indicating a new patient. Why had he agreed to see Kathleen's little sister? So damned hard to be objective. Kathleen had described her as the proverbial black sheep of the family. Liz was a rebel with too many causes. And they were usually half-baked fads that pushed her farther and farther from the mainstream. Things had finally seemed to turn around when Liz shocked everyone and joined a religious order. Peter hadn't seen her since she was sixteen or seventeen. She had shown up at his wedding with blue-and-orange streaked-hair and a hairy-chested biker.

Liz hadn't smiled or said a word since entering his office. She had edged her chair back a good two feet from Peter's desk and now sat rigid, arms folded, a large tote bag covering her lap. Twenty-nine years of age, the tall, willowy woman looked to be in her mid- twenties, maybe younger. She had a model's face and figure without the anorexic frailness common to that profession. And the fox-trimmed suede parka and white cord slacks did little to hide her sensuous figure.

An enormous wooden pendant rested against Liz's chest. Three or four inches wide and about eight inches long, it dangled from a thick, gold necklace. The octagon-shaped pendant showed an ivory cross and three ancient, bearded figures in separate glazed panels. One panel sat on top of the cross's horizontal bar and the other two panels abutted the vertical bar.

Heavy makeup gave Liz's face the appearance of a Mardi Gras mask. A hard shell of white, penetrated by two cold diamond eyes. And wearing that bizarre necklace? Paranoid schizophrenic? Dear God.

"I know this is awkward," Peter said. "Maybe I should refer you to—"

"No, it's dear Kat's idea, so I'm sure it's perfect. You married her, so you know what I mean. She'll be eager to get your report on my sorry, sorry life."

"Everything you tell me is confidential, Liz. You know that."

The frigid eyes didn't waver.

"So would you like to tell me a little about your..."

Her lips turned upward in a semisnarl that gave her mouth a wolfish grin. The grin proclaimed, all bite—no bark.

He retreated to the brown chart. "I see that you mentioned something about depression on the intake form. What, ah, seems to be the problem?"

"Depression."

"So you feel you—?"

"Yep. Just like on the talk shows."

"Problems eating, sleeping?"

"And living. Do I get my Prozac now?"

The stained glass windows darkened as if to confirm her diagnosis. Blinking cranberry spots on the pale yellow carpet faded to unmoving gray shadows.

"How long have you been feeling this way?" He put the file down and took off his reading glasses.

"You want the full Freudian version from when I was slam-dunked at baptism or just the latest stuff?"

"Why don't we start with more recent things?"

"Okay. I was fired from a company specializing in—ah, make- believe. You've got a big one in Orlando, but nothing like this sucker. I kept the books."

"Kathleen never mentioned a company."

"It's international. Offices all over the world, headquartered in Rome."

"Is it—?"

"The Catholic Church, incorporated."

"Oh, yes." He scribbled a note on the yellow pad. Light rain hummed against the north window just behind his desk. "I knew you had, ah, been a nun. Kathleen talked about it quite a bit. Didn't you send a postcard a few years back, from Mexico?"

"Yes. My sister and I just love to stay in touch. Especially when I'm being a good girl. Anyway, when I left fantasyland, I went downhill almost overnight, so I moved back in with my mother in Orlando. I'm sure Mom told Kat I was there, even though I told her not to."

"Do you think you were really depressed?"

She smirked. "When you drag yourself out of bed every morning unable to breathe, puke your guts out, and hope a tornado hits your bedroom, I'd say things aren't going real good. Got a job with Sterns and Tregor, you know, the big-eight investment firm. But keeping busy didn't help either."

He nodded.

"Then one of the senior partners invited me to the dog track, out on Corey Boulevard. I think he had his money on me to win, but I didn't show him much."

Peter smiled.

"Know what? It was better than my fantasy job, much better. I loved it. The smell of the track, the energy of the crowd. I went ballistic. Then I graduated to horses, jai alai, and stud poker."

"The depression was—?"

"You bet. Next stop, Las Vegas. Every other weekend for a year. Ever been there?"

"No, but I've read about it, of course."

"Well, let me tell you. The Horizon has a baccarat room that won't stop. A hundred crystal chandeliers, velvet paneling, and invisible port-o-lets."

"Invisible—"

"It smelled like urine half the time. Hard to leave those tables. Impossible."

"What, uh... how did you do financially?"

She rummaged in her black patent leather tote bag. "Ha, that's the perfect question, Peter. I was opening cash accounts in units of eight to ten thousand dollars and did okay for a while. But you can probably guess the rest."

"You started to borrow money when your luck ran out?"

"Yep. I took a few no-interest loans from some of my bigger accounts and sent them fat statements showing a good return. Naturally, that didn't help my depression any. I started to feel guilty again. Real guilty." Liz pulled a diamond-studded mirror from her purse and inspected her face.

"That's when I met Barrett. He's paying for these sessions. Barrett Spangler. You know the name?"

"You mean the baseball owner?"

"Yep, and the hockey team and the basketball team. Videos— he's the video rental king. One of his guys figured out what I was doing. To make a long story short, Barrett bailed me out."

"And now you're, uh, engaged?"

She snapped the purse shut. "How delicate. Yes, I'm living with him, but it's more than that. He wants to marry me. We spent two months visiting the watering holes of the rich and famous, but the depression is still there."

"Do you care for him?"

"I... I don't know. Can't figure why he trusts me. I sure as hell don't trust myself."

He waited for the tears, but her face was a rock. "Kathleen said you might be interested in some volunteer work."

"That sounds like Kat. Volunteer work reminds me of my do-gooder days, religious servitude and all that stuff. I've grown up a little since then. Barrett insisted I give it a try, so I'm doing some accounting work out at the Good Soil. You know, the rehab place. They do reading and math tutoring and drug rehab. It's part of the school system so they've got good accountability. And they're doing some cool stuff out there. The drug program is great. Barrett's staff worked the numbers. Something like a 95 percent cure rate. Unbelievable."

"I know it's supposed to be good. Kathleen did an article on them a few months ago. She was concerned about brainwashing, but there was no clear evidence of any wrongdoing."

"Ha." It wasn't really a laugh, more like a cough. "That figures. If I like something—anything—my big sister is bound to shred it. Is this ever going to end?"

"What about Barrett?"

"He's a good guy. Wants me to have a baby but, ah, I can't. Screwed up my insides from some of my, ah, preconvent adventures. I'm not up to kids, anyway. In fact, I'm not up to much." She looked toward the window. A single persistent tear fought to work its way out.

"I guess it's really tough to think about getting close to people, making a commitment."

She turned her head in a slow arc and surveyed the room. Her eyebrows inched up when she got to the cracked radiator. "You could use a little help out here. You know, I majored in finance and accounting at Georgetown."

"We could use your help, no doubt about that. But psychological ethics don't permit outside dealings. Especially when you're in active treatment and even after that. I wish we could—"

"That's too bad. Barrett's money wouldn't hurt you a bit. The Good Soil just about went nuts when they heard about my Barrett Spangler connection. And they've got a billion-dollar grant coming up in the next couple of weeks. Can you believe it? A billion dollars."

"I know about the grant. We're competing for it too, but we've got seven weeks until the hearing."

Liz shook her head. "Aren't you being a little naive? I know what that tastes like, because I've gorged myself at that unholy table more than once. Barrett says the school system is politically connected with everyone and his brother. Liberals, conservatives, you name it. Who do you think builds those massive factories they call schools? It sure as heck isn't Jimmy Carter and his do-gooder volunteers. Barrett says some white envelopes must have changed hands to let the Good Soil milk the big money cow. Each kid is worth thousands, so the school system isn't going to give them up to outsiders without some kind of kickback."

Red and ochre prisms danced again on the faded yellow carpet. "Well, they've got people from HRS, the school board, and bureaucrats by the bushel, all running around in circles," Liz said. She looked at her watch. "By the way, my dear sister invited me for dinner tonight. Did you know?"

Peter put his legal pad on the desk. "No, she hadn't—"

"Probably because I haven't been too receptive in the past." Liz fingered the wooden pendant. "The only reason I took Kat's advice is because of you, Peter. You've never put me down. Not even when I was down, like at your wedding. Thirteen years ago. Jesus."

Liz stood. "Anyway, tell her I'll be there. Sometimes, if you're not careful, you get what you ask for." She almost smiled.

Peter started to get up, but Liz turned, walked to the door, and let herself out. He sat back in his chair, took a deep breath, and shook his head. Then he reached for the white conference phone and punched in the numbers.

"Hello, Dr. Gerry. This is Peter Sheppard. How are things in Washington?"

"Just like Miami Beach. Even got my beach towel with me. Should hit a high of thirty, so things are warming up. Could be downright hot by Easter."

Same squeaky voice, same sarcastic manner. "I've heard some rumors down here about the grant. I assume it's still—"

"We're moving the administrative hearing up. We want you ready by Wednesday, the twenty-seventh."

"What? That's just two weeks from tomorrow. No way we can make that."

"No way?"

"I mean—it's just not possible... and, and it's not fair. We've been gearing up for April twenty-third, not March twenty-seventh. You know that. We've been following the guidelines to the tee, and now, at the last minute, you're moving the date? Were you even going to notify—"

"It all has to do with budgeting. Congress can and does change its mind from time to time. Apparently, Dr. Small, one of the new administrators at the Good Soil, snuggled up to some lobbyists. I don't know why they moved it up. Surprised me too."

Peter's throat tightened. "To put us out of business, that's why. Could—could you at least tell me who this Dr. Small is?"

"He's new, all right. Haven't seen his name before. The D-twenty shows him as, uh, assistant clinical director under Dr. Benjamin Wolf. Of course Doris Dantakovic is the overall honcho down there, near as I can—"

"What? Wolf and Dantakovic? Running the Good Soil?" He shook his head. Wolf, in St. Petersburg? And Doris, still with him? He tried not to picture her. Doree... Would he ever shake those memories? "What happened to Norm Steward? He started the whole program."

"Don't know. Just go by the paperwork. Let's see. Benjamin Wolf, M.D., and Doris Dantakovic. On the forms since January one. Well, I've got work to do. The new date's solid, and there's no way to change it."

Peter clenched the phone. "Look, we'd like to comply, but do you realize that some forty people will lose their job if this doesn't go through? We've been planning this thing for two years. You can't just play with lives like this."

"Attorney Reardon will be expecting you on the twenty-seventh, Doctor."

Click.

He shook his head. This was a major blow. They'd been so optimistic about their chances. Too optimistic? The Good Soil was getting a lot of money from the school system. He knew that. But this was hardball. He was suddenly faced with the reality that these people had connections you only heard about. And knew how to throw the switches when they needed to. There was no time left to prepare the necessary reports.

His Center for Children relied on private donations, while most other non-profits like The Good Soil operated with federal funds. But with those federal funds came rules and regulations that worked against the kids. He had wanted the freedom to give each child the best help possible. But this federal grant was different. Up to a billion dollars, it was the biggest school grant in U.S. history. And even better, the chance to work on prevention.

And then there was the big loan for his son's operation. The new surgical procedure could give Mark more mobility, but the costs were horrific. If the grant didn't come in, his center would fail the audit, and Peter couldn't show reliable employment. The loan depended on it.

Chapter 3

Dear God. What was going to happen to her? Jenny Grant squeezed her eyes shut and jammed her feet against the floor. If she could just keep her knees from shaking. Scalding hot lights turned the insides of her eyelids tomato-red. Last night's scene in the cemetery had been terrifying enough, but this was—it was the pits. A summons from the Good Soil head office was every kids' worst nightmare.

"Okay, let's try it again. Who put you up to it?" It was the Hammer's voice. Couldn't be anyone else.

"Like I said, it was my idea—"

"Yes, of course. You're really something, you know that? Always covering for your goody-goody friends. How did you get into College Park High, anyway. The public schools on Selby Isle are for for rich daddies' girls, not a cop's kid. Unless, of course, your ole man's on the take. Hey, maybe he slips drugs to your debutante buddies."

She covered her face with her arms.

"What about Lifewater? Was he in on it?"

"Lifewater? I don't think I know—No, I—"

"Bullshit. You know who I mean. Lifewater, squaw John, the Tonto boy." He unfolded the wrinkled piece of paper and smiled. "'Please call my dad or Mr. Cleary. Tell them we're prisoners in here. Tell them we're being abused.'" He looked up. "Oh, my... how dreadful." He raised his fist over his head. "Who's Cleary?"

Jenny took a deep breath and squeezed her eyes shut. "He's Terri's advisor on the school paper. He wanted to interview her. It was for drug prevention week and to see when she'd be back at school."

"Did you really think you'd get this out? Right under the noses of our monitors? Arrogant little nymph, aren't you? Now, we both know what's going to happen to Miss Terri Johns. She's on the waiting list. It's just a matter of time."

Jenny took another deep breath and shook her head.

"Scared, aren't you? Little hot stuff. Regular teen queen." The Hammer laughed. "What about Doctor high-and-mighty Peter Sheppard? Your memory come back yet? Or do you want us to warm up our generators? You know what I mean. If you're no good to us, you sure as hell won't be helping the enemy."

She flinched, his cool spittle spraying her face. "I don't know. It's all so hazy. Maybe he touched my, ah, front once when I was baby-sitting, but I think it was an acci—"

"No accidents. He fondled you, didn't he? After he picked you up on the chat line. You get off on married men, right? But that's no excuse for Mr. Do-gooder. I think your memory is starting to come back, don't you?"

"Oh!"

Powerful hands reached across her shoulders from behind and twisted her ears into knots. Coarse thumbs jammed deep into her ear canals and jerked her straight up. Jenny gasped. Grinding, stinging bolts of pain burned her ears. He dropped her, and she slammed against the back of the chair.

"Well, your memory starting to come the hell back?"

She took a deep breath... and nodded.

"That's good. That's excellent. Might as well get used to it, 'cause you belong to us now. By the way, where's your daddy, the big-time cop? He's a real Boy Scout, ain't he? Kinda like Doctor Big-Shot, Sheppard. Why doesn't your daddy come to the rescue? His all-American sweety pie sure as hell needs help, big-time."

Jenny shivered. There was someone else in the room. Or something. A faint outline just over the arch of light. Something big, like a mountain of hate. She could feel it. The scorching lights grew brighter. The Hammer must have stepped behind them again, probably to talk to whoever else was in the room. She could hear them whispering.

Silence.

"Okay, Miss Goody, Goody. Just keep your mouth shut. And don't go near Terri Johns. Otherwise, you might get another trip to the cemetery. Only this time you'll be out there permanent-like. Got it? And get your story straight on Dr. Peter Sheppard. It better be academy award stuff."

Jenny covered her eyes with shaking hands and nodded.

~

At five-thirty P.M. Peter cruised south on I-275 past the Suncoast Dome. The ten-year-old Volvo Turbo was his only indulgence. He had purchased it on the day he left the county guidance clinic to enter private practice. Peter tightened his neck and shoulder muscles, then let them go. He often used relaxation techniques and deep-breathing exercises to calm his anxieties.

Peter's left hand touched the worn and frayed black rosary that rested just inside the left door handle. Although he didn't pray the rosary much anymore, he knew the secrets of the old prayer beads. The thick, silver cross opened in the back to reveal a storage chamber containing ancient soil from beneath St. Peter's Basilica in Rome.

Tissue-thin paper, attached to a dark brown particle of soil, spelled out "Terra Catacomba." Block letters on the back of the still shiny cross read "Roma." On the front, the figure of the crucified Christ had turned to orange rust. The broken inscription above the crucifix created a jagged edge, which he fingered gingerly.

Peter touched the beads of the first decade without praying, yet felt an immediate flood of relaxation. The sensation was quite different from the psychological techniques of self-hypnosis and was undoubtedly conditioned by childhood experiences and years of habit. But... well, somehow it worked.

A swerving Land Rover careened past at breakneck speed. Tires squealing, it cut in front of him. Peter jerked the wheel to the right and applied the brakes with a pilot's instincts. He caught a fleeting image of shimmering pink lips and teased blonde hair that danced in the sparkling sunlight. The pulsating rhythm of heavy metal shouted its defiance at the plodding flow of rush-hour commuters.

The 1990s' pleasure wagon followed the Bay Way exit and headed toward the Don Caesar Hotel and St. Pete Beach. Two bumper stickers proclaimed the good news: "Wanted: Meaningful overnight relationship" and "Party Naked."

Peter sighed. He needed to see his family. Turning left onto Pinellas Point Drive, he admired the newly resurfaced pink streets. He swung around tiny Bay Vista Park and pulled into the wooded driveway of his tri-level home. Discovered by Kathleen, the shaded waterfront house sat on a pie-shaped lot with sixty feet on the front and a hundred and seventy-five feet facing Tampa Bay. It had increased in value, but they had refinanced it twice just to keep up with Mark's medical bills.

For Peter it served as a refuge from people problems and opened a door to St. Petersburg's semitropical outdoors. Mix in a happy, loving family, and it spelled home. Let the critics knock it, but until they came up with something better... He opened the side door from the garage and had only one foot in the entry way before Marie attacked. She bounded down the stairs from the elevated dining room-kitchen area and leaped into his arms.

"Oh, you're getting too old for this." He held the chubby little girl and twirled her around and around. Peter had suffered a deep sense of loss when Marie went off to school and came home happily jabbering about newfound friends. He knew a series of separations would follow, and he knew he was an enabler. But he was none too eager for her to give up the role of Daddy's girl.

On the way to the kitchen he stopped and squeezed ten-year-old Mark's shoulder. Mark did not look up. Textbooks and crumpled homework papers fought for space on the dining room table. Unlike his plump, babyish, and impulsive sister, the slender boy was quiet and serious. And cerebral palsy kept him from playing ball or even riding a bike.

Intellectual testing showed gifted abilities, but Mark's grades did not reflect his I.Q. Embarrassed by his condition, he was often mocked by peers. Mark stayed close to his family and lacked any ambition to achieve. If permitted, he would watch TV from the moment he returned home from school until bedtime.

When they eliminated the tube during the school week, Mark retreated to the enclosed sun porch and watched fishing boats pass before the great picture window. He would sit for hours at a time peering through Peter's old Minerva binoculars. He loved the stately cranes, whistling plovers, and dive-bombing brown pelicans.

They had enrolled him in numerous classes and activities, but he remained melancholy. Even counseling with one of Peter's associates had not brightened Mark's spirits. And medical costs were formidable. An experimental procedure at Johns Hopkins offered hope, but the surgery was risky.

Kathleen had written a special story for the *Times* on endangered animals. Along with the Audubon Society, Kathleen lobbied to convert the V.A. Hospital woods to a wildlife habitat to protect it from developers' bulldozers. Her article sparked Mark's interest, and he was determined to protect a family of southern bald eagles nested atop a seventy-five-foot pine tree. Hunters had wounded the baby eagle, and it was not expected to live. The crusade for the birds he loved freed Mark from his homebound solitude, but his lethergy remained.

Kathleen stirred a spicy gravy over the gas-top stove. The aroma of curry sauce tickled Peter's nose and watered his mouth. He marveled at the array of salts and spices covering the counter. The noisy kitchen and the warm, savory air made him feel lucky. So lucky to be a part of all this. He hugged Kathleen and gave her a soft, slow kiss on the cheek.

The doorbell rang.

"Oh, goody! Aunt Liz is here!" Marie scrambled down the steps to the front door.

Kathleen turned to Peter. "Be good," she said. "She's been through so much. This is our chance to help."

Peter smiled. "Yes, dear, I hear you." He licked spicy brown sauce from his fingers.

Marie came charging up the stairs, pulling Liz by the hand. "She's pretty, and she brought Mark and me presents." Stacked one on top of the other, two Florida Marlins baseball caps balanced precariously on Marie's head. Liz was actually smiling. Marie could do that to a person.

Kathleen wiped her hands on her apron and gave Liz a hug. Liz leaned her head forward, but her arms stayed at her sides.

Marie waved the hats in circles and ran toward the dining room. Peter laughed and shook his head. "Welcome to Mariaville. You ready for that martini, Liz?"

"Good man, Peter. Just go easy on the vermouth. And try not to bruise the gin." She looked at Kathleen. "In fact, make it straight up. More bounce to the ounce. Join me, Kat?"

"No, ah, but I'll have a glass of wine with dinner."

"Yes, of course. Much more proper for the doctor's wife." Liz tilted her head and winked at Peter. "Well, here we are. Did Peter tell you about Barrett Spangler? That's where I got the hats. Hockey, baseball, videos. You name it, and I can get it."

"No, of course not," Kathleen said. "Peter wouldn't discuss..."

Peter handed Liz the frosted glass. She dipped her fingers into the icy liquid, then tossed the olives into her mouth and took a noisy gulp. "I hear you've got some problems with the Good Soil, Kat. Peter tell you I volunteer out there? They've got the best cure rate in the Southeast, maybe in the whole country. Not bad for a public school facility that's only been open a year or so."

Kathleen looked at Peter and bit her lower lip. Then she turned to Liz and spoke in low, even tones. "I did a story on the Good Soil—a series, actually. Some of the people I interviewed were worried about blockbusting. That's where they go into a neighborhood and tell the parents that all the kids on that street are hooked on something. That way they get kids who have mild problems or no problems at all. Naturally, they show good results with that population of youngsters."

Liz put down her empty glass and folded her arms.

"Now, don't get upset, Sis," Kathleen said. "I'm not saying they don't do some good work out there. But there were some other rumors as well. Some of the kids have run away. And they claim the Good Soil goes overboard on discipline, kind of like brainwashing. And the Miami Herald did a piece on sweatshops in Mexico City. Some of the wicker furniture was headed to the Good Soil for their fund-raising projects. I'm only saying this because I know you'll read the articles sooner or later. I'm not putting you down for—"

"Jesus Christ, I knew it. Just like home. Nothing ever changes." Liz looked at Peter.

"Whoa." Peter held his hands up, palms outward. "Let's eat dinner and get on another track. I've got to work late on the big grant. It's a never ending process."

Liz set her empty glass on the kitchen counter. "I asked Barrett about your scholarship program, Peter, and he says it's really a voucher. Barrett says we have vouchers for everything like food stamps and housing and even college tuition on the G.I. Bill, but the teachers' unions want to keep control over the money and the programs."

"Does Barrett support the scholarship program?" Kathleen asked.

Liz eyed the gin bottle on the counter and ran her tongue along her lips. "No, he's worried that if vouchers go to private schools the government will start messing with private education and kill it, too. And he doesn't think some of the private schools will want lower class kids. Same thing with parents in the yuppie public schools like College Park High."

Kathleen looked at Peter. "Are those legitimate concerns?"

"Yes, some folks are really worried about government interference. We'll probably hear more about this tomorrow night at the awards banquet. I don't suppose you want to attend, Liz?"

"Heck, yes. I'll be there. I'll probably be sitting on the mayor's lap. Don't forget about Barrett. He's already on the Good Soil's board of directors. I think they're after his money, actually." She almost smiled. "But who isn't?"

Chapter 4

Peter gazed across the Spanish colonial tile roof toward boats docked at the foot of the Vinoy Hotel. The monuments to privilege bobbled lazily under a Wedgwood blue sky and massive white clouds.

He and Kathleen sat near the center of the yacht club's open terrace on the second floor. The Saint Petersburg Yacht Club hosted the prestigious mayor's award banquet each spring. Winning recognition here could give his grant application a real boost.

"He won't come," Peter said. "You'll never get Sterk Trump in a monkey suit."

"You're wrong this time." Kathleen looked toward the outside stairs. Attired in a wrinkled black tuxedo, Sterk climbed the steps behind his wife, Polly. He carried an apple green box tied with a white silk ribbon.

"I don't believe it," Peter said. Then he saw the shoes—and laughed. Black tennis shoes. Sterk definitely liked life in a brown paper wrapper. He often referred to himself as a "meat and potatoes guy." And his face didn't match his body. Drooping cheeks, a long, thin nose, and close-set eyes gave the appearance of a funeral director, British politician, or depressed bloodhound. The 1950s' one-inch crewcut had never met a barber's clippers and didn't complement his upper-crust face.

Polly pulled the detective along by his tuxedo sleeve, obviously trying to cover the tattooed hula girl that was permanently affixed to the back of his hand.

Sterk peered upward and jabbed a stubby finger at the flagpole. "Why's the flag at half-mast?"

Peter smiled. "I hear it's because Polly got you to wear a tux. End of an era, I'd say."

Sterk raised his eyebrows and looked at his wife. "It ain't so bad, hon. Really."

"Actually, I overheard the manager mention to Commodore Fisher that the pennant's stuck," Peter said. "Rotten timing, what with the mayor's regatta to Key West tomorrow. They hope to get someone in here later tonight to fix it."

Sterk tipped his head toward the makeshift bar in the corner. Peter stood and followed him across the room. Several people waited in line to order drinks. Sterk looked both ways and then whispered in Peter's ear, "I heard about the Mendola kid blowin' his top. I was afraid of that."

"You were right about David. Something's not quite—"

"Hell, I know you gotta keep things confidential, but this gang thing's big-time, Peter. I mean, this isn't friggin' L.A. or even Miami. If little ole St. Pete goes, Jasper, Indiana, and Sioux City, Iowa, go, too."

"You think it's all gang-related?"

"Hell yes, I know it is. Look, we got us two honchos here, David Mendola and Billy Ray Thomas—"

"Billy Ray—Billy Ray? Didn't he play ball for Lincoln Middle? You sure you got the name—"

"Yeah, an' I'm Charlie Chan. These guys are fightin' over the Bloods and the Cripts. They're sworn friggin' enemies. But get this, they're both put out of commission on the same weekend, and they're both involved with the Good Soil. Billy Ray was probably beat out."

"What?"

"Chrissake, the only way you can get out of one of these gangs is to have the crap beat out of you. The girls are gang-raped. You're never really out, anyway. Didn't you read Kathleen's articles?"

"Of course, but here in Saint Pete? Do they really—?"

"Hell, yes. And the friggin' Soil's mixed up somehow. Got three clients, runaways. Two of 'em last seen at the Soil, and now they're gone, zippo. We managed to get the other one out, a sixteen-year-old. But he's a zombie, amnesia or somethin'. Parents are home-schooling him, an' he can't even do the friggin' alphabet." Sterk chuckled. "Seem kinda accident prone out there. Like to see their workman's comp reports."

Peter ordered two red wines and a white wine. Sterk pointed at an ice bucket filled with cans of Budweiser. "Billy Ray Thomas is over at Park," Sterk said. "Why don't you just go check him out? Jenny Lewis can get you a consult. Got to get your hands dirty on this one, Peter. The Good Soil is out to win the billion bucks, and I don't think they give a rat's ass who you are. They'd as soon walk on your butt as smoke a joint. I'll cover you as much as I can, but you gotta go on the offense."

"I know I need to do something, but I'm kind of tied down with—"

"Goddam it, Peter, you sit back and the fat lady will be singing up your ass for sure. You'll feel like the Grand Canyon's blowin'—"

"Okay, okay, I get the idea. Thanks."

They turned and headed back to the table. Television lights snapped on, illuminating the mayor and his party who sat on the stage fronting the banquet room. Liz sat with Barrett Spangler, just to the right of the mayor and his wife. The superintendent of schools and two aides sat to the mayor's left. Regal yachts, obscured by the dusk of evening, sent flickering points of light across the placid waters of the Vinoy basin.

"First, it is my pleasure to announce the runnerup," the mayor's wife said. "These groups were judged to be outstanding service organizations and should take immense pride in their contributions to the city. When I call out the names, will the directors please stand?

"Mrs. Margo Burns, League to Aid the Retarded. Ms. Sylvia Rotti, Woman's League Thrift Shop. Dr. Peter Sheppard, The Center for Children."

Sterk reached out a muscular paw. "Congratulations, Doctor. That sure as hell won't hurt the cause none. At least the local folks know you've been doing a great—"

"But now for the big one," the mayor said. "The 1991 Mayor's Award and a check for ten thousand dollars go to... the Good Soil."

The audience stood as the band struck up "School Days, School Days, Good Old Golden Rule Days." Peter and Sterk stared at each other and shook their head. Kathleen covered her face with her hands. The mayor held the check above the microphone for a clear media view. "From the people of St. Petersburg with our profound gratitude." Channel Ten cameras zoomed in as Doris Dantakovic reached for the gold-colored, pelican-embossed check.

Doris Dantakovic. Over twenty years, Peter thought. Still so beautiful. So lovely. Doree...

Dantakovic stepped to the podium. "On behalf of our director, Doctor Benjamin Wolf, our clinical director, Mr. Eric Hamlier, our administrator,

Dr. Harold Small, and our hardworking board of directors, we say thank you. Thank you so much. And a special note of thanks to Ruth Gomez and her late husband, Pablo Gomez. If it hadn't been for their generous start up grant, the Good Soil would not exist. They were willing to give the new kids on the block a chance."

Dantakovic turned to the superintendent of schools. "Without the cooperation of the McDill County School Board, our educational efforts would be seriously compromised. Because of Superintendent Arnold and his staff, we can help those other new kids, the ones who are new to drugs and academic failure."

Dantakovic pointed a jeweled finger at the now hushed audience. "Even as we sit here tonight our staff is training girls from the slums of South American cities. Little girls of only fourteen or fifteen who have been exposed to every imaginable abuse and deprivation. We are teaching these youngsters to be more than love objects, more than empty vessels who are used and then thrown away like yesterday's trash. We are teaching them to become objects of hope, objects of faith... and objects of respect. Thank you."

The audience stood and applauded. Benjamin Wolf stepped to the podium and presented Dantakovic with a bouquet of Easter lilies.

"They make a handsome pair, these tireless workers for the future of Tampa Bay," the mayor said, smiling.

Peter was turning to sit when he noticed Sterk's empty chair. "What the... ?" Ten feet up the flagpole, with a can of Budweiser in one hand, the powerful body with the bloodhound face surged upward without apparent effort. Sterk's black tennis shoes squeaked against the flagpole, and his white fluorescent socks marked his steady progress.

Finally he stopped his climb and struggled to untangle the club's pennant. Then, with the pennant in hand, he eased himself down the pole while still holding the full can of beer. His performance garnered a smattering of applause and not a few raised eyebrows. Polly's face turned pink, then crimson.

"Heck, they needed to get the flag down, and there wasn't much else going on," Sterk said, shrugging. Polly grabbed Sterk's arm and pulled the bewildered detective down the marble staircase to the protective cover of darkness.

"Hey, you forgot your box." Peter waved, but Polly just shook her head and kept on going. Peter reached over and opened the trap door on the top of the exquisitely decorated box.

"Popcorn."

"Popcorn?" Kathleen reached for the box. "At the Mayor's Ball?" She covered her mouth with her hand and broke into convulsive laughter.

"Popcorn and martinis. Great idea," said a voice from behind them.

Peter and Kathleen looked up. Liz pulled back a chair and sat. "And I guess congratulations are in order, Peter. Or are they?"

"I don't think so, Liz. We won the top award three years ago, but this was when we really needed it. I don't want to be negative about the Good Soil, but this gives them a big boost with their grant application."

Liz scooped a huge green olive from her glass and ran it along the edges of her red, glossy lips. "Maybe I've got some good news for you, brother-in-law." Her voice seemed thicker than usual and her head rocked gently, like one of the yachts in the basin.

Liz looked at Kathleen. "I told Barrett about your suspicions, Kat. So, he decided to hold off on the big fund-raiser. He was going to donate thirty cents on every video rented during the Good Soil drug week. It was supposed to start next Sunday and run through Easter weekend. Naturally, Dr. Small is pissed off royally. Oops, sorry, Kat. I wasn't saying that to pi—ah, to make you mad. Really."

"I don't know if that's really being fair to those folks," Peter said. "There's no solid proof that the Good Soil—"

Liz reached across the table and took Kathleen's hand. "Here's the best part, Kat. Maybe even a silver lining. Dr. Small wants you and me to go to Mexico City to check out the rumors." Liz looked at Peter. "Kathleen can check out the sweat shops and I'll check the banks for money laundering. The Good Soil has a charter deal, so we can fly out tomorrow morning and come back on Monday."

"Oh, Sis, get real," Kathleen said. "I couldn't do that. I just, I would have to plan for something like that. There are all kinds of things I need to—and what about the kids?"

"I think you should go," Peter said. "It's about time you did something on the spur of the moment. I'll get the kids to school. There's only tomorrow and Monday. And you two gals need some time together."

"Come on Sis," Liz said. "We can even dig for artifacts. Remember when we did those Indian mounds in Safety Harbor with Dad? Barrett's got all kinds of connections down there. He can set it up."

Kathleen shook her head and smiled. "I can't believe I'm saying this, but..." She raised her glass. "Stand back Mexico City, here come Evita and her little sister, Liz."

Chapter 5

Peter shook his head. The outcome of the awards banquet the night before had given him a jolt. Doris and Wolf had moved into the higher levels of St. Pete society both quickly and effectively. Almost too quickly. What was their secret?

David' Mendola's whistling serve interrupted Peter's reverie. Considering the rough surface of the plywood board that covered the old pool-table, it was a strong serve. But David wasn't quite up to the skill-level of a squadron of pilots who had a lot of time to kill. David blasted the ball with powerful strokes but poor accuracy. Peter picked up the ball each time David sent it sailing beyond the end of the table.

"Wow, you really whacked that baby."

David's eyes twinkled as he watched Peter retrieve the ball from the piles of toys and games scattered across the playroom floor. On one shot Peter smashed the ball, and it careened off the punching bag and onto a shelf just behind David's head.

"Hey, okay." David hit the ball straight at Peter, who returned the shot in midair, driving it into a side wall. David and Peter pounded the ball against the walls. Peter tossed in two more balls, and before long a half dozen balls careened around the room, bouncing from walls to ceiling and back again.

"Hey, good idea," Peter said. "You're really good at this."

When one of the balls plowed into some plastic toy soldiers perched on a high shelf, Peter picked up a dart gun and blasted several of the soldiers. The grimacing figures twirled to the floor and bounced high into the air. David grabbed a gun and fired high at three others.

Peter looked at his watch. "Oh, Lord, only fifteen minutes left, and you wanted to finish up the F-101." He reached to a high closet shelf and pulled down the ten-inch model. David started to hum as he uncapped small bottles of paint.

"Doing rolls and all that, what if you had to toss it, you know, airsick and all?"

"We'd pull off our oxygen mask, unzip our suit, and let it go, then zip up and get back to work."

"Cool."

David used a tiny brush to dab plastic silver paint onto the wooden fuselage. The odor of wet paint and fresh glue filled the air. David looked up, his eyes seeming to feast on Peter. Peter noticed that David's hands were steady. Quite an improvement.

"You know, we never talked about the gangs."

David's knuckles turned a bluish white as he tightened his hand around the brush.

"I know, Dr. Sheppard, but that's a whole 'nother thing. Real heavy stuff. And the Good Soil… it's, it's in the middle."

"The Good Soil?" Peter steadied the airplane stand and bent his head closer.

"I want to talk, but I really got to think on this one. You know anybody big? Like the governor or someone?"

"Well, I don't know. I—"

"This isn't just about me. It's a lot bigger. But I'll tell you one thing, I don't do street signs. And I'm not in any gang. Never have been. Going to see you tomorrow?"

"Sure. I promised, remember?"

David's eyes filled with tears. "With my dad and all, I—I just…"

"It's okay, it's okay. We can talk tomorrow." Peter put his arm around David's shoulder and pulled him close.

~

After David left, Peter stepped over to the bay window facing Fifth Avenue North. David stood on the corner between two orderlies. A Good Soil van pulled up and they got in. The Good Soil's in the middle? Of what? Maybe Kathleen was on to something, after all. But the *Times* hadn't found anything conclusive.

Peter took a deep breath. He felt so damn sorry for the kid. Clinical training had taught him to be open to his own feelings rather than fear them. It was one of the real perks of being a psychologist. Most men, shaped by a few million years of survival training, had learned to cover their emotions. Like an internal barometer, his feelings whispered silent messages that were seldom wrong.

But he knew he had to be careful. David seemed to be opening up, but he might be St. Pete's premier gang leader. Was David coming along too fast? So easy to blame his father, the Soil, or the school system. Sterk Trump had warned him. This kid will tell you what you want to hear.

He looked at the door to the waiting room. A faint knocking sound and none of the usual noises—the radio, Linda's typing. Legs stiff and heavy, he pushed himself up and opened the carpet-covered door. Mrs. Bitty Dalton sat on the floor with her legs crossed and rocked from side to side. She held a book titled Karma and You, and chanted in a rhythmic, high-pitched voice.

Peter looked to his left, where Linda usually sat. Astrid and Starlyn Dalton, ages fourteen and sixteen, crouched behind Linda's desk and shared her earphones. They were listening to Peter's confidential therapy tapes. Bitty looked up from her book and smiled, her face aglow.

"Come on, my darling daughters. Stop playing with Mrs. McCall's computer. It's time to see the doctor."

Peter followed a dull, pounding sound down the hallway to the visitors' bathroom. Propped under the doorknob, a metal chair wobbled from side to side. He slid the chair back and swung the door open. Linda emerged, red-faced and perspiring. She frowned and mumbled something about "kids today needing a good licking."

"Okay, folks, let's get started," Peter said.

Starlyn sauntered past Linda's desk. She wore a red sweatshirt emblazoned with identical messages on front and back: Eat me Raw—St.Pete Oyster House.

White shorts peeked out from under the sweatshirt, and black silk stockings encased her model's legs. Earrings shaped like skeletons smoking a joint dangled from pink, dainty earlobes. A tattooed heart with wings and the number six were inscribed on her left arm, just below the elbow.

Peter shook his head. The tattoo was a symbol of the Folk or Cript gangs. He followed Bitty and Astrid into his office. Astrid walked straight to Peter's desk and opened the top drawer. Starlyn held an old air force photo showing Peter in the cockpit of his F101A Voodoo.

"Starlyn, Astrid. You're wasting the doctor's time," Bitty said. "This is costing me a hell of a lot of money."

Astrid opened another drawer.

"Okay, girls, let's get seated," Peter said softly. "You know it's against the rules to play with my personal things."

"We're not girls," Astrid said. They took seats on either side of their mother. Starlyn still held Peter's photo.

"All right, so what's happening? I know the girls can be a handful, but this behavior is totally inappropriate."

"Nothing much, Doctor. Their father moved out, but that's old news. And good riddance, I say. Macho man bites the dust." She winked at Starlyn. "Tom just couldn't keep up with the times. He'd get his bowels in an uproar over any little thing. The man would rather clean house or work in the yard than hit the beach bars for a little fun. He should've married one of those fifty's types. You know, like Loretta Young coming down the stairs with his pipe and slippers or some crap like that."

Astrid looked at the ceiling while she fingered three silver crosses that dangled from her left earring. Starlyn stared at Peter's photo. He sighed. At least they could have given the girls real names.

"What do you think, Starlyn?" Peter asked.

She lifted the photo over her face. It hid her mascara-encrusted eyelashes. "He was real bossy, like out of it, really out. Bitty dissed him bad, man."

"Yeah, and he wouldn't let Billy Ray stay with Starlyn no more," Astrid said.

Peter raised his eyebrows and looked at Bitty.

"They're both on the pill, Doctor." Bitty shrugged. "I don't like Billy Ray staying over, I really don't. He dropped out of school, but he's nice enough. She could do a lot worse, what with drugs and all out there."

"Billy Ray's got a uniform." Starlyn's long, lacquered nails outlined Peter's air force cap in the photo.

"And Bitty spanked me," Astrid said.

Bitty sighed. "I told you a million times to stop snatching cigarettes. What if you get caught? Then what? We'll have cop cars all over our house, that's what. Our holier-than-thou neighbors, it'd make their day, the nosy bastards."

"But you know I can't buy 'em. I'm not old enough."

"Well, get somebody older to buy them. We do have laws, you know." Bitty shook her head.

Peter closed his eyes. Had times really changed that much? Ten years ago the most common complaints were anxiety and depression, and it was the rare kid who was completely obnoxious. Today, most of the kids were pushing the limits, while those around them suffered the anxiety.

"Isn't that right, Dr. Sheppard?"

Peter blinked. "What's that?"

"Like I said, the girls need to come see you, but if they won't, there's nothing I can do." Bitty's rounded arms circled the girls' waists and pulled them close. Starlyn stuck her thumb into her mouth and looked at Peter with a wide, innocent smile.

"Let's talk alone for a moment, Ms. Dalton."

After the girls left the room, he turned to face Bitty. "You're going to let them quit? Have you seen Starlyn's report card? All Fs except P.E. Doesn't that scare you?"

"Sure. I'm worried about their schooling, Doc. East Shore is the dregs, I know that. We can't afford the nice areas where the best schools are, and it seems like all the dumb kids are on our side of town. East Shore has almost three thousand students. What a zoo. They bus a few rich kids in, but their classes are on the top floor. They're in gifted and that International Baccaterial program or whatever it's called, and my kids are watching movies on the first floor with the blacks and L.D. kids. I complained to the teachers, but they can't help. And Astrid's history teacher is really just an art instructor."

"Look, Ms. Dalton. If you don't follow any of my other suggestions, please at least do this one thing. Take the girls in for drug testing."

Bitty pulled back and crossed her arms. "You know something, Doc? It's easy for you to sit here in this office where everything is quiet and nice, but it's a whole 'nother thing to put up with these kids. I've tried to raise these girls as best I could, but I got no help from their father. No help from anyone."

"But you—"

"No way, Doc. I'm getting tired of all this advice from everyone. I don't have time for drug checks and such nonsense. Hell, I'm lucky if I can get them to school on time. And what about me? Don't I have some rights? Cleaning up after two little brats isn't my idea of the good life. If I had one of those vouchers everyone's talking about, I'd send them off to military school where they wouldn't take any crap. Yes, sir, they'd be long gone."

Peter sat back and crossed his arms. "I don't think military school is the answer for these—"

"Biggest mistake I ever made, having these kids. And Starlyn wasn't even an accident. What in hell was I thinking?"

"I know you're frustrated, Ms. Dalton, but Starlyn has serious problems. If she doesn't get help soon, it could be too late."

"No, I'm not frustrated, Doc. I'm mad. And besides, Billy Ray's a drug counselor. He'll look after Starlyn."

"What?" Peter bent forward. "What's his last name, this Billy Ray?"

"Billy Ray Thomas. He works at the Good Soil. Starlyn just about lives out there now. I don't want to hurt your feelings, Dr. Sheppard, but Starlyn wants the Good Soil for counseling. Says you're too old." Bitty smiled. "Sorry."

Hot wisps of sweat inched down Peter's neck. "You mean Billy Ray Thomas, the gang—"

"Billy Ray fell off his bike or something, out at the Good Soil. It's part of the school system. He's in a coma now."

The room was perfectly still, thanks no doubt to the old home's thick walls. The circular mantle clock ticked with demanding urgency. Peter put both hands flat on the desk.

"The main thing is, get her started in some real counseling. She needs to see a psychologist."

Bitty pushed her chair back and stood. A broad smile split her face. Then, without a word, she turned and exited to the waiting room.

Peter pulled himself up and stepped over to the stained glass window on the west wall. He tried to focus on the Dalton's collision course with tragedy, but the big grant intruded like a hovering thundercloud. He had never set out to get government grants or reform the school system. His mission, pure and simple, was to help as many kids as possible. But casualties were piling up, with no end in sight. Wounded children scurried through a cross fire of neglect from indifferent school bureaucrats and me-first parents.

Peter had counseled hundreds of school kids as well as public school principals, counselors, and teachers. They told him the schools were too large and too unstructured, and that teachers were demoralized because of mountains of paperwork and unsafe working conditions. Little of the budgeted money reached the classroom and even less went to the failing schools. And the really good teachers refused to work in those failing schools.

He felt like a psychological ambulance chaser waiting for the next fatality. He was dealing with symptoms, not causes. Prevention was the key, and prevention meant fixing the parents or fixing the schools. People like Bitty Dalton couldn't, wouldn't, budge. So the only hope was to change the school system. Help the five-year-olds now, and in fifteen to twenty years there would be a new generation of parents… and children. That was why he had to win the grant. No second chances. This was it.

Linda buzzed. "Mrs. Dalton didn't leave a check. Said she didn't like the advice she got."

Chapter 6

Red and green banners hung above Mound Park Hospital's main entrance, proclaiming its fiftieth anniversary. Located only ten blocks south of Peter's office, the venerable, old hospital carried the heaviest load of charity patients in the area yet remained St. Petersburg's pre-eminent health care facility. Its broad mix of ages and economic levels allowed Peter to work with children and adults.

Peter took the One West elevator to the second floor, where he crossed orthopedics and climbed the service stairs to Three South. He looked at his watch. Friday the fifteenth, 8:30 A.M. Hopefully, Small and other Good Soil staffers wouldn't show up prior to visiting hours at eleven o'clock. No sense making waves, he thought.

Peter slipped into the nursing station and sat behind the rotating chart stand. No Billy Ray Thomas. He turned to the duty nurse.

"Billy Ray Thomas?"

"Excuse me?"

"His file, Billy Ray—?"

"Oh, Halleran's got it." She smiled and raised her eyebrows. "Down in three-sixteen. If you can make it through the National Guard."

Three uniformed officers sat on straight-back chairs behind two powder-blue cafeteria tables that blocked the hallway to 316. As Peter approached, a muscular officer in a black uniform stood. He hitched up his pants with his forearms and shook his head.

"Sorry, sir, no visitors in this section."

"I'm a doctor."

The policeman stretched his fingers and smiled. "Could I see your license, sir?"

Peter handed it over. The officer glanced at the hospital ID-card and quickly returned it. Then he looked at the others. "He's a doc, okay. See if he's on the list."

An older officer, a man in his fifties at least, checked the hospital register. He took his time and hummed quietly as he turned the pages. An FDLE patch identified him as a member of the elite Florida Department of Law Enforcement. Peter knew that Sterk Trump consulted with the FDLE from time to time.

"This you?" The FDLE officer held the book open to expose Peter's picture. "Says psychologist. Dr. Wolf won't allow interrogations just yet. Sorry."

Peter crossed his arms. "You better call Dr. Lewis, Officer. She's chief of staff. It has to do with the closed head injury." Peter peered at his watch. "I don't have a lot of time."

The policeman pulled at his double chin and stared into the faces of the FHP officers. The FHP captain scratched his wrinkled nose with his index finger and waved down the hallway. "Let him go, Sully. It's okay with us." The captain smiled. "Won't have much time anyway, what with all them little nurses around."

The man with the double chin smiled and pulled a chair aside. "Sorry, Doc. Just trying to be careful."

Peter looked toward the nursing station. Still no sign of Good Soil staffers. "I understand perfectly, Officer. We've all got a job to do."

Student nurses in crisp apple-green uniforms blocked the door to room three-sixteen, but he had no difficulty seeing over their heads. Cynthia Halleran towered above the reclining patient. Her eager students crowded around her for a better view. He had heard about Halleran. Nicknamed the Iron Cactus, the crusty old warhorse usually ran the cardiology unit. He wondered why in the world she'd been assigned to the psychiatry-neurology wing.

"Mr. Thomas, do you hear me?" She glared down at the young man who stared back at her with unblinking eyes.

"Yes," he said, his voice flat and mechanical.

"Let Nurse Davis take your pulse."

"Yes." But he kept both arms at his sides.

"This young lady has a job to do, Mr. Thomas. If you don't cooperate, you won't get better."

Billy Ray continued to glare at Halleran.

"We've had just about enough of your games, Mr. Thomas." Blotches of red covered Halleran's neck. Her students smiled and exchanged furtive glances.

"Let me see the chart." Two students scrambled to unhook the chart from the bottom bed rail.

"All right, listen up. Maybe we can learn something after all. Billy Ray Thomas, age twenty, fell off his bike. An assistant counselor at the Good Soil, a drug program on the north side." She squinted and shook her head. Billy Ray stared back.

"Seven on the Glasgow Coma Scale. In a coma for two days and post-traumatic-amnesia of two weeks. Apparently fell on the back of his head. The first forty-eight hours the patient claimed he was attacked by demons and ghosts. Dr. Wolf prescribed Xanax." She smiled. "That stopped the ghost stories."

Peter nodded.

Halleran jerked open the pages, almost tearing them from the metal-encased chart. "Night duty says he's totally uncooperative. Patient claims we won't feed him meat." She peered down at three wrinkled crisps of bacon on his plate. The repugnant odor of cold hospital food filled the room. Only the scrambled eggs had been touched.

"When we got him to the cafeteria last night he dumped mashed potatoes on his tray until they overflowed and covered his feet. Just stood there and spooned them on. About ten servings before someone noticed what he was doing." She looked up. "But now he won't eat. I think you've wasted enough of our time, young man. When you're ready to cooperate, just push your call button. We're not jumping through your hoops, Mr. Drug Counselor." Halleran waved a crinkled finger in his face and turned to guide her students to the hall, but stopped when she saw Peter.

Peter looked down at the brooding patient. "Billy Ray, I'm Dr. Sheppard. Dr. Lewis asked me to stop by and see how you're doing." He spoke in a low, gentle voice. Billy Ray remained expressionless.

"How are they treating you?" Peter asked.

"No—ah—meat." Billy Ray's calloused finger shook as he pointed at the gray plastic tray.

"That's not all," Halleran said. "He refuses to cooperate. And he—he won't get proper care until he cooperates with my students." Eyes wide, the red-faced woman stared at Peter.

"Let's take a look." Peter picked up the chart. "Hmm, the Reitan and Luria point to frontal and midbrain damage. The EEG was negative."

"Are you Dr. Lewis's associate? I don't believe we've met."

"No, I'm a psychologist. Dr. Lewis asked me to take a look."

"Oh—well, counseling won't do him any good. Believe me."

"I won't be doing psychotherapy, at least not now. I've been asked to assess the locus and degree of brain damage and its effect on his behavior."

Halleran raised her eyebrows and shrugged. "Well, can you help us—uh, Doctor?"

"What's the problem?"

"He won't eat. That's pretty basic—huh, Doc?"

Peter sat on the bed next to Billy Ray and peered into his eyes. "Billy Ray, take your hand out from under the blanket."

Billy Ray stared back. Silence. A student nurse cleared her throat.

"Billy Ray, take your hand out." Billy Ray inched his hand from under the cover and raised it, palm up, to his face.

"Pick up the spoon." With a shaking hand Billy Ray wrapped his fist around the base of the large soup spoon.

"Now put the spoon under the eggs." Billy Ray lowered the spoon and edged it under a small chunk of scrambled eggs.

"Now put the spoon in your mouth." The machine of a man slowly opened his lips and stuffed the spoon into his mouth. The student nurses smiled. Halleran did not. Billy Ray chewed three or four times and stopped.

"Take another bite," Peter said. But Billy Ray just stared.

"No meat... no meat." Tiny bits of egg spattered the tray when he spoke.

Peter looked at Halleran. She raised her eyebrows and smiled. He again studied the chart. Then he nodded. He reached over and picked up the tray. Then he turned it to position the bacon on the left side.

"Ah... meat... meat." Billy Ray reached for the bacon.

Peter turned. "Anything else we should be doing?"

"How did you manage that?" Halleran's voice boomed.

He led the group from the room to the hall while Billy Ray munched on a cold strip of bacon. "We don't have the CAT scan or MRI, but his behavior is consistent with frontal damage. Pretty severe."

"But wasn't he hit in the back?"

"Most injuries are frontal or temporal because of the bony nature of the skull in those areas. Even though he took a blow to the back of the head, the frontal area of the cortex got banged around because the cortex is driven forward. That's why he's so flat emotionally. And patients of this type often have trouble with sequences, so we need to break behavior down into smaller components. Hand out from under the blanket, then spoon, then open mouth, then take a bite, and so on."

"But what about the meat?"

"Well, neuropsych tests showed a right visual field deficit, so he couldn't see the bacon on the right side of the tray. Actually, I should say he saw it since there's nothing wrong with his vision, but his brain just couldn't register it. With the tray turned, the meat shows up in the left visual field, which connects with the still intact right side of the brain, which is less impaired."

Halleran smiled and pointed her charges down the hallway.

Peter watched them shuffle toward the nursing station. Then he looked both ways before ducking back into the room and closing the door. Peter stepped over to the bed. A thin strand of uncooked bacon fat clung to Billy Ray's chin. Peter took a greasy napkin and wiped it off.

"Billy Ray?" No response.

"Billy Ray, it's Dr. Sheppard. Remember me? Dr. Sheppard. I helped you find the meat. I can help you."

Billy Ray looked up, eyes unfocused.

"Who hurt you?" Peter bent and cupped his hands over Billy Ray's left ear. "Who hurt you? Good Soil? Ghosts? Who hurt you? Billy Ray. Tell me. Tell me now. Who hurt you?"

"Eric." A soft but clear utterance.

"Eric? Did Eric hurt you?"

Billy Ray nodded and tongued his chin where the bacon strand had been. He looked down at the food tray.

Open! The door crashed into a chair and sent a bedpan clattering against the wall. Peter bolted to his feet. A figure in white framed the doorway. Billy Ray stared at the intruder, and his head shook with a palsied tremor.

About Peter's size, the muscular young man was in his twenties. He had a long, thin nose that marked an angular, horsey face and a wide ribbon tied back his shoulder-length brown hair, sixties-style. Three glittering diamonds formed a triangle on his left earlobe.

"Open. Door remains open at all times. Dr. Wolf's orders." He stared into Peter's eyes and smiled, exposing only his lower teeth. It was more grimace than smile, as though he was using unfamiliar facial muscles.

"I needed it quiet for my examination," Peter said. "But I'm finished now." He stepped around the young man, careful to avoid a widening pool of urine that inched its way from the bed pan.

An arm shot out, blocking the door. "I'm Eric Hamlier. Folks call me the Hammer." He smiled.

Peter looked along the top of the Hammer's arm and then directly into his eyes. "I know your mother. It's great that you're back, Eric. So the two of you can work together."

"You didn't come here to talk about my mother, did you?" The Hammer kept his arm rigid and turned his head toward Billy Ray. "Did he talk to you? Listen up, boy. Did this guy ask you any questions?"

Billy Ray, eyes wide, slowly pulled the sheet to his neck.

The Hammer inched his face closer to Peter. "He talk? You been talking to this brain-dead kid?"

"My report will go to Dr. Lewis. Now please step aside."

Stiffening, the Hammer froze in place. "Your clients aren't too lucky, are they, Doc? First that little druggie, Mendola, and now this brain-dead stooge." The Hammer kicked the door with the back of his boot, and it slammed shut.

"I think you need to move out of the way," Peter said.

"It all gets back to the grant, don't it, Doc? You're up here snooping around, trying to make us look bad. If you're a friend of my mother, then she don't need any more—"

Bang, bang, bang! Someone pounded on the door. The Hammer jerked it open. A roundish head peered in. It was Mallory, the officer with the double chin.

"You leaving, Dr. Sheppard? You got a call down at the nursing station. It's your wife."

"Just leaving, Officer."

Peter slipped past the Hammer and into the hallway. The door slammed shut. He heard a muffled voice echo from the room.

"It's me. Eric. Me, Billy Ray."

Peter shook his head. There wasn't a whole lot he could do about poor Billy Ray. He hurried down the corridor, past the barricade, to the nursing station. A nurse pointed at a telephone receiver on the side counter. He picked it up.

"Hello, Peter?"

"Hi. Are you at the airport? What's going on?"

"No, but I've got good news. Dr. Nelson is in Tampa, just for the day. I'm taking Mark over, and he's agreed to see him. And the operation is scheduled for September, at Hopkins. Isn't that great? Maybe this one will turn Mark around. Oh, and the bank called. I'm afraid they're insisting on a full audit of the center before they'll commit on the loan."

Peter rubbed his forehead. "A full audit? God almighty. . . Don't worry, we'll do it. Somehow."

"I know you'll figure a way. You always have."

"What about the trip? Are you and Liz going later?"

"No, and I'm really sorry about that. Naturally, Liz is upset. But she couldn't wait. Said she'd go by herself."

"That's too bad. You folks have some fence-mending to do."

"I know. But she'll be okay once she has time to think about it."

He hung up and stared into space. The bank would never lend them the money, not with the center's negative cash flow. Not when they realized his job was in jeopardy. With the big grant the center would prosper. But without it... ?

Chapter 7

Peter decided to skip the elevator and hurried down two flights of stairs to the main hospital cafeteria. Sterk Trump, wearing his customary flowered silk shirt and plaid Bermudas, waited at a back table. The two men had a standing arrangement for Friday coffee, but their hectic schedule rarely permitted them to meet. Sterk waved his right hand up and down like a checkered flag at a motor speedway.

Peter sat and nodded at his friend. "Anything up?"

"Hell, yes. Last night I'm out on Bayway Isles. Here's this twenty-eight-year-old pretty boy in his million-dollar castle. And guess what? He was the friggin' school counselor at Tampa Beach Middle School for the past five years."

"You think that's what he was really doing?"

"Think I was born yesterday? This guy retired at twenty-seven, for Chrissake. But this poor sucker and his honey can't even leave the house to buy a joint 'cause there's always an Ybor City produce truck or a Busiglia Dry Cleaner's van parked down the road. Now I'm standin' out there last night in the garage of this druggie wigwam with my shotgun, jumpy as a tic on a coon dog, and I'm thinkin' here I am protecting a drug dealer from the Mafia. This any way for a straight and narrow Baptist boy to make a living?"

Peter believed everything his friend said. The thirty-six-year-old detective took on assignments that would terrify most folks in his profession. And people meeting Sterk Trump for the first time were astonished by his appearance. He didn't fit the law enforcement stereotype. More than that, he just looked odd. From the neck down, if it wasn't for his attire, he could have easily passed for a private eye. At five-eight and 190 pounds, the stocky man was all muscle and little body fat. A former all-American guard at Eastern Alabama Institute, he had lightening-quick feet that moved under bulky shoulders like a dancer after five cups of espresso.

Sterk had developed the nervous habit of hiking his shoulders during his glory days of football because his shoulder pads had never fit. Now he inched his shoulders up and down, adjusting the invisible pads in anticipation of danger. A plug of Bandit long-cut tobacco pushed out one sagging cheek. The peppery juice had been used more than once to blind or intimidate an enemy.

"I hear you got some big-time competition for the grant—a shrink and his honey."

Peter winced.

"That might start to explain what in hell's been going on around here. I checked 'em out. Been here since January." Sterk munched on a sugar-coated donut and fingered a small brown puddle next to his coffee cup. "Hell of a stir on Selby Isle when Wolf bought the Chandler estate and moved in with this little gal. Started going to Vinoy Presbyterian. Dantakovic even tried to get into the Easter Belles League. Naturally she didn't make it, but they couldn't keep her out of the church. At least the guy knows what he wants, and they say he's a pretty good shrink."

"That's true, and it's tough for me to say that. I had a bad time at State, back in the seventies, so I can't be objective. But he really goes all out to cure his patients even if he lacks a bedside manner."

"Wanna tell us about State? Sounds like a little ole mystery." Sterk smiled.

"It's a long story, but if Dr. Wolf ever offers to teach you hypnosis, I'd suggest you take a rain check."

"My, my, my, look who's here." Dr. Benjamin Wolf's ebullient voice cut through the cafeteria din as the rotund man barreled toward their table. Peter hadn't seen his old nemesis since the early seventies. And now he appeared, just as they were talking about him.

Back in those days he had looked more like a waiter at a beer hall than a dashing medical student. Five feet, nine inches tall, he had weighed close to 270 pounds. His pinkish, white cheeks were soft and rounded, and he was nearly bald. Many adversaries thought he was just soft vanilla, but they lived to extract tire tread from the high-speed ice cream truck that hit them broadside. Peter could vouch for that.

The figure bearing down on Peter's table now was pie-faced, with a cue ball head, and he carried at least twenty-five additional pounds. Impeccably dressed, he wore a tailored herringbone sport coat and a silk paisley tie. The expensive wardrobe covered Wolf's bulging midsection and projected wealth, success, and unquestioned power.

A thin, hawk-nosed man in his mid to late thirties followed him closely. His polyester suit, brown loafers, and white sweat socks were no match for Wolf's sartorial elegance.

"Nurse Halleran says you put on quite a show on Three South," Wolf said. "I remember a few years ago when you psychologists were making your move on psychiatry. Now it looks like you're going after neurology, too." The big man giggled beneath raised eyebrows and brushed cookie crumbs from his elegant hand-knitted shirt.

"It looks that way," Peter said. "Maybe next time we'll get into hypnosis." Peter immediately regretted the remark.

Wolf threw back his head and giggled. His bald head glowed pink in the glare of the cafeteria lights. "That's a good one, Peter." He turned and smirked at his companion. "That's an inside joke, Harry. Hey, Peter, I'm not trying to one-up you," Wolf said. "But I just got back from Houston—big personal injury case. This guy, Joe Barney, said he had brain damage from an auto accident and couldn't concentrate long enough to hold down a job. A psychologist tested him and said Barney was faking. I testified the poor guy was truly brain-damaged. Well, to make a long story short, the judge ruled against him, and Barney emptied a thirty-eight magnum into the psychologist's head."

Wolf convulsed with laughter and slapped his knees. "Later, Barney was killed in a shootout with the police and the autopsy showed the psychologist was right—no brain damage. That psychologist was dead right. Dead right, get it?" Wolf's hawk-nosed companion crossed his arms and smiled.

Peter shook his head. "Have you met Sterk Trump?"

Wolf emitted a "hi, hi, hi," staccato burst and turned toward the main doors. "Enjoy the grub. I'm headed over to the Vinoy. Need a few of those old-fashioned apple turnovers."

A tremulous hand reached out for Peter. "I'm Dr. Harold Small." Small's limp, bony hand collapsed inside Peter's grip.

"You don't even remember me, do you, Peter? Unbelievable. But it figures. Met you a couple of times at State. Hal Klein was my supervisor."

Peter stared at the man. It was starting to come back now. Small was the guy who got dates for his patients. The guy they had nicknamed the lonely hearts counselor.

"St. Pete is a great town, Dr. Small. I hope you'll make some positive contributions—"

"Oh, I intend to, Peter. Especially when the Good Soil wins the billion-dollar grant. It's too bad you missed out on the mayor's big award. That would have given you an edge."

Sterk folded his arms and spat a wad of tobacco into his empty coffee cup.

Small beamed and pointed his beaked nose at Peter. "By the way, Dr. Wolf has arranged for some of my Good Soil trainees to get involved at the V.A. Hospital. I hear you consult out there. And I'm impressed that you got a nationally known figure like Roger Carlson to do grand rounds. He was your therapy supervisor at Wisconsin, right? How fortunate for you. You might want to fully prepare for the famous professor's visit. My education students wouldn't want to embarrass you in front of the great man.

"Gotta go, gotta go." Wolf elbowed his way toward the exit doors. Small turned and followed him. The smartly dressed physician and the scarecrow-thin man seemed oblivious to the common folk who were left in their wake, like tugboats behind the yacht Britannia.

"Those sons-a-bitches. How could you shake hands with that little weasel, Peter? That guy's out to nail you good. And Dr. Fatso's right there with him." Sterk sniffed the air like a bird dog picking up a new scent, and his shoulders moved to escape the confines of his sport shirt. "Wolf, Wolf. Now I remember. Talked to a lawyer the other day who was working on a spouse-abuse case. They brought this guy Wolf in for expert testimony, and right off he says, 'Which side you want me on? I can go either way.'"

"Yes, I'm afraid that's the Ben Wolf I used to know," Peter said.

"And remember, he's Small's boss. You better be damn careful out at the V.A., Peter."

"True enough. Wolf will knock us cold if he nails Roger Carlson."

"Then you sure as hell better do the knocking. You only got five days until that grant hearing and your chances don't seem to be improving none."

Peter shook his head. His mind flashed back to grand rounds some twenty years earlier. Better to leave those painful memories in the past. Even Wolf wouldn't dare bloody Roger Carlson. The big man was arrogant but not stupid. And no hypnotic tricks this time. Wolf and Small would be tough competitors, but the federal government was rigorous and unyielding when it came to grants. Peter's center still had a good chance to win the grant, and somehow it would. Somehow.

Sterk's cell phone buzzed. He held it to his ear for just a second. Then he handed it to Peter.

"Hello, Peter? It's Liz."

"Liz? Are you still going? Where are you?"

"Hell yes, I'm out of here, brother-in-law. I'm sitting in a Delta wide-body sipping Bloody Marys. It's a little early for booze, but what the hell. I'm going to have a ball even if my big sister can't make it. As usual."

"I'm sorry about that, Liz. I know Kathleen wanted to go, but with Mark—"

"I know. Sometimes I'm a little hard on the old girl. I can see that. Anyway, I'll check out the banks and the so-called sweatshops. And you can damn well bet I'm going to a dig. Barrett set it up. Should be fun. I'll bring you back an artifact. Maybe something to dress up your office a little bit."

"Okay, Liz. Be careful."

Chapter 8

"Dammit, dammit, dammit!"

King-sized pillows muffled Liz's words, but the pounding would not go away. She glared at her diamond-studded watch. Luminous digits blinked 3:45 A.M., Sunday, March 17. Who in hell is crazy enough to be up at this ungodly hour?

She slipped out of bed and pulled on a black lace gown. If it's the front desk, why don't they just ring? Clenching her fists, she marched with short strides to the door. Her feet cut through the lush mauve and black carpet. She wrinkled her nose at the stuffy odor of stale gin and sweet body powder. San Miguel Hotel. Should have named the place after a bandido, not an archangel.

Liz checked the safety chain. Then she cracked the door and stared down at a diminutive, dark-skinned man. She recognized the green uniform of the government archeological bureau.

"What do you want?"

"Forgive me, Senorita Blair. I am sorry to tell you this, but the, uh, the tour, it is not to go today."

"The expedition's been canceled?"

"Si. The government census, it starts today."

"A census? Why in hell are you having a census now, for God's sake? Wasn't this planned?"

"There, uh, there have been some bad things going on. Some of the artifacts are missing, and there is worry that they have been taken from our country."

"Dammit, everything's been screwed up from top to bottom. You people can't even make a decent martini in this so-called world-class hotel." She shook her head and took a deep breath. "Forget it. I'm digging for artifacts, and that's that. You've got the problem, Mr. Bureaucrat. Not me. This was set up with your government, and good money changed hands to give me a virgin dig."

The shrunken man glanced at his watch. "I am sorry, Senorita, but there is another dig in the southeast district."

She stared at him. "Why didn't you say so? What's the problem then?"

"I am very sorry, but the district is five hours by special bus. To arrive at Santa Maria in time, you must leave now."

"Now?"

"I am sorry."

"You said you were sorry a dozen times already. I'm sure that fulfills all departmental regulations in spades."

"Senorita?"

"Never mind. I'll be in the lobby in thirty minutes."

"No, the bus. We need to leave in ten minutes to catch it. I have been up here already five—"

Liz slammed the door. How dumb can you get, sister? What in hell was she doing here, anyway? A lifetime of volunteering, and what had it gotten her? Nothing. She had to be nuts.

~

Five hours later Liz peered through the sooty, mildewed window as the small, rusted bus jolted its way down the broken streets of Calores, Mexico. She fingered the heavy gold necklace. Maybe it would bring her some luck. Better late than never. It had been a gift from her great-aunt Mary, a sister of the Incarnation. Aunt Mary had taken the necklace from her own neck and handed it to Liz.

"This icon graced the home of Finn O'Griffin," she had said. "He was a martyr and saint at the time of Oliver Cromwell. And it is said the icon was blessed by Pius the Seventh, the pope who helped defeat Napoleon Bonaparte. Of that we cannot be sure, but it is fact that in each generation the icon delivers a religious to the church."

It all seemed like a soap opera now. Her brief religious life, Las Vegas, Barrett Spangler. And, of course, big sister Kathleen. Peter was a dear, though. That she had to admit. Well, at least the Good Soil checked out okay. The bank records were in decent shape and, the furniture shops were far above average by Mexican standards. Kat had gone a little overboard with her articles for the *Times*, but that was understandable. Liz smiled. Hell, maybe she was easing up on her big sister. Maybe.

When she stepped off the bus in front of a run-down gas station, she expected a government official to meet her. Initially she felt foolish and conspicuous sitting on hand-stitched leather suitcases from Harrod's of London. The cost of her luggage alone was more than a peasant made in a year, maybe ten years.

The dirt, poverty, and sinister appearance of the isolated village didn't match the photos of colorful towns featured in the travel section of the *St. Petersburg Times*. An hour later she began to regret her impulsive decision to try the Santa Maria dig. Where in the heck was Santa Maria, anyway?

She looked across the hot, steamy plaza. A thin film of sand lined her dry, swollen tongue. Gusts of wind stirred the stench from open sewers running nearby. A blind Indian boy played a little wooden flute on the street corner while tiny children pushed their way toward her with pornographic postcards. Other little ones competed to shine her shoes.

She agreed to several shoe shines and gave generous tips, but this only increased the children's frenzy and excitement. They crowded in, ever so close, and eyed her heavy purse and expensive luggage. She mumbled a shaky prayer and looked around for help.

Suddenly, the children's eyes moved upward in unison. They turned and scampered away. Liz peered over her right shoulder, directly into brilliant sunlight, to see the dark silhouette of a huge man. She bolted from her perch on the suitcases, but her left ankle caught in a suitcase strap. Jerking her foot free, she felt a needle of pain shoot up her left leg.

"San Pedro, importante. San Pedro, importante." The giant continued to mumble as he moved toward a large fountain at the far end of the plaza.

That was the last straw. She forced herself to stand erect on the painful ankle and brushed off her clothes. Signaling the smallest of the children, she waved a handful of pesos and pointed at the front of the gas station. A dozen ninos, like a colony of ants toting a piece of bread, dragged her suitcases inside. She followed them in and gave each child a fifty-peso bill. Much to her relief they closed the door and disappeared into the square.

The gas station seemed to be abandoned. She peered out a filthy window toward the square. The odd giant stood barefoot in the circular stone fountain that backed up to the base of the mountain on the east side of the plaza. Well over six feet tall, he was dressed in a dusty brown robe tied with a rope belt. He seemed to be blessing the natives as he filled their containers. Occasionally he would wave his arms and shout, "San Pedro, importante, San Pedro, importante." How pitiful. The poor, demented man must think he's some biblical prophet, crying in the wilderness.

She looked around. There had to be a toilet here somewhere. Labeled "Senoras," a greasy, discolored sign pointed toward the rear of the station. She pushed her way through a broken door with the bottom hinge missing and followed a crooked dirt path through overgrown brush. A turn in the trail revealed a crumbling old shack with chipped and peeling paint. Covered with fat, buzzing horseflies, it pitched to one side like a sinking ship. Liz pulled back in disgust and turned to leave. That was when she first spotted something moving along the path.

Looking back toward the west, she was blinded by bright sunlight. She shielded her eyes with her hands and saw three figures behind her. They stood, silent and unmoving, across the path.

"What—What do you want?"

The one in front stepped toward her. "Dinero, dinero. We no going to hurt you."

He looked to be about seventeen. Greasy pools of black hair hung to his right shoulder beneath a blood-red bandana, and huge muscles bulged under a tight, black T-shirt. His companions wore identical red bandanas. A gang? They smiled and edged closer to their leader. He peered at her from beneath sleep encrusted eyelids. Liz pulled back and covered her throat. She fingered the octagon-shaped pendant.

The young leader slammed her with his powerful forearm and drove her backward into the splintered wood of the outhouse. Her head snapped back, and her knees buckled, but somehow she stayed on her feet.

The boy slowly unsheathed a wide, flat knife that flashed in the afternoon sunlight. He raised the blade to her face and laid its cold metal flush against her cheek. A tattooed arm tore the hand-stitched purse from her hand. Another arm reached around the leader's shoulder and jerked the ancient pendant from her neck, breaking the chain. She fell to a sitting position just inside the foul and suffocating outhouse. The muscular leader slipped the knife back into its sheath while his two companions quickly pocketed her money and jewelry.

"Yes, take it all," she whispered. "Just let me go. Just leave."

The leader smiled and moved closer. He carefully placed one foot on either side of her body. Looking down, he slowly and methodically opened the silver buckle on his leather belt. The other two laughed and crowded into the narrow doorway.

"Sister Justine... Now it is time."

Oh, God. They knew her religious name! This was no accident. Someone wanted her dead. Liz recalled TV reports about Mexican bandits. Stories of rape, murder, and missing women flashed before her eyes. She was going to die—she was going to die.

Liz tried to remember the short courses on rape prevention, but her mind and her voice were frozen. The sky started to spin, and everything darkened. She thought of death—and worse. Clamping her eyes shut, she gasped for air.

A rough hand twisted her hair and pulled her head upward. The young man's shrill, mocking laughter rang in her ears. The hand tightened, but despite the searing pain she kept her eyes closed. Oh, God. Let it be quick.

"Bastante! The laughter was cut off by a deep, thunderous shout. Liz looked through watering eyes and saw a towering figure behind the young men.

"Bastante!" The giant preacher moved toward them, his jittery, opaque eyes staring upward. Good Lord. Was he blind?

"Bastante," he said again, softer but even more resolute.

The other two grabbed their leader's arms and struggled to pull him back.

The dim-sighted man stepped past them and reached for Liz. "Santa Maria," he said. "Santa Maria."

She stared into the occluded eyes, and a strange tingling sensation swept through her body. Then she heard the sound of retreating footsteps and saw the three predators scurrying into the hot, dry undergrowth.

Chapter 9

Liz buried her head in the giants' chest. She was safe. She was safe! Her body shook with the full realization of her brush with death, and she gratefully let the bear-man fold her into his huge arms.

They moved slowly, step by short step, toward the plaza. Her knees shook as she stumbled again and again on the dry, rocky soil. Warm arms pressed around her while native children watched and giggled. He found a place for them at the side of the fountain and shooed away the mischievous little ones. The preacher held her forehead with one hand and pressed a cold cloth to the back of her neck.

"Vamanos, vamanos." He looked across the plaza and pointed toward a tiny bus sitting near a run-down hotel. Cracked windows, an exposed engine, and peeling red and green paint reminded her of the abject poverty of the area. Squawking chickens peered down from small wire cages that crowded the roof. She blinked. Strapped firmly to the top, her elegant luggage supported the cages of cackling chickens.

The preacher took her arm, and they trudged slowly across the plaza to where the bus stood. He swept her off her feet and lifted her into the bus. Inside, a dozen or so colorfully dressed peasants sat on the few bench seats that still managed to cling to the floor. They greeted the odd giant with boisterous shouts of welcome.

"Juan, Juan!" Smiling and laughing, they stood and clapped. The towering man threaded his way down the narrow aisle, hugging and kissing the men. The driver, a red-faced little man, engaged the ancient transmission with a grind and a suspicious thunk. Dressed rather ceremoniously in a serape and wide-brimmed sombrero, he shouted "San Pedro!" and waved his broad-rimmed hat at no one in particular.

"San Pedro—Santa Maria!" they shouted. With a loud hiss, the bus lurched forward. Even though she was penniless, surrounded by a dozen strangers, and headed for an unknown destination, Liz began to relax. The aroma of berries, oranges, and cantaloupes blended to create a sweet perfume as the brave little bus shook off the dirt and dust of Calores and climbed to the cooler mountain heights.

While obviously poor, the peasants were clean, happy, and extremely well mannered. They spoke no English, but she gradually pieced together their story. They had come to work on the restoration of the Santa Maria Church. The fishermen in the group would provide the food while those skilled in carpentry worked on the church itself.

The narrow trail hugged the steep mountainside. Then she heard thunder. Within minutes a storm moved westward and formed a black celestial cloud some thirty thousand feet high. Torrential sheets of water pounded against the cracked windows and blocked her view. Screaming winds pushed the lurching bus close to the sheer cliffs that abutted the narrow, curving road.

While the passengers tried to ignore the driving rain, the little bus began to hesitate, its engine emitting a high-pitched whine. Finally, it came to a jolting stop. Giving a final defeated shutter, the engine died. A split radiator hose sent clouds of steam upward, as if to appease the angry gods.

Exiting one by one, the peasants fought the buffeting winds and removed their meager belongings from the roof of the bus. Liz, Juan, and the driver were the last ones out. Fearing cave-ins and landslides, the group abandoned the road and began to hack their way through the dense mountain jungle. To keep the weight off her swollen ankle, Liz leaned against Juan and one of the carpenters.

Finally, some two hours later, they reached a small clearing. The rain continued to hurtle down in thick sheets. Juan talked to a short Indian farmer who was sitting out the storm under a primitive lean-to. A faded orange billboard advertising Carta Blanca beer anchored the roof of the swaying shelter.

Juan pointed to a huge brown mule. Liz raised her eyebrows in surprise when the farmer untied the animal and led it to her. Her newfound friends piled small straw bags onto the mule's back. Juan's massive arms plucked her from the rain-soaked grass and effortlessly placed her on the loaded-down mule. Then he turned and dropped a bag of coins into the toothless Indian's outstretched hands.

An hour later, the black, rolling clouds began to dissipate. Edging their way up the final ridge, the travelers reached a treeless grassland near the top of the mountain. The sun broke through a bank of thick, green fog and flooded the valley below with luminescent green light. It looked as though only one spectrum of the rainbow had emerged to engulf the valley.

Atop the swaying mule, Liz was transfixed by the brilliant shades of green. It seemed as though she was deep in the forest, the sun filtering through thousands of deep green leaves, and yet there wasn't a single tree overhead. Liz slowly lowered her eyes from the emerald sky and saw a palacelike church with gold-leaf spires and sky-blue mosaic walls sitting on an island surrounded by indigo-blue water. The fog lifted and hung over the small but princely church. Some of her peasant friends fell to their knees and raised their voices in prayer. Others danced in circles and sang about their God.

"El Dios Verde. El Dios Verde!"

While her limited Spanish kept her from singing the words of the songs, she hummed and clapped her hands with the others. In halting English Juan explained the exuberant and prayerful celebration. According to local legend, the Virgin had appeared near this spot on Easter Sunday seventy-five years earlier, and her image had been burned into a peasant's cloak. A crude grotto was built in her honor, and the church of Santa Maria, constructed entirely by peasant labor, grew up around the grotto. The miraculous cloak still hung near the front altar.

The Virgin had allegedly told the three children to pray for Russia. Pray that the holy names of Christian saints would again be honored in the cities and towns of her beloved people. If the faithful did as she instructed, she promised other signs for the seventy-fifth anniversary of the shrine, which was now only a few days away.

Liz shook her head. Just like all the other shrines, each with its own miracle. Each with its own promise. It was a moving scene, but her gullible days were far behind her. Thank goodness.

Juan took her arm and led her down a steep, grassy slope toward the lake. Two small rowboats sat snugly side by side on the muddy bank.

Were they going to visit the church? Juan turned, and they stepped into a tree-enclosed ravine. There in the distance someone sat on a broken tree limb that ran parallel to the ground. As they got closer she saw a smiling Mexican boy, probably fourteen or fifteen years old.

"Good evening, Ms. Blair." Had she given Juan her full name? She didn't think so. Maybe they got it from her luggage tags. Up close his left leg seemed stiff and wooden, and his mouth tugged slightly to the side. A beggar? Would he ask her for money? Was this the usual shrine trick for American tourists?

"Buenos dias," she said.

"I hope I have not worried you. I am Jesus Gonzalez. My friends call me Gonzie."

"No, I'm not worried. Not now, thanks to Juan." She turned, but Juan was nowhere to be seen.

"Yes, sometimes we try to divert ourselves and do not face our problems directly."

She raised her eyebrows.

"Juan. He says you are from Florida."

"He saved my life. He's an extraordinary man."

"Yes. We are fortunate. He tries to help others when he is not working in the fields with my parents. How do you like living in Florida? My mother says it is a beautiful land, but with many unhappy people."

"I suppose there are unhappy people everywhere, but Florida is probably like most places when it comes to happiness. How did you learn to speak such perfect English?"

"When the Incarnation Nuns left, the Harvest Temple missionaries taught us..."

Liz felt the heat move up her neck to her ears. As the assistant auditor for Mexico she had pushed for the order to leave the country. Good money after bad, it just hadn't seemed practical.

"My father says the use of drugs is quite high in Florida, and there is also much delinquency and promiscuity."

She felt herself pull back. Did he know what the word promiscuity meant? She recalled TV images of Bible-Belt children spewing Old Testament verses under the watchful eyes of their fundamentalist parents.

"You feel my father's observations are too severe?"

She took a deep breath. "Would you like to come to Florida sometime, ah, Gonzie?" He would be perfect for the Good Soil's visiting scholar program. The highly publicized project brought children with leadership potential to St. Petersburg to expose them to drug prevention techniques. The visiting scholars would also serve as mentors for less fortunate children. Gonzie would be an ideal role model for those poor South American girls Doris Dantakovic had talked about at the awards banquet.

"You have many of our people in Florida. They work as migrants. They are trapped in failing schools, but the Virgin has promised to help them."

Those deep brown eyes—there was something, uh, something there. He looked so bright, and he could learn so much in the States.

"My parents would worry about my travel to America, but my uncle would like this. He was waiting for you to come."

"Juan. Is he your uncle?"

"Yes. How did you know?"

"I just knew. I, ah..." She smiled.

Gonzie struggled to stand and finally pushed himself up. He raised his hands, palms upward, and stared into her eyes. "If my father permits, I will go to your land."

Chapter 10

Peter checked his appointment calendar. Monday, the eighteenth. He and his staff had worked all weekend, but they were still far behind. The new date was a killer. A real killer. Peter cracked the door to the waiting room. Linda looked up.

"David's not coming," Linda said. "Just got a call from the Good Soil. They canceled the whole series. Said he's in some kind of lockup or something, and he's going to stay out there permanently."

"You sure? Who'd you talk to?"

"Eric, I think. Eric Hamlier or something like that."

"Call the judge's office, pronto. I'll call David's mom and see if she knows what's going on." He stepped into his office and picked up the phone. Amy Mendola worked checkout at the South Pasadena Cash and Carry. He had to push his doctor title to get her to the phone.

"David didn't show today, Mrs. Mendola. I'm worried about him."

"I'm sorry, I should have told you right away. A man from the Good Soil called last night. Said they had to put David into the ninety-day closed ward. That means no visitors. I called out there this morning, but they won't let me talk to him."

"What? How the heck—"

"Well, they say he's still on drugs, and they think he's in one of those gangs you read about. I just wish his father hadn't left us. The man, a Mr. Hamlier, said some of the druggies in our neighborhood had named David. He said David was selling drugs from inside the Good Soil, so they had to Baker Act him. A whole bunch of kids have gone in there. Not just poor kids from our neighborhood, either. A pretty little gal named Jenny Grant used to work here at the store, and somehow she got bused to that College Park school on Selby Isle. Did real good out there I heard, but she had a drug problem too. A lot of them are the top kids. Shame that they're wasting their lives on drugs."

He bit his lower lip. He had seen Jenny Grant for testing a couple of years back. A beautiful young woman who suffered from a learning disability. A year of remedial tutoring had really turned her around. She had even baby-sat with Mark and Marie from time to time. Peter shook his head. Another casualty in the war against drugs?

"They said it was best for David. Said the courts would go easy on him, and since they were part of the school system they could protect him from the gangs. Said counseling with a psychologist couldn't help a drug problem."

"Okay, Mrs. Mendola. Don't worry. I'll check on how he's doing, and we'll work something out."

"Did I do the right thing, Dr. Sheppard? I know I should have called you."

How could you be so naive? How could you?

"No, no, it's okay, Mrs. Mendola. I'll be in touch later."

Peter hung up the phone. "Oh, my God. Dammit." He picked up the phone and dialed.

"Hello, the Good Soil, Terri Johns speaking. May I help you?"

"This is Dr. Peter Sheppard. I'd like to speak with Doris Dantakovic, please."

"The general is out of town for a week. Can I take a message?"

"The general?" Peter peered at the telephone. "Must be some mistake. I need to talk to the director, Doris Danta—"

The line clicked dead.

He dialed again. Won't win any PR awards out there, that's for sure.

"Good Soil."

"Yes, could I speak with someone in rehab, perhaps an administrator?" The phone started to ring on the other end. His fingers traced an orange and blue seal on the manila envelope that covered a stack of unopened mail. A twenty-year reunion at the University of Florida. Twenty years. Hard to believe.

"Dr. Small."

"Ah, Dr. Small. This is Peter Sheppard. We talked at the hospital. I'd like to check on a patient of mine, a David Mendola. David didn't show today, and his mother says he's now in your isolation facility—"

"Well, as a licensed psychologist, I'm sure you know we can't disclose confidential information without permission. Do you have a signed release from his parents?"

"Well, no, but I saw David twice last week, and he is, or was, my patient. I've got a court order, and I just talked to his mom."

"Hey, let's stop playing games, Dr. Sheppard. You and I both know you're our major competitor for the grant."

"Well, that isn't—"

"You'd love to stir up some trash prior to the NIMH grant hearing. A rather desperate ploy isn't it, Dr. Sheppard?"

"Look here, Small. My only concern is for the welfare of one of my kids."

"Yes, yes. I'm sure you're a lot more worried about one sixteen-year-old druggie than a billion dollars. Do you psychologists really think we educators were born yesterday? Your so called vouchers are just an underhanded way to divert public school money to rich private schools. You think we're back at the university? This isn't 1971, Dr. Peter. You had your shot with David and failed, so why not give your ego a rest?"

"Wait a minute—"

Click.

Peter white-knuckled the phone and started to redial. Then he shook his head and put down the receiver. Never before had a professional treated him that way. But the NIMH hearing could be a factor. Small was right about that, and he was also right about David Mendola. David was no longer Peter's patient.

Linda buzzed. "A Doris Danta-crat-nic, or something like that, on line three. Says she's returning your call. Could be a salesman. Should I have her call back?"

Peter ran his finger along the inside of his collar and peered at the top row of books on his bookshelf. "No, I'll take it." He pushed line three. "Doris?"

"Hello, Peter. The Good Soil said you called." She sounded businesslike, but had the same sweet voice. "I've, ah, been wanting to call you, Peter. But somehow, well, we just got here in January."

"I saw you at the awards ceremony," Peter said. "It's been a long time. Twenty years. Are you doing okay?"

"Yes, I'm fine. Thanks for asking." Her voice softened. "I hear you're married and have two lovely children. Maybe someday we can..."

"That would be nice. Let's try and work that out sometime. I've thought about you and hoped you were okay. It was a long time ago. How's Belle doing?" He laughed. "She was a pistol, as I recall."

Silence.

"Doris?"

"Sorry, Peter. I haven't seen Belle for over seventeen years. Her father took her. One of those parent abductions you read about. It was shortly after Ben and I got, ah, got together. It's a long story and I won't burden you with it, but I did get Eric back. That's been a true blessing. In fact, that's why Ben and I are here. Eric set the whole thing up. He and some friends got the grants and then connected with the school system. Of course he has his own life, and I don't see him much, but still... What did you call Dr. Small about? I'll help if I can." Her voice took on a harder edge.

"It's about David Mendola. I don't understand how he could be selling drugs from inside the Good Soil. I was seeing him in therapy, and he seemed to be moving along rather nicely."

"I don't get involved in the clinical side of things, Peter. My job in mainly PR and marketing. Ben is clinical director, but he's only out there for a couple of staff meetings a week. Dr. Small and my son, Eric, are in the trenches on a day-to-day basis. Would you like me to have Ben call?"

"No, that's okay. It—it was good talking to you, Doris."

"Good-bye, Peter."

He sighed and let himself sink into the soft leather chair. Wolf and Dantakovic. Doree. Hard to believe it was twenty years. He peered down at the University of Florida paperweight and closed his eyes. The sweet scent of rain-washed magnolias drifted through the open window.

~

Moss-laden trees bent low and painted soft, purple shadows across the grounds of the lovely old campus. Just inside the main entrance stood Building E. Born of World War II and originally a part of Vet-ville, the firetrap of an old building was marked by sagging hallways and a distinctive musty odor. In August 1971 it provided temporary space for the growing departments of psychology and architecture.

Peter sat alone in the psychology chairman's office and peered anxiously at stacks of files on the secretary's desk. Eager to start his career as a psychologist, he hoped for a favorable internship placement. After a stint in the Air Force and five years of graduate school, he had only one year of training left.

He heard voices behind the closed door of the chairman's office, but the air conditioners obscured the words. The rattling window units gave little relief from the blistering summer humidity but matched the condition of the old building perfectly. When the compressors kicked in, the convulsive robots quivered and shook before belching cooler air into the hot, creaking room.

A gray, bloated tomcat peered through the bay window. The ghost of Freud, no doubt. Probably wondering what Peter Sheppard was doing in a place like this. The door creaked open, and he looked up, expecting to see the secretary. Instead, a tiny girl of six or seven stared at him with unblinking brown eyes.

"It's raining, it's pouring. You're going to be so boring." She skipped and pranced in circles, golden pigtails flying. He stared at the precocious little demon. What was this, some kind of test?

"It's not raining, and sure as heck not pouring, so maybe I won't be so boring," Peter said.

"No! Stop!" The little elf broke into heavy sobs, then ran full speed into the department chairman's office just ten feet away.

"Mommy, Mommy, he hurt me."

Peter stood, mouth open, and heard the muffled voice of Wilbur West, the department chairman. "There, there," West said. "I'm sure he didn't mean to."

In a few seconds the girl emerged, wiping her wet cheeks on her sleeves, accompanied by one of the most striking women Peter had ever seen. His mouth dropped another inch. Flowing blond hair framed a face thick with mascara and eye shadow. She stood at least six feet tall in her five-inch stiletto heels. Soft mounds of flesh conveyed an earthiness that fit her frame perfectly. He swallowed and bit his lower lip. Hardly an orthodox representative for the department chairman.

"Don't mind Belle," she said. A flowery perfume filled Peter's nostrils. "She's full of the devil like her father, and everybody around here spoils her rotten. I can't keep the students or faculty away."

Peter smiled. It was the mama who drew the flies, not this little monster. He bit his lower lip even harder when the woman bent over, straight-legged, to pull open a file drawer and exposed perfectly rounded buttocks in a tight knit skirt. He knew he should look away, but didn't. The dark seam in her black stockings accentuated the length and curve of her legs.

The feather-light touch of fingers on his thigh interrupted his thoughts. He looked down to see little Belle staring at him with an impish smirk. The tears were gone and sunshine again filled her pretty face. She snuggled her head under his arm and pressed her face into his rib cage.

"Let's play." Belle grabbed his shirtsleeve and pulled him to a chair just behind her mother, who chose that moment to straighten and shake herself like some exotic dancer at a roadside strip joint.

Belle jumped onto Peter's lap and folded her hands in prayer. "Here is the church—and here is the steeple. Open the doors and see all the..."

Peter smiled. "Peop—"

"Penis!"

"What did you say?"

"Penis, you bore head." Belle stuck a finger in each of her dimpled cheeks and gave him a doll-faced grin.

"Belle, that's enough out of you. Don't mind her. Professor Sidney thinks children shouldn't be sheltered, so he and Mrs. Sidney are totally open in front of Belle. We've lived with them since we came over on a work-study visa. I work for the department half-time and take hospital marketing over at the health center. And you, of course, are Peter Sheppard. How does it feel to be the, um, how do you say, the number-one draft choice?" Even Belle quieted down with this supreme benediction and stared at Peter.

"Well, I don't know about that." He stood and brushed wrinkles from his slacks while his eyes searched the files and stacks of mail on the secretary's desk.

"Phi Beta Kappa and magna cum laude? Don't be so modest, Mr. Sheppard. You can afford to be a little arrogant. How do you get every answer right on the quantitative SATs except one and then have the test-makers agree that your solution was better than theirs? It's all here in the file." She held up a manila folder.

Peter smiled. He wasn't about to stop the flattery.

"I'm Doris Dantakovic, by the way. Belle and I are from Poland. My father was a full professor at the University of Krakow."

He noted her near-perfect English. "What about Belle's father?"

"He couldn't decide between the Nazis and the Soviets. Not a nice man unless you think spying on priests is a civilized form of conduct."

Peter glanced at Belle.

"I know I shouldn't talk in front of Belle, but she's got to know these things. The man joined the S.S. after Auschwitz. He was only seventeen. And he thinks he's a baron, for God's sake, related to Queen Victoria through the kaiser. Can you believe it? Worst of all, he kidnaped Belle's brother. I haven't seen my son, Eric, in four years." Tears wet her eyes and smudged thick layers of mascara.

Why was she telling him all this? His psychological training warned him to be wary of people who opened up too much too soon.

Doris bent and held her daughter's face in a beautifully manicured hand. "And he was mean to us, wasn't he, Belle?" A dark shadow crossed Belle's face. For a moment Peter thought she was angry at her mother, but the shadow lifted before he could be certain.

"Well, he won't bother us anymore." Doris stood and brushed tiny wrinkles from her green knit skirt. Then she bent over her desk and picked up a long, narrow envelope. "I was just going to mail this, Peter. It's your transfer to the teaching hospital for the '71 academic term." Doris smiled at Peter through perfect white teeth.

"But I signed for the Webb-Davis Children's Home. There's got to be some—"

She flashed him another blinding smile. "I know, I know. I just work here, as they say."

"But, I—"

"No buts, Mr. Sheppard," Wilbur West said. West shot across the room carrying two fishing rods and a thick volume of statistical abstracts. "I know you signed for Webb-Davis, but two of our guys got Sloan fellowships and need to stay another year. You'll get your shot at Webb-Davis. I'll see to it. That's a promise."

"But—"

"And we're putting you in with the chief resident. That's definitely a feather in your cap. I'm sending our best students to work with the psychiatry residents. Can't let them show us up, right, Sheppard?"

Peter shook his head. This couldn't be happening. Not after all his careful planning. The hospital was bad enough, but sharing an office with the chief resident? He'd be working under a microscope. He'd have to watch every move he made, every word he uttered. And the chief resident, Benjamin Wolf, had a reputation for slicing up psychology students and cooking them for lunch.

He looked down. Belle smirked and tilted her head. Now what? If he transferred it would raise questions on his transcript, and he'd lose a year, maybe two. And the tuition money wouldn't last. His family had sacrificed enough. Shrugging Belle off, Peter stood. He pushed his fist into the pit of his stomach and opened the door. He'd seen a toilet on the way in, down near the Coke machine. He ran.

~

Peter took a deep breath and ran his fingers along the edge of the orange and blue envelope. It had been a tough year. An awful year. Wolf had seemed to delight in badgering him. And when Wolf used posthypnotic suggestion to embarrass him at grand rounds, it almost ended Peter's career. The bastard. Peter stood and reached to the top of the bookcase. He eased the book down and dusted off the jacket. The Prophet, by Kahlil Gibran. He opened the cover.

> Dearest Peter,
> I send this book to you alone. For today and all the days of our future.
> Lovingly yours,
> Doree

She had marked the chapter on friendship, but they both knew it had meant much more. Who knows? Maybe things would have... But Wolf made sure they didn't. He used quick-fix drugs and God knows what else to ease Doree's anxieties about her son. Just when she was starting to understand herself—starting to fall in love with Peter.

Chapter 11

Peter backed the Volvo out of the office parking lot and took a quick right onto Fifth Avenue North. He smiled and shook his head as he peered at the old St. Petersburg Coliseum and its ubiquitous shuffleboard courts. Friends and family had questioned his move to St. Petersburg, Florida, to open a child and family clinic. Back then, in the midseventies, the city on the peninsula had the reputation of a genteel town run by and for senior citizens. God's waiting room. (The old folks really lived in Fort Myers, but their parents lived in St. Pete.)

Peter knew better. Pinellas County now boasted the sixteenth largest school system in the United States and had experienced a phenomenal growth rate. The rapid transition had produced a kind of midlife crisis in a city that was not confronting the stresses of growing old but rather those of growing young. Because of its limited living space, sociologists called the city a natural habitat for sociological research. They probed the water-locked peninsula, searching for answers to vital questions about America's future.

But Peter thought of it as an elegant city. Its grace, beauty, and architecture were so different from Tampa, its brawling big brother east of the Howard Franklin Bridge. St. Pete's majestic hotels, pink brick streets, and sandy white beaches brought together the regal traditions of the Old South and the relaxed lifestyles of tourists from around the world.

Brother Tampa was not so pretentious. He'd bounce back from a bloody nose and return to enjoy the fight. St. Petersburg yearned for some of Tampa's rugged energy and sometimes wondered if a bloody nose might indeed be worth the effort.

Peter looped around St. Jude's Cathedral to Twenty-Second Avenue North. Tourist traffic, headed for the beach, clogged roads leading to the Tyrone Mall. Just ahead he spotted the Veterans Administration Hospital. With its back to Boca Ciega Bay, the massive tripartite structure stared defiantly at approaching motorists. Flanked by two low-slung buildings, the recessed twenty-story structure reminded Peter of a mighty throne. Built in 1944 to care for damaged and broken G.I.s, it was still the largest wooden building in Florida.

A two-passenger service elevator took him to the third floor. He stepped down the narrow hallway to the main psychology office. Through the open door Peter could see his old mentor, Lane Travis, sitting with his hands folded behind his head and his hiking boots anchored to his desktop. Florence Cohen, chief psychology intern, made notes on a yellow legal pad. When Peter stepped through the doorway, Lane narrowed his feet to form a leather gun sight and peered at Peter. "Hey, you're lookin' mighty serious, Dr. Sheppard." Lane gave Peter a crooked smile.

"It's a big day." Peter pulled out a chair next to Cohen. "Hi, Flo. You ready for the seminar?"

"I, uh, I think so, Dr. Sheppard, but I was just telling Dr. Travis that something's up with Ed Blevins."

"Is that the new chief resident? How do you read it, Lane?"

"According to Flo, our old friend Wolf is stirring up the pot. He's only been supervising the psychiatric residents for a couple of weeks, but Blevins is all of a sudden real competitive."

"He's going to challenge Dr. Carlson at the seminar this morning," Flo said. "The patient is Starlyn Dalton. I believe you know her, Dr. Sheppard. They're determined to get this little gal into the Good Soil once and for all. She was taking some counseling out there, but that was strictly voluntary. Her father called several times. He wants her out of there pronto. He told me Starlyn's mother is some kind of New Age space cadet who couldn't care less about her kids."

"Uh." Lane shook his head.

"Sorry, Dr. Travis. I, uh, she is, uh, perceived to be a highly unfocused person who is pursuing extreme lifestyles that could, uh, impact negatively on her children."

Peter smiled.

When Flo Cohen left, Lane turned to Peter. "Deja vu—1971."

"I know, and it's pretty clear why."

"Yep," Lane grunted and swung his feet to the floor. "You've been nominated to head up the Behavioral Research Unit. A psychologist has never held that post at the V.A. Only psychiatrists up to this point. And you invited Carlson to lecture. Show up the great professor and you show up Peter Sheppard." He stared into Peter's eyes.

"If I don't win the top research post the grant's in big trouble. You could be right, he'll probably use the students to get at me."

"I know he will. And if Carlson holds his own, he'll try something else." Let's face it, Peter. Psychiatrists are M.D.s, and this is a hospital. As Ph.D.s we'll never be fully accepted. Blood is thicker than water, and we're not even close relatives."

"Our training is as good or better than theirs'."

"You're right, Peter. But unfortunately we ain't in the family and that's the rub."

~

The ten o'clock seminar usually took place in the third floor research library. Peter scanned the large, airy room. Some forty feet long, a narrow conference table separated a bank of windows from rows of bookshelves on the inside wall. Dr. Carlson would interview the patient at the north end of the table, near the door, while eight psychiatric residents, two psychology interns, and an education fellow observed from the other end of the table. Faculty supervisors were also welcome to attend.

Psychiatric residents had completed basic medical training and faced three years of instruction in mental disorders. Clinical psychology interns had completed five years of graduate training in human behavior and mental disorders and still needed two years of pre-doctoral and post-doctoral internships. School psychology fellows came from the college of education. They were the new kids on the block.

Monday morning rounds had an adversarial feel. While senior staff attempted to keep a lid on this natural competition, occasional turf wars were intense and bitter. The professors looked on with embarrassed grins, eyes darting from side to side, when one of their protegees scored a point. Their demeanor reminded Peter of the little girl who taunts her brother into screaming and then assumes an angelic pose for her parent.

Dressed in snug-fitting jeans and a black T-shirt, Starlyn Dalton entered the room followed by an orderly. Letting her eyes scan the room, she crossed her arms and pulled her shoulders back. When she made contact with Wolf, she quickly looked away. Dr. Carlson stood and pulled out a chair. He patted it gently and smiled. Starlyn yanked the chair back, away from the table, and threw herself down.

"What is your name, young lady, and why are you here?"

"I'm Starlyn. And I want the hell out of this place. Okay?"

"I take it you're really feeling very unhappy about being here, Starlyn."

"That's right. Wouldn't you be screwed if your father kicked you out of your own house. Wouldn't let you have any friends?"

Peter knew Carlson and the trainees had received file copies showing that Starlyn had a record of drug abuse, school truancy, and sexual promiscuity.

"I sense you are very angry and unhappy. You feel your father has been totally unfair."

"You're damn right. He don't care about me. All he wants me to do is school work, stay at home, and live like a hermit. He's a goody-goody, just like my mom said..."

"You feel that he's never given you freedom and a chance to be yourself."

"That's right. Same thing's true in this crappy place. I can't even write a letter without somebody checking it. And those shrinks are watching me every minute." She turned and stared, eyes pointed, at the white-coated students.

"I guess this place reminds you a little bit of home. You're feeling kind of angry and frustrated."

"Yeah, I—uh, think you understand." Her face softened. "Can you get me an outside phone?"

Blevins snorted and looked gleefully at the other residents.

"C'mon, Doc, I just need to get off this floor for a little while, make a few calls." She bent forward and fingered Carlson's coat sleeve. "This place is getting me down—I'm getting real depressed." She glanced at Wolf. "I could hurt myself."

"I guess the constriction and rules here are pulling you down in terms of your feelings."

"Yeah, I know—that's what I said, but can you help me out or not?" Down the table Blevins snorted again. Several of the residents stared at Carlson, their arms folded.

"No, I can't change the rules, Starlyn, but I really do know how you feel, and I'm hopeful your behavior will convince people around here that you deserve a another chance."

Starlyn lowered her head to the table and broke into quiet sobs. There was complete silence in the room. The students' stone-like faces seemed devoid of feeling, but Carlson held nothing back. Voice warm and muted, his lips quivered. "I hate to see you feeling so miserable, Starlyn. It must seem like nobody cares about you at all."

"You bastard"! Eyes wild and dilated, Starlyn stared at the great doctor. "You're just like my father. All this means nothing. You're just a liar like my father. He says he wants to help me, but he doesn't. He just wants to keep me locked up. It's like Dr. Wolf told me this morning. You won't give me shit no matter how hard I try."

This was the only time Carlson's eyes left his patient. He peered at Wolf who slouched in his chair grinning like a fat Buddha. Carlson looked back at the girl, warmth and empathy outlined across his face.

"I guess you're feeling angry and really mad. You feel like all this talk is just a lie. A way to keep you locked up."

"You're god-damned right I do! I want out of here." Starlyn pushed her chair back and stared at the door.

"I guess you feel this has been a waste. But I want you to know I respect you as a person and sincerely want to help you feel better."

Wolf raised his eyebrows and looked at the ceiling.

Carlson moved his head closer to Starlyn. "You may go, Starlyn, but remember that I care about you. If you want to talk again—I'll be here." She stood with a jerk, threw her head back, and pounded out the door, followed by the aide.

No sooner had the door closed than it opened again. Wide-eyed, the orderly leaned his head into the doorway. He looked toward Blevins and Wolf.

"I forgot—didn't know if you wanted this now or not, but Nurse Lewis said she couldn't find the key. She did a strip search up on Six-South. Said you wanted to know right away since it's the key to the whole hospital. If Starlyn, ah, the patient has it, she sure hid it well."

Blevins turned bright red. "No, that's—ah, that's all right." Wolf leaned back and closed his eyes.

"What's this about a key?" Carlson asked. "It could impact on her counseling."

"I believe it's your key, isn't it Dr. Blevins?" Flo Cohen crossed her arms and stared at Blevins. "At least that's the word up on six."

Blevins glared at Cohen. "Now you just wait a minute."

Peter looked at Wolf. How in heck had Starlyn gotten the key from Blevins? The master key controlled the security area, the medication cabinets, even the front door to the hospital. Then Peter pictured Starlyn in her tight jeans. He shook his head. Of course. What other leverage did the poor little gal have?

Squirming bodies accentuated the feelings of embarrassment that hung over the silent room.

Carlson faced his students. "As you can see, this little girl has been hurt deeply. She feels betrayed and holds a lot of anger. She feels abused and rejected, so it's important to accept her as a person without any conditions or qualifications to that acceptance."

Blevins raised his hand. "Can I say something, Doctor? Something's funny here, because MMPI research tells us this girl's a psychopathic deviate, without feelings, and a person who is highly manipulative. We saw this with the key thing. She's pretending to have the key to the whole hospital. Trying to play one father figure against another. A typical ploy of someone like this."

"I think we can help her by reaching her feelings. Even though she manipulates others to find superficial pleasures, it's just a way of filling that deep hole she feels inside. She—"

"C'mon, Dr. Carlson, I don't believe you can sit there and pretend to sympathize with this girl when she's obviously trying to manipulate you. Isn't that being a little dishonest?"

"I guess you're feeling kind of frustrated and maybe a little irritated. You feel this girl is pulling the wool over my eyes—that I'm not really helping her."

"That's, ah—exactly right." Blevins looked to Wolf for support. The uneasy shifting of eyes and feet was interrupted when the conference room door flew open. Spread-eagled, the aide blocked the doorway with his body and shouted over his shoulder.

"She wanted to come back in and I, uh—didn't know if you wanted to see her or what to..."

Starlyn squeezed past the aide, ran to the table, and swooped into Dr. Carlson's arms. She clung to his neck and buried her head in his chest. Tears streamed down her cheeks.

"I just wanted to let you know," Starlyn said between sobs, "that you're the first person who's listened to me. I'm going to turn things around and start over."

"I'm happy for you, dear. A chance for a new start and some hope for the future."

"Yes," Starlyn said softly. She turned to exit with the orderly.

Peter shook his head. That was too quick, too easy. But Carlson was a master at conveying his feelings. That's how he had become world-renowned. Then again, Blevins and Wolf had a point. This girl was a master, too. A master manipulator.

Wolf stood and put his hands on his hips. The rotund man took a deep breath, and his face reddened. He stomped his fist on the table. "You can't let her get away—"

But the tinkling sound of metal interrupted his diatribe. There, under a crumpled paper cup, in front of Carlson, glowed the gold master-key. All eyes focused on the key. Carlson looked at Wolf. The old professor conveyed the same kindly expression that he had bestowed on the young girl.

Wolf looked down, then shifted his eyes toward Peter.

Peter realized he was smiling ever so slightly. He regretted the personal indulgence, but it was too late. Wolf clenched his jaw and glared at Peter through squinting eyes.

Carlson thanked the group, and the seminar ended. Surrounded by other faculty members and a few students, Peter and Lane Travis headed down the crowded hallway. They had just reached the staff elevators when Peter heard someone call his name. He looked up to see Dr. Harold Small skipping down the steps, a devouring smile stretching his ears.

"My, my, just like the old days at State, Peter. Only difference is the outcome. Starlyn's headed back to the Good Soil." He laughed. "That means she can't open her pretty mouth about anything. She just loved Billy Ray's counseling. Now she's going to get more of the same."

"What? We made it clear she needs counseling here, and, uh—"

"Nope, take a look." Small's bony hand waved a sheaf of papers in Peter's face. "Court order and subpoena, just got 'em from the school board attorney. Ninety days in the Soil's solitary unit for observation. And Judge Rolfson wants to know why she needed an evaluation over here. Hope you have a good explanation. Hear he's kind of irritated."

"Rolfson? He's the one that ordered me to evaluate—"

Lane stepped between them. "Wait a minute, Dr. Small. This is all wrong. It's—"

"And another thing, Dr. Peter. If there's any way I can be of service, please don't hesitate to ask. I realize my students aren't at your level of training, but we've managed to help a few people in our own clumsy way." With a toothy grin and a low bow, the skinny professor twirled about and marched down the hall, a noticeable bounce punctuating his step.

"What lake bed did that guy slither out of?" Lane asked.

"Don't you remember him?" The two men were silent during the short walk to the psychology office. Lane closed the door.

"I don't believe it," Lane said. "Same old manipulation. Just like the seventies, only then it was hypnosis."

"We never proved it. If Wolf did induce me he's got some secret—some powers unknown to this world. The scientific world we know, anyhow."

Lane hung his white lab coat on the door-hook. "He did it, and I don't doubt that for a minute. We almost lost you, then. You realize how close you came to ending your career?"

"Well, cackling like a chicken in the middle of grand-rounds didn't endear me to the psychology staff. But naturally, the psychiatrists loved it. You were there. I'm sure you'll never forget it."

"I won't," Lane said. At first I thought you had a seizure, then I thought of Tourettes'. As I recall, you had a deal with Wolf. You'd show him how to interpret psychological tests, and he'd introduce you to hypnotic techniques. But he obviously had a hidden agenda."

Peter nodded and took a deep breath. "I've always believed in Roger Carlson's theories about trust, but I learned that you can't trust everyone. I learned that the hard way."

"But to use the courts—our friends, the lawyers? Once they get in here, it's all over." Peter tossed his note pad onto the desk and sank into a faded, brown leather chair.

"Wolf always seems to find a way. I'd better put the research post on hold. No way I'll get early confirmation now."

Lane looked away. "You're right. When the hospital board gets this subpoena there's going to be fall out—embarrassment, at least. I knew Wolf could be competitive, but this is too much. He's just pushing it..."

Peter stood and walked to the large open window. Down below, patients in dark blue fatigues raced around a softball diamond. Occasional shouts and curses drifted upward through the humid salt air.

"Yep, Ben sure knows how to push things," Peter said. "He seems to operate outside the rules. The day-to-day rules we take for granted, anyway. But this time he has to lose. There's just too much riding on it."

~

Jenny Grant sat at her usual spot in the Good Soil cafeteria. She pushed parsley and cooked carrots around her plate while she read the note. An order to return to her room signed by Breaker Mitchum. She slapped down the carton of milk and pushed her food away. This could only mean trouble. Mitchum was one of the real nasties. Usually her orders were verbal and came from the enlisted ranks.

She took brisk steps down the long tile corridor. The distinctive, sweet odor of marijuana grew stronger as she approached her room. Halting near her door, she saw willowy strands of grayish blue smoke billow into the hallway. Fanning the pungent air with her hands, she peered inside. A muscular youth with three stripes on his epaulet sprawled on her bed. Had to be a captain, at least? Breaker Mitchum sprawled on the red love seat, sucking a clay pipe.

"All right—it's about time." Mitchum leaned back and crossed his booted legs.

"There's a special meeting. It's, uh, the Hammer..."

"That's later." Mitchum blew a ring of wobbling smoke in her direction. "We've always got time to reward one of our top officers, don't you think?"

She glanced at the young man and tried not to stare. He had blotchy red cheeks and looked stiff and uncomfortable. Maybe even scared?

"You're not high, what gives?" Mitchum asked.

"Uh, I'm just not up to it, not feeling real good."

Mitchum pushed himself up from the chair and staggered toward her. "Too good for the program, I guess. Maybe putting you on report will help." He stuck out a plastic bag filled with white powder.

She knew her transformation would appear abrupt and unnatural. "No, I'm up now, really turned on." She snorted the cocaine.

"Yeah, I'll bet. Well, it don't matter. Just show the Major a good time." Mitchum stomped out and slammed the door.

A tilted black and silver name tag glimmered on the night stand and stared like a voyeur's eye.

"Major David Mendola."

Chapter 12

Peter listened to the intercom buzz, again and again. Linda wasn't going to give up. He picked up the phone.

"Ms. Blair on two, doesn't sound like herself." Linda's high pitched, squeaky voice signaled her concern.

"Liz Blair? Back from Mexico?"

"She called twice this morning and sounded really upset, but since you were tied up at the V.A., I thought..."

He punched the outside line. "Hi, Liz. How are you doing?"

"Oh, Peter. Fine, just fine. It—it was really something. I've got to talk to you. Just a few short days, but it's like, well, I'm starting to change. Really. I know it's hard to believe."

How many times had Kathleen told him stories about her little sister's sudden conversions? One time it was mountain climbing, even though there wasn't a single mountain in Florida. Another time it was a 'Save the Manatees' group. None of Liz's obsessions had lasted for more than a month or two.

"We do need to discuss your sudden improvement. If it's legitimate, it should stand up under a little scrutiny."

"Oh, it will, Peter. But that's not the only reason I'm calling. I brought back a Mexican boy."

"Back here?" He doodled a series of question marks on a message pad. Then he jotted down the word "impulsive."

"Yes, he's a crippled child but very bright. Barrett Spangler got him through the red tape so he could come back with me. I arranged for him to join the exchange program at the Good Soil, and I took him straight out there this morning."

Peter raised his eyebrows and shook his head. "How's he doing?"

"That's just it. When I got back to Barrett's place, I called to see if he needed anything, but they said he wasn't there."

"What do you—?"

"He's just not there, Peter. I talked to admissions a dozen times. They said he must have left as soon as I drove away. I talked to a supervisor, uh, Eric Hamlier. He said Gonzie never officially entered the program. I've tried calling Mexico but his parents are migrant workers, and there's no phone service anyway. I even called the police, but they just turned around and contacted immigration. A customs guy said they were tracing his green card and student visa. School board gave me the name of an assistant superintendent who works with minorities, but she hasn't called back."

"How can I help, Liz?"

"I remembered Kat saying you guys knew a private detective. I wonder if I should go that route. I feel so responsible, Peter. If anything happened to that boy, I don't know what I'd do."

"You're still on the board out there. Can't you get some inside information?"

"Actually, it's Barrett that's on the full board. I'm just relegated to the foundation. I never served on the actual board of directors."

"I'm sure there's a logical explanation. Why don't we give it a few days? Look, if Linda can work you in we'll talk some more this afternoon."

"I don't know Peter, he's such an innocent kid. And with his physical problems, who's going to look out for him?"

~

Three hours later, Peter peered across his desk at his beautiful sister-in-law. She sat on the edge of the tufted-wing chair, her hands folded on his desk. "You were right Peter, it's the little things that bottle you up, make you a prisoner. Even Gonzie, a Mexican peasant, knew I had my priorities screwed up. Take last night, after we got back from Mexico. I've got a whole new outlook on life now, but I still needed a haircut. I'm not going to the extremes any more but my hair, it..."

"You don't have to feel guilty about getting a haircut."

"I know, but I got to the Coffee Clutch ten minutes late, and Arnold was one unhappy camper. He can't stand it when I'm late, and of course I don't dare have anyone else touch my hair. I remember the Ascot trip with Barrett. Alexander of London gave me a quick cut, and when I got back Arnold blew a gasket. And he wouldn't try any of the new styles from Harpers & Queens. Of course, none of that matters now."

Peter put down his pen and sat back. "What's wrong Liz? This isn't why you called. Are you finding it hard to talk about the boy—ah, Gonzi?"

She shook her head and looked down. He was amazed to see real tears blotting her eyelashes. Maybe she had softened some.

"It's a long story."

"I'm here," Peter said.

"Actually, it turned out great. If it hadn't been for... I wouldn't have met Gonzi. And his uncle, Juan. I was lost in this horrible little town, and Juan took me on a bus to the mountains. So beautiful. The Church of Santa Maria. An anniversary of the shrine. The Blessed Mother said to pray for Russia, that the saints' names would be restored to their cities. And that green light, so indescribable. El Dios Verde, the peasants called it. Such good people. Of course I'm still not buying it completely. Same old stuff. Virgins' promises and all that. But it got me wondering. Somehow it's helped me think more about myself and what's important..."

"Liz?"

She raised her hand to her mouth, then put it down. Face pale and drawn, she edged forward. "They, you can't, ah... They tried to kill me in Mexico."

"They what?" He leaned forward and peered into her lusterless eyes. "Who tried to kill you?"

"I don't know for sure, young peasant boys with red bandanas. And they knew my religious name."

"Where did they—?"

"In Calores. My dig was called off. They claimed there was a special census, so I had to take a bus to another dig and landed in Calores. A horrible little place. Those knives. I'll never forget—I just, I don't want to talk..."

Peter stood and walked around the desk. He bent and put his arm around her shoulder. "It must have been horrible. If you can't talk right now it's okay. I—"

She looked up. "I think the Good Soil was involved."

Peter straightened. "What? Surely, they wouldn't—"

"Only you, Barrett, and Dr. Small, knew about the trip. And Kathleen, of course. Then the sudden change of plans in the middle of the night and that awful bus ride to the wrong village. A place where I was stranded, even after all the careful arrangements. I didn't put two and two together until Gonzie disappeared."

"But surely you could have been attacked right here in Saint Petersburg? Why would they follow you down there and why would they want—?"

"I know, but it was such a desolate area. People would have thought I'd gone off on another lark. Screwed up ex-nun and all that. Think about it, Peter. This was a spur of the moment trip. You look astonished, and I know it sounds far fetched, but my body is sending me vibes on this one, and I'm starting to listen to my feelings."

"But, I—"

"No, the Good Soil is involved somehow. Jesus, and I brought Gonzie back here, to that screwed up place. How could I be so dumb? The banks were okay and the shops checked out, so I just thought Kat had gone overboard with her newspaper stories."

Liz's cheeks took on a pink hue. "Maybe I was even hoping she was wrong. But after this morning, after Gonzi's disappearance, I started to wonder. That's why I called you, first thing. Barrett has lots of connections. He's even got video stores in Mexico City. His people did some snooping. Guess what? There was no census. It was all a lie. Just a trick to get me on that bus."

"Uh—I don't know."

"And Gonzie? Is he going to disappear like I was supposed to?"

"Why would they want to hurt the boy?"

"I don't know, Peter. Maybe he was a witness. He saw me there. Maybe they were going to try again. And another thing. When I reminded Dr. Small of Kat's newspaper series, he didn't like it one bit. And then Barrett pulled out of the drug-week fundraiser. I think they're after Barrett's money. Maybe I was getting in the way."

"I suppose that could be a motive." Peter found himself dropping the role of therapist. "Anything else you can think of?"

"No, not really. Well, they did take my antique pendant and gold necklace. The pendent shows the trinity. My great-aunt Mary gave it to me. She's a Sister of the Incarnation, too. That necklace led me to the religious life, but I'll never wear it again. I just know it." Tears cris-crossed her cheeks. They reminded Peter of the Randkluft chasms he had seen in Norway. Chasms formed by receding ice.

"I guess the pendant's worth a lot of money but not enough to kill for. I'm running scared, Peter. And it's not just for Gonzie. It's for me. What am I going to do?"

Peter looked into the unblinking blue eyes and felt tired, very tired. It was like a dozen soft quilts had been piled on his shoulders and were slowly pushing him down. The preliminary grant meeting was only a few days away. David Mendola, Starlyn Dalton, and the V.A. fiasco. Now the threats to Liz and the Mexican boy.

"Okay Liz. I'll call Sterk Trump. If he comes up with anything, I'll let you know. Sterk knows agents with the FDLE, the Florida Department of Law Enforcement. They'll keep an eye on you."

"I trust you, Peter. And I trust Kat, believe it or not. That's something else I'm finally starting to learn. But we have to move quickly. Maybe the open house is a place to start."

"The open—"

Barrett has arranged for me to attend the Good Soil open house tonight. It's restricted to parents, but I'm riding on Barrett's clout. Can you come? Please?"

Peter sat back on the edge of his desk and ran his fingers through his hair. "It's not what I usually do, Liz. But then again, what's been usual about this whole crazy thing? I'll be there."

Liz stood and gave him a tight, cool kiss on his forehead. Then she turned and took quick strides to the door. She looked back, but did not smile or even acknowledge his presence. So much for her quick recovery.

Peter stepped over to the big stained-glass window and waited. Liz came out the front door and walked to her green Jaguar sedan. What a striking figure. Liz looked both ways and slid into the driver's seat. Now what?

Line one blinked. He bypassed Linda and pushed line three.

"Peter? This is Lane. We've got problems. They've delayed your nomination for the research post, want a committee to review the whole situation."

"There was no mention of a committee before."

"I know, and that's not the worst part. The committee's going to be made up of mostly M.D.'s, and some of them are cozy with Wolf."

Peter shook his head. "It figures."

Chapter 13

Peter steered the Volvo through the ancient fort's east gate and into the large brick quad. Towering stone walls formed a rectangle around the fort, with the chapel on the north side and a three-story housing complex on the west side, facing the bluffs.

"This place looks like a prison," Peter said. "Those walls have to be at least thirty feet high."

Liz sighed and crossed her arms. "I've heard the whole damn spiel. They even wanted me to give PR tours to potential donors. Let's see, the U.S. Army built this place around 1842, right on top of the old Indian burial mounds. And the Spanish had some kind of facility out here, too. Bellair Bluffs is the highest point in the county, seventy-five feet above sea level, so naturally it made a great spot."

"That high? I didn't know—"

"They had dungeons under the fort, but no one is allowed down there now. Problems getting insurance or something. And the old Indian burial mounds are under there, too. Kind of spooky, if you ask me."

"But these walls, isn't it unusual to have—"

"That's the funny part. Back when they had the big malaria epidemic, the army built these higher walls to keep the mosquitoes out."

Peter looked at her.

Liz laughed. "Cross my heart, that's what they thought. Look closely and you'll see half-timbers about fifteen feet up. That's the original wall. The rest is the addition. And the Good Soil put up the barbed wire. Anyway, the Confederate Army added the Jackson Chapel in 1863. Stonewall Jackson, a man who never went to battle without his bible."

They got out of the car and walked over to the chapel. Three young men in Good Soil robes checked Liz's tickets, and then a tough looking cookie with a closely shaved scalp waved them in. His name tag read "Breaker Mitchum."

They followed the flow of parents into the chapel and found two seats in the back row. Peter kept his head down. Mitchum hadn't flinched when Liz handed over the passes. He either wasn't on the ball, or Barrett Spangler was indeed the ultimate power broker. He'd have to bet on Spangler.

Absolute silence. If it weren't for the occasional sobs and sniffles Peter would have questioned whether the hissing speakers were even working. Two hundred people, all trapped in limbo. Separated by fifty feet of creaking hardwood floors and Good Soil rules, parents sat in pews near the old confessional at the back, while their children sat on the stage, up front.

Wearing faded jeans, stylishly torn, and washed out prints, the youngster's faces glowed. But did they really know? Did they get it? Where had these pretty aliens come from?

And in the back, the real losers. Parents of the kids on stage stood across the back holding hands. Shoulders hunched, eyes bulging, they looked scared. Scared their kids would say nothing, scared their kids would say too much. Scared of what they would see in themselves. And all the psychologists' horses and all the unearned sports cars couldn't put Johnny back together again.

Despite the half-timbered wall, the building had a stately, formal appearance. More church than chapel, it had to be at least a hundred-and-fifty-feet long. Peter stared at the ornate confessional hidden in shadows near the chapel's front door. A spectacular work of art, the black mahogany confessional looked to be eight-feet across and fifteen-feet high.

Liz touched his arm. "Incredible isn't it? The Good Soil hadn't planned on any religious stuff in here. But Pablo Gomez made them take it, along with his five-hundred-thousand. He's the guy Doris Dantakovic was talking about at the awards banquet. Actually, that's not the confessional he gave. There was some kind of mixup, and this gorgeous thing was headed for a Russian Basilica in New York or New Jersey."

Peter nodded.

"But once it got here they couldn't very well send it back. Bishop

McFarlane sent a delegation to bless it, and the next thing you know the other religions wanted to get in on the act. Dantakovic and Wolf had to purchase all kinds of liturgical gear from protestant and Jewish groups, but I haven't seen any of it around. They probably keep it in one of the storage rooms." She smiled and peered at the forbidding structure. "But they can't hide that baby."

Peter noted the pride in Liz's voice. Would this lady ever get her stuff together?

"Hash, grass, ludes, coke, booze, speed, crack." Peter looked up to see Starlyn Dalton standing at the microphone. She spoke over the muffled rumble of motorcycles. Juvenile druggies circled the complex to give moral support to comrades inside. No emotion showed on the doll-like face, a bloodless machine and stranger to her family. She clearly enunciated each word, her voice a trance-like staccato.

"I love you, daddy." A ripple of sighs rolled over the parents. Peter shook his head. Daddy? Bitty Dalton always claimed the girls' father had no relationship with them. But Flo Cohen had reported that the father called several times.

Liz's shoulders shook. She was sobbing. Peter put his arm around her, but she pushed him away and stood. He followed her to the entryway. A smiling Eric Hamlier bowed and held the door open.

"If there's anything I can do, Ms. Blair, I, ah..."

Liz took Peter's arm, and they stepped through the door and into the high-walled courtyard. The sobbing woman seemed to be somewhere else, in a world of her own. Once inside the car, Liz covered her face with her hands and continued to sob. Peter waited. Finally, the shaking body quieted. Liz wiped her eyes with a tissue. She glanced at Peter, then looked away toward the Belleair Bluffs.

"I had a baby."

Peter reached over and took her hand.

"Well, almost. I had a miscarriage during the fourteenth week. Kate doesn't know. Nobody knows." That's why I went on one super guilt trip and became a nun."

"I'm sorry, Liz."

"I'm the sorry one, Peter. I couldn't stop smoking hash and screwing around. Not even to have a baby." She looked up. "I guess you know the syndrome. It's called 'me first.' Probably better that she wasn't born. That girl, Starlyn, looks a lot like me as a kid. My daughter could have looked like her.

"I guess you wonder what it would have been like if—"

"You got it, Mr. Psychologist. But we can't go back, can we? I even tried to get close to poor Gonzie. Maybe I was thinking of adopting him or something. Screwed him up, too. Royally. Everything I touch turns to shit." She crossed her arms and stared straight ahead.

Peter could feel her withdrawing behind her protective shell.

"I wonder if there's anything left out there I haven't fucked up?"

"I'm meeting with Sterk Trump tomorrow, and I promise you this. If your Gonzie's out here, we're going to find him."

~

Jenny Grant watched from behind a thick glass viewing partition along with five other level-one Soilers. Level-ones weren't trusted to interact with parents, but the partition permitted them to learn their roles for future performances. Show time, the Hammer called it. "Make the simpletons cry and bring in that ever lovin' green stuff."

Jenny hadn't seen the new girl, Starlyn, at the mike before. How could they trust a newcomer to speak at an open meeting? And how could she jump to level six so fast? The Hammer strutted up the side isle and joined a dozen level-nine Lions who stood just behind the podium. The public knew him as Eric Hamlier, but inside the Good Soil he was called the Hammer. The bastard who ran everything.

The Hammer squeezed the girl's shoulder. His black-gloved hand contrasted with her white level-six robe. Some of the girls even thought he was cool in a perverse sort of way. Maybe it was the way his muscles rippled under his snug blue shirt. Or maybe they were just giving up.

The Hammer thanked everyone for coming and the meeting ended. Soilers and parents stood to sing "God Bless America." Jenny pushed open the heavy glass door and hurried to join her group. Her mother stood near the ornate confessional. If only her mom knew. Jenny stared straight ahead and marched with military precision toward the stage exit. Tough love and boot-camp discipline. You can't have it both ways, Mom. Her dad would've known better.

She caught up with her squad of twelve, and they marched down the long hall that connected the chapel to the dormitories. Two rights and a left took her to "Acorn Three." Furnished with couches and love seats that circled a 50" TV screen, the living room glowed with bright primary colors, mostly reds and yellows. A single hallway led to six bedrooms.

Jenny and the others stood at attention while their eyes followed the Hammer. The brawny young man strutted back and forth, smacking his open palm against the side of his jopper-style pants. He pointed at Jenny.

"Now look at this sorry mess. Jenny Grant. Jenny, you're lower than a cockroach. No, you are a cockroach. Your old man ran off, and your mother says you broke his heart. And you lied about Billy Ray. Even your teachers are happy you're gone. Miss—oh, excuse me—Ms. student-council president. Cheated on the election, didn't you?"

He stepped in front of Jenny. "Now I hear you even squealed on one of your own. Turned Terri Johns in, didn't you? Was she too much competition, or was it extra make-up to feed your pretty little face?"

Jennie felt the heat on her neck and ears. Don't blush, not now. That would prove the lie.

The Hammer laughed. "You're a greedy one all right. Bottom line is, nobody trusts you. Isn't that right Soilers?"

The shivering girls responded with darting eyes and a barely audible, "yes."

"Hear that? But we don't hate you. Know why? Because you're not important enough to hate. Even your name's old fashioned. Jenny. Old lady, Jenny." Grabbing her chin, he held it in a vice-like grip. "Kinda pretty though." He moved his face closer and closer. Finally his nose rested on her forehead. He licked his lips and smiled. Then he used his nose and forehead to push her backward, into the oval love seat.

"No!" A deep voice just behind her. She looked up. John Lifewater, the muscular Indian boy, stood over her. Where had he come from? John squeezed her shoulders. "No, this is wrong. Stop this. Now." John stared into the Hammer's face.

"Kiss my ass, if it ain't Squaw John," the Hammer said. "America's answer to chicken shit." The Hammer clicked his fingers. "Get this Tonto out of my sight before I give him a few glass beads for his cow-dung state of Oklahoma."

Four husky officers converged on Lifewater. He struggled with the Lions, but they yanked his arms behind his back and jerked him down the hallway toward the chapel. The Hammer chuckled. "You little queens got any ideas? Just remember, the general invites each and every one of you to visit the lab. And now you get to see how Terri Johns is going to fry."

He pressed the video remote-control. The TV screen pulled Jenny in like a giant, luminous magnet. A dark-haired girl, sixteen or seventeen, squirmed beneath leather straps and tattooed arms that held her flat against a narrow bed. Face flushed and perspiring, her tear-flooded eyes darted back and forth. She chewed through thick adhesive-tape that covered her mouth and circled her head.

"Please—please..."

A Lion's black-gloved hand squeezed the metallic lever and inched it down. A patient, methodical motion. Shackled by restraining straps and thick muscular arms, her body flinched, then shot up and down like a rodeo bull-rider. Yellowish-white eyes floated in manic disunion.

The fourteen-year-old, just in front of Jenny, stiffened and dropped to her knees. She careened off the back of the red velvet love seat and crashed to the floor. Jenny struggled to reach her. This can't be happening. This just can't be happening.

When Jenny finally looked up, the young blonde stood next to the Hammer, one arm draped over his shoulder. Her fingers played with his shiny leather belt, and a bare leg peeked from under her white, silk robe.

"Oh, yes, almost forgot. Join me in celebrating a big time promotion." The Hammer's right hand inched around Starlyn Dalton's left shoulder. "Starlyn, a real star. An academy award show out there, Starlyn. Promoted to level seven, as of now. Let's hear it for Starlyn."

Jenny struggled to clap her hands.

Starlyn smiled and ran purple iridescent fingernails across the Hammer's chest. He snapped open a shiny gold lighter and lit the joint that dangled from her lips. Starlyn turned and walked to the door. She didn't look back but gave the novices a demure wave of her fingers.

Jenny waved. What a pitiful human being. Does she have any idea what a class-A bitch she is?

The Hammer was radiant. "Starlyn wants you to enjoy. You performed well tonight, or at least your parents seemed to fall for your little routine. As a reward, I've agreed to go easy and let you have some fun. So lighten up and earn your way to level two. The level-three newcomers want a real blowout to celebrate their promotions. So let her rip!" The Hammer winked at Jenny and stalked out of the room, followed by Starlyn.

Major Breaker Mitchem lit joints and passed them around. Jenny sucked the musky smoke into her lungs, but it did nothing to ease the heavy weight that pushed against her head and chest. Mitchem sat next to her and opened a fresh bag of white-powdered cocaine. She took a deep breath and shrugged her shoulders. What the hell, what difference did it make? Jenny swallowed the sweet, heavy smoke and held her chest tight. Another powwow—another show.

She pushed herself up from the deep cushioned love seat and staggered down the hallway to her bedroom. When she got to the door, she hesitated and peered inside. A young man sat on the edge of her bed. Through the haze he looked crippled and disfigured. Jenny shook her head and rubbed her eyes. But he remained thin, unattractive, and physically bent.

Why resist? Maybe it's not so bad. A new life. She took a deep pull on the joint.

"Okay," Jenny opened the top button of her robe.

"No."

"No?" She swallowed hard and stared through the bluish smoke. Little sobs caught her breath. "If you're trying to break me down, it, ah—it's working. I'm not even good enough for that, am I? Not even with a cripple."

The deep brown eyes seemed to stare right through her. He reached out with both arms…

Chapter 14

Peter looked at his friend and smiled. Sterk Trump sat hunched over the wheel of his brightly painted surveillance van. Psychedelic peace signs gave the vehicle a 60's look, but Peter knew it was a killer machine. Sterk turned the handle of the mounted pan-and-tilt camera. Satisfied, he let the motion-detector begin taping while he fiddled with the parabolic microphones.

"Ah, loud and clear."

Peter heard a buzzing sound, then soft shuffling noises. Sterk squinted at the mud-streaked window. "Bison-balls. Damn friggin' Soil. That's a good name for 'em, all right. Soilers. Can't even keep their windows clean."

They had found a parking spot at the front of the employee parking lot, but it was still a good fifty feet to the lunchroom window. Sterk spat a thick wad of brown juice through the side window and put his feet on the dashboard, revealing hairy legs and white tennis socks. He pushed his straw cowboy's hat over his eyes, folded his arms, and waited. Peter cocked his head, but heard only scraping sounds. Then someone spoke.

"I wouldn't take that crap from anyone, Patti, blood relative or no blood relative."

"But they're only staying two weeks. It's not like they're moving in."

"No, Dotti's right," said a resolute voice.

"Jesus, Peter. Is that all gals talk about?" Sterk raised the brim of his hat and spat out the window. Then they heard louder scraping sounds, as the chairs were pulled back from the table.

"Who gave the tip yesterday? I'm out of quarters."

"Christ, give 'em a dollar, you cheapskates, and get movin'," Sterk muttered. "We don't have all day."

The women finally stepped out of the cafeteria door and plodded toward a dusty blue Dodge Dart with rusted bumpers and a bashed in left-fender. Sterk waved his straw hat. The woman, in her mid-twenties, turned and glanced at Sterk's van. Then she bent to get into the car.

"Patti? Patti Hassup? Ms. Hassup, dear."

She straightened and peered at Sterk. Then she gave her friends a hurried wave and took hesitant steps toward the van. Stopping a few feet away, she twisted her head and eyed both of them suspiciously.

"How do you know my—uh, other name?"

"That's not all I know, toots," Sterk barked. "Get in."

"I don't know you—uh, do I?"

Sterk flashed his badge. "Remember Lee Smyth, bond bailsman, Levy County, Georgia? Get in."

She waved at her friends again and stepped around to the passenger side. Peter moved to the back while Sterk reached across and opened the door. Patti hesitated, then slipped in beside Sterk.

"How did you get my name?"

"How does a felony drug pusher get a job in a school drug program?"

She fingered a white plastic lighter and lit a Marlboro. "Got to eat." Chipped and uneven, her fingernails showed traces of faded pink polish. Purple scratch marks ran along her neck, just behind her ears.

Sterk pointed to her neck. "Birthmark or hubby?"

"My live-in can play rough when he's drinking and, uh..."

Sterk glanced back at Peter. His face said it all. Sterk didn't approve of this gal's life style, and he would probably tell her that before he was finished.

"My grandmother didn't send you did—?"

"Nope." Turning his head, Sterk delivered a perfect shot of juice out the passenger side window. Patti stroked her face but Peter knew she was dry.

"Nope, but some other granny did. See, we got us a nice innocent kid in the Soil, don't want no damn records going to Tallahassee and Christ's sake friggin' Washington."

"Sure, I'll bet." Patti took a long drag on the Marlboro and smiled. "What can I do for you?"

"Easy. Give me the layout, no surprises, make me look good, and deliver the kid's file."

"That all?"

Sterk peered into the woman's face and gave her a soft smile. He slipped some bills into her shirt pocket.

~

Jenny Grant looked at her watch. Two-thirty A.M., Wednesday, the twentieth. She sat on the hard wooden floor and watched John Lifewater pace back and forth in the darkened room. Occasionally he would stop and look at one of the religious items scattered around the small annex.

Located at the back of the Good Soil chapel, the twenty-by-thirty-foot storage room was rarely used, but it proved useful as a place for the escape committee to meet. Most of the Lions disappeared on Tuesday night, leaving a skeleton force to guard the compound. Whispered rumors had them in Rebel County on a drug run. But Soilers were in no position to follow up on the rumors or even question higher level novitiates.

"Where did all this stuff come from?" John sat next to Jenny.

"The man that gave them the money to start this place wanted it to be a religious thing. At least that's what I heard. And now they've got school board money."

John shook his head. "He sure goofed on that one. Big time."

"I know." Jenny peered at open bins stacked along three of the walls. Bibles, chalices, priestly vestments, and other liturgical items filled every nook and cranny of the room. "That's where that humongous confessional came from. Terri Johns told me it was shipped here by mistake." Jenny wrung her hands. "Poor Terri."

"This whole place was a mistake," John said. "I wonder what's keeping the bothers?"

Jenny liked the boy from Oklahoma. A born leader, he kept the fragmented group together. "How did you get all the way out here, John?"

"Don't know, mixed up I guess. My coaches wanted me to play on both sides of the ball." He looked at her. "That means offense and defense. And I had a bunch of offers from colleges. Had ten calls in one week."

"Wow."

"Yeah. But the coaches don't think I hit hard enough. I won't spear a kid with my helmet. Could hurt 'em bad, real bad. And I... I like to dance."

"You like to...?"

"I came to Florida to dance at Native America '91, the biggest pow, uh... get-together of Indian tribes since the Europeans came. My ancestors came from Georgia. The government made us move cause they thought there was gold up there. We won in court, but they force-marched my people West. They called it the trail of tears. Put us on top of black gold—oil. And they never found gold in Georgia."

Jenny chuckled. "I don't remember the last time I laughed."

"That's good. But me, I'm scared to death. This isn't like captain of the football team or Boys State. This is a nightmare. Crazy. We could end up dead. I'm supposed to lead the breakout, but I'm more scared than anybody. Maybe coach was right. Maybe I am a chicken."

She took his hand. "We'll get through this somehow, John."

The door squeaked open and shadowed silhouettes, one-by-one, eased quietly into the darkened room. With a light-footed stride, John glided to the door and pulled it shut "Okay, let's see who's here."

"Hal Jacobson said he was sick and couldn't come, so I asked Gonzie to take his place," Jenny said, pointing at a thin, physically bent boy with deep brown eyes.

"Gonzie?"

"It's okay," Jenny said. "I'd trust him with my life."

"You are."

"Gonzales, from Mexico."

"Welcome to the group," John said. "Jesus Christ. Danny O'Brien here? Nope, I knew it. We've all got to be here. Otherwise, somebody could nark. We're all in this together."

"Yeah, I even worry about Hal Jacobson," Jenny said. "Says he's got the flu. But all of a sudden they have him on the Miami drug detail. A plush job, even if you're a Lion. It looks bad, and we're all dead if they got to him."

The fat boy from Israel was an unlikely candidate for the Lions Corps. But what if he had turned traitor to protect himself? Jenny wondered. Jacobson had been preparing to study for the Rabbinate when the chance for a trip to Florida came up. His uncle, a Rabbi in Miami, had heard about the Visiting Scholars Program. Jenny felt sorry for the clumsy overweight youngster who the Hammer had dubbed the "bowling ball."

"Before we go any further, let's find out who's here and how they got here," John said. "We can't play rotating chairs and expect to get anywhere. Let's start with the right side, over by the door." One by one, in faltering voices, they told their stories.

"It was after the big playoff game," Jenny said. "Lakeside High, good team, but we won. Everyone headed to the big blow-out. My folks wouldn't have let me go, but SADD was putting it on."

"SADD?" John said.

"Students against drunk drivers. They helped pay for our yearbook. Then the skaters started coming in, must have had twenty kegs."

"Skaters?"

"Skateboarders. You, know. They hang together."

"You get boozed up?" A voice from the back.

"No, we stayed in our tent. We had lemonade and, ah—chocolate chip cookies."

Chuckles erupted.

"I know, I know, but back then we were clueless. By the way, we're running out of room in the broom cabinet. Three cookies a day really adds up. You've got to flush 'em down the john or something. The Hammer won't be happy if he finds them. Anyway, things got real loud, and the police showed up. Big FDLE paddy wagons, like out of an old movie. Elliot Ness or something."

"What's the FDLE?" John asked.

"Florida Department of Law Enforcement. My dad works for them."

"For Christ sake, is that all you've got to piss about?"

"Who's there?"

The guttural voice was harsh and grating. "Sonny Shutten, skater and low life. I'm little, they call me Tiny. Counselor said I had a chip on my shoulder. Screw her. I love all these stories—how you was all railroaded in here. But that's not me. I've sniffed, snorted, smoked, and pushed. Got x'd out on some good designer stuff. Loved every damn bit. 'Bout to buy a Porsche, what a rad piece-a-machine. No way I'm like you goody-goodies and Ivy Leaguers. No way. You birds sound like my social studies teacher. 'We all live in a big democracy.' Well, excuse me, but she never put me in for honors and gifted, 'cause my mother didn't drive a Caddy. Her husband did though. Chiropractor with big bucks. Course, I didn't go to College Park like Jenny did."

"You sound like you should be on the other side," Jenny said.

"I'm Jonesing for a real hit, but don't worry. I'm with you guys all the way. These pussies can't make me walk the line. You know, this place is like a big tomb. Reminds me of my school. Can you believe they make me go to a tomb everyday? A place where no one gives a shit? And if you don't go you can be arrested? Hell, I never even learned how to read in that tomb. Good place to learn about sex and drugs, though. No, I'm headin' back to the street, but I'll work for myself. Just don't give me your bleedin' heart sob stories. Let's get our asses out of here."

"You're right, Tiny, we've got to get moving," John said. "And by the way. If you're willing to work, you're welcome here." He was whispering now. "Well, what do you all think?"

"We've got to run for it," Jenny said. "Maybe if enough of us get out it will—"

"John crossed his arms. "That won't work. They'll just bring us back. We're druggies and delinquents, remember? We've got to get something on these creeps. Something we can show people before they drag us back. I don't know, I don't know..."

"Kenny Haas got out," Jenny said. "The newspaper wanted to do a story and everything, but his dad brought him back. Said he couldn't be trusted. Called him a liar and a druggie. Said his mom couldn't take it any more."

"Okay." John Lifewater stood. "Okay." He put his hands in the back pockets of his jeans and bent forward. Turning his head slowly, he seemed to peer directly into each of their eyes. He took his time and seemed unaffected by horror of their situation.

"Okay. Here's what we're going to do. I want each of you to see me before you leave, because I'm going to give you an assignment. Some of you work in the administrative offices, and Jenny, you've been on the laundry detail. Billy Potter was on the trash crew last week, and that's like panning for gold. We've got to get hard evidence, real stuff that will hold up in the newspapers. Photos sure wouldn't hurt, either."

John straightened and crossed his arms. "We can do it gang. We're going to do it—and nobody's going to stop us... Let's hit it!"

⁓

Little scratching sounds—a cat's claws on linen sheets—tugging, pulling. Jenny bolted up in the pitch-black darkness. She rubbed her eyes. Was she at home? Then she felt the pressing weight at the bottom of the bed. Eyes wide, she pulled the sheet to her neck.

"Jenny?"

"Who's there?" The odor of perspiration fought against the sweet scent of body powder.

"It's me, Starlyn. Can I, uh, come to bed with you? I really need someone... kinda scared in fact."

"Let me turn on the light, Starlyn, and—"

"No, don't. Please. I'm not supposed to be here."

She took Starlyn's hand. Starlyn's skin was damp. "I thought you—uh, could go where you want," Jenny said."

"That was before, Jenny. That's why we have to talk, cause you're next.

You're next. But now I just got to be with someone so I can sleep. I haven't slept in—I donno, days, I guess. I'm scared Jenny. So scared."

Jenny pulled back the sheet and let the trembling girl slip in beside her. Hot, wet cheeks pressed against Jenny's rib cage. Starlyn turned and pushed her back into Jenny's chest. Then she wrapped Jenny's arms around her. Starlyn's body shaped itself to hers. Jenny peered at the clock. Four-twenty A.M. She held Starlyn tight and felt the girl relax. "What's this?" Jenny's fingers circled a crusty zigzag of cuts on Starlyn's soft, silky shoulder.

"We're all doing' it, at least some of us, with a razor."

"Starlyn, you're bleeding."

"Good."

"But what will that do? The Hammer's not going to like it. Starlyn?" The sheet muffled Starlyn's sobs.

"I don't know, it's just—just something of our own. Something we can do ourselves. Something private."

Jenny sighed.

"I can't stand it, Jen. I used to think I was bad, really hot stuff. But that was before they—they did things."

She stroked Starlyn's hair.

"I spent yesterday in an airplane."

"What?"

"I didn't see much. They put me in a big box with airholes. I was totally zonked out, or I wouldn't have done it. It was shiny pink and had a big ribbon around it. When they finally let me out there were all these guys in uniforms, dark blue with little shields over the pockets. They were laughing and carrying on. They made me dance and took a lot of pictures." Starlyn choked back a sob. "Then they poured beer on me."

Federal drug and alcohol? Jenny's father had brought some of them to the house.

"The worst part was that I was never alone. Never. When we landed, someone said De Revo or something like that, in Texas. Then another bunch got on, and we flew back. Same thing, only worse."

Starlyn was shaking again. Jenny covered her with the blanket.

"I thought you were protected?"

"No, he's tired of me, talks a lot about you. Talks about your hair. Says he hates blondes."

Jenny pulled back. "But he promoted you and said you were—"

"He calls me the dumb-bunny. Says I'm only good for one thing. Tonight, after we—afterwards, he took my rank. Says I'm nothing, not even a level one. Believe me, Jen, you've got to be careful. Wish Billy Ray was okay, he'd help us. Poor guy had an accident, can't remember things. You know him?"

I know him, you little dope. "Look, Starlyn—"

"Call me Star, that's what my dad calls me. All along I thought it was my mom that cared, but it was my dad. My mom just freaked out and ran off to California."

"Okay, look. We've got to get out of here, and you've got to tell me everything."

"Yeah, before we disappear." Starlyn snuggled closer.

"Disappear?"

"Don't you know? Those girls they bring in from South America. They're gone. Even some of the Soilers are gone. And after Easter, the rest of us."

"We go, too?"

"They're afraid of people getting away. We're going to the Baron's lair. It's in a foreign country. Europe, I think. A castle or prison or something. And I think I know where they're keeping the others... down near the Indian cemetery." Starlyn pulled the sheet over her head.

"Listen, Star. Listen to me. We're going to make it. I'd given up too, 'till I met, uh—a Mexican kid. But you've got to take me down there. We need everything we can get for John and the committee. I... Star?" Slow rhythmic breathing. The warm body was quiet and at peace. Jenny bent and brushed the scar with her lips.

"Sleep tight, little sister."

Chapter 15

Liz watched her sister sort the black and brown video tapes into neat stacks on the table. Kathleen insisted on doing it herself. Naturally. The girl was so damned organized. Is that what had plagued Liz all these years? Simply a lack of organizational skills?

They had cruised up Alternate Nineteen in Barrett Spangler's shiny, black limo. When they pulled into the Good Soil, Eric Hamlier greeted them at the security check point with an exaggerated bow and they followed him down a long hallway to a classroom marked ARROWS. After they were seated behind the teacher's desk, Hamlier went for the girls. The round institutional clock read two thirty-five. Wednesday, the twentieth. Only a week until Peter's big meeting.

"This is risky." Kathleen's fingers played a nervous melody along the tops of the tapes.

"Life is risky, Kat."

"I know, Sis. But as a reporter, I'm bound by some very specific rules. And this is way outside of any rules I learned at Missouri. Life is scary enough without taking big chances. And if we mess up, what happens to Peter's plan?"

"The tape recorder was your idea, Kat, and a great one. You sure about the Grant girl? Barrett said we could see anyone we wanted. Of course, they still claim Gonzie isn't out here."

"She's a fine young gal even if she did experiment with drugs. And she was a very responsible baby-sitter." Kathleen turned her head and raised her hand. The door opened. Jenny Grant and Starlyn Dalton followed Eric Hamlier into the room. Bowing, Hamlier peered at the two girls.

"Jenny and Starlyn, these two ladies are here to help you. Our good friend, Mr. Spangler, is doing a fund-raising project for us. Ms. Blair and Mrs. Sheppard will tell you about it. Remember what I said before I brought you down here. Don't be afraid to answer any questions they may have about any aspect of our program. Mrs. Sheppard is a reporter, and we always go out of our way to cooperate with the press."

Hamlier bowed in Liz's direction and walked to the door. "If you need me, ladies, just send one of the girls. Despite what you may have read, we're very open and relaxed here." Kathleen's eyes narrowed and her cheeks turned a soft shade of pink.

Hamlier closed the door quietly behind him. Before the lock had even clicked shut, Liz turned to Starlyn. "I saw you in the chapel on Monday night. Did you really try all those drugs?"

Eyes wide, Starlyn leaned forward, her ash blonde curls dangling over her forehead. She started to speak—then stopped. Starlyn peered to her left, toward the silent TV monitor in the corner of the room.

"Star has had some problems," Jenny said. "Her father wasn't around for a while, and now her mother has left her. But her dad's back and wants to help, doesn't he, Star?" Jenny took Starlyn's hand and pulled her close. Starlyn nodded, her eyes filling with tears. She looked so pitiful. Liz felt her own tears coming and tried to hold them back. But she couldn't.

"Are you doing okay, Jenny?" Kathleen asked.

"We're treated fairly here, Mrs. Sheppard. I hope to be out before too long."

Jenny's eyes kept moving to the left. Was the room bugged? Were they being taped? Sweat gathered along Jenny's hairline. Maybe Jenny was nervous about the interview, or was she coming off drugs cold turkey? Jenny used to babysit for Kat and Peter, but could she really be trusted? What if she was in with Wolf? What if she just took the hidden recorder to Wolf or Dr. Small? Don't screw up this time, Liz. Just don't screw up again.

Liz reached across the desk and pulled Starlyn closer. "We've heard stories about students in confinement, uh, locked in a small room without even a window. Is that true?"

Jenny and Starlyn looked at each other. Neither spoke.

"We can't help if you don't—"

"There are a couple of bad kids out here, Ms. Blair," Jenny said. "Sometimes they're put in time-out, but I don't know about any rooms like that. Actually, we like the discipline because it keeps some of the troublemakers in line. Isn't that right, Star?"

Starlyn nodded, but said nothing. Tears coursed down her soft, rounded cheeks.

"Okay," Kathleen said. "We're also here to talk about these tapes. Ms. Blair's friend had them made especially for the Good Soil. They show the problems drugs cause. They're animated, ah, like cartoons. And they're funny. You might really like them."

Starlyn sobbed.

"We brought twenty," Kathleen said. "Mr. Hamlier says you have twenty Mighty-Oak Teams, so there's one for each team to watch."

Liz put her hand to her chest. She really missed the old wooden pendant. She was accustomed to fingering the blue and gold likenesses of the trinity whenever she was really anxious. It gave her something to do and helped clear her head. Liz sighed and reached into her purse. Here goes, now or never. She pulled out a package of Marlboro's. Shaking the pack from side to side, she held it at eye level.

"Now look at this, you two. And look hard. This is how it all starts. Look at the cowboy on the front of this package. Looks real cool, doesn't he? Mr. Independent. Mr. Free and Easy."

Jenny and Starlyn looked at each other. Starlyn peered at the package and licked her lips.

"No, look, dammit. Look!" Liz stood and leaned forward. She held the package only inches from Jenny's face. "See his shirt pocket, see the buttons? Looks cool, huh? But underneath is a black hole. The black hole of cancer."

Jenny's eyes widened. She glanced to the left before looking back at the package. Liz took a deep breath and sighed. She saw it. Jenny saw it. Liz started to pull the package away, but Jenny took hold of Liz's wrist.

"I see what you mean, Ms. Blair. It was right there all the time." Her eyes moved to the left. "I thought I was better than the other kids. That I could handle it. That I wouldn't get hooked. Now I know that's not true. No one ever made me look at it that hard. To see what was really inside."

Starlyn cocked her head. She looked puzzled. That was okay, maybe even better. Jenny was the one they had to reach. The one they could trust.

Liz pushed the package of cigarettes deep into her purse. Inside tape # 18. Kathleen had printed it, over and over, until it was perfect. She had used almost a carton of cigarettes before she got it small enough.

Kathleen looked at her watch. "I think we've used up our allotted time. We'd better get going."

"We'll be back," Liz said. "And we hope to see two fine girls who have gotten deeply into the real meaning of things. Not the shallow stuff that leads to big time trouble."

~

At eleven-thirty Peter pointed the black Volvo toward St. Petersburg Beach. When he passed the Treasure Island bridge, he spotted the Florida-cracker bungalow. Above the front porch, raised letters in faded orange paint spelled Tampa Bay Investigators. A gray heron stood on one spindly leg and looked down from the orange slate roof. The rear windows of Sterk's surveillance van glowed with a bluish gray light. Sterk was proud of the mobile fortress. Unlike some others in his business, Sterk loved his job and the lethal hardware that set it off from off from more civilized occupations.

Peter recalled the tour his friend had given him after the Ybor City drug bust only a few weeks earlier. He had never seen the hyperactive detective so animated. Sterk had pulled a Remington model 11-49 chrome-plated shotgun from the overhead rack. His words peppered the van like hot slugs from an automatic weapon.

"Two shells of number three buck followed by a rifled slug, another buck and finally a rifled slug. Good medicine for close-in firefights, even if the friggin' druggies got automatic weapons. Number three buck and a rifled slug will penetrate most cars.

Hell—put down an African Cape Buffalo."

Peter held up his hand.

"The days of the old .38 calibers are gone, except as a hidden back up. I like this Air-Weight thirty-six with the hammer shroud—fits my boot holster real nice. When I'm in deep do-do, I keep an unloaded gun in my waist holster and carry the loaded backup in my boot."

"Wait Sterk, hold it. Slow down." Peter laughed. "We need to get you on Ritalin. You're going—"

"No, just a sec, here's the really big gun." Sterk opened a case that was jammed between a small refrigerator and a chemical toilet. "I use this Colt model number fifteen-caliber 5.56 mm with a thirty-round clip and an Aimpoint sight. Some folks are stickin' with Uzi's, but I like this baby. It has one drawback though, shots can go through the target. They used it in the FBI gunfight in Miami. Killed a couple of bystanders."

Sterk finally stopped to catch his breath, and Peter concluded the tour was over. Climbing down from the portable armory, he had noticed the bumper sticker: "Insured by Smith and Wesson." One heck of an understatement.

Peter turned the turbo sedan into the weed-covered driveway and pulled up next to Sterk's van. The van's side door opened, and Sterk peered out.

"Got two boxes here, gotta get these back in a jiffy. Help me carry 'em in."

Peter picked up one of the thick cardboard boxes and followed Sterk onto the porch of the bungalow. Sterk led him to a small kitchen in the back and pointed to a vinyl card table. They handled the heavy containers with little effort, but the card table wobbled under the weight of the boxes. Peter opened the first box. It held about thirty dark-brown, laminated files. Each file had a name typed neatly on the bottom tab.

"Don't get revved up on these things, Peter. They're sure as hell not personnel records. Looks like some kind of test profiles. It was around ten o'clock when I finally got in. Patti had hauled 'em down a dumb waiter to an old kitchen in the back. I don't know how she got around security, but that friggin' place is locked up tighter than a Baptist with a bottle of moonshine. Got a full alarm system and guards dressed in boots like the damned gestapo. Anyway, wasn't 'til I got this stuff loaded up, I noticed they was testing files. Don't know if they're gonna help, but I got to get 'em back before five when the early shift comes on."

"Let's see, MMPI's on their staff." Peter held a testing graph close to the light. "Uh, they look pretty good, not too many elevations here."

"Never could figure out all those squiggles." Sterk peered over Peter's shoulder.

"Ten clinical scales altogether, but it's the way the scales interact. It's not just the elevations. See, here's one on a female staffer with the initials' J.G. Shows elevations on scales one and three and a dip on two. She's probably an internalizer who converts anxiety into the body. Probably has stomachaches or headaches from the stress she's under. But she's a relatively healthy lady. Were these taken when they were hired or later on?"

"What do you mean hired? The box you're lookin' at has the Soiler profiles, not the staff."

Peter shook his head. "That's not possible. Either they're the best bunch of liars around, and sophisticated test takers, or they're pretty healthy folks."

"No, here's the box with the staff." Sterk pushed the second box toward Peter. "See here where it says Good Soil... staff testing?"

Peter spread a dozen profile sheets on the table and sorted them into stacks. He shook his head again. "No, they're in the wrong box. These are the Soilers all right. A lot of elevated profiles and a lot of acting out, really psychopathic-looking stuff along with depression. This mix-up will sure as heck raise some eyebrows when it gets to Tallahassee or Washington."

"Hell, they're hiring druggies to work in the administrative offices," Sterk said. "Screw-ups like this are bound to happen. You'd think the school system would do some background checks."

"No, this is a private company," Peter said. "They're against money going out in vouchers for the kids, but they contract privately all the time." Going back to the box marked Soilers, Peter pulled out more profiles. "Yep, this has to be a mix-up. Just look at some of these. Here's one that's incredible, has to be a staff member. No indications of lying or faking good and the clinical profile is almost flat along fifty. Heck, this guy isn't just lacking in pathology, he's super healthy."

"Then there's these neuro—uh, neuropsych profiles," Sterk said. He dug through the box marked "Good Soil—Staff."

Peter let out a low whistle. "These profiles show the beginning stages of brain deterioration. But why in heck would brain pathology show up, even on the Soilers? Drug problems and personality disorders, yes, but not chronic brain syndrome."

"Well, I don't think they're mixed up, but if they are, then suckin' drugs would sure as hell mess up those kids." Sterk's shoulders began to quiver and he fired a thick, red stream of tobacco juice through the kitchen window.

Peter shook his head. "Yes, I guess. Something about these neuropsych profiles, though. Something really odd here." Peter let the files slide through his fingers, one by one, into the box. "Oh well, this whole thing's been a mess from the start."

Chapter 16

Darkness obscured the Good Soil Chapel. The only sound echoed from the gurgling baptismal fountain. Jenny peered through an opening in the confessional window's thick velvet curtains. Cramming them into the old confessional was John Lifewater's idea. Brilliant.

Jenny had studied it during the parent-night powwows. At least eight-feet-across and fifteen-feet-high, the rigid, heavy style of the ornate mahogany confessional clashed with the warm, modern tones of the chapel. She had heard it was shipped by mistake, along with the other religious items now hidden in the small storage room.

A four-foot-high figure of Saint Peter stood in the center of the confessional. The ancient disciple held two, one-foot-high keys in his right hand, and his left hand held a globe of the earth. Two penitent rooms flanked the confessor's room, and above the confessional, winged cherubs looked down playfully from a mahogany roof.

Jenny couldn't see the other kids' faces in the darkness, but she knew John Lifewater and Tiny Shutten shared the confessor's room with her. She had seen Gonzie and Starlyn earlier, on the way to the storage room, but didn't know if they had made it to the confessional.

"Okay." It was Lifewater's voice. "Look, we can't stay crammed in here very long, but with the storage room locked it was the only option. You called the meeting Jenny. Tell us what you have and make it quick."

"I think we've really got something this time. Star, are you—?"

"I'm here, Jen, and I've got—"

"Star? Wait a minute, Jenny. You can't just keep bringing anybody you like to these—"

"No, it's okay, John. Just listen up. Star and I met with two ladies today and they want to help. One is Dr. Sheppard's wife. I used to babysit for her. She works for the newspaper, so she can—"

"How do you know they want to help?" John asked.

"Okay, Star. Pass it through."

Jenny pulled at the privacy screen that separated the penitent's cubicle from the priest's station. It wouldn't budge. She used both hands and strained to open it.

An ear splitting screech echoed across the chapel!

Almost simultaneously, footsteps scraped across the large stage at the front. Jenny dropped to her knees. Only the sound of labored breathing filled the confessional. The steps grew louder. They moved down the main aisle toward the back, where the confessional stood.

Jenny pushed herself up and peered through a narrow slit in the confessional's heavy curtain. Shadowy figures lurched and wobbled down the center aisle. Hal Jacobson had turned them in! She knew it, she just knew it.

Silence. No one moved and no one breathed.

"Wait, it's over there," the tall skinny one said.

"Awesome. What in hell?" his short, stocky companion said. The pair stepped back and peered up at the confessionals' wooden spires.

"It's one of them grandfather clocks," the tall skinny one said. "Wood and all that. Hey, you think it's a speaker? Earth Watch and Dead Alive had speakers that big over at Lakeland."

"Nah," the short one said. "You know? It could be a church."

"What?"

"Yeah, a church."

"Funny looking church and awful small. How do they get the people in there?"

"It's got to be a proto."

"A what?"

"Yeah. You know, like that Car of Tomorrow at Disney, a proto."

The stocky one was Breaker Mitchum, a tough guy with a long rap sheet. Jenny shivered. He really enjoyed hurting people. The tall kid was

Billy Ray Thomas. Jenny hadn't seen Billy Ray since their ill-fated trip to the ancient cemetery. Now the Hammer called him Dumbo, the elephant without a memory.

"Yeah, it's a proto of a church," Mitchum said.

"Okay, I guess it's a little church," Billy Ray said. He wove from side to side and peered through bleary eyes at the ominous structure. "Hey, man, let's get out of here."

"You ain't scared, are you?"

"No, course not." Billy Ray kicked his foot toward the silent sentinel, but his boot fell short of touching it. "Churches are for suckers. My mom still goes to church, and it don't help her none. Still has to work two jobs. She wanted me to be an altar boy but I couldn't remember all the different things you had to do. Yeah, it's for suckers. We got our freedom here, we're on top."

"Yeah," Mitchum said. "That's right, we're the top dogs. And the Hammer says there's lots more good stuff comin' our way."

Only the drip, drip, drip, of water from the baptismal font broke the silence of the dark chapel.

"What's inside?" Mitchum pushed Billy Ray toward the paneled center doors. "Don't be a nerd, it won't bite. Open the friggin door."

Billy Ray inched his hand down.

Jenny held her breath.

Silence.

"You sure we should be doing this?" Billy Ray stared at the grimacing gargoyles that peered down from the massive structure. Their bloated eyes blinked in the weak light.

"Hey, there's a sign on the front," Billy Ray said. He sighed.

"Huh, I don't see nothin'. What you scared of?"

"No, there's a sign, Breaker. I can feel it. Come over here."

Mitchum edged one foot closer to the inlaid inscriptions. "What's it say?"

"You know I can't read. I get the letters mixed up and backwards."

"Ah, one of them brain dead dyslexuns." Mitchum peered at the dark, wooden letters. "Go on, Dumbo, you can read it."

Keeping one hand behind him, like a runner poised for the starting gun, Billy Ray's calloused fingers traced the raised wooden letters. Streaks of white cocaine helped illuminate the words.

"They—even—brought babies..."

"Babies?"

"Yeah," Billy Ray whispered. "Babies to be—uh... torched by him."

"Torched?"

"The—disciplines saw this, they scalded them… around, but Jesus called the child-ren. Let the little child-ren come to me. Do—shut them off. The king-dom of, ah—belongs to… some of them."

"Jesus," Mitchum said." He torched and scalded the babies in a ring to discipline them? Jesus."

"Where you goin', Breaker?… Oh, okay."

Squeaking sounds as the silent figures turned in unison. Then steps, gradually withdrawing steps. Jenny wiped clammy beads of sweat from her forehead. Total silence. Total blackness. The steps faded, leaving a profound sense of relief inside the confessional. Jenny wasn't Catholic but she was willing to bet that no one using a confessional ever felt any better than she did at that moment. "God, that was close." Jenny took John's hand.

"I wet my pants," Freddy Sloan said. High-pitched giggles pierced the heavy air.

"You can't pee in the confessional," Ester Edwards said. Edwards was a high school senior from Washington, D.C. She had registered for pre-law at Howard University prior to joining the Visiting Scholar's Program. More giggles. Jenny took a deep breath. She felt a lot better, a lot more in control.

"Here it is." Jenny pulled the object through the confessional window. Her fingers touched John's in the pitch-darkness.

"What is it? A portable radio?"

"No, it's a little tape recorder. There's nothing on it, but it's got sixty minutes of clean tape. Dr. Sheppard's wife hid it inside one of those nerdy videos they gave us. And that means she's suspicious. They're sticking their necks out, big time, so they'll really listen if we come up with something solid."

"You take it, John, get the proof we need," Edwards said.

"I don't know. Don't know if I can. I admit I'm really scared, but I'm willing to do it. It's just that I think they're watching me. And with Hal Jacobson not showing tonight, I wonder if I'm the right one."

They sat in silence, except for the uneasy sounds of shuffling feet.

"I'll do it."

"It's Gonzie," Jenny said. "I told you we could count on him."

"Me, I'm scared too," the Mexican boy said. "But maybe I'm a good one to help. I am still only a phase-one Soiler. I know they expect little of me because I am Hispanic, and they think I speak only a little English."

"Well, your English is excellent," Edwards said.

"Okay. It's your baby, Gonzie," Lifewater said. "It's probably voice activated. Just leave it in your shirt and hope for the best."

"What about the puddle on the floor?" someone said. Once again, nervous giggles spread through the confessional.

"They've got holy water in the baptismal fount," Gonzie said. "Maybe we can wash it down with some of that."

"Good thinking. It won't be used for anything else in this place," John said.

Quiet footsteps cut short the frightened banter. Bodies froze again in silent pantomime. A strangled voice whispered though the confessor's front window.

"It's okay guys. Just me, Danny O'Brien."

"Where have you been?" Anger tightened John's voice. "Were you with Jacobson?"

"No, had to pull guard duty at the file room, but I hear Jacobson's on a drug run. He's definitely on the fast track to promotion."

"That's what we're worried about," John said. The boy leader from Oklahoma whispered into the darkness. "Okay, everyone know the plan?" After a moment's hesitation, the barely audible voice replied.

"I am the one. No one will suspect me."

Chapter 17

Peter watched as Sterk's brightly painted van pulled into the Good Soil parking lot and stopped next to the Volvo. Peter waved. Sterk got out, looked both ways, and stepped to the driver-side window.

"No need to come in, Sterk. Just a nice polite inquiry about Liz Blair's young man, and maybe see if David Mendola and Jenny Grant are okay. Kathleen and Liz are hoping I can get some feedback on the tape recorder. If things don't open up, that's fine, but I've got to do something. This is the twenty-first. The grant meeting is less than a week away."

"You gotta be nutty, Peter, that's a tough bunch in there. When Liz and Kate asked you to do something, they weren't asking you to commit friggin' hari-kari."

Peter opened the door. "Even if you're right, Doris Dantakovic wouldn't let them pull any rough stuff. I know that lady, and she's okay."

Sterk spat a wad of tobacco. "Okay. I'll just park my boots here and have a little chew. But if you're not out in ten, I'm comin' in. That's a fact. After talking to Liz, I think we got some psychos out here. And maybe some killers." Peter hadn't told Sterk about his run-in with Eric Hamlier at the hospital.

Peter laughed. "You wouldn't loan Mother Teresa a quarter for a phone call. That's an occupational hazard with you folks. If you weren't suspicious of everything that moved, you wouldn't be nearly as good at your job."

"I'm just seeing people for what they really are. If I was as trusting as you, Peter, I'd of been six feet under, long ago. Go ahead, give you ten minutes and not a second more."

Over a wide brick archway, worn, chiseled letters spelled out "Fort Washington." Anchored to the barrel-vaulted door, a white plastic sign with blue lettering said: "The Good Soil. A McDill County School Rehabilitation Program. Your tax pennies for progress are working for you." Peter entered and walked across a gray tile floor, his footsteps echoing against rows of cheap metal chairs. A pert little receptionist with a well-scrubbed complexion smiled and looked up. Her gold name plate spelled out: "Terri Johns, Trainee."

"I'm Dr. Peter Sheppard. I'd like to talk to Ms. Doris Dantakovic, please."

"What would you like to talk to the general about?"

"We're old friends. I've seen some of the youngsters here in the program. I'd like to visit them and see how they're doing."

She ran her fingers through thick auburn hair. "I'm afraid we don't usually allow visitors, except for the parents, of course. The parents attend the powwow meetings once a week. Are you with the newspapers?"

"I know all about the program, but I'll take it up with the administrator. Is she in?"

"Please have a seat over there, Dr. Sheppard." She looked in the direction of the waiting room. "I'll be happy to check for you."

"Well, well, the infamous Dr. Peter Sheppard." A loud voice boomed from the darkened hallway. Dressed in a simple white robe, Eric Hamlier sauntered into the deserted waiting room.

"Still raking in big bucks on Fifth Avenue North? Didn't know I was down at your office when you saw the Mendola kid, did you? Gotta keep our eyes on these juvenile druggies when they're in the early stages of treatment. Had a phase one Soiler go out the back window of a doctor's office. Just can't trust the little buggers at all." He laughed. A forced laugh.

"David was starting to turn around," Peter replied. "I don't think we should talk about it out here."

"This will do, Doc. This will do just fine." The Hammer peered over Peter's shoulder toward the main door. "You can't trust that little son-of-a-bitch as far as you can throw him, Doc."

Wide-eyed, the receptionist turned and buried her head in the appointment book. The Hammer leaned into Peter's face. "His old man wised up and ran off with some nice, young honey. That kid's got to learn his old man wasn't so dumb after all."

Peter pulled back. "He had stopped using drugs."

"Yeah? And I'm the sweet little tooth fairy." The Hammer thrust his face even closer.

Peter could feel warm air from the Hammer's flaring nostrils. He pulled back "Look, this is ridiculous, I just came here to—"

"You bloody liar!" The Hammer grabbed Peter's suit coat and jerked it under his chin. Two Good Soil staffers appeared from nowhere and blocked the front door. Another white-gowned staffer lowered the window blinds.

The Hammer continued with a staccato burst of profanities, spittle flying everywhere. Peter stared into the young man's eyes. Flat, black eyes. Shark eyes. Peter's instincts told him a line had been crossed. It had happened in an instant. The time for talking was over. But wait, it didn't add up. Why the roughhouse? Why give Peter more proof? The logical conclusion slid into place like the click of a massive bank vault. Click, click, he wasn't leaving. He wanted to swallow , but didn't. Click, click… he was dead. Liz was right. Sterk was right. Kathleen was right.

His breath stopped halfway up his throat. It was like taking a football helmet in the stomach. Don't swallow, don't breathe, stall for time. Numbing heat rolled behind his knees, across his stomach and up his arms.

Suddenly, the Hammer relaxed his grip. His eyes wobbled as he stared over Peter's shoulder. Peter turned to see Sterk Trump, head down, barreling through the front door. He parted the band of staffers, which had grown to six, like a fullback brushing aside tackling dummies.

Nine-millimeter Glock in hand, Sterk flew past Peter with lightening speed, grabbed the Hammer, jerked him around by the front of his robe, and eased the barrel of the mirror-plated cannon into the Hammer's face. It came to rest on his upper lip, an inch of the barrel fitting nicely into in his left nostril.

Peter took a deep breath. "I haven't had much success talking with this young man."

"You're right, Peter. Saw him grab you. Now I'll do the grabbin', got it?" Sterk turned to the Hammer whose ruddy complexion had gone gray white. "We're gonna have a look-see around here before you wet your pants, tough guy."

"No need for that, sir." A mincing, high-pitched voice echoed from the back of the waiting room. "As you know Dr. Sheppard, I'm the acting administrator while Ms. Dantakovic is in Washington," Dr. Harold Small said. "Even though you have no search warrant and have frightened my staff, I will be most happy to give you a quick tour of the facility, just to quiet any doubts you may have about our program." Sterk eased his grip on the Hammer and wiggled the polished blue barrel from the Hammer's nostril.

"We're not here to make trouble," Peter said. "I just asked to meet with the administrator, and I'm afraid this young man got carried away. There's a youngster from Mexico who seems to be missing. Here is Liz Blair's file on the Gonzales boy."

Small took the ragged manila folder and slowly paged through it. "No, nobody by that name." Protruding eyeballs and a greenish skin- tone gave Small the look of a person who was not long for this world. It dawned on Peter that each time he saw Small, the man looked more debilitated. Small turned, with much apparent effort, and led them slowly down the hallway past several offices.

"No, no, talked to all the boys. No one from Mexico. Takes a special immigration card because of recent problems with border crossings. I'm sure that delayed his journey, if he's headed to our program." Small handed the file back to Peter.

"But Liz dropped him off right here, at this building. Didn't she tell you that?"

Small looked down and shrugged. "Ms. Blair is a marvelous person. She and Mr. Spangler are great supporters of our program. I will do everything possible to assist with her inquiry."

Small led the entourage, followed by a red-faced Eric Hamlier. They stopped a short distance from the waiting room at a door marked ARROWS. Small pushed open the door and they filed in. A serious looking young woman, dressed in a tweed jacket with a purple blouse, lectured some twenty adolescent girls. The students sat, shoulders back, with their hands folded demurely on their laps. When they noticed Dr. Small, they sprang to their feet and stood at attention.

"That's all right, Ms. Johnson. We're just taking a little tour. Have the students be seated." Small placed his hand on the shoulder of a girl seated near the door. "This is Jenny. What are you learning today, my dear?"

She looked older than he had expected, but Peter recognized her immediately. Jenny Grant. Thick auburn hair crowned large velvet-brown eyes. Her lips turned upward, but she stared straight ahead, without the least hint of emotion. It was like someone had reached in and turned out the lights. Smiling depression?

"We're learning about drugs," Jenny said. Sterk shot Peter a look.

"Yes, drugs are what we're all about," the teacher said. "Right girls?"

"Yes Ms. Johnson!" the students shouted.

"Would you like to hear the girls recite?" Like soldiers in boot camp, the adolescents responded with a rigid, stylized chant:

"Drugs, D—don't cut class.

"Drugs, R—report all druggies.

"Drugs, U—understand your parents.

"Drugs, G—go to church.

"Drugs, S—study, study, study!"

"Thank you, Ms. Johnson." Small wrinkled his hawk-like nose. "Let's continue our tour. I want you to see everything."

In a classroom with a blue Peace Pipe sign on the door, young women read patriotic speeches. In the next room, a smiling young nurse demonstrated resuscitation techniques and first-aid procedures. Students were taught to analyze urine specimens in a classroom identified as TEPEES. The instructor said these Soilers would someday work in school clinics, the front lines in the fight against drug abuse. Peter noticed David Mendola sitting toward the back of the class studying something under a microscope.

"Dr. Small, is David Mendola okay?"

Small sniffed. "Yes, of course. He's doing fine, no thanks to you. Poor child was using drugs the entire time he was seeing you, but thanks to Dr. Wolf, and hypno-therapy, he's now perfectly clean."

So that was it. Hypnosis. Wolf was up to his old tricks. So easy to induce false memories.

Peter crossed his arms. " So I've heard. Just to satisfy my mind, let's do a quick urine check right now."

Small stiffened. "That would be quite irregular. I don't think I could permit it."

David looked up. "It's okay, Dr. Small. I'd like to show Dr. Sheppard that I'm completely clean." We have some cups next door, and I can do it in a jiffy.

"I'll probably catch hell from the General and Dr. Wolf," Small said. "But I'm going to permit it on the condition that this completes our tour. And if David checks out okay, you will apologize to both of us."

Peter nodded, and David stepped into the hallway. He returned a few seconds later with a plastic specimen container.

"I'll just step into the toilet here," David said, but barely got the words out when Sterk Trump, shoulders twitching, began to frisk him.

"What do you think you're doing, Detective? This boy is under our care and supervision, not yours," Small said.

"Well, he may be part of your little family, Doc, but these folks have been known to switch specimens. Just don't want no hanky panky. He's squeaky clean, Peter, but I'll go in and stand outside the stall after I give it the once over."

A few minutes later Sterk returned holding the specimen jar. Peter put his hand on David's shoulder. "I don't know what's going on, David, but I want you to know that I'm still here for you. If you need me for any reason just call me at the office or my home. I'm in the book."

David looked toward the Hammer who hovered in the hallway just behind Small. Taking a deep breath, David turned and walked to his seat. Peter followed Small and Sterk out the door. On the way back to the waiting room they passed an office with a small white sign on the door: General Doris Dantakovic. Doree, hard to believe she'd be mixed up in anything illegal, let alone unethical.

When they got to the waiting room, two St. Petersburg police officers stood in front of Terri Johns's desk. Flashing lights from their cruiser blinked against the stark waiting room walls.

"I want to sign a complaint to have this so called detective's license removed," Small said. "He carried a gun into a public school facility and frightened our staff and disrupted our program. We need to stop people with a bully mentality. I, for one, won't stand for it. There are mandatory sentences for carrying a weapon into a school facility."

The sergeant shook his head, a crooked smile creasing his face. "For Christ's sake, Sterk, you know you've been warned before..."

"Just took it out 'cause it needed some lubrication, Sarge." Sterk grinned and chewed on a thick lump of tobacco. "Didn't want it to rust, had to wipe it on something."

"But not on a citizen's face, Sterk."

"He's no friggin' citizen, believe me, Sergeant—"

"Okay, that's it," the sergeant said. "We'll work this out downtown. Dr. Small, I assure you these people won't bother you again."

Chapter 18

Prodded along by Breaker Mitchum, Jenny took hesitant steps down the concrete stairway. Cold, damp air rushed up to greet her when she got about halfway down. An open area the size of four tennis courts separated a modern wooden building from a row of cells, faced with steel doors. The Good Soil must have modernized some of the old dungeons. Was this where they had sent John Lifewater for time out?

Mitchum muttered something about the ceremony and stomped off toward a timbered archway some twenty yards away. The black hole coughed up strands of bluish smoke that hovered and watched like curious ghosts. It reminded Jenny of an old railroad tunnel, but the gnarled black cross standing just to the right of the entrance marked it as the Spanish Chapel. That's where the ceremony would take place.

Jenny stared down at a dusty monument. It had been erected in the sixties when tourists were still allowed to visit some of the dungeons. She read the faded message on the rounded cement slab: "You are now standing in the Tocobaga execution room. Several layers of human skulls and bones, along with longbows, arrowheads and pottery shards, were discovered by a team of anthropologists in 1947. Local tradition has it that Panfilo de Navarez, the Spanish conqueror called Red Beard, slaughtered some two thousand members of the Tocobaga Tribe near this spot."

Jenny studied the ceiling. No vegetation. No bats. She shivered. Was the old cemetery nearby? She bent and brushed red-orange dust from the shallow, chiseled letters.

"Legend also persists that the first holy man to die in the New World was buried alive in the great conch burial cavern. Shocked by the atrocities of the early conquistadors, Father Luis Cancer de Barbastro, a Dominican priest, hoped to win over the Indians with love and patience. He wanted to free them from suffocating superstition and Spanish mandates, but the ruling council feared that too much knowledge and freedom would weaken its control.

Beaten while praying on his hands and knees, clutching his crucifix, the priest was buried by Indian converts who thought he was dead. Even now his spirit is said to roam the burial cavern which is below the fort. Because of rotting timbers and shifting terrain, the conch hall was permanently sealed in 1962."

Jenny still had terrifying dreams about that night in the underground cemetery. She had really lucked out. A staffer told her they had found Billy Ray, out cold, head bloody and swollen, near Barbastro's tomb. Billy Ray had raved to nurses about prehistoric flying monsters with feathered wings. Breaker Mitchum told the slow-witted boy that it was the old priest, Barbastro, still stalking the burial cavern, still trying to escape the martyr's tomb.

She walked to the chapel and took hesitant steps through an open archway of rotted timbers and compressed shells. Dressed in gleaming white cassocks, about thirty Level I and Level II Soilers stood near the north wall of the damp, gloomy chamber. Jenny was surprised to see a handful of girls toward the back. She knew they would never become officers. John and Gonzi waved. Thank god, they had saved her a place. She sat quickly, not wanting to draw attention to herself. David Mendola, Danny O'Brien and Breaker Mitchum sat alone in the front row. So it was O'Brien. She swallowed hard and peered into John's eyes.

Dressed in starched blue shirts, burnished buckles, and polished leather straps, twenty Lion officers sat stiffly just behind O'Brien. Incense swirled from a gold chalice near the front of the altar, filling the room with a musky odor. Next to the chalice three silver medallions with intersecting triangles glistened in the murky light. Two candles, one black and one white, lay next to the medallions.

"Jesus," John said.

"What?" Gonzi turned and took Jenny's hand. Dressed in a black monk's tunic, a figure stood silent and unmoving behind the altar. It had appeared from nowhere. A dark wooden pendant hung from a thick gold necklace around the monk's neck. The large, octagon-shaped pendant showed an ivory cross surrounded by three glazed panels. The figure raised its arms. Slender, graceful fingers waved the three candidates forward.

Mendola, O'Brien, and Mitchum formed a perfect column. Only the whispered cadence of polished boots could be heard in the silent chapel. Stiff-kneed, they paraded around the towering black candle and stopped before the altar. Responding to a faint command, they knelt in unison.

Jenny hugged Gonzie and took a deep breath. It wasn't the spooky chapel that terrified her. It was the chilling realization that these people would do anything to frighten innocent teenagers. Unbalanced. They had to be out of control. The black-robed monk stepped in front of the three kneeling officers.

The Hammer, resplendent in his smartly pressed colonel's uniform, bent and placed the silver medallions around the graduates' necks. Then he turned toward the novitiates and swung his arm in a wide arch. "Someday, the rest of you will learn to honor the general."

The monk stepped to the front of the altar and picked up the candles. Reaching into his jacket pocket, the Hammer produced a polished gold lighter. He flicked it, and a three-inch flame shot straight up. The monk held the candles over the flame and the wicks ignited. With the black candle in one hand and the white candle in the other, the monkish figure stepped slowly around the young captives. Soilers shrunk back, close to the rough damp wall.

The concealed figure stopped abruptly, then turned. It moved straight toward Jenny and Gonzi. Halting in front of the Mexican boy, the monk circled his face with the black candle. Jenny had a clear view of purple, serpent-tongued sleeves on the monk's robe. The octagon shaped pendant glimmered in the shadowy light. Inside the three glazed panels she could see blue and gold carvings of bearded men. Could these be the leaders? The crazies? She had to remember those faces.

A serpent-tongued sleeve brushed her arm as it moved toward Gonzi. The candle came to rest against the boy's chin, the white orange flame almost touching his eyebrows. Unblinking, Gonzi did not waver. The flame dipped and danced in circles before faltering and finally going out. Wisps of cold, damp air fingered Jenny's ears. She squeezed Gonzi's arm, but he continued to stare at the shadowy figure.

An escalating tremor moved up the hooded figure's body. Emitting a low whimpering sound, the monk turned, tore off the gold necklace, and hurled the chained pendent into the dark recesses of the chapel. Jenny felt Gonzi move, but quickly looked away as he made the sign of the cross. The Hammer folded his arms and stared at the cloaked figure. He smiled. Then he turned and faced the Soilers.

"Many of you lack the confidence and self-esteem to become Lions. You don't realize that you carry seeds of greatness. Now we will nourish and cultivate those seeds. First, you will learn how to stand before your peers and speak with authority. I have chosen a brief passage for each of you to repeat. Speak clearly, and by all means, use your natural voice. I assure you that anyone who refuses to cooperate will regret it. Let me repeat myself. I want this to go smoothly, without any hesitation or difficulty of any kind. I want each of you to recite the following: "I am the one. No one will suspect me."

A low murmur ran through the teenager's ranks. Jenny squeezed Gonzi's hand. Starting with Hal Jacobson, in the back row, each Soiler stepped to the front of the chapel and turned to face the assembled group. Then they repeated the statement verbatim.

When it came to Jenny's turn, she glanced at John Lifewater who was just to her right. Lips trembling, he met her eyes for only a second, then looked away. Several Soilers stuttered and stammered through the brief recitation, but when Gonzie's turn came he smiled and spoke in an even voice.

"I am the one. No one will suspect me."

Danny O'Brien smiled and nodded.

The Hammer pointed toward the chapel entrance. A shrill whistle called Soilers to attention. A Lion sergeant held a long billy club by a smooth leather thong and barked out orders.

"Right, face! Forward, march! Hut two, three, four, hut two, three, four." Soilers marched out of the chapel and stood at attention in the open area between the chapel and the metal-faced cells.

"Just think of the poor people who were killed here," Starlyn whispered. Jenny shook her head and stared at Starlyn. Clueless. She had to be clueless. Or coming apart at the seams.

Danny O'Brien, resplendent in his tailored Colonel's uniform, sauntered up behind Gonzie, who stood in an outside column. He threw his arm over the boy's misshapen shoulders.

"Don't think we've met, you doin' okay?"

"We've met."

Soilers marched to a low slung building, maybe forty-feet-deep and sixty-feet-wide. It looked new. White fiberboard walls, probably prefab, connected to a flat green roof. A white plastic sign over a double doorway spelled out: "Communications Bunker."

"Halt."

A lieutenant tapped Gonzie on the shoulder. "This way." He took Gonzie's arm and pulled him to where the Hammer stood. Two Lions held Gonzie, while the Hammer and David Mendola searched his pockets. The Hammer pulled the micro recorder from Gonzie's shirt and wiggled out the tiny cassette. He smiled and handed it to Mendola.

"Take this to security, and have it destroyed. Also, call the general's office and get a verbal okay on Dr. Wolf's standing orders for electroshock."

Mendola's eyes widened.

"You heard me, Colonel. Get a move on."

Mendola looked sideways at Gonzie, who stood motionless, head down. Two muscular officers, walking ramrod-straight, dragged the limping Mexican boy up a steep stairway.

Danny O'Brien executed a perfect left-face and took brisk military steps along the silent column. He pointed out other Soilers. Jenny, Starlyn, John Lifewater, Billy Potter, and David Jacobson were ordered to stand aside.

"These unlucky five are returning to the chapel," the Hammer said. "We have some unfinished business with these traitors."

Chapter 19

Starlyn Dalton's sunken eyes retreated behind dark, fleshy pouches like a world hunger poster-child. She squeezed Jenny's hands and made shallow whimpering sounds. Jenny tried not to look at the other committee members. Bent over on his knees, John Lifewater fought to maintain his balance. Breaker Mitchum, Danny O'Brien, and two lower ranking officers straddled the powerful young athlete and twisted his long, muscular arms. A broad smile covered the Hammer's face. He slowly inched his mud-caked boot into John's face.

"Lick the boot, Tonto! I want your so-called committee to see what a brave little squaw you are."

John pulled his lips into a tight line and slowly shook his head. Mitchum laughed and thrust his heavy boot into John's side. The dull sound of hard leather against muscle and soft tissue made Jenny dizzy. Mitchum kicked him again. And again. Jenny hugged Starlyn and tried not to pass out. O'Brien jammed John's shoulders down. John managed to turn his head, his face just an inch from the Hammer's boot.

"No heart. No guts. And you thought you could lead this spineless group of cowards? Well I say you're nothing but a chicken, Tonto. A chicken that likes to dance around in pretty costumes like a drag queen." He laughed. "Just an Okie-fried chicken."

John's elbows jutted into the air like wishbones, ready to snap. Jenny covered her face with her hands and peered through her fingers at John's wet hair and flushed face. Why didn't he just give up? What was he trying to prove?

"I thought you Tontos' loved nature." The Hammer's boot rubbed against the boy's face, but John continued to clench his mouth shut. The Hammer crossed his arms, looked at Jenny, and smiled.

"Start licking Tonto, or Jenny gets electroshock. Now."

"No! Don't do it, John. Please don't do it." Jenny reached for John, but Mitchum pulled her back.

John hesitated for a moment, took a deep breath, then bent and ran the tip of his tongue across the Hammer's muddy left boot. Jenny looked away, tears flooding her eyes.

"That's more like it, you little red papoose. You heard me. Nothing like a little papoose to keep our shoes bright and shiny. "Hi ho, Tonto, away!"

Danny O'Brien smiled the smile of a schoolyard bully. "Hi ho, Tonto, away!"

The Hammer jerked his boot from John's face and pointed to the prisoners' cells across the way. "Put these traitors over there, and let them think about the lab."

Jenny reached to help John, but Mitchum yanked her back. He twisted her fingers and she fell to her knees. Dear God, she couldn't stand the pain. She peered at the Hammer for help... and immediately felt ashamed.

The Hammer reached behind Jenny and pulled the back of her robe. "She's been into this committee thing up to her earlobes, but we'll bring her along. Might be fun." Still holding the loose material, the Hammer lifted Jenny to her feet. The thin linen robe tugged against her large, rounded breasts. The Hammer stared hard and laughed. He released his grip and pulled a three-by five-inch picture from his tailored jacket. He pushed it into Jenny's face.

"Oh... my dad. Where did... is he okay?"

"He'll be all right as long as his pretty little daughter plays ball." The Hammer giggled and looked upward. "You got it, honey, or do I got to draw you a picture? Hey, come to think of it, pictures might be fun."

He looked down at Starlyn. "Take her back to the dorm. I think she's just about used up." He smiled. "It sure as hell doesn't take long." Jenny glanced at Starlyn, but the bent and broken girl stared downward. Jenny paused for only a second before moving to the Hammer's side. Her fingers caressed the back of his neck.

The Hammer's gold bars and silver Lions' emblem glittered in the murky light. "You newly anointed officers have succeeded by force and ingenuity because you're under the general's powers. Tonight, the general has christened you full colonels in the Lions Corps. As such, you are privy to the secret workings of the corps and will receive unlimited power and un-imagined pleasures of mind and flesh. You will work on the hierarchy of human needs from the bottom up."

Jenny fingered the black ribbon that held the Hammer's ponytail and stared into the eyes of the Lion officers. Standing at attention, with perfect posture, they looked like West Point Cadets. David Mendola, that bastard.

"As you know from the classified parchments you received earlier, the most basic need is security. And that's why spreading the use of addictive drugs is critical to our cause. It's not just apathy we're seeking. It's the high level of crime and insecurity that drugs create. Our time bombs are sociological, not chemical."

The Hammer pushed Jenny's hand from his ponytail. "And speaking of insecurity, what about our gangs? And I do say our gangs. The Bloods, the Cripts, the Trenchies, call them whatever. But they belong to us. Ever wonder how they grew so fast. Ever wonder where they got their money? The Good Soil is the gang, folks. We are it. These gang members are just our hired help."

The Hammer gave them a condescending smile. He seemed to be enjoying himself. "By teaching our value system through the public schools we'll indoctrinate the future citizens of this country. With rampant crime, uncontrolled drug use, and a dropout rate of 40 per cent, our school system is the perfect host for our seeds of destruction. And we can infiltrate without detection because the public schools are really private. If we tried this stuff in a private school the parents would raise holy hell. No, the public schools are private, and the private schools are public. That's good."

Breaker Mitchum raised his hand. "Public schools are a piece of cake. We nailed their ass—"

"Yeah, the bureaucrats and politicians were easy 'cause the teachers unions have them well conditioned, but the teachers are another story. Too many teachers want to be heroes, teacher of the year and crap like that. Damned ants. Step on 'em and they keep coming back. And for what? Can't be the money." The Hammer chuckled. "Hell, if they want to be martyrs we'll be happy to feed them to the lions." He bent over with laughter. "Feed them to our Lions, get it?

Tears wetted Jenny's eyes. The Hammer reached over and pinched her cheek. "And speaking of money, now comes desert. Because we've been such good little boys and girls, we get to pass Go and land on Boardwalk. Oh, my, a billion dollars. And are we going to use the grant money to help the little kiddies in our public schools?"

He looked at Billy Potter. "You're a Colonel now, Potter. What do you think?"

"Well, ah, I, ah—"

"Of course not. Some of that money will continue our programs here, but most of it is going to jolly old England to ah—let's just say to help us reinvent the human race. My father will be flying high. A billion from the grant, fifty million from a not-to-be-named country for our work in U.S. public schools, and another fifty million from blackmailing a few not-so-proper members of the upper crust. That ought to be enough to keep papa happy."

Jenny and the three officers followed the Hammer along a narrow stone corridor. He stopped in front of one of the many kerosene torches that illuminated the hallway and turned the base of the torch in a clockwise direction. The moss-covered wall pivoted to one side revealing a brightly lighted passageway. They pressed through the opening to a modern, carpeted hallway. Large windows ran along each side of the darkened corridor. Behind the windows, Jenny recognized the brilliantly illuminated classrooms.

"You must pay strict attention," the Hammer said. "Each of you will be responsible for one of these training groups."

Inside the first window, under a sign marked: Arrows, eight students sat straight, shoulders back, at small wooden desks. Jenny shook her head. Ms. Johnson's tweed jacket, purple blouse, and gold antique broach matched her pinched face and resolute jaw.

"Now here's the main thing, girls—listen up! This is behavior modification." The teacher stood with her hands on her hips. "That means we need perfect timing and a 100 percent response. Kind of like the Rocketts except we don't synchronize, we pulverize."

Taking quick steps across the front of the classroom, the teacher waved her arms and addressed the students in a loud voice. "'Mary Todd, Mary Todd.' The voice would speak to her through the walls. 'Mrs. Lincoln, your husband will die tonight.' Mary Todd cried and prayed to be released from her terrible dreams." The teacher pulled at her hair and imitated the anxious cries of the President's wife.

The class slumbered.

Slowing her pace, the prim little teacher spoke in a dry, quiet voice.

"Mrs. Lincoln liked biscuits for breakfast. She spread the salted butter with an old silver butter knife and sometimes warmed the biscuits in the oven. She liked jam too. Strawberry jam and sometimes honey. And sometimes raspberry jam and sometimes she ate toast."

The teenagers sat up, grinned, and gave her direct eye contact.

"Not bad, girls, not bad at all. Teachers are used to bored students, but with this technique we can send them straight to the hospital. Burn out, they call it."

The Hammer turned to the group. "Johnson used to teach in a New Jersey public school. But that was before a seventh grader took a shot at her. Now she's one happy lady—and a main-liner."

They moved along the corridor to a room that looked like a crating or shipping department. A technician in a blue lab coat showed four students how to pack book marks into black Gideon Bibles.

"Packaging blotters of lysergic acid diethylamide in the good book isn't always the best way to go," the technician said. "But sometimes we're forced to. Trick here is to use middle-school kids and keep your backsides covered. And use a downtown post office box where you can watch the pick-up."

In the next classroom, labeled: Tepees, large metal coffee urns pushed clouds of steam into the air. Jenny wrinkled her nose at the sour and acidic odor. Ten to twenty students watched teachers in chef hats and white aprons siphon dripping liquid from enormous pots.

"What is it, Colonel?" Mitchum asked. "Don't smell so great."

The Hammer lifted the lid from a large metal pot and rinsed several fingers in the golden liquid. "Best way to know that is to try the blessed stuff." He shook his hand and put his index finger in his mouth. "Ah... the future of the Good Soil."

The young officers dipped their fingers into the pot and sucked loudly. His eyes filling with tears, Mitchum held his hand over his mouth and coughed, again and again. The Hammer slapped his back with an open palm and laughed.

"Not bad," Mitchum said.

"Yep, not bad at all—for urine." The Hammer gave him a mocking grin. "If you hope to progress, gentlemen, you'd better keep your eyes open. I didn't suck the fingers I put in the pot. Just wanted to see if you were awake. And Christ Almighty, you weren't.

The Hammer pointed at the steaming pots. "No, you won't want a steady diet of this golden beverage, though our chefs know their business very well. Freeze dried, a real breakthrough. Parents and doctors always insist on urine tests and they really had us rocking in our boots. But the General discovered how to freeze-dry clean urine. So now we reduce it to the size of a button. Our druggies can go into the john any old time and come out with clean stuff. No fuss, no muss, and a hell of a lot easier than sneaking someone through a window. Right, Mendola?" David Mendola smiled and gave the Hammer a lazy salute.

"You should see parents' faces when our bleary-eyed druggies come up with 100 percent clean urine. Want to make you cry. And while the stuff cools, we make our famous chocolate chip cookies. Soilers get 'em with every meal. M.J. cookies, delicious. Get yours today, Jenny?" He chuckled.

The Hammer strutted down the hallway. "Hang onto your hats, gang, and follow me. As my beloved father would say, here's where we separate the serfs from the royals." Eyes dancing, he smirked from behind pointed teeth.

Chapter 20

Jenny followed the Hammer and the three colonels into a small, narrow room. They sat on a cushioned bench and faced a one-way mirror.

"You are six-teen, go-ing on sev-en-teen, ba-by it's time to think. Bet-ter be-ware, be can-ny and care-ful, Ba-by, you're on the brink!" A medley of tunes from the "Sound of Music" tumbled out of a brown plastic radio, and brilliant light bleached the room in shades of white. An enormous man, dressed in a wrinkled surgical gown, bent over a reclined figure.

Jenny didn't want to look. She knew who it was. Only partially covered by a thin white sheet, Terri Johns lay flat on her back on a stainless steel table. A small, bloodstained pillow cushioned her head. The music reverberated against the small chipped windows. "How do you solve a prob-lem like Ma-ri-a? How do you catch a cloud and pin it down?"

Terri's right eye stared like an iced fish-eye, her eyelid propped open by the surgeon's plump index finger. Jenny tried not to stare at the heavy blue eyeshadow and garish painted lips. Terri never wore makeup. Sick. So sick. And the glittering purple nail polish... The sour taste of bile filled Jenny's throat.

"Terri, Terri... Terri, it's time to go to school. Can you remember the golden rule?" The fleshy man chuckled and reached to a glass-topped side table for a bottle of Jack Daniels'. Wiping cigarette ashes from a dirty plastic cup, he emptied what was left of the bottle into it. The brown liquid disappeared in one gulp. He closed his eyelids and tilted his head backward.

Belching softly, he picked up the icepick and cradled her head in his left arm. He pulled her eyelids apart with his thumb and sausage-like index finger and slowly worked the gleaming point into the pink folds of her eye socket. "Ah… there we are, Terri. Oh, yes, there we are." He released her eyelid and slowly rotated the bloody shaft back and forth, up and out. Straightening, he wiped his wet brow with the back of his hand, and a smile spread across his face.

"Terri, Terri, you'll be glad, no more memories to make you sad." The obese man stepped back and dropped the icepick into a jar of clear liquid. Visible above the rim of the jar, the icepick's orange wooden handle showed a crude drawing of two blue ice cubes: Central Ice—Beer to Go.

"Girls in white dress-es with blue sat-in sashes, snow-flakes that stay on my nose and eye-lashes." He flopped into the oversized chair. It squealed under the weight of massive buttocks, while rolls of fat searched for equilibrium. Shoulders hunched, he reached for the desk drawer, pulled back on a rusted gold knob, and removed a small transparent bag. Nicotine-stained fingers held the plastic bag open while he brushed in the auburn eyebrow and long, dark lashes.

When he opened a leather-bound calender, Jenny could see an inscription and a picture of a large tree on the cover.

> "Acorns Into Mighty Oaks"
> The Good Soil
> (A Florida Nonprofit Corporation)

Head bent, the corpulent man flipped the stiff, heavy pages. "Now here's a pretty one. My, my… yes. Starlyn Dalton. Hi, Starlyn. Peach ice cream and pigtails. You're on my list, dear. Oh good! Right after the big show on Easter Sunday. A little electricity to calm your nerves and then my… ah, loving touch. The Hammer must be tired of his little plaything." He giggled. "You've been a naughty girl. Or maybe not naughty enough."

He wiped saliva from his bloated lower lip and turned the page. "I should get time-and-a-half. Not even the Good Lord works on Easter Sunday. Jenny Grant. Gorgeous. A model's face. Another Easter Sunday girl. And those must be your proud parents. Ah, Florida Department of Law Enforcement." He quickly turned the page.

Jenny stiffened and tried not to react. Had she heard that right? She let her eyes drift toward the Hammer but did not turn her head. Good God, was this all part of the torture? Was this just a threat, or...?

"Liz Blair. Must be late twenties, early thirties? How unusual. Ice-cold blue eyes. Interesting. Yes indeed, the eye is truly the doorway to the soul." He snorted. "So many beautiful ones. And when the big education grant comes through there will be one a week, maybe two. And then the Hammer is taking me to Europe. Yes, they'll accept my research over there." He reached to the radio and turned up the volume. "Climb ev-'ry moun-tain, ford ev-'ry stream." Then he settled back into the cushioned chair.

The Hammer rubbed his hands together and smirked. "Everyone enjoy the performance? The old Doc knows when he's got an audience and knows how to put on a show. Come on, I'll introduce you." Jenny squeezed out of the narrow room and found herself in front of a door labeled: Lab. The Hammer opened it.

The massive lump of a man sat in his soiled surgeon's gown and sucked on a limp marijuana cigarette. In his late sixties or early seventies, the fleshy giant cocked his head and gave them a soft, sweet smile.

The Hammer bowed almost to the floor. "May I present Dr. Porter Stroud, a highly distinguished surgeon, indeed." Another soft smile crossed the obese man's face. He waved, but only his fingers moved.

"How's about showing us around your laboratory, Dr. Stroud?" the Hammer asked.

"Oh, are these candidates? "The gargantuan man spoke in a tinny, high-pitched voice. The smile quickly turned to a smirk. Dr. Stroud stood and shuffled over to Terri John's reclining body. Scooping up the icepick, he straightened and patted the restraining straps. The soft smile was back. Jenny shivered.

"You saw the show. It's really quite simple. I just slide in this little miracle worker. Snip, snip, snip. A little tissue from the frontal lobes and my, what a difference it makes." He flourished the ice pick and cut the air like a conductor leading an orchestra.

"Hell, I did a thousand of these babies in Baton Rouge over a ten-year period." Stroud's eyes gleamed, and a catlike grin revealed bleached-white, artificial teeth. "Don't use an anesthetic, don't need to. Just electro-shock. Catch 'em while they're still dazed. Perfectly safe. Another little technique we've developed allows us to put our operators into a deep coma, then bring 'em back to life when the heat's off."

Stroud smiled at the skeptical expressions on the faces of the new officers. "There's no way you can tell they're still alive. When they recover, days later, they're in a dream state. They can't hurt us 'cause all they remember is bit and pieces. Our beloved general brought this stuff back from El Salvador. Believe me, it works."

"I understand the State Board of Examiners boogied you right out of the State of Louisiana, Dr. Stroud," Mitchum said. Jenny shook her head. Just promoted and already starting to flex his muscles. Did anything seep through that drug-soaked brain?

"It was all politics, young man. No one made a peep when we used it on kids and retards who were giving their parents a rough time. Or even the honeys of some of our politicians. After all, some things are better off not remembered. But as soon as we cut a black man, all hell broke loose. That candy-assed bastard was trying to blackmail the lieutenant governor of the sovereign state of Louisiana, by God."

Stroud smiled and lowered his voice to a conspiratorial whisper. "Blabbed about their—uh, special relationship. We figured a little memory loss wouldn't hurt. I admit I took more out than necessary, but conducting surgery in the back of a Lincoln Town-Car during the half-time of an L.S.U—Alabama game? Not real easy, my friends."

Jenny felt swirls of heat and perspiration dance along the back of her neck. "Some of those young predators in training, just down the hall, will do a real good job out there," Stroud said. "But the time may come when their memory needs shortening. That's when I turn them into mighty pretty secretaries who are great on an hour-to-hour basis, but who can't remember a damn thing about the day before."

Speckles of blood dotted Stroud's stained lab coat. He pulled a whiskey bottle from nowhere and lifted it to his mouth. "Hell, yes. I'm the world's leading expert. You won't find me in the medical journals because I'm not considered politically correct by a few spoil sports." He smirked. "Can't imagine why? Yep, just a little snip here and a little snip there. You want 'em to forget men's names or just ladies' names? What happened a week ago Thursday? Just let me know." His stained, chubby fingers cut the air with his imaginary scissors, "Snip, snip, snip."

Jenny saw Terri Johns' head inch to the left, and the dazed girl moaned softly. The radio buzzed with static, then cleared. "Your Golden Oldies, 860 FM, is proud to present Tulsa's own, Miss Patti Page, with that all-time favorite classic, 'How Much is that Doggie in the Window?'"

Jenny couldn't breathe. She felt like she was in a boiling-hot furnace. And the smell of blood and ether was everywhere. She focused on the blue ice cubes on the icepick's stubby handle. Don't pass out now. Don't end up like Terri.

The Hammer raised his hand. In unison, the officers turned and marched out. Leaning against the door frame, the Hammer looked back. "That was a pretty good show, Doctor Stroud."

The old man gulped down more whiskey. A tiny drop of moisture blotted his left eye.

Jenny shook her head. That poor guy, his—

A shrill laugh shattered Jenny's thoughts. The Hammer's mouth lifted to reveal widely spaced, pointed teeth. Intense rolling eyes signaled a maniacal lack of self-restraint.

The man's crazy, daddy... just crazy. Daddy, where are you?

Curling his hand in mock salute, the smartly dressed officer did a parade ground about-face. Then he strutted down the hallway, a renegade toy soldier from a child's worst nightmare.

Chapter 21

Peter surveyed his cluttered desktop and pressed the telephone against his ear. His hand shook. "What? I don't believe it. Today's only Friday, the twenty-second. It was already moved up once. This is just, it's—irresponsible."

Yep, we're moving it up," Dr. Gerry said. The Washington bureaucrat sounded a bit uneasy. "I really can't figure this one myself, Dr. Sheppard, and I've been around here awhile. I shouldn't be telling you this, and I'll deny that I said it, but I've heard rumors that a big celebration is planned down there for Easter Sunday. Maybe they want to—"

"You mean risk the future of kids all over this state just to create a P R circus? And squander a billion dollars in the process?"

Gerry's voice went up an octave. "It wouldn't be the first time. Easter's a slow news day, and giving out money on a religious holiday makes everybody look good. They'll probably tie it in with Passover or anything else that plays well."

"So I've got an hour to get to a meeting in Tampa. A meeting that was originally set for April twenty-third and rescheduled for next Wednesday? How about the Good Soil? Were they just notified too, or did someone tip them—"

"I really can't go into that, Doctor. Good luck."

Click.

Peter sighed. Why did he always end up looking into the phone mouthpiece when he talked to Washington?

Linda's poked her head around the door. "Bad news?"

"The big meeting's in forty-five minutes. Give Kathleen and Liz a shout, and tell them to meet me at the Tampa Bay School Board. I've got to get a move on, and I'm going to need some reinforcements."

Peter stuffed his briefcase with files from his desk and hurried down the hallway to the back door. He jogged over to the Volvo and tossed the briefcase into the backseat. Edging into heavy traffic on Fifth Avenue North, he headed west, toward I-275. He checked the rearview mirror for police cars. Then he punched the accelerator and felt the turbo kick in. If he could get past the tourist traffic on the Howard Franklin Bridge, he'd make it on time.

Weaving in and out of three lanes of traffic, Peter streaked past the West Shore Shopping Center exit in just under twenty-five minutes. He took the downtown exit and worked his way through heavy traffic to the school board building. He arrived with ten minutes to spare. Liz Blair sat on the hood of Barrett Spangler's stretch limo, smoking a cigarette. The limo occupied three reserved parking places in front of the school board garage. Peter shook his head and grinned. A policeman stood next to Liz with his hands on his hips, but his smile gave him away.

A young man with a carrot orange ponytail, wearing a gray double-breasted suit and chauffeur's cap, ran over and opened Peter's door. Peter got out and stepped to the limo. Liz scooted off the hood and took his arm. Then she turned and blew a kiss at the policeman. Peter and Liz headed for the front door.

"Dear Kat probably won't get here in time. Same old story." Liz looked him up and down and giggled. "Maybe we ought to hook up. We seem to be the action guys." He could smell alcohol on her breath. Despite Liz's claim that she had turned the corner, her drinking had increased.

"There it is," Liz said. "A damn twelve-story monument that cost us taxpayers close to twenty-six million dollars." She smirked. "Of course I don't have a quarter to my name, so I guess it didn't cost me much."

They crossed the Italian marble lobby and rode the quiet, carpeted elevator to the fifth floor. The doors opened, and they stepped into an atrium filled with exotic plants that extended from the lobby to the twelfth floor. On the south side of the atrium, a large room with floor-to-ceiling glass windows filled the entire width of the building. Signs on the windows announced its purpose: This is Your Professional Multimedia Center, Teachers. Don't be Afraid to Use It!

But the huge library was empty. Cutouts of bunnies carrying pink and blue Easter eggs adorned the plateglass windows. Like ghostly puppets, school librarians glided in circles around long, neat rows of carefully indexed reference books. Peter and Liz walked alongside the atrium and past offices marked Assistant Administrator, Administrator, and Assistant Superintendent. Thickly padded carpeting quieted their steps.

"This furniture would be the envy of any Fortune five hundred executive," Liz said. "Never had anything like this, not even at Sterns and Tregor."

Peter peered down at her. "Yes. Maybe that's why we're here."

The door to Room 538 stood open. A hastily scribbled sign read: Paula Reardon, Hearing Officer. They stepped into a noisy conference room that was forty feet long and twenty feet wide. As they entered, the chattering voices quieted. A fortyish woman in a tweed business suit sat at the head of a long, highly polished table.

Behind her, a court reporter adjusted a small black transcriber. Along the far side of the conference table Peter counted twenty people with briefcases, tape recorders, yellow legal pads, and stacks of files. Prickly heat danced along Peter's back and neck. Someone had tipped them off. No other way they could all show up prepared and on time. Not with just an hour's notice.

Reardon turned to the court reporter. "You ready, Henrietta? Looks like everyone's here, so let's get started. Now, you all know we're here today to explore these two proposals. Witnesses will be under oath, but these procedures do not carry the full weight or formality of a court of law. This hearing falls somewhere between a group deposition and a debating society, except that everyone has to be truthful. I ask that each of you maintain a civil and courteous tone. Now why don't we go around the table and introduce ourselves so we can all find out who's here. Dr. Sheppard, why don't you start?"

"Peter Sheppard, psychologist and administrator of the Center for Children."

"I'm Liz Blair, and I'm, ah, I'm related to the guy." She grinned and rolled her eyes. "Let's just say I'm along for the ride."

Peter stared at Liz. Good Lord, how much alcohol had she put away? Just what he needed.

"Okay, thank you," Reardon said. "Now let's hear from the other side of the table."

With shaky hands, Dr. Harold Small used a large white handkerchief to wipe perspiration from his forehead. The frail educator's eyes darted from side to side. Peter knew anxiety when he saw it. Maybe even fear?

"I'm Dr. Harold Small, assistant administrator of the Good Soil project. I'm sitting in for the director, Doris Dantakovic. I might also add that our consulting psychiatrist, Dr. Benjamin Wolf, is running late. But I'm sure you'll understand. He has a very busy schedule."

Reardon pulled back her shoulders and stared at the frail counselor. "Well, let's hope your consultant gets here, Dr. Small, or his input will be rather slight. Let's go with the people who have managed to find their way up here on time."

"A stocky young man in a black suit lowered his head and smiled. "I'm Judson Browne, legal counsel for the Good Soil." He looked to his left. "Jack Barns and Ralph Starling are attorneys from our Washington office. And next to Ralph is Mark Shelton, assistant school superintendent for Tampa Bay county. He's here with three associate superintendents." Peter had debated Shelton at a Tampa Junior League meeting. He had seemed like a decent enough fellow.

A large black woman dressed in floral square-neck dress spoke in a deep, booming voice. "Pearl Truby, NAACP, and two members of our executive council. We also got Freddy Jakes, child placement supervisor, HRS district six and Betsy Willy, HRS, district four. She's also child placement and adoption supervisor."

A muscular man in his forties with coffee-colored skin and long delicate fingers waved at Reardon. "Ed Martinez, AFL-CIO teachers union. Also with me are State Representative Devon Washington, chairman of the state of Florida legislative panel on public education and Harold Timis, legal counsel to the Tampa Bay School Board."

Reardon smiled. "Thank you very much, ladies and gentlemen. I didn't expect to see so many people here with the Good Soil program. Reminds me of being called to a school conference when one of my daughters was in trouble." Liz giggled, but the Good Soil representatives responded with stony silence.

"All right, let's keep it simple and direct. And remember, we're only allotted three hours for this entire proceeding. As I said before, the purpose of this hearing is to flush out details of the two competing proposals. While my recommendations will carry considerable weight, the final decision will be made at the National Institute of Mental Health. Dr. Sheppard, why don't you get us started with a summary of your proposal?"

"Thank you, Your Honor," Peter said. "The Center for Children offers a unique approach to drug prevention. Rather than spending huge sums of money on antidrug programs within our schools, we would like to focus on reforming the schools themselves. Our teachers are looking for a better place to teach. A place where they can feel safe and productive. To achieve this end, we need true reform. The parent scholarship program will give vouchers worth $3,400, much less than the public schools spend on educating students, to parents so they can choose the best schools for their children. These scholarships will create a climate of competition which will improve all schools, public and private. This program will greatly benefit minorities and the disadvantaged because they are in failing schools. But it will help all children."

Liz put her hands behind her neck and stretched. Several of the men eyed her shapely body.

"We believe that a positive school culture and positive peer pressure can have a more significant impact on drug use than most so-called antidrug programs. Our research project, Your Honor, will cost only twenty million dollars—not the billion dollars requested by the Good Soil."

Judson Browne, legal counsel for the Good Soil, yawned and smiled at Reardon. The hearing officer stared straight ahead.

"We are the freest country in the world, and yet our parents are denied freedom of choice in this most critical of all areas, their children's education." Peter nodded and sat down.

"Thank you, Dr. Sheppard," Reardon said. Now let's hear from the Good Soil proponents. Dr. Small?"

"Dr. Sheppard's proposal is a cruel joke, Your Honor—nothing but a bunch of conservatives pushing an old idea that's never worked and isn't at all realistic. What happens to our quota system and court-ordered integration of the school system? Parents will just pick the school that has the best football team. They're not prepared to make heavy professional decisions for their children. Can you imagine the average parent telling us how to run our schools?

"These people want to destroy the melting pot that has given this country its cohesiveness. You will see private school classrooms filled with KKK children sitting in white sheets, being taught racist ideas with taxpayers' money. What about diploma mills—"

"Excuse me," Reardon said. "Your opening statement should emphasize the positive points of your own program. Mr. Browne, I suggest you advise your client to proceed in a manner appropriate to this hearing." Judson Browne leaned over and whispered into the pale educator's ear.

Small straightened. "I apologize, Your Honor. The Good Soil believes American children deserve the finest education in the world. Not only that, they deserve free day care and head-start education from the age of three months. Public schools will be the center of the child's community and encompass all services needed for the child's proper development. Sex education, health clinics, school physicians, psychological services, culturally sensitive curricula, and even drug services modeled after the exemplary Good Soil program. Actually, most parents are satisfied with the schools their children attend. We're doing a great job now, and with this billion dollar grant we—

"Listen you little twirp." Liz stumbled to her feet and pointed an unsteady finger at Small. "If you think your schools are so great, why are you scared to death of a little competition? You think we'll pull one brick from that Berlin Wall of yours to let a couple of poor kids smell some freedom, and that whole damn wall will fall down like Humpty Dumpty? And why do more public school teachers send their own kids to private schools than–"

"Hold it." Reardon pounded her gavel and glared at Liz. "Do I have to remind you–"

Laughter echoed from the hallway. The door sprang open to reveal a portly and animated Dr. Benjamin Wolf, who backed into the room while still waving toward the hallway. He turned and said to no one in particular, "Mighty fine secretaries in this building, I'd say. Yes, sir, mighty fine."

The blimpish man bent and squeezed Harold Small's hand. Then he plopped into the chair next to Small. Dressed in a blue plaid sport coat with a Burbury's of London logo, charcoal gray slacks, and a pink silk tie and handkerchief, the psychiatrist exuded a rich and forceful image that seemed alien to the assembled group.

"Sorry I'm late," Wolf said without giving Paula Reardon the courtesy of eye contact. "Up in Gainesville. Yep, up in Gator country. They needed somebody to tell them that son of a bitch Pichard massacred five students. He tried to play crazy, but the guy's a real shark. We're gonna cook him up good in the hot seat. Stew him like gator meat."

Liz frowned and glanced at Peter, but the two HRS representatives sat wide-eyed and smiling. Peter's main focus was the small mustard stain on Wolf's silk paisley tie. Someday the man's impulsiveness would do him in. He compared Wolf's current level of manic excitement to the mildly hyperactive chief resident he had known twenty years before.

"By the way, I don't want to rain on your parade," Wolf said. "But after my modest testimony in Gainesville, I hopped over to Tallahassee on the Good Soil corporate jet." Small and Browne closed their eyes and inched down in their chair. "And talked to the governor's liaison with Washington. Guess what? Looks like the parent-choice dream boat just went kerplunk." The pudgy man's giggles pushed folds of fat up and down his elegant mint green shirt.

"According to the governor's chief aide, John Bostick, the dream boat over there"—Wolf paused for effect and pointed at Peter—"is going to have to file official requisitions through all the agencies representing the Good Soil. And they have to be submitted today." He smirked and stared into Peter's eyes.

Peter turned to Reardon. "What? That's impossible. What does this mean, madam hearing officer? We weren't asked to submit proposals through these other agencies. I don't think they've submitted them either, have they?"

With synchronized precision, the representatives on the left side of the table pushed a dozen bound documents forward. The two HRS proposals were at least five hundred pages each, and the NAACP proposal easily reached a thousand pages. The proposals formed a straight line down the center of the conference table.

Judson Browne spoke in a low, soothing voice. "I'm truly sorry, Ms. Reardon, but we weren't sure what the outcome of Dr. Wolf's meeting would be. We were advised some time ago that our proposals might be needed for this meeting."

Reardon slammed her fist on the table. "My instructions speak to verbal presentations and two written proposals, one from each group. I know nothing about these other proposals or the time limits you have indicated. Surely you are mistaken, sir."

She pushed back her chair, stood, and marched to the door. "I want the administrators and consultants in my office. Now." She pointed to the stenographer. "You stay where you are."

Peter, Liz, and the others followed Reardon down the carpeted hallway to her office. Once they were all inside, Reardon slammed the door. "All right, Mr. Browne. What's going on? And mark my word, this had better be good. I don't care if the governor or the Queen of Sheba gave you orders. If I find foul play, I'll report it to NIMH—and the White House, if necessary."

"I apologize again, Ms. Reardon," Judson Browne said. "But we really had nothing to do with this. Apparently, a grant of this magnitude weaves its way through many layers of review within NIMH as well as the new drug czar's office. It wasn't until last week that we heard rumors about needing applications from all agencies. We let them know about the rumor, but did not, I repeat, did not ask them to prepare reports. I'm completely surprised myself that they came fully prepared."

"Can we cut through some of this, Jud?" Wolf asked. "The bottom line is that those people over there need to have proposals in that cover all agencies involved by midnight tonight."

Peter heard a growling sound and looked at Liz. She lurched forward and grabbed Wolf, her nails clawing at his stylish sport coat. "You bastard! Now it's all coming together."

Peter reached for Liz and struggled to pull her back. "Hold on, hold on!"

Reardon stood and removed her glasses, her face just inches from Wolf's. "This is outrageous. I'm washing my hands of this whole affair. This is a setup, and I've been used. We've all been used. I'm calling the governor now, and I'm going to put a stop to this charade. Certainly the governor is not involved in this kind of travesty."

"Well, my dear, I'm afraid that won't help," Wolf said. The governor has agreed to give a pot full of money to the Good Soil on Easter Sunday unless those other proposals are in tonight. I suspect that's going to be kind of tough." Wolf looked at Peter and smiled. "Especially when just getting the right forms takes about three weeks."

Reardon stared at the fat man. Then she turned and took slow, measured steps to the window. She stared down toward the street. Even Wolf held his tongue. After a few seconds she turned and faced the group. Reardon spoke in soft, quiet tones. "Thank you, Dr. Small. Your people may now go back to the conference room where you will wait for me." The trio bumped their way quickly through the door and closed it carefully behind them.

Reardon shook her head. "It looks impossible, Dr. Sheppard, but I have a plan. I'll extend the deadline to this Sunday, the twenty-fourth. That gives you two and a half days. I'd give you more, but the Feds need at least a week to shuffle the papers, and let's face it, Easter Sunday is just next week. If they reject your proposal, which they may very well do, you'll have grounds for appeal through legal channels that bypass the politicians. Between the legal process and the media, I think we can get a hearing."

"But what about the proposals? Peter asked. We don't even know the requirements of all those agencies. It would—uh, require a huge team of experts to put the applications together."

"I'm afraid my hands are tied, Dr. Sheppard, but extending the deadline may give you a chance to defeat that group of conniving—Don't get me wrong, I'm not necessarily endorsing your proposal. But I am endorsing your rights and your freedom. This high-handed approach smacks of the very bureaucratic manipulation you oppose in your grant. And if the school system is involved, so be it."

Liz crossed her arms and shook her head. Reardon sighed. "I know it isn't much, but it is a chance. You have just three days to do what ordinarily takes months to accomplish. But if your belief in the private enterprise model is valid, perhaps you can pull it off. Good luck."

Chapter 22

Linda stood just inside the back hallway door to Peter's office. Her hand rested on the reinforced carpet that served as additional soundproofing.

"I think the incredible one has arrived. Ms. Blair wasn't kidding."

"What does that mean?"

"Well, I'll tell you. If Mrs. Sheppard calls, I'll just say you're tied up with a government official." Linda smirked, eyes dancing.

"Okay, thanks for the warning."

He took brisk steps into the waiting room, but slowed his pace when he saw the woman. In her early twenties, she reclined in the deep recesses of the overstuffed couch, arms stretched across the top of each section. Attired in a white, pristine rayon coatdress with large white pockets, she had dramatic red-orange hair that hugged her shoulders. A glowing sunset, the almost garish hair mirrored her fresh, flawless skin. The clean, classic fragrance of geraniums was a bit overdone, but the flowery perfume punctuated the woman's sheer physical presence. A confident smile played across her face.

"I'm Dr. Peter Sheppard."

"Oh, yes, I know, Dr. Sheppard." She extended her hand and smiled, displaying toothpaste-commercial teeth. "I'm Bonnie Freeman, Liz Blair told me all about you. And her big buddy, Barrett Spangler, speaks highly of you also. I'm ready to get to work."

He caught Linda's expression from the corner of his eye. She always hid the yearly swimsuit edition of Sports Illustrated because she felt it was inappropriate for a family practice waiting room. Where was she going to hide this sexual fantasy?

Peter tried to hold back rising feelings of despair and irritation. It had to be a mistake. This honey was gratifying to look at, but... He shook his head. It was like Kathleen had always said. Liz could be well-meaning at times, but you couldn't count on her in a pinch. Did Liz meet this gal in some bar?

"Are you sure Liz, ah, Ms. Blair, filled you in on the position?"

Bonnie floated across the carpet toward his office. "I know. You wonder if I have the goods."

She had the goods, all right.

"Where am I going to work? Time is of the essence."

"You sure you can organize this thing? I've lined up a dozen typists, and I can get backups, but this is going to take an enormous amount of organization to have any chance of working."

"Look." Bonnie lifted a stack of forms from a large straw purse that looked as if it belonged on St. Pete Beach. She pulled out another sheaf of official-looking documents and handed them rather imperiously to Peter. One by one he flipped the pages. When he had worked his way through half the stack, he looked up.

"Where did you get these applications?"

"I know I look young, but for the past three years I've been an assistant to the Florida Commissioner of Education. As soon as Liz and Barrett filled me in, I borrowed the state computer in Tallahassee and ran off copies of applications similar to your Pilot Scholarship Plan."

"My God, with these applications we might still have a chance."

"I've got the black caucus committee report that set up the first voucher program in Milwaukee. You'll also find successful applications for child-placing agencies, day care centers, and the latest public school budgets for Interbay and McDill counties. I've even got the teacher's union strategy plan that helped defeat the voucher amendment in California. It's still a long shot, but point me to the word processor, sir, and stay out of my way. I don't need typists or anyone else. Just give me room."

Peter folded his arms. "I'll stick around, though, and answer questions."

"No, that will come tomorrow. Let me get all of this in shape tonight. Tell you what, get me a sixpack of Heineken and some Hershey bars. I'm really gonna burn some energy here. Then you can go about your business. And tonight you can go home to the wife and kiddies."

She gave him a mocking smile and snap of her head. He wondered how much Liz had told Bonnie about his family. Maybe that was Liz's way of protecting him from this centerfold with brains.

"If you want to come back tonight around eight, I'm going to need a break, especially if I pull an all-nighter. Hey, this is Saturday, I'll definitely need a break."

"Are you going to work uh, uh, like that?"

"You mean in this?" She gave her hips a suggestive move. "No, I've got these." She slipped a pair of apple red satin shorts from the colorful straw bag and held them high in the air.

Bang, Bang! Linda hammered on the door. It always sounded like she was trying to break it down. She cracked the door and peeked in. Raising her eyebrows, she peered at the red shorts, then at Peter. "I can show her the computer room, Dr. S., and they just dropped off more statistical data from USF." Peter nodded. He had finally found a research design that could prove the validity of vouchers. Bonnie followed Linda out, and he closed the door.

Now what? He didn't usually work on Saturday afternoons. Marie had a Brownie outing, and Mark was supposed to attend St. Paul's annual fair. Mark probably wouldn't go, anyway. Poor kid. No, he had to stick it out here and work on the grant. And tonight, and tomorrow, and tomorrow night, if necessary.

As the afternoon progressed, he found it difficult to concentrate. All of his golden eggs were in one pretty basket. Could he rely on a complete stranger to pull the project through? What choice did he have? The other volunteers meant well, but...

~

Purple shadows fell across the stained-glass window. Peter checked his watch. Seven o'clock. Hard to believe. Linda buzzed. "Maybe I'd better stay, Dr. S., just in case, ah, Bonnie needs some help."

"No, that's okay." He didn't need a chaperone... or did he? He glanced up at the book. Peter hung up, stepped over to the bookcase, and eased the thin little book from its unmolested spot on the top shelf. He pulled the book to his face, still hoping to pick up that enchanting scent. Doris—Doree. So beautiful. Wolf, that bastard. No, it had been his own fault. He sighed. Well, no sense reliving the past. Looking at it objectively, he knew Kathleen was the right partner. It had worked out for the best.

He stretched, pushed himself up, and walked to the side door. He opened it and peered along the dimly lit hallway. Had Bonnie left? Then he saw a sliver of light glowing softly under the back office door. Peter switched on the hall light and stepped down the corridor. He turned the knob and cracked the door.

He started to go in, but hesitated, his hand still squeezing the turned knob. A thick lump filled his chest and throat. Seated on a quilted pink pillow, head and back positioned squarely over the keyboard, the striking redhead's long, porcelain fingernails skimmed the keyboard at a blurring and impossible speed. In red satin shorts and a wet, clinging T-shirt, the siren moved trancelike, in rhythm with the machine. Massaging, playing... assaulting.

He shook his head. Why did he feel so anxious? His body shouted. "Run!" He recalled the James-Lange theory. Does the body respond to feelings of fear before the mind even registers them? Crazy. Just an attractive female. A glorified secretary he was paying to work on a project. Then it dawned on him that she hadn't mentioned a fee. Barrett Spangler had probably covered it. Good old Liz. She had a good heart, despite herself.

Linda must have gone out for refreshments because three empty cans of Heineken beer sat on the metal side table. The typing stopped, and Bonnie inched her body toward him. Framed by deep red circles, her sunken eyes stared straight through him. Hypnotically, she continued to turn toward him, her wet, pink tongue licking melted chocolate from her wine red lips. Then, a mask-like smile.

"I'll be out here," he said. Peter took slow steps down the hall and into his office. He collapsed onto the soft leather chair in front of his desk. This was totally unnerving. And so unexpected. The lady was just in there typing, that's all. He took a deep breath.

It seemed as though an hour had passed when he heard a knock on his door. He checked his watch. Only ten minutes. The door opened and Bonnie sauntered in, burnished orange hair framing her vibrant, cheerful face. Her whole demeanor had changed from the woman at the computer. It was more than the fresh makeup and the unwrinkled alabaster suit. It was like another person. Multiple personalities?

"Happy hour, happy hour," she chanted like a college sophomore at spring break on Clearwater Beach. " And meat. I want some meat." Her eyes twinkled. Peter let the comment pass. At least he was starting to relax.

"First, let's see what you've accomplished."

Bonnie pulled back her shoulders and gave Peter a mock salute. "As soon as we get back, I'll show you, sir. Can't go in there now. When I don the red shorts, I'm superwoman. But now I'm just a soft little pussy cat."

He shook his head and held the door open.

⁓

A St. Petersburg landmark, Ted Peter's Restaurant specialized in hamburgers and smoked fish. Undiscovered by tourists, it remained a secret hideaway for locals. By eight-thirty the families had gone, and the restaurant became a haunt for fishermen, truck drivers, and college students.

Over the bar a life-size bronze pelican hung from the ceiling, suspended by black fishing line. A dozen brown lacquered tables faced the bar, and another row of tables ran perpendicularly toward the smokehouse. Sixteen heavy-duty ceiling fans hummed in unison, stirring humid beach air. Signs behind the bar gave visitors much-needed information: "Draft Beer, 13 Ounces. Mug $1.25. Please Do Not Feed the Birds."

An assortment of males jammed the forty-foot-long bar. They watched the NCAA basketball semifinals on a fifty-inch TV and wolfed down hamburgers and smoked fish. With her shoulders back and her head up, Bonnie eased into a slow strut. Peter smiled. Each head, ostensibly glued to the TV, turned eyes right with the precision of a military drill team. The turning stools squeaked a blue-collar tribute as the hip swinging queen reviewed her troops.

One acne-faced young man wearing a "Divers Do It Deeper" T-shirt slipped off his stool and had to be rescued by his leering companion who was dressed in iridescent pink shorts with footprints on the buttocks. "I done died and gone to Nashville," his bearded buddy muttered.

Bonnie led Peter to a table at the far end of the bar. She sat and pulled her chair sideways, exposing her crossed legs to the thigh. Even the teenaged waitress treated her like a celebrity. When the food arrived, Bonnie attacked the meal with the same intensity she had showed with the typing. Peter watched her polish off a smoked mullet, three scoops of German potato salad, a dozen sweet onions, and a jumbo hamburger. She washed them down with three Molson beers.

Bonnie begged him to have at least one beer, and he finally agreed to a Miller Lite. The slow table service gave the young exhibitionist an excuse to wiggle her way to the bar for iced mugs and refills. When Bonnie admitted she could eat no more, she retreated to the ladies' room while he paid the bill and faced the envious stares of twenty men.

Back safely in the Volvo, he could again smell the fresh scented perfume. Bonnie sat closer than necessary and let her dress coat creep above her knees.

"Are we near the beaches?" A little girl's voice.

"Just over the Pasadena Bridge. About a mile I'd say."

"Believe it or not, I've never seen the beaches down here. And you're going to take me out there—right now. No beaches, no speeches, written or otherwise."

Looking sideways at the alluring nymph, he shook his head. He started the engine and headed south down Pasadena Avenue. They crossed the South Pasadena Bridge and drove west to Gulf Boulevard. Peter saw a vacant strip near the old Hilton and maneuvered across a sand-covered road to the beach.

"Oh, the moonlight on the sand," Bonnie said. "It's like snow. Look at the glow on the water. I'm going to walk right on top of that glow, all the way to the moon." She peered into his eyes. "I know. Let's go for a run on the beach. Maybe we could even go for a swim."

"What?"

"Well, maybe not a real swim. You could roll your pants up and I could just tie this skirt back a little. No problem at all."

"Uh, I think we'd better stay in the car, Bonnie. I need to get back pretty soon."

"You know, I'd like to live in this part of the state. I haven't had a very easy life, living in foster homes and all."

"Ah, I didn't—"

She turned her head and stared into his eyes, her mouth only inches from his face. "I've never had anyone who really understood what it was like to move from place to place and never have a real home. I just want someone to be nice...."

He knew where the conversation was headed. The aroma of flowery body powder sweetened the salt air. "That must have really been tough." He retreated behind the protective shell of therapeutic words, but she edged even closer.

Absolute silence. He stared straight ahead at the moonlit gulf. Shallow waves lapped against the shore. The soft sound of a siren's call.

Then he felt it. The incredibly light touch of long, lacquered fingernails resting on his thigh. Bonnie inched closer, the sweet scent of geraniums heavy in the air. Cool fingers on the back of his neck pulled him down to her lips.

"Ow! What in hell?" Bonnie threw her head back and twisted her body sideways. "What in hell is down here?"

She reached under her thigh and then raised her hand. The old black rosary, silver cross reflecting the bright moonlight, swayed beneath her outstretched hand. Bonnie yanked her arm back and hurled the beads at the windshield. They smashed against the glass, clattered to the dashboard, and slipped to the floor. She peered down at her left thigh.

"Dammit, I'm bleeding! That thing cut me. "What are you doing with a goddamned rosary?" Droplets of blood dotted her torn, wrinkled dress.

She pulled up the hem to reveal a crosshatched scratch on her upper left thigh. Just below the cut, thin brown streaks extended down her leg, the crumbling martyr's soil contrasting with her milky-white skin.

"It's mine." He reached down and picked up the rosary.

"Put it away." Bonnie bent and pulled off her left shoe. "Broke my heel, too. Dammit, these are brand new." Tears streaked her mascara. He picked up the dark blue shoe and set it on the dash.

There was no conversation during the twenty-minute ride back to Peter's office. WUSF played Monteverdi's Vespers by the Canadian Brass. Only an occasional sob interrupted the sweet instrumental and the quiet hum of the engine.

When he pulled up to the office, he saw Kathleen's old Chevy wagon near the back door. Peter and Bonnie entered through the front door. They found Kathleen and Liz in the typing room examining a dozen reports all neatly bound in legal folders. Liz continued to look down at the reports, but Kathleen stared at Bonnie, her eyes wide.

"Jesus, Mary and Joseph." Liz made an exaggerated sign of the cross. "How in hell did you do it?"

Kathleen just kept staring at Bonnie.

"And the bibliography," Liz said. Where did you get all this information?"

Peter turned to Bonnie. "We have a chance, don't we?"

She laughed. "Remember this, Dr. Peter Sheppard. With me nothing is ever as it seems. If I go all night and most of the day tomorrow, we can have it in before midnight. I know I can do it."

"This is truly incredible," Peter said. "Unbelievable." Kathleen finally shifted her gaze from Bonnie and gave him a bewildered smile.

"I knew Barrett had connections, but this is—this is awesome," Liz said. "We've got ourselves an angel here." Liz bent over the computer, but Bonnie arched her eyebrows and pointed a long, straight finger toward the door.

"Everybody out. Time for Wonder Woman to pull on her satin shorts and get back into the meat grinder."

Her eyes pointed and intense, Kathleen again peered at Bonnie. Peter smiled at Kathleen and gave Bonnie a crisp salute. Finally, a good night's sleep, he thought.

Chapter 23

Peter turned and buried his head in the pillow, but the piercing sound was relentless. "Hello? Hello?" Kathleen nudged Peter with her elbow and handed him the phone. "It's Sterk Trump, and he sounds worried."

Peter rolled over and looked at the alarm clock. Only five-thirty. It had to be Sunday. What—

"Hi, Peter. At your office. Better get down here pronto. A break-in. I got a call from Sheriff Harris's office 'cause he knows we're—"

"A break-in?" He shook his head and peered at Kathleen. "Is the girl there? Uh—Bonnie?"

"Nope. Nobody here, and this place is a damn mess."

Peter stumbled out of bed. "There's been a break-in at the office." He knew that Kathleen saw the pain in his eyes. He loved her for saying nothing.

When Peter arrived at the office, rotating police lights illuminated the faces of a dozen retirees from the Lutheran Towers Center just across Fifth Avenue. Mesmerized by the oscillating red- and-green lights, the old folks stood along the sidewalk in their pajamas and nightgowns like travelers waiting for an AARP spaceship to carry them to the promised land.

An officer dusted for prints on the back door. Inside, chairs were overturned, and pieces of the computer monitor littered the floor close to the east wall. Down on one knee, Sterk sifted through a stack of shredded papers.

"Any sign of the young woman?" Peter asked.

"No, but it looks like someone was dragged out this door," a slightly built officer said. He looked young enough to be in middle school. "Found the heel from a woman's shoe in the alley."

Peter sat on the cracked typing chair and buried his head in his hands. "I didn't think they'd go this far."

"Huh?" Sterk's shoulders shifted slightly.

"The Good Soil wanted to stop us. Looks like they finally did. But to kidnap Bonnie? That's just—It's just going too far."

"That's the problem, Peter." Sterk exchanged glances with the policemen. "They think this damn thing is an inside—"

"Nobody broke in here," the little-boy policeman said. "It's hard to believe she'd leave the back door open, and all the windows are locked. It was someone she knew, that's for sure."

"Wait a minute. Surely you don't suspect the young woman—or, uh, me?" Peter looked at Sterk.

"We found this blue high-heeled shoe in your office closet, Doctor," an overweight sergeant said. "Take a look. The heel is broken off. And the heel we found outside matches perfectly. Look familiar?"

"Well, yes, I, uh—"

Sterk eyed the policemen. "Close it up, Peter, wait 'til you talk to Rothman. That's what we pay lawyers for."

"We don't even know a crime's been committed, Doctor. But you need to come down to the station in a couple of hours and answer some questions."

"But I haven't done anything. Sure, I met with—"

Sterk stepped between Peter and the two officers. He pointed his index finger in Peter's face and stared at him through squinted eyes. Peter shrugged and looked down.

~

After the police cars left, Sterk turned to Peter. "If you're in some kinda trouble, please tell me. Now. I don't give a hill of beans what you—what happened. I'm your bud, you know that."

Peter covered his eyes with his hand. He could feel the wetness. Tears of fear? Tears of fatigue? Tears of self-pity? "Dammit!" He bolted from the stool. "You've got me now, totally confused, totally—"

"Take it easy, guy. Take it easy." Sterk threw his arm around Peter's shoulders.

Peter swallowed hard. "Sorry, Sterk, just not up to it. They come into my office and think I'd hurt that girl, hurt anyone. It's just not my—"

"I know, Peter. I know."

"And the project's sunk." Peter laughed. "What a joke. I hate to think of breaking it to Kathleen. Poor Kathleen."

Sterk walked him to his car. He got in and pulled onto Fifth Avenue North. Heading for I-275, he drove slowly down the deserted causeway. Breaking it to Kathleen? How about breaking it to himself? How about breaking it to Mark and Marie, and his banker, and the board or directors? Peter pumped the brakes and pulled the Volvo onto a narrow service road. He turned off the engine and leaned back against the headrest.

Real trouble. Peter repeated the words over and over. He had never really been in trouble. He had always played it by the book. So mature and understanding. Yep, he was the great man, all right. The original goody two-shoes. Valedictorian of his high school class, Keynes scholar, and second string All-American football player. Jet pilot and squadron commander. It had all come so easily. He had only wanted to give something back to the community. But it wasn't that simple.

And Kathleen was perfect, too. Attractive, well educated, supermother, supervolunteer, super, super, super. They were a pair, all right. Like Ken and Barbie dolls, they starred in a fantasy world. A plastic world. Every community had them—the just-right people.

His cell phone buzzed.

"Peter, that you?" It was Sterk. "We're in deep do-do. They found Bonnie."

"Great, now we can—"

"No, it ain't great. She's at the friggin' morgue, and she's wearing a shoe that matches the one at your office."

"No. Are you sure?" Peter peered down at the door handle and the rosary's silver crucifix. "That poor, pathetic little gal. No self-esteem, just no self-esteem—"

"No time to worry about stuff like that. It's your ass what's on the line now. This could be murder one. You hear?"

"The police station's only five minutes from here. I'll head straight over and get this thing ironed out. I can't afford to be out of commission now. Not with the grant—"

"Listen up, Peter! You got to forget the goddamned grant. And you're not going to the police. I talked to Joe Carlson over at the FDLE, and I'm still gettin' bad vibes. Real bad vibes. Did you know Jenny Grant's dad had gone undercover with the FDLE? And he's still missing. This whole thing is startin' to stink like my pet pig, and you're sure as hell in more danger inside the jailhouse than on the street. Your home may not even be safe. I'm gonna have to move in with Kathleen and the kids."

"Come on, Sterk, don't you think you're over doing this whole—"

"Hey. You're still not listening. You heard of the Bumper girl? I know damn well you ain't. Two of Sheriff Harris's plainclothes guys came on a van that got itself stuck trying to cross an I-275 median. The two bozos in the front were smashed out of their friggin' minds but the big thing was what Harris' boys found in the back... a teenage girl all wrapped up in adhesive like one of them friggin' mummies. She'd been dead for a while, and they said she was disfigured real bad."

Peter swallowed and stared into the phone. "What—"

"I dunno. Scotty, my bud, wouldn't talk about it. Said it made him sick. He said she was from some place in South America, but she had one of those jackets from Bumpers Restaurant covering her."

"Bumpers?"

"Christ, what world you livin' in, Peter? It's one of them soft porn family restaurants. Friggin' families used to pray together, now they ogle white girls in short-shorts with big boobs."

Peter shook his head. Sterk could be crude and outspoken ,but he was the world's biggest prude. Freud used to leave the room when a dirty joke was told. Maybe Sterk and Sigmund would have hit it off.

"But what does that have to do—"

"That was two months ago, and nobody, I mean nobody, knows about it. Not the D.A., not the Saint Pete Police, and not the Saint Pete *Times*. An' that's cause the damned Attorney General stepped in and put a gag order on Sheriff Harris. We're talking State of Florida here. Harris is real pissed. Figures the FDLE is behind it. Had to put Scotty and his bud on administrative leave. Now here's the friggin' punch line. Get this. It was a Good Soil laundry van."

"That's hard to believe, Sterk."

"Ain't it, though. You know if it had been the Scientologists, the *Times* would've been up their ass with a roto-rooter word processor. So here's what I think. I think your life's on the cuttin' block. Your life, Kathleen's life, even the kids'."

Peter sat up and checked the rearview mirror. Wedged into the front seat of a blue Ford Bronco, two heavyset men stared at the Volvo. Were they already parked there when he pulled in? "Okay, Sterk, I hear you. What do you want me to do?"

"I think the bastards are on my tail right now, so don't say nothin'. Just meet me where we went to lunch that one time when the waitress spilled the cucumber salad on your shoes. Remember?"

"Yes, I—"

"See you pronto. Get a move on."

Peter headed east on Second Avenue and turned right onto Bayshore. He scanned the rearview mirror but didn't see the Ford Bronco. Apropos Restaurant anchored the entrance to the St. Pete Municipal Pier. When he pulled up he saw Sterk standing next to a shiny VW Beetle parked in front of the closed restaurant. He had probably called from there.

Sterk walked over. He looked both ways, then opened the passenger-side door and eased in next to Peter. "You're gonna stay in my Aunt Trudy's trailer. It's a double-wide, and she's up in Mobile at a family wedding. You got it for a week."

"I can't be tied up for—"

"Hells bells, Peter, I'm goin' straight to Attorney Rothman. This could take hours, or it could take days. The longer it takes, the more we'll know I'm right. We got to get Sheriff Harris involved. He's a real pro. Grew up in Plant City and played ball at Bethune Cookman. An he's sure as hell no fan of the FDLE. Need the St. Pete PD, too."

Sterk handed Peter a letter-sized envelope. "Trailer park is off Ninth Street South, across from Lake Maggorie. Nobody's gonna look for you down there. Clean your car out and leave it here. You can use Trudy's bug. Damn thing's forty years old, but she washes it two or three times a week. Runs like hell. If anyone comes around, you're Trudy's nephew, Larry, from Little Rock. I got the whole thing set up. Damn fast work if I do say so myself."

"Okay, Sterk, thanks. But hurry this thing up. Our only chance is to prove the Good Soil cheated on the grant and terrorized some innocent kids. And now, from what you said, it could be worse. A lot worse."

"Oh, I almost forgot." Sterk handed him a crumpled brown bag. A thin line of grease ran along the top and down one side. Peter fingered the soft, smooth surface and felt the outline of a gun barrel.

Chapter 24

Liz held Barrett Spangler's hand and peered at Vinoy Presbyterians' barrel-vaulted ceiling. It was Barrett's idea. Kind of a compromise between Lutheran and Catholic. The tower bells chimed. Sunday, eleven o'clock.

Liz blinked, then sat up straight. Only four pews ahead, the hulking figure of Benjamin Wolf dwarfed Doris Dantakovic. That son of a bitch. No, that's not nice, Liz, not in church. But if that son-of-a-bitch was a member of this church, she'd have to find some other church for a middle ground. Liz looked at Barrett. Somewhere between Holy Roller and Buddhist?.

Liz had several friends in high school whose families had attended Vinoy Presbyterian. She recalled the big ruckus about Benjamin Wolf's mother. For some reason the church had refused to bury her in the Selby Isle Cemetery. Why would Wolf come back here? It didn't figure. Maybe it was to make a statement about his mother. More likely it was just to make connections. That bastard. He had really screwed Peter over. And tonight was the deadline. Maybe with Bonnie Freeman's expertise they still had a chance.

"Oh, God." Liz covered her mouth. Barrett peered at her over tinted, wire-rimmed glasses. There, right in front of Wolf, sat the one and only Babsie Courtney-Brown. Kat had always laughed when Babsie's name came up. "Mrs. Snooty," she would say. "With a capital S." And those poor kids. Kat had just talked about them. Muffin? No, Muffet, little Muffet. That was it. And her little brother had a real dorky name, too. Lindell or something. Babsies' husband, Judson Courtney-Brown, was a good old boy and unofficial mayor of Selby Isle. It was rumored that his prosperous real estate firm steered minorities and other undesirables to the south side of town.

Liz smiled. They were oh, so properly attired in frilly Laura Ashley gowns. Intergenerational twins, a mother and daughter surface bonding. But little Miss Muffet looked more brat than yuppie. She took special delight in pulling her baby brother's hair when her mother knelt forward, leaving the two children out of her line of sight.

Wolf looked down at Muffet, who continued to pull her little brother's hair. Finally, the sobbing boy knelt in imitation of his mother. Muffet stared into Wolf's eyes, eyebrows raised, a slight smile playing across her lips.

Later, when Muffet announced in a loud voice that she had to use the bathroom and skipped down the aisle with her mother's indulgent approval, Liz noted that Wolf excused himself and hurried down the aisle after her. Coincidence? What was that egotistical bastard up to?

Ten minutes later, Wolf eased back into his seat next to Dantakovic. He crossed his arms and smiled. Little Muffet still hadn't returned. Mother Babsie edged left and right. Liz shook her head. Babsie was worried about her yuppie puppy, but didn't want anyone to know. Finally, Muffet minced her way back up the aisle.

She looked different now. Glassy-eyed, her expression was flat, but her face was radiant. Almost angelic. She held her hands together in a prayerful gesture, but with each step she jerked her elbows up and down a few inches like the wings of a grounded bird. Nervous tic? Strange. So very strange. When Muffet stepped into the pew she even smiled at her brother. Had Wolf followed her out to give her a lecture? Or turned her over his knee? He wouldn't dare, not even that pig.

"I'm sorry I took so long, Mother dear."

It was time for the communion service. Row after row, parishioners proceeded up the middle aisle to receive the unleavened bread. Babsie leaned back and turned her face as a prominent black physician and his family crossed in front of her.

Finally the grand moment had arrived. Most of the parishioners had received communion and were returning to their pews when Babsie and Muffet, side by side, floated to the altar. Muffet's arms still flinched involuntarily with each step she took. They received the wine and wafer, while celebrating their preeminence with grace and humility. Then they turned in unison to face the congregation and piously retraced their footsteps with a practiced cadence, noble heads held high.

"Quack, oink, ah, do, do, do!" Muffet let out a screech and cackled like a crazed chicken. Actually, it was a mixture of barnyard sounds with quacks, cock-a-doodle-dos, and indistinguishable grunts. Babsie froze. Eyes glazed, she stretched her hands to her daughter. Muffet spun out of her grasp and charged onto the altar.

"Cock-a-doodle-do, ado-ado, ado-ado," she gurgled as she hopped off the altar and did somersaults and side flips up the east aisle toward the back of the church. Babsie Courtney-Brown maintained her composure for a full five seconds before turning bluish gray and passing out cold at the foot of the altar. She landed on her back and bounced twice on the thick carpeted floor.

This was most fortunate because she missed the climax of Muffet's performance. The rudely smiling girl danced to the top step of the altar, pulled down her frilly Victorian panties, and happily mooned the astonished parishioners.

Doris shook her head and whispered something to Wolf. The big man looked down at her and smiled.

~

Jenny and Starlyn crouched in the darkness of the dining hall alcove, the smell of starch and sweet milk heavy in the air. Jenny didn't like it. Starlyn was too calm, too composed. A trap? Did Starlyn know what she was doing? Maybe the Hammer had taken her back?

"Star. You sure this is right? Last time the cemetery was down some stairs, way down below." Starlyn didn't answer. She floated ahead, zombielike, through the dining hall, across the kitchen, and into an unlighted pantry. Jenny followed her billowing white robes through the darkened room.

A bloated, gray rat lumbered across loaves of bread and boxes of breakfast cereal that stood ten deep, floor to ceiling, along the walls. On the far side, a crack of vertical light divided hinged swinging doors. Starlyn walked to the doors, her body erasing the center strip of light.

"Good, it's Larry Lander. Nice kid, at least he used to be. Did pot on weekends but never hurt a flea. The Hammer puts him down all the time 'cause of his big ears. I even tried to line him up with Astrid, but he had a crush on me. Still does. He'll do anything as long as he, uh... you stay here, Jenny."

Starlyn squeezed Jenny's hand and pushed through the padded doors. Jenny stepped up and put her eye to the crack. It was one of the main hallways that formed a rectangle around the third floor. Lander stood in front of a huge painting of an Italian villa surrounded by orange groves. A large bronze plaque under the painting spelled out: "Pablo and Ruth Gomez. Gracious, Gracious, Gracious."

Hands on her hips, Starlyn glided across the carpet and into Lander's arms. Starlyn stood on her tiptoes and whispered in his ear. Blushing, he gave her a half-grin and reached for the hem of her robe, but she pushed his hand down. They laughed together like old friends. The willowy nymph scribbled something on a small card and tucked it under the polished belts that crisscrossed his chest. Red-faced, Lander smiled and stepped out of Jenny's line of vision.

Starlyn fingered the bottom of the frame, and the painting moved. Split vertically down the middle, it slowly parted to reveal a hidden panel. She pushed four buttons on the panel, and the door opened. Then she looked both ways and backed in.

Jenny pushed through the swinging doors and sprinted to the elevator. Starlyn pulled her in, and the door closed. Unlighted except for blinking green floor lights, the elevator moved down. They held hands. Two... one... bunker... terminus.

"You don't have to, Star." Jenny tightened her hands around Starlyn's shaking fingers.

"Yes, I do. I never told you the worst part, Jen." She bent and put her hands over her face. "Sometimes.... Sometimes I like it. It's exciting. I can't say how, but if we don't get out soon, I won't make it. It doesn't matter what the Hammer does. And another thing. They're after Astrid."

"Your—"

"My kid sister's in the newcomer's program. She starts tonight. It'll kill my poor dad."

The elevator eased to a soft landing and stopped. The door slid open. Jenny bent forward and stuck her face into the salty, humid air. Bats' wings fluttered across the ancient graveyard, and she recalled the pitiful yelping sounds. Please, Lord, not again. Not ever again.

Shapes gradually emerged from the silky darkness. She could make out shadowy tombstones about a hundred feet to the left, at the end of an open hallway. Three large double doors stood directly across from the elevator. Doors. That's what the Hammer had asked her—

"It's the one on the right," Starlyn said. "The terminal station. The

Hammer said they send Soilers from there to places all over the country, to different hospitals. He didn't say what they did, but they make lots of money. It's the only place he wouldn't let me go. Got real nasty."

Please be open, please be open. Jenny turned the knob. The thick metal door swung smoothly outward. "Leave it open, Star. We we may need to come back this way."

Starlyn stepped in front of her. "I've still got more pull with Mitchum, or at least they think—"

"No way. I—"

Starlyn disappeared into the dank, gloomy crypt, the soft swishing of her robes barely audible. Jenny looked to the left toward the shrouded tombstones. Nothing stirred. How could they keep kids down here with no guards? Yes, of course. There was no place to go except into the cemetery. The whole horrible place was one big tomb. No air, no escape, no—

What was that? Something there? Hissing. So low... so soft. A tea kettle's warning, but so soft. Yes, there under the bats' wings. Or was it... crying? Then those soft little yelps. Not that again. Please. Sobs... louder now... dear God. No!

Where's Star? She realized she was holding her breath. Too dry to swallow. Slowly, very slowly, she turned her head toward the cemetery. Groaning yelps and heavy sobs swept through dark, shadowed valleys.

Won't look. Don't want to see? But her head seemed to move without her, forcing her face into the salty blackness. Something there? Something wrong? The smell. Horrible. She wrinkled her nose. It had been there all the time. Underneath it all. Like the dead rat at home, above her bedroom, in the attic. The smell of rotting flesh had been there for days.

Jesus, please. Now what? Calm down, calm down. What would Dad do? Get Star and get out... now. The chorus of sorrowful yelps and smell of decaying flesh engulfed the corridor. Immoveable... unstoppable.

Run, Jenny. Run! She slid through the narrow opening and pulled the heavy door behind her. It snapped into place with a reassuring but ominous click.

"Starlyn. Star, where..." Sobbing. It was Star. The sobs came from deep inside the tomb. Jenny raced down the dark corridor, her fingers tracing cold marble walls.

Illuminated by a thin strip of light, Starlyn's face floated, ghost-like. Her soft, rhythmic sobs were not sane. She wasn't crying, she was dying. Hysterical. Jenny remembered her father's police academy lectures. "Got to get this girl moving."

She followed Starlyn's haunted eyes to the lighted open drawer... and the world titled on its side. Did the gagging fist of sour puke erupt in her throat before the ringing exploded in her ears?

It was a hand, all right. A dainty powdered hand... severed neatly at the wrist.

Jenny tried to look away. She didn't want to see the rounded pink nails, the delicate pearl ring on the chubby little finger. Vomit gushed from her mouth and spilled onto the rock pathway that fronted the chamber. She threw up over and over again until nothing was left, not even yellow bile.

Jenny wiped her mouth with the sleeve of her robe and took a deep breath. With huge tears obscuring her vision, she raised her leg and slammed the drawer shut with a powerful kick.

"Come on, Star. Out of here. Now!"

Chapter 25

Liz peered through the bronze-tinted windows of Barrett's limo. An endless line of cars crawled along the circular driveway in front of South Side Liberty High. When she was a kid her parents wouldn't let her go to the south side of St. Petersburg. They had said it wasn't because of the blacks, but she always wondered. Ricky, Barrett's daytime driver, had parked discreetly behind a towering banyan tree near the athletic field. Why did she feel so damn guilty? She was a taxpayer. Or at least Barrett was. This was everyone's school. Watching a class in action should be a citizen's right.

But this was a special school designed for kids who had fallen through the cracks. Kat had found it on the Good Soil grant application. A Good Soil drug unit had operated in the school for several months, and someone at the *Times* told Kat the school was a mess. Kat tried to get in, but the school demanded a three week notice and a seal of approval from the superintendent's review board. So much for the public in public schools, Liz thought. She looked down at the special permit signed by the superintendent of schools. Good old Barrett. Hard to imagine not having his clout to ride on.

She knew she wasn't welcome. At least not while the grant was still up in the air. Afraid of true reform, the school administration sided with the Good Soil and the teachers' unions. Hell, she could understand that. Maybe that's why she had left the Sisters of the Incarnation. The Second Vatican Council had opened the windows to church reform. They said it was to let some fresh air in, but they had let out a ton of holy air in the process.

Liz lifted the sixteen-ounce can of Guinness Draught and took another sip. She had to control her drinking. Peter and Kat were on to her. She'd deal with that later, but for now only one thing mattered, and that was to get something good, something dramatic to help Peter. Especially now that Bonnie was dead and Peter was hiding from the FDLE and the Good Soil. What had happened to poor Jenny's dad?

She really loved Peter. He was quite a guy, and Kat was luckier than she knew. How did her big sister always manage to hit the jackpot? Liz put down the can of beer, opened the door, and climbed out. Cars edged in, bumper to bumper, in front of the school and crowded into the driveway leading to the front door. Faculty transportation was a mixture of junkers and economy, except for a couple of Harleys. Parents' cars were mostly clean and practical, four-door sedans and a few vans. Bumper stickers proclaimed student achievements: "Citizen of the Month: South Side Liberty School." "Principle's Honor Roll," "Go Blue Devils,"

But the student fleet was something else. Powerful, throbbing libidos danced and skidded into the school parking lot. Expensive machines that tooted and winked at the school's claim to authority.

To Liz's right, five girls recited the pledge of allegiance while an ancient black man hoisted the Stars and Stripes up a swaying silver flagpole. The girls wore identical blue sweatshirts with orange letters that spelled "Students Against Drunk Driving," front and back, in five-inch letters.

Squealing brakes shattered the girls' quiet ceremony. A shiny black Lexus LS 400 swerved onto the curb and bullied its way to the front of the group. On the windshield a sticker for Oakley sunglasses boasted "Thermonuclear Protection." The piercing vibration of one-thousand-watt speakers bombarded Liz's ears. Two Live Crew welcomed students, teachers, and parents alike:

"Me so horny,

"Me so horny,

"Me love you long time."

Liz crammed two sticks of spearmint gum into her mouth and walked through the open front door. She set her purse on the conveyer belt and stepped through the arched metal detector. An armed policeman snapped open her bag and looked inside. He kept his head down and made no eye contact when he handed it back. She hesitated, then moved to the reception counter. An attractive but unsmiling young woman peered at her through broad-rimmed designer glasses.

"I'm Liz Blair. I'm here to take a look around." Liz pulled a letter from her purse and laid it on the counter. The woman looked down at the letter, but did not pick it up. She wrinkled her nose as if she had smelled something offensive.

"Do you have identification?"

Liz dug into her purse and handed over her driver's license.

The woman studied it, then looked back at the letter. "What do you want?"

"I just want to visit some of the classrooms."

The woman adjusted her glasses and looked at the letter again. "Are you with the press?"

"No."

"I don't know." She looked toward the policeman. "Gus—you seen one of these before?"

The gray-haired policeman ambled over. He didn't seem to be in a hurry. He took the letter and stared at it for a while. Then he wet his finger and ran it over the signature. He shook his head.

"I think you have to give us some lead time, ma'am."

Liz sighed and crossed her arms. "Shall we call the school board? Now?"

Gus looked at the woman. She raised her eyebrows. "Okay," he said. "But don't be too long."

Liz nodded and moved toward the hallway. According to Kat's map, Room 148 should be on the right. When she passed the girl's rest room, she hesitated, then stopped. Smoke? She knew what it was. Only too well. That was one thing she hadn't confessed to Peter.

Liz pushed open the door and found herself staring at two black students who stood over a wash basin, counting a stack of twenties. A pale, skinny face peeked from the last stall. Rusted hinges showed where the door had hung.

"Uh—shouldn't you gals be in class?"

They looked up and smiled, but didn't move. The skinny-faced white girl laughed. Liz ran her fingertips along her thumbs and felt the sweat on her fingers. "Are you sure this is what you want? What—what would your parent's say?"

"Oh, duh. They'd say shove it up your pretty little ass, Mom," the skinny-faced girl said. She wore tight jeans marked with the letters FTW and spoke in a perfect South St. Pete dialect. "We's got us some business to conduct, me good lady, so let's be on your way." She laughed again.

Liz knew what F.T.W. meant. F—the world. She turned and moved down the hall. She was in no position to cause a ruckus. Liz dug her fingers into her purse and traced the outline of the tiny camera. Try to stay on track for once, Liz. Get something Kat can write about. Something that exposes the Good Soil.

Rubber bands and paper clips littered the hallway in front of an open door. Room 148. Liz hesitated. Should she just barge in? She edged her way into the classroom, but no one acknowledged her entrance, not even the teachers.

Liz shuffled along the inside wall to the back row of the auditorium-sized room. Peter had told her about "open space" or "pod" schools. Huge rooms with no dividers. Peter said they didn't work, but the school board just kept building them. On her right, a boy wore a T-shirt that read "A Mind is a Wonderful Thing to Waste." A picture of the cortex showed where reading, math, and other functions were localized. Each skill was crossed out and replaced with the word Sex.

Forty kids roamed the classroom. They chatted in small groups, slept under desks, and ate french fries. One young man, dressed in a dark trench coat, puffed a suspicious-looking cigarette. A graffiti-covered sign hung above the front chalkboard: "Comp. English 101. No eating or drinking in class."

Down in the pod near the front blackboard, show-and-tell was under way. A girl held up a gold necklace. It formed the letter's Z-A-C-C, as in Zacc Zimmers, the heavy metal star.

"Didn't he break his guitars?" the teacher asked.

"He didn't break 'em, he goosed 'em," the girl replied. She plugged in a cassette and played a song by the Peter Beaters.

"Why are you listening to that stuff?" the teacher asked. The girl turned to her classmates and shrugged.

Three desks over, a pretty little gal with long, red hair wrote in her notebook. She couldn't have been more than twelve or thirteen. Despite the chaotic din and rocket-launched tacks and paperclips, the girl seemed determined to finish her work. If only this sweetheart's parents knew what was happening in here. She wouldn't learn a damn thing in this madhouse.

Another teacher waved. Liz picked her way along the back of the room to where the teacher sat with a dark-haired girl.

"Why do you want to hook up with the Bloods anyway? You know they're bad news."

"If you want to fly with the Bloods, you got to fu—"

"No! Uh—now there, you, uh, don't use the F word. I don't want to write you up, but that's just—you know... It's out."

The buzzer sounded, and the students pushed, shoved, and stampeded their way from the classroom to the crowded hallway.

"Wow," Liz said.

"I know. It's a shock," the teacher replied. "Are you with the Good Soil?"

"Ah, no. I'm just visiting. But I did want to see the Good Soil program in action."

"I'm afraid you won't see them down here. We were supposed to get tutoring and a drug program, but the Good Soil counselors spend all their time upstairs with the advanced kids. They've taken a bunch of those kids into their program, but this is where they could really help. Are you with the school board?"

"No, ah, I'm just part of a citizen's committee. So you haven't seen a single counselor from the Good Soil?"

"Well, there was a young counselor named Mitchum who came by one day when I was out. Maria, my aide, said he wouldn't tell her what he talked to the students about. He said it was confidential."

"That girl mentioned the Bloods. Do these gangs really exist?"

"Absolutely. David Mendola used to be down here. He's supposed to be one of the leaders, but he's locked up at the Good Soil now. Thank God the school board has places like that to help these kids. The Bloods have red bandanas and picadors. That's why we've got metal detectors."

"Picadors?"

"Mexican knives, really sharp."

Calores. The peasant boys. She would never forget that knife. Or the red bandanas. Of course. It's all connected. Just as she had thought. And all engineered from here. Liz sniffed the air. Marijuana and chalk—not good soul mates.

"That girl I was talking to—Lara. She's looking for a home," the teacher said. "Let's see, we've got Geeks, Iveys, Jocks, Stoners, Trench Coats, Pearl Jam, Metal Heads, Skateboard Cowboys, Nintendo Junkies, Gangbangers, and that's only a partial list. Lara's willing to do whatever."

"Gangbangers?"

"No, now it means drive-by shootings. Mostly empty houses. Sad little wannabe bangers."

"Jesus, she just needs some hugs. I know. I was in her shoes when I was..." Liz looked down. And still in those shoes?

"Know something? You're right. She needs hugs and discipline, but we're not allowed to touch the kids. It's school board policy. Can't hug 'em, can't spank 'em, can't pray with 'em."

The teacher looked toward the student parking lot as a mighty roar of exhaust pipes and stereos shook the room. A paper cup danced in tight circles on a student's barren desktop. "Well, another short day for some of our students," the teacher said. "Off to rehab or a work-study program. Hard to teach them when they're not even here." She peered into Liz's eyes. "You sure you're not with the school board?"

"Thanks a lot for your help." Liz shook the teacher's hand and turned toward the empty classroom. Where was that desk? The one where the little redhead had sat? That poor little gal was giving her all to achieve something worthwhile.

Liz stepped across the littered floor. Several wadded-up notes formed an uneven pile under the girl's seat. Liz laid the notes on top of the desk and smoothed out the wrinkles. Only one of the notes looked complete.

> Nance,
> What's up? Not too much HERE—I'm like bummed out. Sorry I haven't been writing, but life really sucks and I'm mad about school—AND my old lady took off with some jerk. You see Breaker Mitchum at the drug rally? Lupe—says he got it—YOU KNOW—got it pierced—Big blue ring—I can see him in the shower now. Wow! He's a god!!! I'll keep his baby—no way I won't—No DOCS this time—And DIG those choc chip cookies!! Breaker says if we join the Soilers he can get us all the STUFF we want. Uppers, downers, you name it—my SIS is out there right now and she LOVES it!!!!
> Can you help me PLEASE?!!!!
> Your true friend,
> Astrid Dalton

Oh, my God! Liz stared at the blurry pencil marks. Dalton? Didn't Peter say Starlyn had a younger sister? This could be the evidence they needed. Yes. Yes! It ties Good Soil counselors to drug use, and they're including this school in their grant application. But the Good Soil doesn't even help the kids who need it. It's like Kat said. They cream off the easy ones to look good and then pull the serious cases in to do—what? Work for them? It didn't add up.

But she knew one thing. She had to find Peter. Kat knew where he was hiding. She said she didn't, but this was too big to keep under wraps. Liz folded the note and pushed it deep into her purse. She teased out the camera and surveyed the room. Huddled together near the front blackboard, the teachers were deep in conversation. Liz took several quick, random shots.

She smiled. Maybe she had finally done something right. Maybe after all her screw-ups she could repay Peter. And her mom. And yes, even her sister.

Chapter 26

Peter stood in the kitchen of Aunt Trudy's double-wide trailer and stared at the phone. Sterk had told him not to answer it under any circumstances. But it had rung at least fifteen times. Finally it stopped. Then it started again. Was someone trying to reach him? Kathleen? Did something happen to one of the kids? He reached over and picked it up.

"Peter, it's me, Liz."

"What's wrong? Why are you—?"

"I had to call. I know I shouldn't. Kat wouldn't give me the number, but today is Wednesday, and time is running out. And maybe this can help you with your—"

"Make it quick, Liz. Someone may tap in—"

"Okay. I went to the Southside Liberty School. You know, the special school for dropouts. Starlyn's little sister goes there, and I've got a note she wrote to a Good Soil counselor named Mitchum. He's giving her drugs to recruit her for the Good Soil. Can you believe it? Kat thinks the *Times* would run the story, but she needs time to check the sources. I told her that we're out of time. You and Sterk need to see it. I know where you are and I'll drop it off. I'll just put it in your mail—"

"No! Wait, Liz—"

Click.

Peter shook his head and stared at the phone. It could be a helpful piece of evidence, but she shouldn't have called. On the other hand, he was totally fed up with the whole hiding scene. It had been three days. Something had to give. And soon.

Peter walked into the kitchen. Five forty-two. He opened the refrigerator and studied the mostly empty shelves. Three yogurts and a few stiff pieces of bread. How much more of this stuff could he eat? Mark needed to learn how to cook. Roasting marshmallows at Boy Scout jamborees wasn't the best preparation for a bachelor's life.

He sat at the small plastic table and dug into the yogurt. Tipping the plastic container, he used a soup spoon to scoop out the last icy pockets of raspberry flavoring. Finally, the six o'clock news started. Time dragged. My, how it dragged. And the evenings were the worst. Peter stared at the twelve-inch screen. Aunt Trudy needed a new TV.

Suddenly, he heard a scraping noise. So faint that at first it sounded like a car door closing. Then he heard it again, in the family room, near the sliding glass door. He took a deep breath and gently set the yogurt cup down. Bending low, he edged his way off the chair. With the dim light he should have the advantage.

Peter crept into the family room, then stopped. He pivoted and duck-walked back through the kitchen to the bedroom. He fumbled with the pillow, pulled out the .45 automatic, and released the safety. Crawling on his hands and knees, with the gun pointed straight ahead, he decided he wasn't cut out for this cloak-and-dagger stuff. What would he do, shoot a policeman? Or Liz? He felt the wetness under his arms.

When he got to the family room, the scraping noise grew louder, but it was still outside. He bent down, his nose almost on the carpet, and used the gun to pull the curtain aside. Nothing.

Then he saw the intruder. A fat brown squirrel sat on the metal mail box, stuffing its chubby cheeks. Peter took a deep breath. He flipped the safety lever on the trigger lock and set the gun on the metal TV table. He slid open the glass door, stuck his head into the warm, humid air and looked both ways. Nothing seemed amiss. The green and blue flag on the bright red mailbox was still down. Peter stepped to the mailbox, opened the mail slot, and peered inside. Nothing.

"Nice of your family to stay in touch, Dr. Sheppard," said a commanding voice behind him. "Sure makes our work a lot easier. Now keep your hands right there on the mailbox. In plain view. I'm Joe Penrod, Florida Department of Law Enforcement. I've got a gun pointed at your back, so I suggest you don't move. Not even a little bit."

Holding his fingers steady on top of the mailbox, Peter stared straight ahead.

"Now move it on inside. Slowly—slowly."

Peter turned and stepped to the glass door. He slid it open and stepped inside. He could hear Penrod close behind him.

"All right, now listen up. And let's make it real quick like. Pick up the gun by the barrel and bring it to me." Peter bent and reached for the gun. But then he stopped, his hand still in midair. Wasn't this an odd way to go about an arrest? And come to think of it, Penrod hadn't even arrested him. Or read him Miranda.

Peter's mouth went dry. A heavy throbbing sensation moved up his chest and into his throat. If he picked up the gun and turned, he could be shot for resisting a police officer. Jesus. Peter took a deep breath and straightened. Raising his arms over his head, he took a half step toward the kitchen.

"Stop or I'll shoot." I'm going to shoot you, Mister. Now!"

Peter stopped. He heard a click and braced himself.

Silence.

"Okay, hold it. You're under arrest." A young woman holding a black machine gun bolted through the guest room door. A tall, skinny man wearing a yellow raincoat with "FDLE" imprinted across the front darted into the room from the back door area. Peter took a deep breath and felt himself relax.

"As you know, Dr. Sheppard, we're dealing with a homicide," the tall agent said. "Please put your hands flat on the coffee table and spread your legs." Peter bent forward, and the policeman quickly ran his hands along Peter's legs and then fingered his shirt. The female officer cuffed his hands behind his back. Standing at the door with his arms crossed, a tall, red-haired man with bloodshot eyes pulled his mouth to one side and stared at Peter. So this was Joe Penrod. Sterk had talked about him many times.

When they got outside, Penrod pushed Peter up some metal steps into a white, unmarked van. The man's clothes reeked of tobacco. Penrod unlocked the cuffs and pulled Peter's hands around to the steel-mesh grate that separated the front seats from the back of the van. He attached the cuffs to the grate and snapped them shut.

The cold metal handcuffs assailed Peter with the reality of the situation. Could these things really happen to someone like him? They drove north and picked up I-275 near Mound Park Hospital. That ruled out the St. Pete Police Station. Perhaps they were headed for the Pinellas County sheriff's office in Largo. Penrod said nothing. Why wouldn't he at least question him? Were they playing it by the book and waiting for him to speak with his lawyer? But they still hadn't read him his rights.

When they took the Clearwater exit and turned north toward the St. Pete-Clearwater Airport, Peter began to feel uneasy. Sterk sure didn't trust these folks. Were they going to fly him to their state headquarters in Tallahassee?

"Oh, shit! Jamaar Harris."

Penrod had finally spoken. Peter smiled. There, next to the airport parking lot, flanked by a Pinellas County sheriffs' cruiser, sat Sterk Trump's psychedelic van.

"Pull up," Penrod said. The van stopped next to the cruiser, and Penrod opened the window. The cruiser door swung open, and a barrel-chested black man stepped out.

"Shit," Penrod said.

The black man stepped over to the window, followed by Sterk. A five-pointed badge glittered above the left shirt pocket of his khaki uniform, and a western-style straw hat sat low on his forehead. Two deputies got out of the cruiser and joined Sterk and the sheriff.

"You planning on going somewhere, Joe?" the black man asked.

Penrod looked up and shaded his face with his hand. "I'm sure Sterk Trump has filled you in, Jamaar. At least his version of things. It's simple enough. This man, Peter Sheppard, is wanted for murdering a state employee. So that puts him under our umbrella."

Harris leaned against the bottom of the window, the brim of his hat only inches from Penrod's face. "That right? Or is your umbrella full of holes from little varmints eatin' at it? Last one of my prisoners I let you put on a plane had some kind of accident, and he don't remember a hell of a lot."

Harris looked past Penrod to Peter. "How's your memory, Doc?" Peter smiled.

"I'm warning you, Jamaar. You need to get your men out of here, or I'll have to take this to the office of criminal justice at the state level. I mean it, so just stand aside."

Sterk inched his shoulders up and down and spat a wad of tobacco juice toward the van's back tire. Harris turned and watched a seagull skim along car rooftops in the parking lot. "Those Tallahassee politicians the same fellas that gave you half our drug funding last year, Joe? Guess they figured us niggers don't know how to spend the taxpayers' money just right."

"You shouldn't be burning bridges like this, Harris. Some day it may come back to haunt you."

Harris smiled. Then he walked around the back of the van and opened the door next to Peter. He got in. Sterk opened the right front door and jerked his thumb toward the sheriff's cruiser. The female agent got out, and Sterk got in. He turned to the driver.

"St. Pete Police Department."

"Shit," Penrod said.

Chapter 27

On the ride to St. Petersburg, Peter could think of nothing but Kathleen and the kids. Jesus. What about Mark and his scheduled surgery? They swung into the St. Petersburg police station parking lot, and the sheriffs' cruiser pulled up behind them. Once inside, Peter was warned that questioning could take hours. He called Kathleen and asked her to stay at the house with Mark and Marie and to telephone attorney Bruce Rothman. He had just hung up when Sterk called from a downstairs phone.

"Listen to me Peter, you got to close it up. Remember what I said. Don't open your mouth to anyone. You haven't been yourself lately and you might say—"

"My God, Sterk. You think I have something to hide?"

"Course not, but you've been under a hell of a lot of pressure lately. Just don't say beans 'til Bruce gives the okay, that's all. I'm still workin' on this mess, and I think we're finally getting somewhere. But watch your backside for sure. Believe me, it's the only way."

Clyde Brandeon, the detective in charge, led Peter to a small room on the second floor. A younger officer sat next to Peter at a small wooden table that was barren except for a black Pioneer tape recorder. Brandeon had attended several of Peter's lectures at the police academy. One talk focused on how to interrogate suspects; nevertheless, Brandeon made no attempt to be cordial and maintained a strict professional demeanor.

The younger officer, a pudgy corporal with uncombed red hair and fresh coffee stains on his snug-fitting sport coat, went overboard to be friendly and supportive. The old good guy-bad guy routine. They should have known better. But as the interrogation continued, Peter found himself giving the corporal more eye contact.

The professional observer of people gave photographic recollections of detail and sequence. The two policemen traded glances, expressing their appreciation for the one-sided self-interrogation. Finally, Peter stopped. "Can we do anything to speed this along and clear my name? Naturally I'm worried sick, but I'm working against the clock on a project that means everything."

"Well... maybe we could run a quick lie detector," Brandeon said. "Don't know if Sayles is around, but I'll try and get him. That could get you out of here in no time."

He accepted the offer. His attorney, Bruce Rothman, wouldn't be pleased, but the galvanic skin response was not alien to Peter. He used biofeedback in his practice and had researched lie detectors while still in graduate school. Standard baseline questions could be disrupted to produce an invalid reading, but he hoped to use the instrument to prove his innocence. The best way to do that? Tell the truth.

He completed the polygraph a little before midnight. Brandeon took him to a third-floor holding cell, where Attorney Rothman waited. Rothman escorted him to a tiny visitors' room. The two men talked under the watchful eyes of a muscular female guard.

"I wish you hadn't taken the lie detector, Peter. These people are going full-out to prove your guilt." Rothman glanced at the big-breasted guard. "They've even brought in some private consultants and two school board attorneys. That's damned unusual."

"Come on, Bruce. What's going on?"

"Well, the FDLE came up with some of your letters."

"Letters?"

"You don't know?" Rothman's eyes narrowed. "A dozen or so love letters were mailed to the St. Pete *Times*."

"From Bonnie?"

"Afraid so, and they, uh... they're rather explicit. And they mention a rendezvous point near the beach. You ever take her to Ted Peter's Fish House?"

Peter took a deep breath and looked at the ceiling. "And on top of all that, I'm stuck in here. Trapped. Any chances for the grant are completely shot."

Rothman stood. "Where the heck are you coming from, Peter? You've got to get on board here. None of that's important now. It means nothing, absolutely nothing. Believe me, you've got to think of yourself. You've got much bigger problems right here."

The door swung open, and the big, black guard poked her head in. "A detective Trump wants to come—"

"Bring him on in," Rothman said.

Sterk barreled through the door, head down, and almost tackled Peter. He gave Peter a huge hug, then looked at Rothman. "How's our boy doing?"

"Not good," Rothman said. "These people are on a crusade." Rothman cocked his head toward Peter. "You had problems with these folks? You're not very popular, that's for—"

Sterk grunted and spat into a soggy paper cup he held in his left hand. "Shit list. He's on their friggin' shit list." Sterk turned and threw the cup against the wall. It smacked against a concrete slab and left a wet trail as it slid into a green metal wastebasket. Sterk wiped his hands on his flowered Bermudas. "A billion bucks and keeping control of the schools. It's that simple. It's that Goddamned simple." Sterk circled the table, then stopped and went the other way.

Rothman reached down and opened his briefcase. "I wasn't going to bring it up right now, but, ah, they've got something else." He peered at Sterk. "You want me to..."

"It's okay, let's hear it," Peter said. He sat back and folded his arms. Sterk leaned toward Rothman.

"It's a sex-abuse allegation. An adolescent named Jenny Grant. They claim you saw her in therapy, Peter, then tracked her through Internet contacts. They say you found her cruising the chat rooms and used e-mail to set up meetings. Even claim she came to your house."

Peter sighed and shook his head.

"And they've called in Pictrosante," Rothman said. "He's their big gun on capital cases. The guy's never lost. He's just chalking up victories so he can pull in megabucks doing criminal defense."

Sterk halted, then restarted his sojourn around the room. "They got no evidence on the sex charge. No friggin' evidence. It's just a goddamn frame."

"Good point," Rothman said. "Seems this Grant girl is unavailable for deposition. Suicidal, they claim. The Good Soil says she really trusted Peter because her father is missing, and she was searching for a father figure. Of course we wouldn't put up with these unsupported allegations in any other area of the law. Florida's child abuse regs are above the law, if you ask me. In the wild blue yonder, in fact."

"Perfect for a frame," Sterk said. "In fact, all they want with the sex thing is to give jurisdiction back over to the FDLE. But I'll tell you something, Rothman. Law or no law, Peter Sheppard's not leaving this building with those guys unless it's over my unholy little body." Sterk stopped and reversed course. "And this place is no three-star Hilton, neither. Maybe they don't figure Peter is gonna leave. Ever."

They stared at Sterk.

"Don't be so goddamned naive, folks. We've had lots of convenient accidents over at the Tampa County Jail. And a couple of questionable suicides, too. And you can damn well bet it didn't take a billion smackers to get that action rollin'. Not with Tampa's screwed up courts.

Sterk shot a stream of tobacco juice across the room into the green wastebasket. Then he pulled up his Bermuda shorts. "Better watch your backside, Peter. This is big time. And it's sure as hell for real."

Chapter 28

"Wake up, Dr. Sheppard. Y'all wake up now."

Comforting, that soft southern dialect. It was the big-boned guard who had remained ever vigilant during his conversation with Bruce Rothman five hours earlier. Fearful for his safety, Peter had followed Sterk's orders and fallen asleep sitting up on the small bed at the back of his cell. Like his wrinkled suit, he was a lifeless and disheveled mess.

"Time for breakfast," the guard sang. She hoisted the food tray like a waitress at a fancy resort. "And you've got an important visitor."

Squeaking shoes? Dr. Benjamin Wolf stared down between the shiny blue-green bars. A power-red necktie dangled in front of a blue denim dressshirt, and silver cuff links sparkled in the colorless gray light. Peter rubbed his eyes and shook his head.

"What in hell are you doing here?"

Wolf chuckled. "I sense you are angry and unhappy, feel like you have no freedom, no chance to be yourself."

"Okay, cut it, Wolf. You couldn't carry Roger Carlson's shoe laces, and you know it. And coming in here to gloat, after your pack of psychopaths murders a young woman, just to win a grant. Unbelievable gall. You're sick, you know that?"

"Hold it. Hold it, Peter. I actually came to help—"

"Help? You'll need all the help you can get when this—"

"Okay, okay, listen." Wolf eyed the guard and lowered his voice to a whisper. "Sometimes I think Doris is still soft on you. Anyway, we've come up with a compromise. I know you didn't kill that gal, but it's not going to look too cool on your grant application."

"A compromise?"

"Yeah. We'll cut you folks in. There's a hell of a lot of money to be had, and we can afford to spread it around."

"Cut us—"

"You got it, pal. We want you folks to run our school clinics and help with the sex-ed and drug prevention programs."

Peter pushed himself up and stood on wobbly legs. "You know we're totally opposed to those clinics. Weren't you at the administrative meeting? How can you come in here for God's sake and offer to buy me off? Which, I might add, is totally illegal. And on top of that ask me to go against my principles?"

"Easy. How does ten million bucks sound? That would pay a few bills down at your center. You could use it for more of those free services you like to dole out to the underprivileged. Doesn't your holier-than-thou clinic want to help the families and little kiddies?"

"I don't know. I—"

"And don't be surprised if your staff has thinned out some while you were jousting windmills. We just hired your chief social worker and Dr. James, your head shrink. Seems your loyal staff members are a little more practical than their boss. Guess they have to live in the real world like the rest of us."

Peter looked away, tears blurring his vision.

"And another thing. I know you hocked your home to keep your center going. How about considering your family for a change?"

Peter slumped back against the concrete wall and closed his eyes.

"Ain't no more time, Doc. Game's up, show's over. You're finished. Kaput, get it? Now, want to accept our compromise or show off in your pretty little fantasy world?"

A few seconds later Peter heard Wolf's pointed Italian shoes tip-tap their way down the cement hallway. Still slumped against the wall, he rubbed his eyes and tried to clear his mind. But it was no good. There was no way out. He sighed. Everyone had warned him. Even Judge Rolfson had said he was a fool to take on the school system. Wolf was right. Just a pathetic fool jostling windmills and still trying to save the world. Maybe it was time he started thinking about his family.

"Peter? Peter?"

Liz Blair stood where Wolf had been only a minute before. Or had it been longer?

"You okay? I met Wolf on the way in, and he was grinning like a fat, pompous toad. Said you were joining the Good Soil. Is it true?"

"I don't know, Liz. I just..."

"Don't do it, Peter. You can't do it. I know you're upset and you've been through a lot, but these people are bad. Don't ask me to prove it, but they're bad. The easy way out never works. Believe me, I know."

"I just—"

"But you stand for so much, Peter. Can't you see that? You've helped so many kids and families."

"The school reform project may be over."

"I'll help, and we'll get other volunteers. We can't give in to these people. I, ah, wish I could offer some money, but Barrett and I are on the outs."

"What?" He tried to shake the dull ringing from his ears.

"Barrett went ahead with the video deal. He's sponsoring the governor's visit and renting Good Soil promos through his video stores. He won't listen, thinks I'm hysterical. We had a fight, and I gave him back his engagement ring. Only had it three days."

"Sorry to—"

"Not as long as he's in bed with those people. Maybe, deep down, he's just another businessman."

"There's just so much going—"

"I know. I know you're tired and confused, but please wait before you decide. Don't do anything now. Please?" She stretched her arm through the bars and squeezed his shoulder.

"Amen, amen." A deep voice rolled out of the stark corridor. The muscular female guard stood with her hands on her good-sized hips. "You don't want nothin' to do with that big fella, Dr. Sheppard. He's big trouble. No other way to read it. Just big trouble."

Peter peered up at the two women. Was this it, then? Group therapy with an ex-nun and a jail guard? He swallowed hard, wiped the wetness from his eyes, and smiled for the first time since his arrest.

"Thanks, ladies."

Chapter 29

It seemed like hours before Peter heard the cell door rattle. He looked up to see Sterk Trump, accompanied by Peter's newfound friend from room service.

"Good news, Peter. Good news." Sterk shook his invisible shoulder pads.

"I've had about all the good news I can take," Peter said.

"No, no, this is different. I used a little friggin' pull and collected a big I.O.U. over at the morgue. The cutter puts this honey's bye-bye a full twenty-four hours before you ever met Bonnie, uh, what's her face?"

"Freeman."

"Yeah, Freeman. And that damn hooker's still alive, make book on it. That good news or not?"

Peter beamed through red, puffy eyes. "Maybe that's why Wolf was up here trying to make a deal."

"Whattaya mean?"

"Never mind, it's a long—"

"Okay, but I ain't through. Called Joe Penrod and told him it was a frame, 'specially with the planted shoes. But that mother is still not buying it. No way. Fact of the matter, he's gettin' meaner by the second. Course when we managed to get you in here instead of going with those state skunks, Penrod was really ticked. And he wouldn't even buy the poly—"

"You got the report?"

"Hell, yes. Went over it myself. Have to admit you know how to play it, but you're a damn fool to mess with that mother."

"What do you—?"

"Hells bells. When they asked if you was a virgin when you got married and you said yes, the damned stylus didn't even wiggle. You lucked out. But like I said, don't mess with the hardware."

"I didn't."

"Well, you sure as hell didn't fool 'em when it came to the Freeman gal. Stylus jumped all over when you denied any, uh, hands-on stuff with that hooker."

Peter smiled.

"So the police analyst said you're a hell of a liar and got it on with Freeman, but the bread-and-butter line is you wouldn't kill nobody, and goddamn it didn't kill nobody." Sterk broke into a toothy grin and jerked both thumbs up.

~

Peter heard a dull scraping sound. He rolled over and pulled the rough blanket around his shoulders. Then he heard it again. Metal? One of the kids? Mark, having another nightmare? Peter's eyes burned, and his stomach seemed to float in acid. Where was he? Brilliant flashes of orange-yellow light danced across the ceiling, illuminating sheets of driving rain that pounded against the tiny, barred window.

What was that? Blurry figures near the cell door? Were they coming in? He sat up and tried to clear his head. One of them carried a long pole. No, a mop. Now they were inside. And they were edging closer.

"Don't worry, Doc. We're just here to clean up from the storm," said a dry, flat voice. Was that a bucket? The one in front carried a large metal bucket. Peter looked at the ceiling. No leaks up there. Why two of them just to clean up some water? And in the middle of the night?

Something under the other one's arm. A pillow? And there, dangling near his leg, a thick, black belt. Peter swallowed hard. So this was it. Sterk had figured it right.

"No, hold it! Not any closer." Peter pushed his back against the wall and edged himself to a standing position. He retreated to the end of the narrow bed and reached back against the cold wall for support.

"I don't think he's going to listen, Toby," said the same hard voice.

Peter flexed one leg. If they had knives, he was out of luck. He could scream, but this whole cell block was isolated. Was this supposed to be an accident or a suicide? He pictured Mark and Marie. Daddy's going to fight like hell, kids.

"Yoo, hoo. Better get your asses out of there, boys." The two men spun around. Peter bent and peered through the bars. The rotund guard stood just outside the open cell door, holding a small black cellphone. "My brother-in-law, Jamaar, he's callin' to see if Dr. Sheppard is havin' a peaceful sleep. Is he, boys?" She smiled. "That's Jamaar, as in Jamaar Harris, sheriff of this lovely old county."

"Shit," said the hard-voiced leader.

Peter took a deep breath and peered at his shaking hands. The two men bumped and pushed their way out the door, their shoes scraping against the hard floor as they took quick strides down the hallway.

Peter dropped to his knees and rolled out of bed. He staggered over to the bars. The big woman smiled and nudged the cell door with her elbow. It snapped shut with an authoritative clap.

"I'm afraid Mr. Trump's hundred dollars didn't buy you a breakout, Dr. Sheppard. But, heck, I would have stayed around for nothing." She smiled and flashed a gold tooth. "By the way, Jamaar really is a distant cousin or something. Haven't seen him in a while, though."

Peter grabbed the bars with both hands and put his face flush against them. "I don't know how to thank—"

"Sleep tight, Dr. Sheppard. And don't worry none. I'll be here. Just you rest yourself now."

⁓

Peter rolled over and peered at the clock. Six-twenty. He had actually gone back to sleep. Thank God. Rain continued to slam against the small elevated window. Strange for this time of the year. Usually the spring storms lasted only an hour or two.

The big black guard punched in some numbers on the keypad and slid the door open. Did she ever sleep? She smiled and waved her arm. He followed her down the hall to the visitors' room. A cup of steaming black coffee sat on a splintered wooden table. The delicious fragrance of nut-roasted coffee filled his nostrils. He vowed he would never again criticize bureaucrats or government workers. Never.

Bruce Rothman barged into the room juggling a thick leather briefcase and stacks of loose papers. "I think we're finally getting someplace, Peter. The murder charge is out the window. Now I'm working on why the autopsy was hidden and where they got their lab work. Even the FBI hair analysis was screwed up. If Sterk hadn't checked it—"

"When am I getting out? Kathleen and the kids have to be worried sick about me, and if there's anything I can do about the grant, it's—"

"You should have been out of here long ago, but I'm afraid we're talking Sunday morning at the earliest."

"Sunday? Easter Sunday?"

"Well, now it's the sex charge. Sterk was right when he said it was just to keep you bottled up. It all boils down to the billion dollar grant. I was reluctant to believe that at first, but—"

"Count me in, too," Peter said. "Especially after last night."

"Yeah, I heard. The guard, Shekita Lewis, called Sterk. She also filed a complaint. No big surprise, they were FDLE agents. Joe Penrod claims they were assigned to plant a microphone in your cell, just in case you discussed your many and assorted crimes with visitors. Pure hogwash." He smiled. "I think Sterk used slightly stronger words to—"

"Beep... Beep... Beep. Rothman reached into his briefcase and pulled out his cellphone. He held it to his ear for a second. "It's Kathleen. Says it's important. Want me to step out?"

"No, that's all right."

Rothman handed him the phone.

"Hi, you okay?"

"It may sound odd, dear, but I've never felt better. We miss you like crazy, but you'll be out of there tomorrow or Sunday. And the really big news is about the grant. I wanted you to hear it straight from Dr. Wolf, so we have a conference hookup—"

"This is Laurie, your GTE conference operator. Thank you for using GTE. If you are disconnected, please dial star, eight, eight, eight. Dr. Wolf is now joining you."

"Ah, Peter, are you on?"

"Yes."

"And Kathleen?"

"Yes, I'm on, Dr. Wolf."

"First, let me say what a marvelous family you folks have. Marie is just as cute as a button. So proper the way she answers the phone and—"

"What do you want, Wolf?" Peter asked.

"I suppose Kathleen told you the good news. I was able to raise the ante to thirty million, even got school board approval. Sure, we'd like to get this thing settled before the governor gets here on Sunday, but it's more than that. We really want to work with you folks. I mean it, Peter."

Peter glanced at Rothman, then looked away. He closed his eyes and saw Kathleen's radiant smile and Mark's uneven gait.

"Oh, and another thing. You've been wanting full admitting privileges down at Mound Park. We both know I've been screwing up your application, but if you join now I can open the right doors. That should help your private practice, maybe let you salt away a little money for Marie's college education. And, uh, Mark's surgery."

"I—I really can't do it, Dr. Wolf. I'm sorry, Kathleen, I..."

"Well, hell, then what in God's name do you want, man? Name your goddamned price. If you're trying to hold us up you're doing a goddamned good job of it. Maybe your assistant, Dr. James, would like to have full admitting privileges at Mound Park. Sure he would, and he will."

"I just can't do it, Ben."

Click.

He could hear a low, muted sound. Was Kathleen sobbing?

"Kathleen, you still there? Sorry, hon. Everything's so muddled. It's hard to know what to do."

"No, ah, it's okay. I just thought you could do something really good with the money. I wasn't just thinking about us, but..."

"I know, I know," Peter said. "We'll figure something out. We always have. Mark will get whatever he needs. I promise."

He handed the cell phone to Rothman. His raw insides clawed their way to his throat. Peter hurried to the large wastebasket in the corner. Bending low, he threw up again and again. He closed his eyes and tried to think, but it was all a jumble. Finally, he stood and wiped his face with a tissue. He glanced at Rothman through watery eyes.

"It'll be okay, Peter," Rothman said. "Once you're out of this place things will seem a lot different. Believe me."

Chapter 30

Liz peered at the flailing windshield wipers. Were they on slow speed? Even a Jag wasn't built for this kind of downpour. She turned left onto Park Boulevard and headed west. Good old Pinellas Park. Home of pick-um-up trucks and country cooking. Aunt Mary's place was only three miles ahead, on Sixty-sixth Street. But with the darkness of night and the flooded streets it could take awhile. Her clock read nine forty-two.

Liz smiled. She hadn't been a bit surprised when Kat told her that Peter had refused Wolf's bribe. If she could just bottle some of his integrity. "Sheppard's Elixir" for the weak of heart.

Poor Kat. And poor Mark. What a great kid. Keeping him involved in the wildlife preserve was one of Liz's better moves. She had to give herself credit for that. Protecting those displaced eagles finally got Mark interested in something. Liz shook her head. Was she still, even now, trying to save the world? The birds seemed more worthy of life than a hell of a lot of people she knew.

Ragged cloud banks rolled in from the west, pushing gale-force winds into her path. It looked nasty. Just the right weather to match her mood. Columns of rain marched down the street behind her slow-moving car. Time was running out. Only one chance, and she knew what it was. Nothing had ever been so clear. Did she have the guts to take it? Kat would call it impulsive. That was always the knock against her. The family's little black sheep, who was hyper and impulsive. But this time there was no choice. If she could get to Patti, the rest would be simple. Sterk had laid the ground work when he got the testing files. But she needed more—a lot more.

She had grown to love the lush green beauty of central Florida, and she knew a storm when she saw one. But this one was special. The cloudy sky turned an eerie emerald green, flooding the landscape with luminescent light. In all of her twenty-nine-plus years of Florida seasons, she had never seen such a mysterious and enchanting sky. The green light reminded her of the church of Santa Maria. Verde Dios. Verde Dios.

She listened to WBVM meteorologist Shelby Stern: "The first edge of the storm moved into Clearwater Bay on Thursday night. By ten o'clock this morning the skies had turned so black that the solar radiation meter at WTOM, Channel 13, registered zero. The unexpected storm packed ninety-mile-an-hour winds. Temple Terrace in Hillsborough County and South Pasadena in Pinellas County were hardest hit as the storm rolled in from the Gulf of Mexico and eventually took its toll on a ten-county area stretching from Hernando to Highlands. Here's Safety Harbor city manager, John Randall:

'This is the worst I've seen in my ten years as city manager. We've had some real hard rainstorms and a couple of hurricanes we thought were big deals. But nothing like this. A couple of cars were buried under roofing from the Surf-Side Condo, and shingles were blown several hundred feet, all the way to Mandalay Avenue. I've lived here thirty-two years, and it's never rained this hard. This is a heck of a lot worse than Elena.'

"Gusts are reaching one hundred and fifty-five miles an hour, but the most unusual aspect of the storm is the smoky green light that has covered much of the area. Hold on. We have a traffic alert. Cars are backed up on Highway Nineteen in Clearwater. Several callers have indicated… Just one moment."

"This is the news director, Bishop King. Our phones have been inundated over the past thirty minutes. Calls from drivers on Highway Nineteen, north of Clearwater, report seeing an image on an eight-story office building just to the east of the highway. This has slowed traffic to a standstill, and the Highway Patrol is advising drivers to avoid that area."

Liz turned up the volume.

"Workers at the Texaco Station at, uh… Santa Cruz and Highway Nineteen report that the image has gradually appeared over the past two weeks, but the storm accelerated its development. Despite torrential rain and dangerous winds, Mexican migrant workers are building a shrine near the building. They claim the image is that of the Virgin and that she had promised them a special sign."

Gonzi's parents were migrant workers. Was somebody up there trying to tell her something? She smiled. Don't go postal, Liz. The Virgin isn't going to do this one for you. Or is she? Liz smiled and reached for the car phone. She punched in the numbers and waited. Static. Finally, an edgy voice.

"File room, Patti Hanson."

"Patti, this is Liz Blair. You know who I am?"

"Sure, everyone knows about Mr. Spangler. They pulled me out of here yesterday to work on the big video promotion."

"That's great. Now listen carefully, Patti. Barrett has a couple of questions, but he doesn't want to go through normal channels. He's trying to find out how his money is spent, and I can't say I blame him. Sterk Trump said we could count on you to help."

"Well, I dunno. I already helped that oddball once, and I'm not so sure—"

"There's five hundred in it. And, who knows, maybe more. Ever thought about managing a video store? Could be some good money in—"

"It's not so much the money. I'd like to help, but some of these folks give me the willies. A couple of real studs out here. I already told, ah, Sterk. This guy Mitchum, he's... And that Hammer guy is a psycho, if you ask me. Is this gonna be dangerous?"

"No. Just the same thing you did with Sterk, plus a phone call. That's all." Liz eased the Jaguar past fallen tree limbs and into the convent driveway.

"Okay, what the hell. Count me in."

A rain-soaked branch clattered against the windshield. Liz cupped the phone with both hands to block out the sound of howling winds. When she finished talking to Patti, she hung up and reached into the backseat for her umbrella. Then she buried her shoulder into the door and after repeated pushing forced it open. She pointed the umbrella into the wind to keep it from turning inside out and raced toward the convent's old wooden porch.

~

An hour later Liz stared in the mirror at her own tear-filled eyes. She had never worn the white headgear and traditional black habit of the Roman Church. Maybe that was another holy thing the church had tossed out when it opened the so-called window of fresh air.

"There, there, child," Aunt Mary said. "You'll ruin all that lovely makeup."

The seventy-nine-year-old nun had rubbed the dark foundation cream onto Liz's face with gnarled but loving fingers.

"Do I look Hispanic? Como esta?"

"You will be perfect, my dear." Aunt Mary struggled to lift her heavy rosary from around her neck. She finally swung it over her black-and-white headgear and laid it around Liz's neck. Liz looked up and smiled. She recalled when Aunt Mary had given her the octagon-shaped pendant so many years before. She didn't have the heart to tell her that the pendant and gold necklace were gone. Liz knew she would never wear them again.

"Please be careful, child."

Liz stood and hugged her aunt. "I'm sorry I haven't visited more often, but I'll be back. Soon." She lifted Aunt Mary's faded black cloak and let it settle over her shoulders. Then she took one final look in the mirror. Satisfied, Liz hurried down the stairs and out the front door. When she finally overcame the unrelenting winds and eased into her car, the dashboard clock read eleven o'clock. She had to get a move on. The late shift changed at midnight.

Liz headed up Alternate Nineteen and crossed Gulf-to-Bay. Flooded roads and downed power lines slowed her progress, and gusting winds jerked the Jaguar from side to side. Finally she saw the lighted walls of the old fort outlined against the purple-black sky. The massive half-timbered structure dwarfed Belleair's elegant homes. Liz checked the dashboard clock. She really needed a stopwatch for this operation.

The barbed-wire gate moved slowly upward. Liz pulled under it and stopped next to the security booth. She snapped on the inside light and opened her cloak. The guard in the booth needed to have a clear view of the habit and headgear. He cracked his window for only a second before slamming it shut. The wind obliterated anything he might have said. Liz raised her hands and shook her head. He finally waved her in.

She pulled a gray accounting ledger from the side door pocket and shoved it inside the cloak, under her arm. Then she forced the door open and let the wind slam it shut. She staggered five or six feet to the security booth and stumbled against the door. The guard pulled it open. His powder blue nametag read: "Sgt. Larry Lander." She let Aunt Mary's cloak slide off her shoulders and watched rainwater spill onto the floor. Hopefully, her makeup hadn't run.

"Buenos dias, Sergeant. I am Sister Justine, Order of the Incarnation. I am sent by the Pablo Gomez estate. We have give you the five hundred thousand dollars to, what you say? start the program. I am here to audit the money records. We must do this, ah, each or every year to show that our, ah, gifts are tax-deducted. Do you understand? Comprende?" Liz looked at her watch. Less than a minute.

"Ah. Oh, sure," Lander replied. He pulled his eyebrows together and stared at her.

Liz smiled. This guy didn't have a clue. "The general, she is waiting. Can you take me to the room file, ah, file room?"

"I'm sorry, ah, lady. Must be some mistake. I got no orders..." He stooped and peered at the Jaguar.

Dammit. Why hadn't she used one of the convent's old rattle-traps? She glanced at her watch. Come on, Patti, come on. "I may look like only a religious, but I am accountant, too. I am C.P.A. Do you know what that means?"

He peered down at her tax ledger and moved his head slowly from side to side.

"That's why I drive a car like that." She jerked her thumb toward the Jaguar. Come on, Patti. Get a move on.

He turned and pushed a bright orange button on the wall just above his desk. She heard a screeching sound and turned her head to see the wire gate slowly descend behind her car. Now she was trapped in here.

"I'm gonna have to call Colonel Mitchum. He's not too happy if it's not necess—"

Ring—ring—ring.

"Sergeant Lander. Oh... Oh... I didn't know... I'm sorry, General. She didn't have a pass and... No, M'am. If it's urgent, I can bring her right up. I'll bring her myself. Yes, General."

Lander hung up and looked at Liz. "Sorry, Sister. We're okay to go up now. I'll have someone take over here and watch your car."

Liz followed him down a narrow corridor to an ancient stone staircase. A gully formed the center of each step. How many thousands of feet had trod these steps over the past hundred and fifty years? When they got to the top, they walked into a wide brick hallway, and Lander stopped. "I got to get back. Over there, see that sign?" He pointed at the second office down.

"Gracias," Liz said. "I no like these audits. Tonight I do inventory while everyone else, they sleep. Finished by tomorrow noon." She waved at Lander and walked straight to the door. Liz rapped twice on the frosted glass panel, and the door swung open.

"Welcome to the Good Soil, Sister Justine," Patti said.

Chapter 31

Wide-eyed, Patti Hanson sucked on a king-size Marlboro and stared at Liz through a cloud of bluish gray cigarette smoke. A dozen half-smoked butts littered the ashtray. Unkempt hair, chipped fingernails and poor posture signaled depression. That was a subject Liz knew well. Patti pointed to a small library carrel that was sandwiched behind an eight-foot metal file.

"It's Friday, don't you know, so everybody hightailed it out of here early. I told Nicole I'd finish up so she could go out with her hubby. It's her old man's birthday. He's probably falling-down drunk by now, but what the hell. Right, Liz? Hey, you sure you're not a nun? Could've fooled me."

Liz smiled. "No, I'm not quite up to—"

"Oh, by the way, today's payday." Pattie raised her eyebrows.

Liz pulled a white envelope from her black habit and handed it to her.

Pattie slit the top edge of the envelope with a white plastic letter-opener. She pulled out the stack of fifties and counted them. "Oh, an extra fifty. That's nice." She gave Liz a sloppy kiss that reeked of stale tobacco and marijuana. "But tell that hard-nosed buddy of yours I'm fresh out of favors. We've heard some stuff around here that's got us bummed out good. It's just not worth the—"

"What have you heard? It could be important." Liz immediately regretted the hasty question.

After a brief pause and a condescending smile, Patti stepped to the door. "I'm lockin' it, but you can open it from this side. Just be sure to close it when you leave." Patti switched off the overhead light, opened the door, and stepped into the hallway.

Liz peered at the luminous dial on her watch. Eleven-fifty. Howling winds still slammed against the sides of the old fort. She felt her way along the metal desk to the tall filing cabinet and the adjacent study carrel. The overpowering odor of dust and cigarette smoke filled the air.

Over the next two hours Liz used her penlight to study drawer after drawer of files. Sterk was right. The so-called file room contained only tests and evaluations. And some of those could be dummies. Perfect for a government inspection but not the real McCoy.

She stepped to the door. Patti had told her the actual file room was the second door to the left, on the other side of the hallway. The door would be marked "Sociology, Drug Research." Liz peered down the dimly lighted hallway. "Damn. A Soiler stood guard in front of the door.

Now what? She had cleverly painted herself into a hell of a corner. She couldn't get past the file room to the administrative office, and she couldn't get into the file room itself. The security guard coughed and turned his head toward the hall light, exposing his face to full view. Liz took a sharp breath and smiled. She paused to make sure her eyes weren't deceiving her.

It was Jenny Grant, the girl she had given the video. The one who had claimed Peter abused her. If she was suicidal, how could she be on guard duty? Whose side was this little gal on, anyway? Did it matter? Jenny was her only chance. Liz took a deep breath and switched on the ceiling light. Then she stepped into the hallway. Holding the door ajar, she gestured as she spoke to the empty room.

"It is okay Senora Debbie. Do not worry. When I am finish with the audit, I will tell the general it was not, how you say it? Not your fault. Just fix it up by next time I come. Gracias."

Liz closed the door and walked straight to the startled girl. "I am Sister Justine. Do you wait a long time for me?"

"Ah, I'm sorry—"

"It is all right. Just open the door. The general is in a much big hurry for the final audit, and I must count everything. Even the paper clips and erasers. She said she would have someone to show me around, so you must be the person."

"I can't, Sister."

"Well, this is not good. I will have to report—"

"No. Please. You don't understand. It's locked, and I don't have the key. They would never give me the key." Jenny looked up and down the hallway. "I'm just up here on a punishment detail. I'll be here all night. I'd really like to help you, Sister." Tears filled Jenny's eyes.

Liz took Jenny's arm. "Is there something you would like to tell me, my dear?"

"Yes, yes." Tears now washed Jenny's cheeks. "It's not what you think, what they do in here. You've got to—"

"Hush, Jenny. It's me, Liz Blair. Remember? I was with Kathleen Sheppard when she gave you the recorder."

Jenny peered at her. "But—"

Liz grasped Jenny's hands. They were cold and clammy. "This is just a costume. Look, I'm here to get evidence. What about the recorder? Did you get any—?"

"Gonzie took it, but they caught him, and we don't know what they—"

"Gonzie? He's here?" Liz felt the tears coming. "Look, Jenny, you've got to help me get into this room. Where do they keep the keys?"

Jenny looked down the hallway. "There, at the end, around the corner. The keys are behind the counter, but there's always someone back there."

Liz didn't hesitate. She turned and marched straight down the hall. Keep your head back, honey, and walk with authority. When she got close to the end of the corridor, she heard the sound of exploding glass and high-pitched screams. A rush of damp, cold air swept along the hall and stirred the sleeves of her habit.

Rounding the corner, she saw a broken window that had buckled under the weight of the storm. It was as if the wind had placed its cold, wet knees in the back of an unsuspecting victim and shook it up and down and from side to side. Silvery beads of water covered the top of the long counter.

Liz ducked around the counter. No one home. Time for the goblins to do their mischief. The first ring of keys was tagged "Second Floor—Administration." She pushed them into her pocket, looked both ways, and hurried back down the hallway.

Eyes wide, Jenny stared at Liz. Liz said nothing. She tried the key marked "Sociology." It clicked, and she felt the lock give way. First time. No problem. Saints be praised. Liz looked back at Jenny. "You stay here and act like nothing's going on. You've got to be my cover."

She opened the door and ducked into a small cubicle that led to a larger room at the back. Within seconds she found David Mendola's file. So easy. Clear blue folders marked with chalklike printing, all in alphabetical order. But what about Gonzie? Nothing in the files. Then she noticed a stack of charts in the "to be filed" basket. Sure enough, the file was on top. She opened the folder and read the most recent entries. "Security violation—taping confidential sessions—eliminate from participation. And stamped on the bottom of the page: "See Confidential File."

Now what? Another dead end? She peered at her watch. Two minutes had elapsed. The Soilers were bound to notice the keys were missing. She might have another minute, two at the most. She stepped into the larger room and saw a small plastic box next to a row of computers. Of course—floppies.

Liz jerked open the lid and dumped the discs onto the table. She fanned them out and found one labeled "Layout." Liz turned on the computer and slipped in the disc. At first the drawings made no sense. The fort was only three stories, yet the map showed five stories. Then it finally dawned on her. An interconnecting network of rooms and corridors lay below the fort. She had heard about the Indian burial mounds during her volunteer orientation, but no one had told her there were two lower floors.

A blinking arrow served as a guide to the underground areas. One showed stairs connecting the general's office to the underground compound. Funny, Dr. Small had shown her Dantakovic's office. There was no stairway. And another stairway started near the dining area. And what was that? An elevator? Sure enough, hidden behind a wall covering of some sort. No, it was a painting. Pablo Gomez. Why would his name be on it?

Liz checked her watch. Another minute had passed. She removed the disc and shoved it into her pocket. Scattering the other discs, she noticed a red-and-black one with a special notation: "High priority—confidential." She slapped it in and waited. Then her lips began to tremble, and her eyes filled with tears. Gonzi, what have they done? And it's all my fault.

"Where's that nun? You see her?" A deep, raspy voice from the hallway.

"Well, no—ah, yes, Colonel Mitchum. What am I thinking? Of course. About twenty minutes ago."

Liz froze.

"Are you up to something?"

"No, ah, she said she was going to bookkeeping. Something about an audit."

"A what?"

"You know, like checking the books. She's with the old man's estate. The one that died and left the money—"

"I know that." He shook his head. "Too bad you got no brains to go with that bod of yours." Liz heard a rustling noise against the door. The doorknob rattled.

"Don't do that, Breaker. Please don't do that."

"Yeah, I guess you're the Hammer's property. I always get the leftovers, but that ain't too bad." He laughed. "In fact I think I'll do a little audit on Starlyn tonight. She's going under the knife on Sunday, so we got to make music while we can. Right?"

Liz covered her mouth with her hand. Starlyn was like her own daughter. It didn't make sense, but that was exactly how she felt. She had destroyed her own baby. And now Gonzie and Starlyn. Why did she always hurt the ones she felt closest to? Would Kat and Peter be next?

"Anyway, we got to find this friggin' nun. Her car's blocking part of the entrance, and it's locked up. She must have the keys with her."

Liz patted her side pocket and felt the outline of the keys. Dammit, would she ever get things right? But at least she had more time. That was a blessing.

"You can go now."

"No, I've got to stay here. It's—"

"Nope, the Hammer will be back from Miami before noon. Wants you to have a good night's sleep." He laughed. "Maybe you're going to get audited, too."

Liz heard retreating footsteps as Mitchum moved down the hallway. Silence. Then the door squeaked open and Jenny slipped in.

"Did you find anything?"

"I'm afraid so. There's another floor or something under the fort, and I've got to go down there."

"No, don't… Please don't." Jenny held Liz's shoulders. "I've been down there. There's nothing good down there. Please believe me."

⁓

Liz took short, cautious steps down the rock staircase that hugged the damp walls of the ancient cemetery. A musty odor filled her nostrils, and lightning flashed through narrow slits high up on the gray walls. She licked her lips, her eyes moving in every direction. The confidential report on Gonzie… It couldn't be. They couldn't be that brutal, they just—

A violent bolt of lightning shattered her thoughts and illuminated row after row of tombs and burial mounds that spread out from the bottom of the steps. She expected to see an Indian warrior rise up at any moment, eyes filled with fury and death. She spotted the shallow grave right away, but wished she hadn't. About six feet long and four feet wide, it was covered with long-haired pelts. Florida panther? Wolf skin? Peeled back at the top, the skins revealed a clear glass window. Why a window? To take pictures? To scare the others?

Liz bent and peered through the foggy, tinted glass. She sat on her haunches, but fatigue and creeping numbness forced both knees to the damp clay floor. Looking through the dim light, she shook her head and stared at the body below.

She rubbed the window with shaking fingers until a clear outline of the boy's face emerged. At first it looked flat, without emotion, like a white plaster death mask. But looking closer she could see intense fear and suffering, as though the boy had witnessed some terrible thing. At the same time, the protruding jaw reflected strength and an unwillingness to submit to the chains of darkness.

She ran trembling fingers along the edges of the window. Brilliant shafts of lightning, followed by deafening blasts of thunder, jolted her back. Heart pounding, she leaned her aching back over the glass cover. The whites of her eyes were reflected in the clouded glass. Fingering the sides of the cold window with both hands, she edged it slowly upward. Liz took a deep breath, swallowed, and shook herself.

The boy's wrist was cool and limp. No pulse. Nothing. Dear God! Reaching under Gonzi's shirt, she massaged his icy chest, searching for signs of life. A flash of light threw dark shadows across the boy's face. Liz tried to scream, but couldn't. Clawlike fingernails cut into her mouth and throat and pulled her head back. Then she saw feathered horns, huge white eyeballs, and piercing black irises. She struggled to hold on to Gonzi's hand, but felt it slipping away.

~

Jenny Grant and Tiny Shutten crouched behind the tomb marked "Padre Cancer de Barbastro." They watched the shadowy figures step over Liz's crumpled body. One of the strangely dressed creatures flipped through the ledger book with long, razor-sharp fingernails. Then he took hold of Liz's hands and feet and lifted her effortlessly into the air. Swinging her as he walked, he and his companion disappeared into the darkness.

~

The storm ended just before daybreak. A soft, pink glow heralded the light of day. Monuments and Indian mounds shimmered under a golden sunrise that projected the shadows of three large crosses onto the vast floor. Translucent, reddish blue light streamed through the weaponry slits, converting them from windows of death to lenses of renewal.

Jenny took a deep breath and stood. She was reaching down to give Tiny Shutten a hand when she heard a rustling noise just behind her.

"Don't be scared. It's me, David Mendola."

Jenny pulled back and put her hand to her mouth. Shutten stepped in front of her.

"No, I'm with you guys," David whispered. "I've had it with the Soil."

Jenny crossed her arms. "That's what you say, but you're a big shot colonel, now. You'd do anything to get us to—"

"People change. Really." David held out his left hand. Nestled inside was the tiny tape recorder.

"You're a druggy. Even if you're trying to do something right, we can't count on you," Jenny said.

"I'm finished with that stuff. Dr. Sheppard, he… Anyway, I'm off the hard narcotics. It just took awhile to sink in. Look, the tape's right here. I never destroyed it. Now we need to plant it on Gonzie."

Jenny felt her chest tighten. "But you gave Wolf the orders for electroshock, and God knows what else. Did you hand him over to that crazy Dr. Stroud, too?"

David looked down and shook his head. "I'm sorry, Jenny, I feel just awful. Please give me—"

Tiny Shutten stepped between them. "We need him, Jenny. It doesn't matter what he did. That was then, and this is now. Let's get that tape into Gonzie's pocket. It's the only damn chance we've got."

Chapter 32

Peter smiled. Where the heck was he? Polished white rocks circled the small, balmy lagoon. A green mist hung over thick purple foliage. Beckoning, the naked young woman splashed languidly while cavorting with smiling dolphins. Her creamy milk skin and bright orange hair flashed in the steaming emerald waters.

He longed to immerse himself in the warm estuary, but held tightly to each smooth rock as he slowly made his way down the steep, rock-ridged bank. When he reached the water's edge, he sat and let his burning feet dangle in the clear, cool water. Peter looked down. He was naked.

The woman had changed into a tiny blonde girl who smiled mirthfully from the back of a huge gray shark. The sinister maneater glided through the flourescent green waters, its flat, deadly eyes like unmoving buttons.

The water exploded with fury. Pounding waves blasted showers of green foam into the air and onto the shore. He felt the muscular arms of the undercurrent pulling him down. Hundreds of enormous gray sharks, their terrible eyes glaring like demonic neon lights, raced through the formerly placid lagoon.

He crashed into icy cold water and tried to cling to the smooth rocks along the bank, but buffeting winds pushed him back. The little girl reached out, but black decay spread through her bony fingers. He screamed and screamed as panic invaded every ounce of his being.

A cool hand covered his feverish forehead.

With just that single touch, he knew he was safe. A voice asked him a question, but he didn't understand. Shakita Lewis sat on the edge of his bed and looked down. "You was having a real bad one, Dr. Sheppard. I had to wake you, anyhow, 'cause you got a visitor."

He looked at the small, barred window. It was still dark.

"It's only five-thirty. But Mr. Sterk, he says it's real important. I'm afraid it may not be good—"

"Wake up, Peter." Sterk Trump stood at the open cell door. He wasn't smiling.

"Got some bad news. They got Liz. She's in a coma over at Mound Park."

"What?" Peter rolled out of bed and stood.

"Yeah, she's been missing since Friday night, but nobody knew it. She had a falling out with Spangler, so he didn't know nothin'. He's kickin' himself all over the place now. She said somethin' to one of the aides at Mound Park about being out at the Good Soil. I called Patti. Sure enough, Liz was out there Friday night, dressed up like a nun."

"Does Kathleen know?"

"She was the first to find out. She woke up to a car siren about two hours ago. Whoever done it left Liz in the Jag with the headlights on and the security alarm goin'. Kathleen didn't know she was missing neither. Thought Liz was with Barrett Spangler or at her mom's place in Orlando."

Peter ran his hands through his hair. "Jesus. And I'm still stuck in here."

"No sir. This is Sunday, remember?" Sterk waved an official-looking document in a blue binder. "These are your walkin' papers. You're out of here. Now."

~

The faint but vibrant sounds of music and clapping hands filled her head. Liz shook off the thick cotton of sleep and tried to remember where she was. What had happened? A white glow, up above. What? Where the heck was she? Then she saw the I.V. bag and the oxygen tent. Hospital? She closed her eyes. Thick and swollen, her tongue filled her mouth.

"You'll be fine."

Someone sitting under the T.V.? Someone in a white robe? It just wasn't clear. Liz blinked and looked at the T.V. A park of some kind? Men in robes with silk sashes and ladies in long glittering purple earrings. A sunrise service?

A fireball exploded and painted the sky and water with a ruby red brush. The clapping and the music stopped. Worshipers stared in awe. And touched one another, and looked and questioned in silence. Liz tried to shake her head clear.

"Praise be the Lord," came a voice from the assembled group of red folks who moments before had been black folks.

"Praise be Jesus," came the response from the ruby, pink, and cardinal choir.

Worshipers sat on the now flame-red grass. A boy of eight or nine, dressed in a black suit with a white dress shirt and bright orange tie, began to sing. He shouted in a high-pitched voice as he moved back and forth with the music. Four men, dressed in conservative black suits with white shirts and orange ties, served as backup vocalists.

"You may be down and feel the Lord has forgotten you. But God has proven time and time again, he will come through. You may not know how—and you may not know when—but he'll do it again.

"He'll calm the storm and find the way, and he'll do it again. He always comes through. You may not know how—and you may not know when—but he'll do it again."

The maroon red earth had turned itself in service to the blood-red sun, and the sun seemed to shatter the earth's watery bounds. A hushed silence magnified sounds of shallow waves lapping gently against decaying boat docks. The TV closed in on wizened commercial fishermen, red-eyed and unshaven, who leaned against their vessel, blank faces betraying nothing.

A powerful soprano voice broke the deathlike stillness. "Like a crippled sapling he grew—a thing despised, reject-ed by men. On him lies a punishment that brings us peace, al-le-lu—ia, al-le-lu-ia.

"Why do you look for the living among the dead? He is not here. He has been raised to new life! He goes now be-fore you—to make all the won-drous deeds of our life! Al-le-lu—ia, al-le-lu-ia."

Liz covered her face with her hands. Tears ran along her fingers.

"You'll be fine, Liz."

The figure in white was still there. He stood close to the bed. Gonzie? Was it her Gonzie? Still alive? But this person looked different somehow. He was dressed in clean white robes, the kind they wore at the Good Soil, and his face was smooth and relaxed. Liz reached out and grasped the boy's hand. It felt funny, like hardened wax. Was she hallucinating? Thank God he was okay. Liz looked into the boy's brown, almost black, eyes. It was Gonzie. Who else could it be?

"Here, this is for you." The fingers of his right hand opened slowly to reveal something dark inside. It looked real.

"What, what is—"

"You will know what to do. I will help you."

Amazing. Suddenly, Liz felt wide awake. Completely alert. She felt as if she'd been awake for a while, even when her eyes had been closed. It was like coming out of a cold storage locker into burning hot sunlight. She stared at the oxygen tent and disengaged I.V. The boy must have done it.

She peered at him. Was he a boy? He looked older now. Why wasn't she afraid? Liz looked down at the tiny tape. Then she peered into his glowing face.

"This is the key, Liz. You must give it to Peter. He will understand everything, when it is time."

No accent at all. With a quiet, gliding stride, the figure turned and walked to the adjoining room door. No hobbling… no limping.

"Gonzi?"

The figure turned and smiled.

"Thanks," Liz said.

~

Luminescent red light flooded through the window. A quiet, almost imperceptible click. Liz snapped her head to the left. Was it just a second or two? Or had she fallen asleep again? The hallway door opened, and Sterk Trump, a plug of tobacco pushing out his cheek, peered through the opening. He slipped around the door and tiptoed toward her bed. Then he stopped.

"Jesus, Liz. What in hell you doing sittin' there like the cat what ate the friggin' canary?" With a wide grin on his face, Peter stepped in just behind Sterk.

"I'm feeling a whole lot better," Liz said.

Peter glanced at the oxygen tent and disconnected I.V. "I talked with Julio Fernandez on the way in. He says you're going to be okay, but I thought he said you still needed—"

"Gonzi did it."

Peter and Sterk traded glances.

"It's okay. I feel so much better now." She looked at Peter's raised eyebrows and Sterk's ever-widening eyes.

Sterk wiggled his shoulders. "You mean the Mexican kid? The one that never got to the Soil?" He pointed his stubby index finger at the oxygen tent. "That kid came in here and took this stuff down?"

Peter sat on the bed and took Liz's hands. "You're going to be fine. Don't worry about anything. If Gonzie's still in there, we'll find him."

"No. I mean it, Peter. Someone was up here, right here. Just a little while ago. Ah, unless..."

"What's that?" Sterk pointed at Liz's pillow. She twisted her head and saw the partially covered microcassette at the edge of her pillow. So she hadn't been dreaming. He had been real. She knew it. It had to be Gonzie. And he was okay. That was the main thing.

"Gonzie gave it to me."

Sterk rolled his eyes and spat a wad of tobacco juice into a Styrofoam cup. "I'm gettin' Doc Hernandez in here pronto."

"No, hold it, Sterk," Peter said. "Do you remember where you were, Liz? Do you remember what happened to you?"

"Let's see. Aunt Mary gave me her rosary." Liz looked up. "Why did she do that? Then I saw Patti what's-her-name. Her husband had a birthday. Poor Gonzie, dead in that terrible tomb. And the lightning. I was so scared. I was in an Indian village, or..."

Sterk looked at Peter and shook his head. Then he stepped over to the bed and picked up the tape. "We gotta go listen to this thing. Just in case there's somethin' on it."

Peter held Liz's hands. "I think Liz needs us now. We can—"

"Kate should be back in a few minutes," Sterk said. She came in with Liz, and she's been here ever since, but she had to take Mark out to the V.A. Somethin' about some eagles." Sterk turned to Liz. "Oh, and your mother's on her way over, too."

Liz sat forward. "I've got to be out there with Mark. We're helping the wounded eagles." She shook her head. "Funny, I can remember that part fine."

"No, you stay put, sister-in-law," Peter said. "We'll talk to Dr. Hernandez on the way out. They found some powerful neurotoxins in your blood work and—"

"Yeah, a South American Mickey," Sterk said. "You get your rest and leave Mark, and the eagles, and Gonzie, or whoever, to us. Oh, and I got one of Sheriff Harris's boys out front so nobody gets another crack at you." He smiled. "Of course he'll sure as hell keep you from wanderin' off somewhere, too. So remember that. We don't need you playin' hooky about now."

Chapter 33

Peter and Sterk shook their head in disbelief. Recordings of Good Soil staff meetings poured out of the Corwin-Vaga speakers with sound room clarity.

"Son of a bitch! I don't believe it." Sterk held a white-knuckled death grip on the van's steering wheel. "Getting kids hooked on drugs. Kids go in there to get clean, and they make true druggies out of 'em. Kids with the AIDS virus and blackmailing judges and congressmen It's, it's—"

Sterk leaned into the steering wheel and jammed the transmission into low gear. The ponderous van squealed in protest and lumbered onto the road, spewing a trail of black diesel smoke. "Goddamn it, Peter. Goddamned bastards, white trash, son-of a—"

"Hold it, Sterk. Hold it." Peter eyed the speedometer, which seemed to have a life of its own—fifty five—sixty—sixty five.

"I should have guessed about the HIV," Peter said. I just wasn't thinking."

"Whattaya mean?"

"The neuropsych reports. Subtle cognitive changes associated with early stages of AIDS dementia complex. Remember the files we looked at? Remember the Verbal Learning Scale and the Paced Auditory Serial Addition? And those elevations on the depression and anxiety scales of the MMPI? All point to subtle neurological complications, but I just wasn't thinking about HIV. Stupid. Just wasn't thinking."

They headed north and made good time in light traffic. Most people were still digging out from the storm or attending Easter morning services. Festooned with colorful balloons, both Good Soil gates stood open. Sterk took a deep breath and pumped the brakes. He pulled into the fort's parking lot and stopped behind two oak trees near the road.

Only a dozen or so cars were scattered throughout the area. Workers carried tables and chairs into the Jackson Chapel. Huge red, white, and blue banners hung above the chapel's main doors, advertising the special parent meeting.

Peter pushed back into the seat and took a deep breath. These people had to be stopped. First it was that poor Mexican kid. How many other children were missing? And Liz could have easily disappeared in Mexico. Next it would be Kathleen and the kids. He looked down at his trembling fingers. "We've got to go in. Now."

"Hold it a sec, Peter. They don't even know we have the tape. And they probably don't know the kid escaped."

"That's right, but the problem is we've got no proof and the tape will never hold up in our courts. We've got to get a confession. We need to use that tape to get them to talk. The police are restricted by the rules of the court, and think of their political clout. You should have been at the NIMH hearing. Believe me, they can just walk away from this."

Sterk crossed his arms and gazed out the window toward the chapel. "Maybe you're right. But what if we're stopped?"

"Look, they're having their grant ceremonies at noon, so most of the Lions and Soilers will be in the chapel with the parents. That's the time for us to go in and try to get some real evidence. If we're stopped we'll pull out the tape and see how far it gets us. We can certainly do more with it than the police. And you know the FDLE is—"

"Say no more, Peter. You got a friggin' convert right here. Just say Joe Penrod or FDLE, and I'm rarin' to go."

Peter yawned and closed his eyes. He hadn't slept much since he was arrested. When would he see Kathleen and the kids again?

"You okay? You look like crap." Sterk reached for his sawed-off shotgun and delivered a stream of brown tobacco juice through the vent window.

"Thanks for the vote of support, Sterk. No, you're right. I don't know whether to run away or fall asleep. But I'm as sick as you are with this whole setup. But one thing, Sterk. No shotgun."

~

Liz peered at the door. It had to be Kat. No one else would bother knocking. Only her perfect sister, bless her soul.

"Hi, Sis. It's good to see you up and at 'em." Kathleen set a small leather suitcase on the floor and gave Liz a peck on the forehead. Liz reached out, pulled her close, and gave her a tight hug.

"I took Mark to the V.A. Hospital," Kathleen said. "Then I dropped by Barrett's and got these clothes and things. You were really out of it when I left, but here's something that will help." Kathleen smiled and held up a toothbrush.

"Thanks, Kat." Liz shook her head. "You never liked that name, did you? Guess I knew it, but I wanted to make you mad. I was jealous, of course. If you want me to drop it, I will." Liz felt the tears coming. "I'm sorry about a lot of things, Kat, uh, Kathleen."

"No, no, it's okay." Kathleen sat close to her, and took her hand. "You call me whatever you like. Actually it's kind of cute, or funny, or something."

Liz looked toward the window. "That red light was incredible. Must have been quite an Easter morning."

"I've never seen anything like it," Kathleen said. "NASA said eruptions of Mount Pinatubo in the Philippines caused the purple-red light. A bunch of folks called nine-one-one. Some of them thought Castro had finally dropped an H-bomb on MacDill. The Air Force even sent some jets up to see what was going on. It was kind of like we had five feet of snow around here."

"Wait," Liz said. "That green light on Friday, it's starting to come back. Verde Dios. That's why I went to see Aunt Mary."

Kathleen cocked her head.

"No, wait. Some of it *is* coming back. I think I saw Jenny Grant and Starlyn. No, maybe... But I remember dressing like a traditional nun. All the religious stuff..."

"It sounds confusing to me, Liz. But I thought about you when I saw the morning paper. Remember how you said the Virgin in Mexico said to pray that Russian cities would take back their saint's names? Well, Leningrad just became St. Petersburg. Can you believe that?"

Liz smiled.

"And that's not all. Have you heard about the apparition of the Virgin out on Highway Nineteen? I went by there last night and it's really—"

"Yes. I remember that, too. On the radio. It's coming back, slow but sure."

"I'm so glad to hear that."

Liz took Kathleen's hand. "There were times I felt you didn't support me, Kat, even when you really wanted to. Like the trip to Mexico. But now I need your help on something big. I want you to do something a little bit daring. It might even be quite a bit daring in your book. Will you?"

"Well, it depends on what it is, but this time—okay, Sis. Just don't get me in hot water like you did when we were kids." Kathleen smiled. "What do you want me to do?""

Liz giggled. "Take off your dress. Oh, and I'll need your car keys. And a dash of your cologne would be nice when I hustle past the guard."

Kathleen's eyes went wide. "Oh, my God."

Chapter 34

The van's location gave Peter a clear view of parents and other guests who had started arriving at eleven o'clock. Lions Corps officers greeted them at the chapel's wide front doors. Sterk had called an old friend with the Bellaire Bluffs Fire Department to telex floor plans of the fort directly to the van. They arrived less than a minute later. Sterk replayed the tape, and they studied the layout. "No sign of a hidden cemetery on this diagram, Peter."

"Poor Liz was really confused, but she also said something about a secret chapel and a communications bunker." While Peter studied the drawings through itchy, burning eyes, Sterk crawled between the two front seats into the back of the van. Peter twisted around to watch the brawny detective take off his coat, strap on a recording device, and slip a microrecorder into his left shirt pocket.

Sterk bent, strapped on his leg holster, and inserted the Walther PPK. He slipped a .38 caliber revolver into his boot and shoved the 9 mm Glock into his shoulder holster. Then he pulled on his yellow and orange polyester sport coat. He was ready for prime time.

"And here's a present." Sterk held up the massive S&W 10 mm automatic. "You won't let me take a shotgun in, but this can blow a damn big hole at close range, so you might as well have it."

Peter shook his head. "No way. I'd be in more danger with it than without it. And so would everyone else."

"Okay. But I want you to pull your pants down."

"What?"

"I need you to keep somethin' for me. Nobody's gonna check you as close as me, so you're my fail-safe guy. Sterk held a tiny automatic in the palm of his hand.

Peter shook his head. Then he loosened his belt and slid his pants down. Sterk used three strands of tape to secure the gun to Peter's inner thigh. Peter pulled his trousers up and buckled his belt. Sterk's shoulders quivered. "Let's go."

They climbed out through the van's rear door and walked around the west perimeter of the parking lot. After stepping through the open gate, they turned left and strode toward the Good Soil main offices. A woman with binoculars waved at Sterk from the roof. "FDLE," Sterk mumbled. "Guess Penrod hasn't spread the word about me yet."

Bright lights blinked from television cameras inside the chapel as technicians scurried to hook up outside speakers for the overflow crowd. Like a long, purple serpent, stretch limousines formed a solid line through the parking lot and down Sea Breeze Boulevard as far as the eye could see. Florida Governor Ray Chavez exited the first limo along with a heavyset black man.

"Know who that is, Peter?"

"No, I don't think I—"

"Judge J. Harry Rolfson the third, or some such crap. Enjoyin' himself, ain't he? Damn, wonder if they even got to the governor."

Peter just shook his head. They took slow, casual steps to the administrative offices. Peter held the door open, and Sterk headed straight to the front desk. The receptionist, awash with cosmetics, was the same secretary who had been on duty during Peter's previous visit. What a change.

Terri Johns. She used to look seventeen, but now she could pass for twenty-five. Heavy coats of make-up seemed to be part of her new corporate dress code. But the flat, dead eyes and blank expression were the most obvious changes. Shark eyes. He shivered. This little gal wasn't just depressed, there was nothing there. Just nothing inside. What had happened to the warm, vivacious girl he'd met on his previous visit?

Head turned toward the closed-circuit TV, the girl did not hear them approach. Sterk leaned over and put both hands flat on the desktop.

"Guess what? Look who's back." He smiled and spit a huge glob of reddish brown juice into a nearby trash basket. "Remember me?"

Terri Johns moved her fingers along the underside of the desk.

"Uh-uh." Sterk waved his fingers. "Nope, this here's a surprise visit, and we're gonna keep it that way. Up. Move." He opened his gaudy sport coat to expose the glistening hardware holstered inside, and his twitching shoulders warned of a preemptive strike. Sterk stepped quickly around the desk and cut the surveillance camera wire.

They each took one of the young woman's arms and stepped quickly down the hallway. After two right turns and a left turn, they stopped in front of a door marked "Doris Dantakovic." Closed circuit TVs continued to blare. "From the mountains, to the prairies, to the oceans white with foam..."

Sterk turned the doorknob and they stepped into the office. Only an empty In and Out basket and a weekly planner, opened to Easter Sunday, sat on the desktop. A modest cardboard sign read: Director.

"See. I told you the general wasn't here," the listless adolescent said. "They're all in the chapel."

Sterk smiled. He stroked the light green desk as if it were his beloved van. "Damned if I know how we got this tape, but it's the key all right." Sterk crawled behind the cheap metal desk and pressed the carpeted floor under the three drawers.

"There's a lump under this small piece of carpet just like the tape said." Sterk pressed it. They waited, but nothing happened. Sterk stared at the small cassette tape and frowned. Then he pulled back the carpet. "Look, a metal button down here."

"Probably to prevent an accidental opening," Peter said.

"But a gal with high heels could open it real easy. Okay, here goes."

Peter looked over Sterk's shoulder. The three-foot-wide fiberboard bookcase inched its way silently into the wall. The stuporous secretary stared at the ceiling, unmoved by this wondrous event.

Peter gasped. The room looked to be at least forty feet long and thirty feet wide. Situated at the far end, the original fireplace had been restored to its white, gleaming marble finish. An inset oval painting of a fox hunt hung above the eighteenth-century mantlepiece. The floor was in a matching white marble and the secretarial desk, easily five by ten feet, was covered in contrasting black polished slate.

He imagined the dazed secretary sitting behind the desk in her black biking gear. Truly an intimidating sight. They walked through the open door to the director's office. The closed circuit telecast was not much louder than the hiss of the air conditioning. "And now, ladies and gentlemen, to officially accept the largest single school reform grant in the history of the United States, the governor of the great state of Florida."

Vintage Victorian, the office had gold ceilings, heavy maroon curtains, and red and gold embossed wallpaper. It was jammed with lamps, ceramic ornaments, knickknacks, and overstuffed chairs. Vases, framed prints, and collections of china were everywhere. Oriental throw rugs abounded, and a polished mandolin hung on one wall. Surrounded by dark red candles in silver holders and leather-bound volumes of Punch, a gold statue of Venus sat on a small table just inside the door. She covered her eyes with the back of her hand.

An eight-by-ten-inch program wrapped with a purple silk ribbon sat next to the magazine. The cover showed a crown, and just below, raised letters spelled "Bury St. Edmunds Abbey." Beneath that, an inscription: "Her Majesty's Holy Trinity Service, Sunday, May 31, 1887. Not Transferable."

Arms folded, the embalmed Terri Johns sat stiffly on one of the red velvet-encased chairs and stared at the two men. Thirty feet away, the director's desk, which faced away from them, sat beneath two stained glass windows. Red and blue family crests glowed in the windows. The chair, with its high, gold-encrusted back, resembled an antique throne.

Sterk barked out the orders. "You take that side, I'll open everything over here. Don't want to miss nothin'."

A soft chirping sound.

Peter looked up. The thronelike chair edged forward, squeaking over the sounds of the televised ceremony.

"Once and for all give all our children a world class education and end illiteracy, school violence, and drug abuse."

~

Liz peered through the swaying pine trees to the sky above. They had waited patiently beneath a massive banyan tree for two hours, and Mark had been on the scene long before that. Blessed. What a blessed morning it had been. Mark said the sunrise was like nothing he had seen before. It was as if crimson food coloring had floated down from giant space ships. Was there room for one more miracle on this blessed day?

Suddenly a cheer went up. The broad-winged eagles zoomed into the bright, golden sky. The injured baby eagle faltered for a breathtaking moment but managed to stay airborne and climb above the tall oak trees. Circling the cheering circle of people, the golden-edged birds soared in majesty above the deep-green forest.

Liz hugged Mark. "Our prayers have been answered." Bathed in sunlight, they danced together in the purple shadows. Liz raised her voice to the heavens with an old Shaker song. "I danced in the morning when the world was begun—and I danced in the stars—and the moon—and the sun."

Chapter 35

Jenny peered down at the first squad of Soilers. They marched in single file from the side door of the Good Soil compound and took brisk steps to the chapel. The Hammer had told her that the T.V. sponsors insisted on a dramatic and symbolic entrance through the main doors of the historic chapel. Looking like well scrubbed but oversized altar servers, the teenagers moved in winding columns under the Lion Brigade's watchful eye.

Jenny leaned out the arched window and filled her lungs with fresh air. Many of the Soilers hadn't been outdoors in months. The storm's heavy rains had scrubbed the trees and flowers to a brilliant glow, and a soft southerly breeze carried the sweet scent of magnolias across the large quad.

Towering red, white, and blue, banners hung from the front of the chapel. Snapping in reproach, the flags reminded Jenny of the power and authority of the state. Her father had been a part of that. She could see agents on rooftops carrying high-powered telescopic rifles. Helicopters hovered above the buildings and adjacent grounds. A massive display of force and power.

The Soilers marched into the chapel. Through the open doors she could hear ringing applause and strains of "God Bless America." Jenny smiled. This was what the people had come for. Here they would see the resurrected youth who had fallen by the wayside. Thank God for government programs and powerful community leaders. And what an honor to be in the presence of the First Lady.

Jenny frowned. What was going on down there? It looked like Soilers were passing messages along the weaving line. A head held back to hear a whispered message, then nodding forward to pass the word. And right in the middle of it all she saw Tiny Shutten. Good old Tiny. Somehow the Hammer had overlooked him. Thank God.

Only ten minutes. That's what the Hammer had said. The First Lady's schedule mandated only a few minutes for the dramatic parent-child confrontations. To speed things up, only one confession would be heard. And the Hammer had suggested Jenny. Something about her all-American freshness or some such rot. And then, of course, her missing father. That's what it was really about. A sob story for the six-o-clock news.

She had seen her mom on "Good Morning America," televised from the St. Petersburg Pier. Eyes red and swollen, her mom tearfully recited the story of her husband's disappearance and appealed to her husband and/or his abductors to think of poor Jenny. Her lovely Jenny who had turned to drugs in his absence.

Jenny cranked the window shut. She sat and stared at her reflection in the mirror. The Hammer had warned her to get the makeup right. Better to put on too little than too much. Freshness, that was the key. She sighed. Not much freshness left. Not now. Not ever again.

She had known the Hammer's offer was more summons than request, but a refusal would have resulted in unthinkable consequences for her friends. John Lifewater waited in solitary confinement for the lab, the pit, or both. And the condition of her adopted sister, Starlyn Dalton? She shook her head. The once energetic and cheerful teenager lay lifeless on her cot. Unable to sleep and refusing to eat, she stared into space. Ravaged by memories of abuse and the excesses of her own behavior, Starlyn was too depressed to cry.

The Hammer warned Jenny that Starlyn was no longer of any use to him, or anyone else. The only solution was a delicate procedure to bury her painful memories. Scheduled for one o'clock, Starlyn would find a new beginning under Dr. Porter Stroud's trembling fingers. But if Jenny performed, and performed well, the outcome could be different. Starlyn would be put under the care of Dr. Wolf and Dr. Small. She would receive counseling, medication, and rehabilitation. Lifewater would return to a regular cell, his visit to the lab canceled.

She had no choice. She couldn't trust the Hammer, and Dr. Stroud had named her as one of his future clients. But she had to buy time. If only they hadn't found poor Liz. One brave woman, no doubt about that. And she seemed so attached to Star. Maybe the tape got through. Maybe someone found it on Gonzi. But would it really help? She shuddered and tried not to dwell on Liz's certain fate.

A knock on the door. The door opened, and David Mendola and Billy Ray Thomas stepped into the room. She looked into David's eyes. He stared back, his face expressionless. They escorted her to the main living area where two makeup artists highlighted her natural beauty for the T.V. cameras.

Sandwiched between David Mendola and Billy Ray Thomas, she walked down the long corridor to the chapel. She was surprised to see a faint smile on Mendola's face. Could she really trust him?

~

Sterk yanked out the nine mm Glock, dropped to a firing stance, and held the gun with both hands. He signaled Peter to take cover and shot the secretary a look to hold her in place. The thronelike chair continued to turn... ever so slowly.

A tiny figure. A child? Then Peter saw the spiritless face of Professor Harold Small, Ed.D. He'd been crying. Peter looked at the little man, lost in the enormous chair and the overpowering room. Peter couldn't help but feel sorry for the ambitious educator. Sterk shouldered his weapon.

Professor Small coughed, again and again. Blood and phlegm covered a wad of Kleenex that he clutched in his bony hands.

"We've got a tape here," Sterk said, signaling the emotionally flat secretary to a forward position in the room.

"I know. I know, for God's sake."

Peter relaxed a little for the first time since entering the compound. "How did this?—"

"I don't know... deserve everything I get. I've got no excuse, just glad you're here." Small sobbed into the wad of mucus and blood. Then he looked up. "Now we can get it over with."

Peter followed the secretary's eyes to a red, velvet-faced door with a large brass handle. He stepped over to the door and slipped into a tiny bathroom. It contained a marble topped wooden sink and decorative brass and porcelain faucets. A collection of thirty to forty prints and photographs of eighteenth-century European royalty and military figures stood above the wash basin.

He held one of the Irish linen hand towels under a stream of cold water. Embossed initials, BVH, over a crest of some sort, were sewed along the top edge of the towel. He backed into the room and handed the dripping towel to Small. The frail professor wiped his face and covered his coughs with the bottom of the towel.

Sterk turned on the recording gear. "Let's start from the beginning, Professor." Sterk's voice was soft, even gentle.

The telecast grew louder. "And now, Soilers, parents, and guests." The governor's raspy voice stuttered with excitement. "Our First Lady. the First Lady of the United States of America." Cheers and clapping accompanied strains of "I'm a Yankee Doodle Dandy."

"It started innocently enough, I guess." Small looked up at Peter. "I guess not, not really... There was this beautiful girl in my class over at the junior college, and the next thing I knew they had videos of us together in bed with, ah—a minor."

Eyes wide, Small glanced at Sterk. "No, it's not what you think. They had me drugged. Even then I didn't connect it with the Soil. I thought just being here was my big break. Doing medical and educational research with Dr. Benjamin Wolf, and seeing my dream-list of programs in the public schools. Then, right after Loretta took the kids and left, I saw what was going on. But it was too late. I tried to resign, but the Hammer told me I was in for life. I wanted to say something at the NIMH hearing, Dr. Sheppard, but one of the HRS assistants worked for the Hammer. She had a gun."

"A gun? At the hearing?" Peter shook his head. How did she get past security and the metal detector?

Small coughed up more blood.

"God-dammit, I knew it." Sterk glared at Peter. "Wish we had the shotgun or even the ten mm auto—"

Sterk was interrupted by thunderous applause for Doris Dantakovic. They watched the First Lady present the director with the President's Service Medal. "The highest award given by the federal government." The Air Force Drum and Bugle Corps played "America the Beautiful."

"My friends, this is a momentous day," the First Lady said. "As you know, some people have criticized the President for spending a billion dollars on a single school reform grant. But I tell you, here and now, and I want to make this abundantly clear. The president will lead the fight to end failing schools, drug abuse, and juvenile crime. And we will win this battle once and for all. It is time for the people to ask not just what they can do for their country, but what their country should be doing for them. Believe me, this government plans to deliver."

Sterk spat into a bone china sugar bowl. "So this general, whoever he is, plans to run the show?"

"There's a show, all right, and it's hurting kids all over America. But that isn't the final goal. What they really want is the money, pure and simple. Just the billion dollars. Their ultimate show is in Europe. I don't know what it is or where, but there's a lot of British stuff here." Small looked around the room.

"So we need to get word to the federal government," Peter said. "Get that check impounded."

"I'm afraid it's a little more complicated than that, Dr. Sheppard. It's actually a letter of credit, and the biggest chunk arrived yesterday. By now it's propping up some brokerage house in Singapore or God knows what—or where. Whatever amount they got has already been spent. You can count on that."

Sterk turned and hurled one of the embroidered pillows against the wall. Terri Johns watched it rebound into a china tea service and send cups and saucers flying. But she remained expressionless.

"It all started right over there," Small said, his scratchy voice like sandpaper. He pointed behind him at French doors that were partly obscured by dark red, velvet drapes.

Peter stepped to the doors while Sterk kept his eyes on Small, the young woman, and the secret passage. Peter looked inside. A lavishly appointed bed filled the center of the room. The bed curtain was eighteenth century red silk damask, and the outside fabric was a glazed chintz in matching colors. All of the room's appointments were bright red including a fully stocked wet bar covered in red leather, which occupied one corner of the spacious room. Just what every drug program needed, Peter thought.

In the background he could hear the First Lady. "Yes, this is a true friend of America and a truly dear friend of mine. The lady who started it all right here."

Doree... such a good caring person. Before Wolf corrupted her very soul. "That bastard," Peter said aloud, not caring who heard.

"You say something?" Sterk asked from the other room. Peter stepped to the doorway and peered at Sterk. When he turned his head to the right, he felt cold metal pressing against his neck. He raised both hands. Sterk fell to his knees and whipped out his automatic.

"Throw down the gun tough guy, or the shrink ends up with a tiny, shrunken head." The Hammer's strong, confident voice filled the room.

Before the gun hit the floor, several blue-shirts surrounded Sterk. A thorough search uncovered Sterk's carefully hidden weapons and the tiny tape recorder. A thick-necked man in his late twenties ran his hands down Peter's legs and searched his side pockets. He patted Peter's left thigh just below the gun. The Hammer opened the recorder and removed the microcassette that Sterk had labeled "Evidence—Good Soil." "Okay Sergeant Bullock, take them to one of the cells across from the communications bunker," the Hammer said. "Got to get back. Only a couple of minutes 'til Jenny goes on."

"The communications bunker?" Bullock raised both hands, palms up.

"Yeah, it's the only safe place for these two. I don't think it matters 'cause they won't remember much. The general will decide on their ah, future. Now move it."

Peter and Sterk made eye contact but said nothing.

Chapter 36

Four Lions pushed Peter and Sterk into the walk-in closet. The back of the closet opened onto a stone stairway that descended deep into the bowels of the ancient fortress. Moist, musty air greeted them about halfway down. The moldy dampness reminded Peter of his boyhood visits to his grandfather's farm cellar in Wisconsin.

Except for the shuffling footsteps of the two men and their captors, profound stillness filled the dark stairwell. Peter had counted thirty-six steps by the time they reached the bottom. They took a right turn into one of the many dark mazes lighted by elevated kerosene lamps and came to a wide gray door.

Bullock pushed it open, and they stumbled into a room filled with dazzling white light. Peter felt like a science fiction traveler moving from the twentieth century to the eighteenth century and then finally to the twenty-first century. The room resembled the flight-operations center of the Middle East Command Headquarters at nearby MacDill, Air Force Base. Five rows of analysts and technicians, perhaps fifty in all, sat behind TV sets, computers, and radar monitors. All wore the now familiar blue gray shirt with crossed leather shoulder straps. Peter had yet to see a female or minority in any position of authority.

A screen covering the front of the room blinked with dates, statistics, and rolling messages, much like a stock exchange. Peter managed to take a sideways glance at the monitors.

"Benson, J. school board—Cincinnati, Ohio. School clinic, + sex ed—contribute $5,000. Hit—Blair, Liz—March 17, Calores, Mexico—abort—reset—March 30. Cocaine drop—Merritt Island, Florida-April 3, 0600 hours—location 736. Starlyn Dalton—March 30—lobectomy—Dr. Stroud. Peter Sheppard—March 27."

Another monitor flashed a list of names under the heading, videotaped and contracted "Reverend James Harrington—Archdiocese of Milwaukee. Senator Lowell Jerrod—Cheyenne Wyoming. Benson Rutledge—V.P.—MCP Corp. Lt. Joe Penrod—FDLE. Goalie Darrell Jones—Montreal Rockets. J. Harry Rolfson III—Florida Supreme Court. Jesse Roberts—mayor—Atlanta, Georgia."

Prodded from behind, Peter and Sterk stumbled through the bunker's front door. Across a wide expanse of red clay a row of ash gray cells lined the wall. A faint sweet odor penetrated the cool, clammy air. What? Couldn't be. Incense?

Peter counted four cells. Carved from a solid wall of fieldstone, each cell had a black metal door with a one-foot opening and three vertical bars. They were headed to the last cell on the left. Several faces peered from adjacent doors. Was David Mendola one of them? And what about the Mexican boy? Was he really a prisoner here? The light was just too dim. To the right, near the first cell, large wooden packing crates formed an uneven pyramid.

Some twenty yards to the left, a grottolike cave with a timbered archway had also been carved out of rock. The black cavity reminded Peter of a one-eyed god of mythology. Bluish smoke drifted upward from the opening. Barely discernible, a small wooden cross was embedded in the top of the archway. The secret chapel mentioned on the microcassette?

Bullock slammed the door behind them. The room was about fifteen feet wide and twenty feet long. Peter guessed the ceiling to be fifteen feet high. Clearly defined rake marks covered the damp clay floor. Bullock glared at Sterk and wiggled his fingers through the bars. "We've got 'round the clock monitoring, so behave yourself. If you get bored, we have a great show going on in the chapel. Better than professional wrestling. Oh, and our fatso doc is busy, too, with a cute little bunny. Let's call her the Star of the Easter parade. She's going to have her memory fixed, real permanent-like. No charge, either." He laughed and turned away.

Peter touched Sterk's shoulder and cupped his other hand to the side of his mouth. "Penrod and Judge Rolfson, did you see? And they already had plans for Liz, even if she hadn't tried to break in here. And poor Starlyn. Liz is really going to take it hard—"

"Those bastards. And that guy Bullock used to be with the FDLE. That means they got some hired guns just in case those snotty-nosed Lions don't know which end is up."

"And Lt. Penrod," Peter said. You were right. Thank God I didn't pick up that gun at Aunt Trudy's."

Sterk pointed to a T.V. monitor hanging from the ceiling just above the door. The video camera's unblinking eye jutted from just beneath the monitor. Sterk's jaws moved slowly and deliberately. A cow chewing its cud. Filling his cheeks to capacity Sterk took only three tries before the camera lens wore a thick glob of reddish brown tobacco juice.

"That ought to improve our privacy a little." Sterk held his index finger over his lips and raised his eyebrows. Then he touched Peter's inner thigh and fingered the tiny gun. He put his lips to Peter's ear. "These sons-a-bitches sure aren't pros. Can't believe our luck."

Peter looked at the barren cell. "I don't feel very lucky."

"God-damn friggin' dungeon." Sterk surveyed the room. "Don't think the prison commission would approve of this place for our modern day bad guys. No racquetball courts, neither."

Peter looked away from the smiling detective.

The only light came from two narrow slits a foot from the ceiling. Six-inches wide and two-feet high, the primitive windows faced west, toward the bay. Sterk searched the ground on hands and knees. "Cleaner than a monkey's ass at the circus parade. Not even a paper clip or a cigarette butt. We're definitely in one of the old dungeons. Walls a couple feet thick, probably used as a holding cell by the Army."

Sterk squatted and used his finger to draw lines in the clay. "Look, here's the way I make it. General's big office is about the center of the fort, but the steps angled toward the bluffs."

"If we're that far underground, why the windows?" Peter pointed to the openings near the ceiling.

"That's what I mean. They built the fort against the cliffs. Part of the fort was actually dug out of mother earth."

"How did they get that communications bunker down here?"

"Its standard prefab, so it wasn't too hard. Not when you got lots of school kids for slave labor. And it's a damn good place to have it. Good security inside and out. I was down here as a kid. All open then, and I recall there was lots of executions in the ole days. Indians and Spanish killed each other off like it was coon huntin' season in Georgia. Did you see the old chapel? Burning incense or some damn thing in there."

Peter shook his head and peered upward. "None of that matters. The main thing now is look out one of those windows and get our bearings. I'll give you a boost up. Maybe you can hold on to those rough edges up there." Peter leaned sideways against the wall and put his hands together to form a step. Sterk climbed onto his shoulders, and the two men wavered precariously. Peter's face brushed against the rough stone wall. He felt Sterk reach higher toward the vertical bar centered in the narrow opening.

"Still can't see out. Gonna put a foot on your head. Hold my ankle, and don't move. There, got hold of the bar." Peter tried to steady his wobbling head.

"I can see a sidewalk and most of the bay. My God, boaters. Sail boats out there. Help! Help! Three or four sailboats, must be a race or somethin'. They're looking this way. Help!"

Sterk's bouncing feet jammed Peter's head against the jagged stone wall, and a hard leather sole dug into his left ear just before Sterk came crashing down. Landing feet first, Sterk rolled across the floor and slammed into the door. He jumped up and brushed damp red clay from his pants. "I guess being a paratrooper was worth somethin' after all."

Cut and bleeding, Peter wiped his forehead with his sleeve.

"But they saw me," Sterk said. "Maybe with the governor being here—maybe some gung-ho bureaucrat will check it out."

"I don't know," Peter said. "This has become a well known drug center. Most folks think it's full of juvenile lunatics on acid or something. Let's hope..."

"Might have a chance to blow our way out with that little cutie you got taped to your leg. Chief Longo and the Largo firefighters know we're here, and folks at the hospital should be able to put two and two together. The Seventh Cavalry will probably arrive in the nick of time." He grinned. A forced smile.

"I don't think so," Peter said. He held his lower eyelid to slow the flow of blood. "With Penrod on the other side we're pretty well cut off. Not even the people at the hospital know much about this place. Kathleen may have put two and two together, but even if she suspects we're out here it won't do much good. The few friends we have in the St. Pete P.D. are either inside the chapel as guests or outside doing security."

Sterk shot a stream of juice toward the camera lens. "Our priorities have changed."

"Huh?"

"We're not out here to clobber these mothers. Our new gig is to save our skins. We're—"

"Bang! Bang! Bang!" They turned to see two pointed black eyes staring through the barred window. "I warned you, Mr. "N.Y. P.D. Blues," Bullock said. The Chamber of Commerce doesn't approve of your big ugly mouth, especially when you're screaming out the window. Hurts the tourist trade. We got two calls already. And spitting your crud on our camera is a definite, for sure, no, no."

The cell door swung open and the muscular sergeant waved Sterk out. Sterk glanced at Peter, and his disgusted look said it all. Sterk followed Bullock out, and the door slammed shut. Peter shook his head. Great. Now what? The passive intellectual guy, the Phi Beta Kappa, who made his living talking to folks and understanding feelings, had the gun. The detective who bled gunmetal and sniffed his way through every kind of hard-nosed calamity was in solitary—without a weapon.

Maybe he should just sit tight. People wouldn't expect him to have the skills or experience to use the deadly pea-shooter strapped to his leg. He had used a .45 for target practice in the Air Force, but that was long ago. Peter sighed and looked at the barred door. Rationalizing. He knew it when he heard it, even coming from himself. Rationalizing to give himself any and every reason to sit this one out—-to protect his own hide.

Peter stared at the cell door and shook his head. He had to decide now. It was Miller Time, as they said in the beer commercials. He had talked big in the parking lot, but this was different. This wasn't like writing a research article on violence. Now he was facing real bullets. Real, flesh burning, blood letting bullets. He knew what he should do. Especially if he ever wanted to face Kathleen and the kids again. But did he have the raw guts to do it? And what in God's name could he do? The damned surveillance camera recorded every nook and cranny of the cell.

Peter took a deep breath. Then he stepped to the corner of the cell opposite the camera and stopped. He unzipped his fly and turned to face the wall. Tilting his head back, he imitated the ritual movements of baseball fans relieving full bladders at Al Lang Field. Reaching down with both hands, he freed the gun from its holster of tape. Then he pressed it tight against his stomach and chest and inched it into his left shirt pocket. Even if he did chicken out, it would still be good to have the gun. Maybe he could get it to Sterk. He had to get it to Sterk.

Chapter 37

Jenny Grant watched the Hammer takes long running strides toward her. "Thought you weren't gonna' make it, Colonel," David Mendola said. He relaxed his grip on Jenny's arm. Beaming, the Hammer jogged up the backstage steps.

"Almost didn't make it, but it made my day. We got the shrink again, and this time we'll finish the job. Even got the redneck." The Hammer cocked his head and stared at Jenny. David bit his lower lip and looked away.

They waited behind the curtain for the final invocation. Jenny could see the speaker's podium, but most of the stage was blocked from view. Dressed in a white linen suit with a southern gentleman's black bow tie, the handsome blond minister would have looked at home at the Kentucky Derby.

"The farmer went out sowing." The preacher waved his right hand above his head. "And some of what he sowed landed on the footpath where the birds came along and ate it. Some of the seed landed on rocky ground where it had little soil. It sprouted immediately because the soil had no depth. Then when the sun rose and scorched it, it began to wither for lack of water." The Reverend Robert Archibald Lee shook his head and scanned the audience.

"Again, some landed on thorns which grew up and choked it off, and there was no yield of grain." Springing to his full height and snapping his shoulders back, he put both hands around his throat and called out in a powerful voice. "Some seed finally landed on good soil... good soil, my friends! And it yielded grain that sprang up at a rate of thirty and sixty and a hundred fold. Hear me! The good soil yielded a hundred fold! Let him who has ears to hear, hear me!"

The Hammer squeezed the back of Jenny's neck. His calloused fingers dug into her skin as he jerked her to her toes. Searing pain took her breath away, and tears stung her eyes.

"Okay, no tricks my little cutesy. Remember your old man."

Jenny took a deep breath and walked slowly up the metal steps to the stage. When she got to the top, the governor and First Lady greeted her with a warm smile. Momentarily blinded by TV lights and flashing bulbs, she turned to face the vast audience.

Her mother sat in the front row dressed in a fashionable tweed business suit. Jenny shook her head. Things had been rough since her dad disappeared, and her mother always watched every penny. God, had her mom sold out too? She blinked her eyes to hold back the tears.

Just over her mother's shoulder she spotted Tiny Shutten standing in the second row of Soilers. Was he smiling? No, he was mouthing something and jerking his thumbs in a victory sign.

"Got it?... God dee?... Gone see?" Jenny smiled, thrust her thumbs high in the air, and took a deep breath. Tears filled her eyes. Then she pulled back her shoulders and turned to face the Hammer. Her smile broadened in response to his puzzled expression. The final strains of "Onward Christian Soldiers" left the packed chapel in hushed anticipation.

Jenny stood before the audience, great tears streaming down her cheeks. "Mother, I love you."

"I love you too, my darling girl," her mother said. "How are you, my dear?"

"I'm happy, Mother. I'm so happy—you know why? Because I'm not a druggie." The audience responded with warm applause. The governor and First Lady beamed their approval.

"I know, dear. You've come so far. We're all grateful to the Good Soil for this program." Doris Dantakovic and Benjamin Wolf smiled and clapped.

Jenny raised both arms to form a giant V. "No, Mother, that's not what I mean. I've never been a druggie."

A stunned murmur swept through the audience. Taut, drawn lines replaced the smug grins of government officials and Good Soil staff.

"All I ever had was two beers. You've got to believe me, Mom. They're trying to make us into druggies.!"

The Hammer bore down on Jenny, his boots pounding against the wooden stage. He grabbed her shoulder and covered the microphone.

"Exhausted—drug relapse, uh, poor girl."

"No, I'm not. Get your hands off me, you Nazi!" She fought to free herself, but the Hammer jerked her around and pinned her arms behind her back.

A deafening roar shook the rafters and jolted the audiance to shocked silence! One hundred and fifty screaming adolescents exploded from the bleachers. Running and shouting, they ran toward their parents and burst through the protective cordon of Lions.

A few parents fought against the Lions to free their offspring, but most parents helped the Lions contain the rebellious teenagers. Two secret service agents threw their bodies over the First Lady, who was forced to the floor along with the governor and other state and community leaders. Agents blocked the back doors. Lions, Soilers, and parents, were trapped within the tight confines of the chapel.

Jenny jumped from the stage and fought her way to her mother. On his back, Tiny Shutten struggled under a muscular, tattooed parent who held Shutten's arms behind his head. Jenny pulled on the man's shirt sleeves but couldn't dislodge him. Appearing out of the jungle of tangled bodies, David Mendola leapt onto the man's back and helped pull him aside.

Jenny glared at Mendola.

"It's okay," Shutten said. "He's with us all the way. For sure."

She shook her head. "We've got to free the committee. Let's move it. Now!"

"What about Wolf and the general?" Shutten asked. They watched Dantakovic and the psychiatrist make their way toward a back exit.

Jenny had to shout above the deafening noise. "Don't worry about them. Let's save our friends." A wave of backup Lions rushed into the chapel and cut off the backstage exit to the hallway. The spectator area was totally chaotic and unpassable. The First Lady and other officials lay stretched out on the stage, covered by secret service agents and the governor's bodyguards.

"Follow me." Jenny pushed her way to the stage and charged toward the governor and First Lady. One of the governor's bodyguards, a white-haired man with a pink, rounded face, raised his gun. But the First Lady pulled his arm down.

"My God, they're only kids. We can't—"

Some twenty Soilers scrambled past the agents who formed a human bridge over the V.I.P. party. Jenny looked back to see three agents spring to their feet, guns raised. The pursuing Lions would have to detour back through the mound of combatants on their way to the backstage exit.

Jenny led the pack of Soilers when they turned the corner into the security area behind the main waiting room. Totally unprepared for the onslaught of charging teenagers, one Lion and two secretaries watched the TV monitor. Shutten and Mendola wrestled the Lion to the floor, and Jenny pulled his sidearm from his holster. "My dad showed me how to use one of these."

Hurtling into the director's office, the Soilers ran at breakneck speed through the Victorian chambers and down the ancient steps toward the communication bunker. Stampeding feet raised an echo of rumbling thunder. They burst into the bunker, and Jenny shouted the orders. "Put your hands on the monitors where I can see them. You along the wall, both hands up there." She pointed the gun at three high-ranking Lions who huddled in one corner. "Hands on the wall. Face the wall, and spread 'em."

A tall, square-shouldered Lion lunged for the back door. One of the girls screamed. Jenny pulled the trigger and a quarter-sized black hole exploded in the prefab wall in front of the Lion's head. The acrid smell of gun powder filled the silent room. "Let's get our friends," Jenny said. She led the white-smocked Soilers through the back door to the old execution field. Shutten and Mendola stayed back to disarm and guard the prisoners. As soon as Jenny stepped onto the clay surface facing the cells, a volley of bullets shattered the windows just above her. Jenny and the others flattened themselves behind a two-foot mound of dirt that surrounded the bunker. Spread out across the field, a dozen Lions fired hundreds of rounds of ammunition into the bunker walls. Splinters of glass flew in every direction.

~

Peter heard the thunder of small arms fire and hurried to the cell door. Twenty yards away, a dozen Lions in firing position formed a ragged line on the clay floor. Peter could see the communication bunker's bullet-ridden facade across the wide field.

The robust sergeant pressed his prominent nose between the bars and smiled. "Looks like some of the Soilers want to be naughty boys and girls. They're gonna be real sorry." He chuckled. "The Hammer doesn't handle stress real well. He's on his way down here right now. Oh, and I just had a little visit with your buddy, Mr. hard-ass. Guess what? We moved him to the lab. Maybe they'll look inside his pointy little head to see what makes him tick. So you're on your own, Doc."

"So are you, Sergeant," Peter replied. He pushed the barrel of the black automatic against the sergeant's forehead and released the safety. "Keep looking straight into my eyes and unlock the door." Bullock hesitated, and his eyes narrowed. Finally Peter heard metallic sounds as the keys brushed against the door. The door inched slowly inward. Peter kept the gun barrel flush against the sergeant's forehead. The door came to a stop against Peter's foot.

Okay, put your hands through the bars."

Bullock glared at Peter. "You're not going to shoot me. I know your type. All talk and no—"

Peter pressed the gun harder against Bullock's forehead. "You're right. I'm not the type. That should scare you. I know it scares me. Now shut up." Peter shifted the gun to his left hand and used his right hand to tape the sergeant's wrists together. Then he shoved the automatic into his pocket and taped Bullock's mouth.

The burley young man peered upward at the unforgiving camera. "That doesn't matter," Peter said. "I think time has run out. What has to be done—has to be done. Now. Before someone is killed." Peter stared at the cell door. Well, this is it. No going back. He checked his watch. Was the darn thing even working? The second hand seemed to stop along the circular path, taking a rest at each point. He tapped its clouded face with a wet finger and shook his wrist. Then he wiped the wet smudge against his shirtsleeve.

He took a deep breath, stepped through the open door, and shouted in an alien voice, "FBI!" Peter raised his arm and pulled the trigger.

Blam! Blam! Blam!

The gun's kick drove his arm down, and the thundering blasts left his ears numb and ringing. The bitter smell of gun powder seared his nostrils. Would they buy this charade? Peter's many years of counseling impressionable young people told him they would… Probably. Wide-eyed Lions stared over their shoulders, and several dropped their guns.

"Okay, drop those weapons, we've got you covered all around. Drop 'em. Now!"

Thump. Thump. Thump. The dull sounds of guns striking the clay surface were the cheerful notes of a victory anthem. Jenny and the other Soilers peered over the low mounds of dirt.

"Come over and get these guns." Peter waved the tiny gun. Would this bluff really work?

Jenny and the other Soilers sent up a shout of triumph. Skipping over the clay surface with arms raised in celebration, they had covered half the distance between the bunker and the squad of Lions when a shot exploded above them!

"Hold it right there, druggies. This is Lieutenant Joe Penrod with the Florida Department of Law Enforcement. You're all under arrest. Drop your guns. You too, Sheppard. Don't make me finish what I started before."

Didn't Penrod know they had spotted him on the computer list? A cold river of sweat washed Peter's forehead. He squeezed the gun butt to keep his hands from shaking. His little .25 automatic couldn't hit the wide side of a barn. He knew that—but even worse— so did Penrod. As though reading his mind, Penrod pointed the powerful nine mm weapon straight at him. Kathleen and the kids, would he ever see them again? He pictured himself pulling Marie around and around in lazy circles, her high-pitched giggles filling his ears.

Silence. Peter and Penrod stared down each other's gun barrels while Soilers and Lions froze, puppet-like, in breathless silence. Even the Hammer, directly behind Penrod, stood motionless. Peter tried to swallow, but his throat was too dry. Would he throw up? He felt tears of fear filling his eyes. His quivering chin would surely give him away?

"Drop the gun, Lieutenant Penrod," said a soft but firm voice from the bunker door. "This really is the FBI."

Peter saw his old friend, Dave Milliken, standing just outside the bunker. The square-shouldered ex-Marine pointed his huge black gun—it looked like a cannon—at Penrod's back. Sheriff Jamaar Harris stood just behind Milliken. Penrod did not hesitate. His gun made a muffled sound when it landed on the damp surface.

But before the gun hit the ground, a roar of celebration rolled across the red clay floor. Soilers hugged each other, jumped up and down, and danced in circles. Like students at a high school pep rally, the teenagers cried and screamed and laughed and touched and hugged for joy. Their eyes sparkled now as they raised their arms to salute their greatest victory.

David Mendola ran to Peter and stretched out his hand, but Peter grabbed him in a gigantic bear hug and pulled him off his feet. Whirling

David around, Peter saw Soilers burst from the other three cells. Peter shook hands with Milliken. "Sure glad you came, Dave."

"So am I, Peter," the muscular agent said. "Got an anonymous phone call that we traced back to Mexico. That led us to the hospital, and things just started falling into place." He laughed. "But we were a bit surprised to find Kathleen impersonating her sister."

"What? What happened?"

"Found her in Liz Blair's bed. Kathleen hadn't let her sister talk her into breaking any rules since they were kids."

Peter chuckled and shook his head. "And then to be caught by the FBI. But what about Dr. Wolf and the gen—ah, Doris Dantakovic?"

"Just got here so I don't know their status." Milliken looked at Peter. "Why don't you head for home? You look exhausted. We'll follow up with these folks. We're searching for a floppy with the layout of this place. Liz thinks she found one when she was out here, but they must have lifted it after they assaulted her. And Kathleen said she was still a little fuz—"

Another chorus of vibrant shouts bounced into the cell block. Covered with a gray V.A. hospital blanket, and followed by a dozen Soilers, Starlyn Dalton rode on Sterk Trump's shoulders. Her eyes were dull and unfocused, and rivets of tears splashed down her pale cheeks. Behind Starlyn, and helping support her, Liz Blair beamed a soft, glowing smile. Peter squeezed Starlyn's hand and hugged Liz.

Liz gave Starlyn a kiss, and Starlyn leaned her head against Liz's shoulder. "This is my girl," Liz said. She looked at Peter. "Star's a little woozy, but we got there before that goon was able to use his ice pick."

"His what?" Peter covered his face with his hands. It felt like someone was sitting on his shoulders and pushing him down. But he couldn't stop now. Maybe it wasn't rational, but he felt personally responsible for Wolf and Doris—and their unholy clinic. He had a hunch. It was a long shot, but he needed to play it out. It was the least he could do.

Chapter 38

Despite police roadblocks, Peter made the trip from the Good Soil to the V.A. Hospital in less than an hour. He slowed and pulled Liz's Jaguar into the hospital parking lot. He really didn't expect to find Wolf's cherry-red Lincoln Continental nearby. If Peter's hunch was correct, he would find Wolf and Doris hiding in the main building. The couple probably drove south from the Good Soil compound, ditched the Lincoln, and hailed a taxi. Maybe Doris wasn't with him. Funny how he had always protected her and hoped she would come to her senses—hoped she would realize Peter was her true love?

He took the small staff elevator to the third floor and walked down the narrow corridor past the psychology offices to the east wing. The old east wing was rarely used now. Not even for research.

It still housed the antiquated amphitheater that had showcased grand rounds back in the forties. How ironic that Peter's memories of Wolf's abusive power had given Peter the clue he needed. When Peter had followed Wolf's posthypnotic suggestions and danced like a chicken at grand rounds in '72, it almost cost him his career. But during those foggy sessions when Wolf ostensibly taught Peter the latest techniques in hypnosis, Wolf would wander off on egoistic muses that covered a multitude of subjects.

One such notion was prompted by the popular T.V. show, "The Fugitive." Wolf maintained that no criminal had ever hidden in a hospital. He further declared that most large V.A. Hospitals had out-of-the-way places that were rarely used, and felons could make nighttime forays to the hospital kitchen for food.

Peter slowly eased open the glass-ribbed fire-door and stepped into the amphitheater. All was quiet. Wolf would probably be holed up in one of the small offices in the back. He wrinkled his nose at the musty odor. Steep rows of brown wooden seats' rose from the stage and gave the room a cold, impersonal feel. No life in this place, he thought, none whatsoever. Gray walls and black metal shelves held bent and broken medical equipment—and human specimens. No light, no tension, no movement. A library without books, an amusement park without people, a morgue without bodies.

Cortical sections floated inside murky bell jars covered with cobwebs. He blew a heavy layer of blue-gray dust from the cover of a glass container marked C.C. 42 and reached in to scoop up a human brain. Rivulets of bluish green fluid squirted from the gray cortex onto brown paper towels that covered the black metal table. The feather-light weight always surprised him. He lifted the awesome matter to his face and examined the soft ridges and clear convolutions. Somewhere in those billions of brain cells the records of a past life were encoded. The senior prom, the fresh smell of autumn—the first flicker of love. Yet all the colors of the rainbow were reduced to the same gray intellectual source. Truly, the common denominator. Peter sniffed the sour air and shuddered. He imagined a body on stage and surgeons in bloody gowns working feverishly over a screaming patient.

He pulled out the tiny automatic and checked the clip. Five rounds remained. When he pushed open the hallway door on the right side of the amphitheater, he was greeted by the suffocating smell of stale, moldy air. Peter stepped slowly down the center of the dark hallway, his steps muted by the worn institutional green carpet.

What was that? Doris's voice? She was sobbing. Peter gulped. No, she was crying her heart out. Was that bastard still abusing her? Peter rounded the corner and saw a light under one of the office doors. He stopped, took a deep breath, and reached for the doorknob.

Crash! The milky glass window exploded in his face, and the door gave way. Someone had given him a powerful shove from behind. He landed hard on his right shoulder just in front of a long metal desk. Doris sat behind the desk, wide-eyed, tears coursing down her cheeks. He peered upward to see Benjamin Wolf towering over him. The rotund man glared down, goggle-eyed. "You're not going to stop us, Sheppard. Not now. Not ever." Wolf pointed his left index finger and raised his right arm over his head. He held a rusty metal rod.

"No Ben. No!" Doris stood and leaned over the desk. "We have nothing to hide, Peter. It's, it's just that we panicked. And Ben thought..."

Peter looked at Doris. Even now with tears streaming down her cheeks, her loveliness tore at his heart. "Pick up the phone," Peter said. He felt the handle of the gun in his pocket, but he had to give her a chance.

"No!" Wolf shouted and took a step toward Peter.

Doris swallowed hard and shook her head. Then she reached for her cell phone. Wolf just stood and watched. Doris tapped in the numbers, and Peter identified the acoustical tones "nine-one-one." Wolf lurched sideways and leaned against the desk before regaining his balance and dropping into a soiled plastic chair. A single tear balanced on his right eyelash. Head bent, he covered his face with his hands.

"I promised to take care of you Doris, but I didn't do a very good job, did I?" Wolf asked.

⁓

As soon as Jenny knew Starlyn was safe, she found John Lifewater and they started to search for the Hammer. Not finding him in the communications bunker or underground classrooms, they approached agent Milliken, who had taken over the general's lavish office.

In the corner near the fireplace FBI and FDLE agents, St. Petersburg police, and Pinellas County sheriff's deputies studied maps of Bellair and the beaches. Reporters and camera crews surged forward, but state troopers formed a barricade inside the receptionist's office to keep them at bay. Technicians were setting up TV cameras and microphones in the general's bedroom for a press conference scheduled to begin in thirty minutes.

"I'm sorry, folks, but Eric Hamlier and a few of his top cronies seem to have escaped in the confusion," Milliken said. "We've cordoned off the whole area from Tarpon Springs to Sarasota. Hopefully he's still out here on the beaches somewhere. Either of you hear him talk about other contacts out this way?"

Jenny looked at Lifewater. "No," she said. "They knew we were trying to break out, so they didn't tell us anything."

The agent turned to speak into his phone. Exiting past FBI agents wearing black jackets and carrying semiautomatic rifles, Jenny and Lifewater headed to the chapel. David Mendola, Hal Jacobson, and Tiny Shutten followed close behind. When they reached the chapel, Lifewater led them past the confessional to the old storage room.

"I know where the bastards are," Lifewater said. "My grandfather taught me how to do some tracking, and with this red clay it was easy to follow the footprints. When they led straight into a stone wall, I knew something was up."

"Yeah, we know about it, too," Jenny said. "I was down there a couple of times. One time with David and Tiny."

"Good, that will help my plans. I scared the hell out of Billy Ray Thomas when he made you go down there, Jenny. He probably still has a headache. We've got to stop the Hammer before he escapes. I figure he'll wait until dark and then try to break out."

Hal Jacobson stepped between Jenny and Lifewater.

"Don't you think we should let the police handle this? Those guys are nuts. And they're armed. Let the cops do their job."

John Lifewater took a deep breath and peered at Jacobson.

"No—it's a matter of honor. If you guys aren't in, I'll do it myself."

"I'm in," Jenny said softly.

"Me, too," David Mendola said, nodding his head.

John peered down at Tiny Shutten.

"Hell yes, Geronimo, bring 'em the hell on."

"You guys ever heard of a safety blitz?" John stepped to the blackboard and picked up a piece of chalk. Moving his hand quickly across the board, he drew lines and patterns that resembled the x's and o's of a football play. John gave each of them an assignment. Then he raised his arms.

"Looks like Little Big Horn, part two, my friends. May the great Breath Giver be with you."

Chapter 39

The Hammer peered at the elevated burial mounds and black cavernous dungeon. His head nodded, and he struggled to stay awake. His elite officers huddled in darkness near the now empty grave. The only reminder of Gonzie's entombment was his white soiler's gown which rested in neat folds near one corner of the shallow pit. The Hammer was desperate for sleep, but knew he couldn't trust these idiots for five minutes.

"This place gives me the willies," Danny O'Brien said.

"Shut up and have a joint." The Hammer tossed the new fledged colonel a crumpled bag of marijuana. "And keep your god-damned mouth shut. I'm surrounded by weaklings, not a brain in the whole bunch. Now listen up. We'll wait until three-thirty or four and take the general's passageway. And when I get out of here, some people are sure as hell gonna pay. Big time." He stared at his huddled officers through squinted eyes.

O'Brien swallowed hard. "I'm not afraid or nothin' Eric, but I saw something when we hit the nun. Something out there where that dead priest is buried. A couple of other guys saw it too." Breaker Mitchum sucked in a gulp of pungent smoke and moved closer to O'Brien.

The frightened young men recounted stories of the walking dead while invisible clouds of smoke billowed upward. The drugs, which had previously led to euphoric silliness, now heightened their feelings of fear and panic. The Hammer laughed. "I think I'll catch a few winks while my hard-nosed, combat ready troops look for fairies and goblins." He rolled up his jacket and eased his head down.

The recurrent nightmare had pursued his dreams since early childhood. Even as he dreamed, he knew it was coming, knew he couldn't stop it, knew he couldn't shake himself awake. Like a nauseating cloud the terrible obsession rolled on and on.

"Run, run!" But he realized once again that this was part of the dream. It had already started. He is a little boy about seven or eight, holding hands with his tiny sister. He follows the big bosomed woman, her blond pigtails bouncing as she inches across the swinging rope bridge. A harmonica's discordant whine screams along the edge of the wind. An old song. An old wartime ballad.

"Mother!" Eric shouts. But she keeps moving and does not look back. He clutches the flimsy, shredded ropes and peers into the deep gorge below. The woman stops and turns.

"Come. Come!" Fierce winds obscure her words.

Then it happens, as it always does. The terrible odor of decay and the pressure bursting inside his chest. The black hairy paw and long painted fingernails tearing at the fragile bridge, sending his little sister down, down into the open mouth of the hideous monster. He watches, helpless, as his sister drops into the purple folds of the wet, foaming tongue.

He can't wake up, and knows he has no choice. No choice but to wait for the nightmare to start again, and again—and again.

⁓

One hundred feet away, obscured by darkness, Jenny Grant watched the Hammer and his men from the top of a ten-foot-high Indian mound. Just below, and to her left, chiseled letters fronted a cracked, mildewed tomb. "Cancer de Barbastro."

John Lifewater crouched on all fours, next to Jenny. She smiled. No one seeing him now could ever question his intensity. Not even his coaches. Would the Hammer still dare to call him Tonto? John's face, blackened with the martyr's soil, gave the illusion of huge white eyeballs and piercing black irises. A thick leather coverlet with protruding buffalo horns encased his head, and feathered eagle wings covered his arms. John had told her that these ceremonial costumes from the chapel weren't authentic Sioux, but they would have to do.

Jenny peered at the circle of men who surrounded the sleeping Hammer. Breaker Mitchum twisted his neck and raised his eyes. Jenny smiled. Mitchum had heard it. Soft yelping sounds from opposite sides of the vast cavern. Louder and louder the pained cries filled the great hall. Mitchum, Danny O'Brien, and Billy Ray Thomas sat stiffly, their eyes darting from side to side as the bloodthirsty cadences swept over the dark expanse of tombs.

Jenny shook her head. It even scared her, and now she knew where the sounds came from. Then she heard running footsteps. David Mendola, and Tiny Shutten came barreling up the side of the steep mound. Gasping for breath, Hal Jacobson lumbered up the mound after them and sunk to his knees.

Breaker Mitchum shook the Hammer and pleaded with him to wake up. Like phobic children terrified of the dark, the Hammer's men looked to their all knowing parent for support. Curled in a fetal position, the Hammer lay still, his eyes closed. John Lifewater looked at Jenny and chuckled. "Live by the grass, die by the grass."

Finally after repeated but tenuous shaking by Mitchum, the Hammer pushed himself to a sitting position. His head rolled lazily, like a ball on a tether. Then he shuddered and reached for his black Uzi.

"Here goes," John said. With rocket like speed the fullback cum-Sioux-warrior hurled himself forward, jumping conch mounds and decaying monuments as he streaked toward the six disoriented Lions. Building speed and momentum John dug deep into the moist red clay and sprinted up the back of a protruding burial mound. Arms to his sides, the human arrow lifted into the air.

"Hi, ho, Tonto. Away!"

Dropping out of the darkness like the black shroud of an avenging spirit, he speared the groggy Hammer's head. The sound of crunching bones paralyzed the Lions.

Rolling to his feet, Lifewater crouched over the unconscious tyrant. As the huddled Lions looked on, bugeyed, he held the Hammer's glorious ponytail straight up before cutting it off with a ten-inch surgical blade.

O'Brien and Mitchum turned to run but were cut down by more human arrows that flew through the air emitting hideous, yelping screams. Homing in on the enemy like guided radar missiles, Mendola, Jacobson, and Jenny Grant were poor imitations of the speedy Lifewater, but they played their parts to the hilt.

"Hi, ho, Tonto!" they screamed.

Tiny Shutten dropped from the sky like a diver doing a cannon ball, tattooed lightening bolts shimmering on both arms. He landed on O'Brien's back and rode him into the soft clay. Then he whirled and kicked Billy Ray Thomas squarely between his legs.

"Enough," said the courageous warrior of strong heart. "Our honor has been satisfied."

~

Jenny stopped at the bottom of the stairs and watched the candle light procession move past crumbling graves and sloping Indian mounds. The steady clinking of the gold censer reverberated through the vault releasing aromatic clouds of incense. The slow, plodding walk of the celebrants, burdened by the souls of the departed, resembled an ancient church ritual.

Jenny shivered. The heavy weight of sin in this All-Souls-Day ceremony was the 180 pounds of Eric Hamlier, lying unconscious on the improvised stretcher. When the weaving line reached the bottom of the stairway, it straightened and moved up the rugged stone steps. Flickering candlelight filled every corner of the dark chamber.

Breaker Mitchum held the front of the stretcher, both hands behind his head as he bent forward under the heavy burden. Danny O'Brien was in the back, his head under the stretcher and his hands above his head supporting its sides.

David Mendola led the slow moving column and swung the censer from side to side. Purifying clouds of smoke cleared the way for the weary band of pilgrims. Immediately behind the stretcher came Jenny Grant and Tiny Shutten followed by three Lions who clutched the cold, wet wall like children who had lost their way.

Following the Lions came Hal Jacobson, grunting and perspiring as he played the ram's horn and eyed the uneven steps and deep chasm below. Notes of the traditional shofar filled the black chamber and blended with the sweet, heavy scent of incense.

John Lifewater trailed the procession by some thirty feet. He seemed unafraid of the sinister tombs and enveloping darkness. Lifewater shuffled a Sioux victory dance, the dance of the Great Plains, of the people described as the greatest horsemen of all time.

Jenny shook her head and smiled. The boy-warrior had shown her his T-shirt. The orange and purple luminescent lettering read "In 1492, Native Americans Discovered Columbus, Lost at Sea." Was he wearing it now?

Jacobson peered back at his Indian friend. In a strong, even voice he repeated the words of an old testament verse. "He shall cover thee with His feathers—under His wings shalt thou trust. Thou shalt tread on the lion and adder—the young lion and dragon shalt thou trample under foot."

Like knights from a much earlier time, the young crusaders had done what they had to do. Not filled with the bittersweet fruit of revenge satisfied, but knowing what was required, they had obediently played out their roles. Now they were ready to go home.

And on the makeshift stretcher the Hammer at last enjoyed a dreamless sleep.

The End

Epilogue

Kathleen handed Peter another ornament. "I can't wait to see the kids' faces in the morning."

"We've been truly blessed, haven't we?" Peter gave her a tight hug.

"And Mark's progress is the greatest miracle of all. A's and B's on his report card, and friends calling every night."

"I know," Peter said. "We'll need to buy him his own phone if this keeps up. But playing goalie in soccer and managing the baseball team? It just doesn't seem possible."

"Maybe the operation had a delayed effect."

"I don't know, but it all seemed to turn around when Liz started helping him with the conservation group."

Kathleen nodded. "It's as though the flight of the wounded eagle somehow freed Mark from his mental straightjacket. Mark just seemed to zoom along with him."

Peter knew it was one of those moments. They had felt them before, but with each renewal there was greater closeness, greater intimacy. It wasn't just love, and it wasn't just happiness. It was a sense of completeness. A sense of things coming together in their rightful order... A tiny glimpse of eternity? They had helped to create a moment, and they accepted that moment with a deep sense of gratitude.

He looked up at the twelve-foot Christmas tree. Perhaps the season itself had something to do with it. But why not? In the background, Mehalia Jackson's voice boomed prayerfully. "Oh Come All Ye Faithful—Joyful and Triumphant."

Little Marie had just scampered up the stairs clutching her giant teddy bear and singing an off key "Jingle Bells." Reprimanded back to her bed several times, she had finally agreed, along with her doting father, that it was time for her to go to sleep.

Peter's hand groped beneath sparkling tinsel waterfalls to a mound of red and green packages stacked neatly under the tree. Evergreen sap filled the air with the aroma of childhood and innocence, transforming the room to a safe, magical place.

"It's an early present. I, ah, wanted you to have it."

Kathleen tugged at the purple ribbon. "It's a book, I can tell. Oh, Peter—Gibran—The Prophet. How lovely. And the inscription." She hugged Peter with gentle arms and buried her face in his neck.

"It, I got one, once, from, ah, a friend. I wanted you to have a new one. You're my friend... and my love."

The sound of carolers filled the front of the house. Peter stepped to the window and watched a candle-light procession wind its way up the sidewalk. Still holding an odd little English ornament, showing a blue and silver mouse jumping out of a box, he opened the door. Continuing to sing, the carolers marched through the entryway and into the living room. A draft of crisp winter air, surprising for Florida, surrounded the red cheeks and spirited voices.

"Welcome," Peter said. "Welcome." But the minstrels would not be denied. They sang an enthusiastic and surprisingly harmonious rendition of "Rudolph the Red Nosed Reindeer." When they finished their song, Kathleen and Peter led them through the kitchen to the sunroom overlooking the bay. They sat around a large circular glass table in front of the picture window. Kathleen poured eggnog.

Liz held up her hands. "I've got a surprise. That's why Barrett and I got Polly to drag poor Sterk out here."

Peter looked at Sterk. The detective didn't smile. "I was workin' on my boat," he said. "You got a beer, Peter?" Despite the unseasonably cold weather, Sterk wore his trademark Bermudas. Peter opened the refrigerator and found him a can of Budweiser.

Liz waved a picture over her head. "It's a Christmas card from—guess who? Gonzie."

"So, he's okay?" Sterk leaned forward. "What did he say in the card?"

"Well, it's written on the back of the same picture I got in Mexico. It shows the Santa Maria Church in San Pedro. I can speak a little Spanish, but I can't read much at all. Anybody?"

After the others shook their heads, Peter nodded and Liz passed him the card. A wave of scarlet and emerald colors from Christmas lights along the top of the north window danced like tongues of flame on the little blue and gold church.

"Dear Miss Blair." Peter enunciated each word in a clear voice, without effort.

"You are my friends. I know you will continue to love the children. Because of this, the project will bear fruit. Stay together as if one.

"I am sorry I did not get to see all of you face to face. But I am back where I belong. I look forward to your next visit. My father and my uncle also send their regards. Wish you were here.

"Jesús Gonzalez.

"P.S. Please bring a McDonald's quarter pounder and large fries when you come."

Liz burst out laughing. Peter studied the new Liz Blair. Her face was no longer the impenetrable rock, split by the sharp needles of a cactus plant. A gentle smile opened like a little girl's grin, reborn in innocence.

"Jesús, Jesús." Peter shook his head. "Now I know where I heard that name. "Jesús, Gonzalez. JG. Sure, that was the name on the perfect MMPI. Never saw one like it."

"I've got another surprise, too." Liz smiled and kissed Barrett Spangler on the cheek.

"Yep, I asked her the big question down at the Saint Vincent de Paul Shelter," Barrett said, holding Liz's hand to reveal a common brass wedding ring. "We ate leftover lasagna off paper plates. Best damn meal I ever had."

Liz put her arm around Kathleen's shoulder. "So, happy ever after, just like in the fairy tales. And the bad guys are in jail."

"May not be that easy," Sterk said. "Latest stuff from Milliken and the others shows Wolf and Dantakovic really didn't know what was comin' down. It's like Dr. Small said. Wolf just made rounds and signed orders. The staff and Soilers were scared to death of Dantakovic cause they thought she was the general. But it looks like she never went near the place. Just a figurehead."

"But if Dantakovic isn't the general, who is?" Liz asked.

"A real mystery all right. Could be years before we nail the top honcho. They sure as hell went out of their way to make Dantakovic look bad, and Wolf too, as a matter of fact."

"What about the Hammer, maybe he was running things?"

"Yeah, he's a bad one all right, Liz, but we don't think he's the mastermind. I have a feelin' he won't tell us a hell of a lot. They say he's got some brain damage after his run in with that Lifewater kid. Peter knows about it. That young shark's gonna live in the big house for a long, long time. And he'll be afraid to blow the whistle on the general, whoever he is."

Liz stood. "I want to say something. Maybe I don't have the right. Maybe I'm just being impulsive." Liz looked at Kathleen.

Kathleen smiled and nodded.

"Well, I don't know where to start," Liz said. "El Dios Verde. Maybe that's as good a place as any. I was so skeptical when I saw that incredible light in San Pedro. It wasn't until Gonzie came to the hospital that I understood what it was all about. The miracles of Easter Sunday. Gonzie rising to show us the way, the flight of the eagles… the newly christened city of Leningrad…. And that glorious red sky. Why then? Why the same day? And the apparition of the Virgin in Clearwater?"

Sterk put down his beer and stared at her.

Liz held out her hands, palms up. "I thought it was just my religious training. I saw religious symbolism in everything. Just another pathetic soap opera. But now… now I know better. It wasn't about me. I'm just one part of a much bigger story. And it wasn't just those glorious miracles because there were bigger miracles by far. Like my finding myself. Like really learning to love myself. And Mark getting better. And finding Barrett. And finding my dear sister, Kathleen."

Tears filled Liz's eyes and she swallowed hard. "And finding Star, the daughter I never had. I didn't tell you, but I've been accepted into the Big Sisters' program to work with Star. And her dad wants me to help. I was accepted immediately." She looked at Barrett. "And I got in on my own. That's another miracle. And Peter. Of course, dear Peter."

Kathleen stood and pulled Liz close. Surprised by two big tears that sat heavy on his eyelashes, Peter wiped his eyes with his fingers. Sterk bit off a plug of Bandit chewing tobacco and shifted his shoulders from side to side. "I think you got it about right, Liz," Sterk said. "But what I don't understand is why here. And why now?"

Liz smiled. "You were the first one to figure that out, Sterk. If it can happen in St. Pete, it can happen anywhere. Sociologists love this place. With an older population and no room for expansion, this little peninsula is like a crystal ball. They say it has most of the problems other cities will face fifty years from now."

Sterk dribbled tobacco juice into his empty beer can. "They was really after the money, and they got most of that."

"But Peter's voucher program is already helping," Liz said. All of the failing schools have improved their test scores dramatically, and the new governor is pushing parent choice like there's no tomorrow."

"Liz is right about the Good Soil," Peter said. "They were more than just a few opportunistic psychopaths. They were well organized, and they were trying out their programs here to see how they'd fly. And it's amazing when you think about it. We all worked so hard. Those kids out at the Good Soil, Jenny, David—and John. And all of you. And even the FBI. But it took a crippled Mexican peasant to finally stop them."

Liz smiled. "And in St. Peter's City, no less. But you're right, Sterk. They got the money, and they'll strike again. I'm sure of that."

Peter heard a faint sound he couldn't identify. Was it the front door chime? Who would be calling at this time of night? And on Christmas Eve? He stepped quickly through the kitchen and down the three steps to the entryway but hesitated as he reached the door. Then he checked the doorlock and peered out the side window. The Federal Express driver looked exhausted and probably had many more deliveries ahead of him. Why was he so suspicious?

Peter released the lock and opened the door to a rush of frosty air. The driver quickly handed over a large gift wrapped box. Signing off on the form, Peter looked at the return address. England? He walked past the living room entrance and into the deserted family room.

Wrapped in gold foil the box was stamped "Fragile." Under the address another stamp read "Open Immediately—Perishable Goods."

Cutting through the heavy gold string with his Swiss army knife, Peter continued to feel rattled. A legion of invisible flies made its way up his forearms. He tugged at his shirt collar. Pulsating heat burned his neck and chest. Was it the eggnog? He tore open the tape, and the suffocating fever continued to rise. A letter bomb? He shook his head. Too many trips to England?

Inside the box a white envelope was taped to a brown paper bag. As he opened the flap of the envelope with his thumb nail, he could smell the musky odor of a vaguely familiar perfume. Cascades of tiny purple flowers of elaborate Victorian design flowed down the left margin of the ivory-white stationery. He held the letter under Kathleen's reading lamp and let his eyes travel over the lavender script. Leaning back he felt prickly heat moving up his chest. Peter kept his eyes riveted on the brief message and took a deep breath.

"Jesus, Mary and Joseph." He sat for a few seconds, then took another deep breath. Finally he pushed himself up. Like an uninvited party guest who claims to be a relative, the embellished paper sat boldly on the glass coffee table,

Peter studied the elaborate script as though staring it down would help. But it didn't.

"Dearest Peter "Here is the church—and here is the steeple. Open the doors, and see all the—pitiful people!

"I must say I'm surprised that someone with your education could fall for the neurotic rituals of the masses—and a rosary yet!?

"The next time we go to the beach you'll get what you've been dreaming about. That is, if you've been a good boy!

"Love,

"General Belle Von Hamlier

"P.S. My dear Father sends his regards."

~

At the bottom of the page a small circle contained two intersecting triangles. Over twenty years, but the memory was clear and chilling. Precocious little Belle dancing in circles, golden pigtails flying. What had her mother said? Full of the devil like her father. Yes, that was it. Like her father.

Peering into the brown paper bag he immediately recognized the bright red-orange wig. Sweat coated his underarms, and his hands shook. Standing, he continued to stare at the wig and letter. Then he placed them back into the box. Holding tight to the railing, he climbed the stairs to his bedroom.

Peter picked up the phone and dialed. "Agent Milliken, please. No, that's okay. Just let him know it's urgent." He sat on the bed and cradled his head in his hands. Now, for the first time, it was clear. Only too clear. He turned his head as though trying to avoid the grotesque reality that faced him. Could people really be this conniving? This evil? It wasn't enough for the so called "Baron" to use Doris' kids, Eric and Belle, to carry out his dirty legacy. But he had used the kids to destroy their own mother, and Benjamin Wolf, the man who had won her heart. The Baron had never forgiven Wolf for freeing Doris from his abusive control.

The phone rang. Peter talked in low tones to avoid waking the kids. "Interpol? I thought that was only on TV. Oh, and Dave, you might want to check on a Baron Von Hamlier, now possibly in England." He hung up.

"Dad?"

Peter stepped into Mark's room and sat on the bed. A silver framed bird sanctuary petition hung over Mark's headboard. The signatures of the president and First Lady were clearly visible. Bending, he took Mark's hand and gave him a kiss on the forehead.

"Who was on the phone? Something wrong?" A tight frown pushed Mark's eyebrows together.

"No, just a business call. Nothing to worry about."

A gold necklace hung over the bedpost near Mark's pillow. The moon's reflected glow showered the necklace with sparkling silver and gold highlights. Peter turned his head. The necklace appeared to hang in midair, like some celestial apparition.

Then Peter recognized it. How could he ever forget? Liz Blair had worn it to her first counseling session. He had worried about schizophrenia. He lifted the heavy wooden pendant. "Beautiful. Looks expensive. Where'd you get it?"

"I've had it for a while in a box under my bed." Mark looked down. "Kind of like a little shrine. Mom thought I should put it up. You know, with Christmas and..."

"It's really impressive. Gorgeous."

Mark sat up. "The Mexican boy gave it to me."

"You saw—"

"Easter morning, when everything turned red. At the bird sanctuary. He said it was an Icon. He said it was worth a lot of money. It's got the Father, Son, and Holy Spirit. See." Mark pointed to the glazed inset panels that formed a triangle on the pendant.

"I thought you were with Aunt Liz and the conservation group on Easter Sunday?"

"I was. But when the sun came up and everything turned red, I got lost for a few minutes. Aunt Liz didn't get there 'til later. The other kids wanted to go through the Boggie Woods up toward the bay, to see better."

"Did you go?"

"I tried. But back then I was, ah, you know—kinda weak." Mark looked away. "I sat on a broken tree limb to rest. That's when I met the crippled boy."

"Crippled?"

"You know, like me. But his was worse. He asked me why I was sitting there, why I wasn't with my friends. I told him I couldn't do much."

"What, uh, what did he say then?"

"He said I could be as strong as I wanted or something like that. Then he gave me the necklace. He said it was special and would help me decide what to do in life."

Peter again fingered the chain and pendant, marveling at the exquisite glazed figures. "It's special, all right."

"I know. Aunt Liz was really excited. When I told her the Mexican boy gave it to me, she said to keep it close and take care of it. She even cried when she held it."

"Cried?"

"She said it would bring me a life of, uh—love and..."

"Oh." Peter looked intently at Mark before getting up.

Mark cocked his head. "Santa arrive yet?"

Peter laughed. "I think I hear him now." He patted Mark on the shoulder and gave him another kiss. Then he walked to the door and looked back into the darkened room.

"Sleep tight, my son."

By day, Mack Hicks works as a child psychologist and operates Center Academy schools for children with learning disabilities. By night, this crusader for educational reform dons his cloak and dagger and gets to work at the keyboard.

In addition to co-authoring the acclaimed child-rearing book, *Parent, Child, and Community,* (Chicago: Nelson Hall), he authored several scholarly publications and wrote legislation that shaped the first statewide parent-choice scholarship program in the United States. He founded voucher and charter school programs in Florida and England and is currently hard at work completing *Peter's Pence,* a second Peter Sheppard thriller and sequel to Martyr's Tomb. The author and his wife live in St. Petersburg, Florida. They have three children.

If you enjoyed this novel, and would like to pass one on to someone else, please check with your local bookstore, online bookseller, or provide the following information:

Name ____

Address ____

City ___________________________State______ Zip_____________

______ copies of Martyrs' Tomb at $14.95 $ ________

Florida residents, please add applicable sales tax $ ________

Shipping: $3.50* first copy, $2.00 each additional copy $ ________

Total Enclosed $ ________

For more than five copies, contact the publisher for quantity rates. Send completed order form with your check or money order to:

Splenium House, L.L.C.
6710 Eighty-Sixth Avenue North
Pinellas Park, FL 33782-4502
Fax: 727-544-8186

Order Line: 1-800-247-6553

web site: www.martyrs-tomb.com

*International shipping is extra. Please contact us for shipping rates to your location, if outside the United States.